A Promise unBroken

A PROMISE UNBROKEN

AL LACY

For my darling wife, JoAnna (Joni to me),
whose tender love has been the inspiration for
romance in all my novels,
and whose ideas, suggestions, and help
in historical research over the years have been
invaluable.

PREFACE

While studying American history in high school I was struck with a strange fascination for the Civil War. That fascination grew stronger when I studied it again in college, especially since the bulk of my college education was obtained in southeastern Tennessee, where Southerners old and young are still fighting the Civil War (at least in conversation).

Known also as the War of the Sixties, the Great Rebellion, the War Between the States, the War for the Union, Mr. Lincoln's War, the War for Separation, the Second War of Independence, the Lost Cause, the Last Gentlemen's War, the War against Slavery, the Yankees' Invasion, the War for Abolition, the War of Secession, the War of Southern Planters, the War against Northern Aggression, the Confederate War, the Union War, the War for Southern Freedom, the War of the North and South, and the Brothers' War, the compelling four-year conflict has continued to enthrall me until at last I have become a full-fledged Civil War buff.

My personal library is quite extensive, and among literally hundreds of volumes are dozens of books on the Civil War. My enchantment with this dynamic period in American history has lured me to many of the sites where the battles took place.

I have spent a great deal of time in the Rich Mountain area, and have explored the meadows and forests that make up the battlefields of Chickamauga, Gettysburg, Chancellorsville, and Fredericksburg. I have stood on the narrow streets of Harper's Ferry where troop and supply trains met along the Shenandoah River—a strategic town that once held a Union arsenal—and I have walked on the very ground at Winchester, Virginia, where General Stonewall Jackson launched his campaign across the Shenandoah Valley. I have watched the vagrant winds toy with the tall grass on the slopes of the Bull Run battlefield, and I have seen brilliant sunlight dance on the surface of Antietam Creek, along which was fought the bloodiest one-day battle of the war.

It was a special treat for me not long ago to visit Appomattox Court House in Virginia, where General Robert E. Lee signed the documents of surrender before General Ulysses S. Grant. I stood on the front porch of the restored Wilmer McLean house and looked into the parlor where the two great military leaders brought the war to an end.

When I eagerly entered the village bookstore, I was amazed to find that it carries books only on the Civil War. After strolling about for some time, my eyes strayed to a display of booklets describing the individual battles of the war. Each booklet (of about thirty pages) gave the place, dates, facts about military leaders, how many men on both sides were killed or wounded, and other details of import.

The thought struck me: What a fantastic series of novels those battles would make! I could build stories around the battles, molding fictional characters with real ones (as I had often done in my previous novels), filling them with romance, suspense, intrigue, heart-wrenching sorrows, espionage, cowardice, courage, and the blood, smoke, fire, action, and excitement of battle. I discussed this with my good friend Thomas Womack at Questar Publishers, and he bought it. You now hold the first novel in your hands.

Not all historians agree on every detail of the war. I have long been a subscriber to the *Civil War Times Illustrated* magazine. In almost every issue, there are letters to the editor that take exception to a story or article in a previous issue. Some readers are unhappy that a writer has made a "mistake" on a date, military leader, type of weapons used in a particular battle, and so on. In checking out some of these complaints, I have found that both the writer and the person sending the letter have solid basis for their arguments.

The same thing could happen in this series, so I ask for some tolerance from my readers. I will do my best to be accurate on all historical points, but if you find a discrepancy, please save yourself the price of a postage stamp and understand that these things happen. I remind you that the books in this series are novels based on history, not historical textbooks.

The series is written for the simple pleasure and enjoyment of my readers. If the stories thrill you, excite you, stir your emotions, and give you a better appreciation for America's great heritage, my extensive research and long hours at the word processor will be worth it.

PROLOGUE

When that first Confederate shell arched through the predawn sky and exploded behind the walls of Fort Sumter on April 12, 1861, it touched off one of the greatest points of crisis in the history of America. Not only did the Civil War quickly develop into a bloody conflict between two societies with opposite views on slavery, but it moved inexorably toward something almost unthinkable—a tragic clash between families. Brothers battling brothers.

In the century between the end of the Napoleonic Wars and the commencement of World War I, the most catastrophic military conflict fought anywhere was the American Civil War. Some historians have alluded to the Civil War as a combination of "The Last Medieval War and the First Modern War." I agree. As the first modern war, it ominously foreshadowed the horrors of warfare that have followed in the twentieth century.

The Civil War introduced trench warfare, propaganda, warfare of psychological attrition, aerial observation, naval blockade, economic warfare, iron-clad ships, and the Gatling gun, as well as the horrible impeding influence of filthy, disease-ridden, prisoner-of-war camps. Compulsory enlistment for military service was also put into use for the first time in American history.

The Civil War brought about many other firsts. It was the first war to have photographers taking pictures on the battlefield. It was the first war to employ repeating rifles and to use railroad artillery, naval torpedoes, flame throwers, land mines, electrically exploded bombs, telescopic sights for rifles, fixed ammunition, the wigwag signal code, and periscopes for fighting in the trenches. During the Civil War, the bugle call "Taps" was first played, naval camouflage was invented, and the Congressional Medal of Honor was introduced.

With all of its firsts in modern warfare and the hatred that raged between the North and the South, the Civil War cost more American lives in the four years from Sumter to Appomattox than the two World Wars, Korea, Vietnam, and Desert Storm combined. The carnage that took place between April 1861 and April 1865 was appalling. Of the three million men who saw action afloat and ashore—Union and Confederate—more than a million were casualties. Well over 600,000 lost their lives as a direct result of combat (including those who were wounded, then died of infections and various diseases). Another 400,000 were wounded, but lived to tell of the horrors of the war.

This caldron of blood was spread wider than the casual follower of the Civil War realizes. According to government authorities, there were some 95 major battles, 310 minor battles, and over 6,000 skirmishes, some of which the soldiers themselves called "squabbles" or "dust-ups." If a man died in a dust-up, he was just as dead as if he had been killed in a major battle. The bulk of the fighting took place on Southern land. However, a few battles were fought on Union soil, including two of the bloodiest—Gettysburg and Antietam. Blood was shed in land-fighting as far north as Vermont, and as far west as the Pacific coast. California saw 6 skirmishes, Oregon 4, and 19 occurred in New Mexico Territory. There were other skirmishes in the territories of Washington, Utah, and Idaho.

The fighting in Vermont was a result of Confederate raiders striking the town of St. Albans. Other Rebel raiders shed blood in

Illinois, Minnesota, and New York. The southernmost fighting happened between Union and Confederate forces on a sandy beach in Florida known today as Cape Canaveral.

The seeds of war over slavery were planted in this country long before the first shot was fired upon Fort Sumter. When Spain conquered a large part of South America in the late fifteenth century, they made slaves of the Indians and forced them to work in the mines and in the crop fields. The Indians, however, began to die off quickly because of exposure to European diseases and harsh working conditions. To remedy this problem, Spanish king Charles I began to import slaves from Africa in 1517. The idea slowly caught on in other lands. The first African slaves arrived at the English colony of Virginia aboard a Dutch ship early in 1619.

Almost immediately pressure began to build between northern and southern colonists over slavery, and it grew worse as the decades passed. During the Revolutionary War, slavery was a hot issue amongst the colonists, and it did not subside when the thirteen colonies declared their independence on July 4, 1776. For the sake of unity political leaders on both sides of the issue agreed to not allow their ideologies to divide them. This worked fairly well until the mid-nineteenth century, when a fatuous abolitionist zealot named John Brown led a band of men on a killing spree in Kansas, murdering proslavery leaders in cold blood. Although Brown controlled his thirst for blood in the months after the Kansas ritual murders in May of 1856, he was anything but inactive. He gained more recruits for his crusade against slavery as time passed, and moved eastward. His scheme was to set up a base in the Alleghenies from which he could invade Virginia, free a multitude of slaves, and make them part of his army.

It took Brown over three years to prepare his small band of men for the invasion. On the night of October 16, 1859, Brown and his men took over the Union arsenal at Harper's Ferry and held several hostages. Word of Brown's plan had been sent to thousands of slaves, whom he expected to rally around him. Once he had armed them with the guns and ammunition from the arsenal, he would lead them in a march of liberation.

The slaves did not show up, but the United States Marines did. When the fighting was over, only John Brown and four of his men remained. They were captured and were hanged in Charles Town, Virginia, on December 7, 1859. Southerners angrily accused the North of plotting to end slavery by instigating a giant slave rebellion. The accusations flared tempers in the North. When the Northerners disclaimed any connection with Brown, Southerners called them liars...and the situation grew worse.

News of the Harper's Ferry incident spread to every state, including Massachusetts, where famed poet Henry W. Longfellow resided at the time. On the same day John Brown was hanged, Longfellow penned these prophetic words:

> This will be a great day in our history; the date of a New Revolution—quite as much needed as the old one. Even now as I write they are leading old John Brown to execution in Virginia for attempting to rescue slaves! This is sowing the wind to reap the whirlwind which will come soon.

When John Brown was being escorted from the Charles Town jail to the public place of execution, he handed a note to one of the guards that incredibly coincided with Longfellow's presage of the national calamity that Brown had done so much to make inevitable. It read: "I, John Brown, am now quite certain that the crimes of this guilty land will never be purged away but with blood."

One hundred and twenty-six days later, the whirlwind of blood had its beginnings at Fort Sumter, South Carolina.

Events might have been vastly different had the nation been more mature. At the time John Brown was inciting civil unrest, the United States was less than a hundred years old, barely an adolescent as nations go. The people of the two philosophies concerning slavery had much to learn about each other.

The economy in the northern states was much stronger and more stable than the economy in the South. The Northerners, according to southern leaders, failed to understand the situation.

At the close of the eighteenth century, profound economic changes were taking place in Great Britain and all over Europe. There was an increasing demand for cotton, but the climate in that part of the world prevented the growth of the product. Hence, clothing manufacturers from the Continent crossed the Atlantic Ocean and met with southern cotton producers, placing large orders. The plantation owners were elated with the new business opportunities, but found that the only way they could make what they felt was a fair profit was to use slave labor.

The South was already providing virtually all of the cotton needed by the growing textile mills in the northern states. The added demand from the Europeans meant the need for expansion in cotton production in the South, which also meant the expansion of slavery. Cotton and slavery became inextricably intertwined. Apathetic about the economics of it, northern newspapers and periodicals were concerned only with the baneful practice of slavery. They blasted the southern cotton producers, saying in essence, "To sell cotton in order to buy Negroes—to produce more cotton to buy more Negroes—is immoral, and the practice should be outlawed by the Congress of the United States."

The attitude of the North embittered Southerners, who retorted in their own publications that the rich Northerners were ignorant and should mind their own business. Thus, the adolescent nation, driven by the winds of bitter debate over slavery, took a set course toward bloody conflict.

Fuel was added to the fire by reports that filtered northward concerning the brutal treatment of slaves by the southern plantation owners. Political leaders in the South readily admitted that there were slave owners who were short on compassion toward their slaves, feeding and housing them poorly and often abusing them physically. They were quick to point out, however, that such slave owners were in the minority.

The same politicians hastened to denounce the arrogant Northerners for being in the dark about the constant danger of slave revolt. Even the decent and compassionate slave owners found it necessary to exercise strict discipline on their human chattel to keep them in line.

The plantation owners remembered the slave revolt near Charleston, South Carolina, in September of 1739, when twenty-five white people were killed before the rebellion was crushed. They also had not forgotten the massive slave revolt in Haiti between 1791 and 1804 when a collective army of six thousand vengeful slaves, brandishing guns, machetes, spears, knives, and clubs created a massacre. Marching behind a standard—the body of a white baby impaled on a spear—they killed their white masters, violated their wives and daughters, and shed the blood of whites anywhere on the island who stood in their way.

Also remembered were conspiracies to revolt that occurred at Richmond, Virginia, in 1800 and at Charleston, South Carolina, in 1822. Although these two plans were thwarted, it caused the slave owners to take precautionary measures. Fresh in the minds of plantation owners was the slave revolt in the summer of 1831 at South Hampton County, Virginia, when fifty-seven whites were killed, resulting in the hanging of nearly a hundred slaves.

When southern newspapers tried to make it clear to Northerners that slave owners lived in the shadow of revolt and had to use "fear tactics" to keep their slaves in subjection, the northern newspapers answered back, "Free the slaves and your impending danger will be gone!"

Thus, the contentious exchange between North and South raged until John Brown came along and lit the fuse that exploded the verbal conflict into full-scale war. The four years of carnage brought about an acceleration of maturity. America grew up.

The conflict ended at Appomattox Court House, Virginia, on Sunday afternoon April 9, 1865. Slavery ended in the United States later that year with the passage of the Thirteenth Amendment to the Constitution.

When General Robert E. Lee mounted his horse and rode away from the McLean house that fateful day, followed by hundreds of weeping Confederate soldiers, the Civil War was over. The bitter memories and deep sorrows of the four-year struggle, however, lived on. As time passed, it eased the sorrows, but the memories were rooted in the soil where the blood was spilled. Although the guns were silent, in the minds of both Northerners and Southerners, the war would never end. The memories would continue to burn in their hearts until, like their brothers and friends who died in the conflict, they too passed through death's dark door.

Having laid this brief historical foundation, I now tell my version of the Civil War's first major battle, which took place on July 11, 1861, at Rich Mountain in western Virginia.

CHAPTER ONE

Web Steele whipped his head around as the flat report of the shot carried to him through the cool mid-October air. Jerking hard on the reins, he drew horse and buggy to a halt in the middle of the road. While the breeze carried the small dust cloud away, he peered past the imposing archway on his left that housed the gate to the Jason Hart plantation.

Letting his gaze follow the narrow, winding road that led to the mansion and its complex of buildings nestled in a thick stand of trees, he listened for any further sound of trouble. The gunshot seemed to have come from that way, but the pounding of the horse's hooves and the whir of the wheels had suppressed the report enough to make it impossible to be sure.

Pulling his gaze from the Hart mansion, Steele looked up the road ahead of him as his horse blew and stamped a hoof. The Virginia sky was clear, and the brilliant light of the early afternoon sun revealed no movement in that direction. The John Ruffin plantation lay two miles further on, but the shot was too loud to have come from there.

Turning around on the seat, he looked down the road behind him. The Steele plantation—from which he had just come—was nearest, but it also was too far away to have been the source of the shot. There was no sign of life except for the birds that hopped about in the branches of the towering trees that lined both sides of the road. Sunlight danced on the orange and golden leaves as they fluttered in the autumn breeze.

Steele looked to his right across the rolling hills toward Richmond, but saw nothing moving.

Suddenly there was a second shot, followed by a third. This time he knew it was coming from the Hart place. The gate beneath the archway was open. Snapping the reins, he sent the horse galloping under the archway, following the narrow, winding road. Another shot rang out, and Web felt a vast hollow in his stomach. Instinct told him that what he had been expecting to happen on both the Ruffin and Hart plantations was now in progress directly ahead of him.

The mansion was a quarter-mile from the road. As the buggy bounded into the spacious yard, another shot reverberated through the air, the sharp sound coming from the rear. Guiding the horse along the path to the backside of the house, Steele saw Jonas Hart and his two sons hunkered behind an overturned wagon, facing the tool and wood shed, which was close to the barn, about forty yards from the rear of the mansion. There were splintered places on the wagon where bullets had chewed wood.

Drawing the buggy to a sudden stop, Steele saw Mabel Hart, her oldest daughter, Mary Ann, and daughter-in-law, Chloe, collected on the back porch of the mansion with the butler and the maid. All were wide-eyed with fear.

As Web Steele jumped out of the buggy, he saw that Jonas was holding a revolver with one hand and a bleeding shoulder with the other. Sons David, twenty-two, and Daniel, twenty-one, were not armed. A group of slaves could be seen at the edge of a clearing some fifty yards further back, where their small cabins huddled in a circle. They too looked frightened.

Steele knew his instincts were correct. Hart had a slave revolt on his hands. Some of them were holed up in the tool and wood shed, and were armed. The absence of Hart's sixteen-year-old daughter and fourteen-year-old son might mean they were being held hostage.

Jonas Hart shouted, "Web, take cover! We've got real trouble here!"

Steele took one look at the open window next to the shed's only door and saw the barrel of a revolver glint in the sunlight. He dashed to where Jonas and his sons were clustered behind the overturned wagon. "Please tell me that Darrel and Melissa aren't in there!"

A gray pallor was on Jonas Hart's pain-pinched face. Even his lips were colorless. At forty-four, he owned the large plantation and had done well, but Steele knew that Jonas was sometimes unnecessarily harsh with his slaves. He had come close to warning Jonas about it on several occasions, but the man was sixteen years his senior, and he could not bring himself to do it.

Jonas's voice was tight as he replied, "They're in the shed, all right, Web."

"How many slaves in there?" Web asked.

"Two."

"Do I know them?"

"Yeah. Dexter and Orman."

Eyeing the blood that was running between Jonas's fingers as he gripped his shoulder, Web said, "You'd better get to the house and let Mabel tend to that wound."

"Naw," growled the plantation owner, "it's only a scratch. It'll be all right. Main thing right now is to bring this situation to an end."

Looking back toward the shed, Steele said, "Dexter and Orman, eh? What do they want?"

Gritting his teeth in pain, Jonas replied, "To go free. They say if we'll let them go, they'll release the kids when they're a safe distance from here."

"What brought this on?"

"Nothing special, they just—"

"Tell him the truth, Pa," butted in David, who was slave overseer for his father. "I've been warning you this was going to happen."

"Shut up!" snapped Jonas. "If you'd be a little more stern with these lazy whelps, it wouldn't make me look so mean when I have to discipline them."

David Hart had been developing a distaste for slavery for the past two years. He and his father had had many heated discussions about it. Jonas accused him of becoming an "abolitionist Yankee" in his heart.

Before David could respond, a voice came from within the shed. "We's gettin' tired of waitin', Massa Jonas! We want those horses, and we want 'em right now!"

Web Steele recognized the voice of Dexter, whom he had known for several years. In a half-whisper, he said, "Jonas, Dexter knows me well. So does Orman. Do you think it would help if I talk to them?"

"Couldn't hurt, that's for sure," spoke up Daniel. "Both of them like you."

"What about it, Jonas?" pressed Steele.

"Go ahead. Talk to them. Like Dan said, it can't hurt for you to try."

"Massa Jonas!" bellowed Orman. "We saw Massa Web come in. You can do yo' talkin' later. We want those horses, or we's gonna be forced to hurt dese chillin o' yo's!"

Jonas's anger broke. "You harm my kids and you'll wish you'd never been born, Orman!"

There was no response from the shed. Setting his gaze on Steele, Jonas said, "Well, do your talking."

"First I have to know what David meant when he told you to be truthful with me."

"Aw, I just found it necessary to give them both a good belt-whipping, that's all. They've been getting lazier by the day. David won't chastise them, so they just get continually worse."

"How bad did you whip them?"

"Not too bad."

"Did you draw blood?"

"A little."

"Pa, you expect too much of them," said David. "Their bodies get tired like ours do. If you'd only ease up on the load—"

Jonas swore, cutting off his elder son. "Young and strong as they are, they oughtta be able to do a whole lot more than they've been doing! There are other slaves on this place who put out more work."

"Yes, and there are other slaves who'll be doing this same thing shortly, too," responded David.

"Not if I make an example of these two," Jonas growled, sending a heated glance in the direction of the shed.

At that moment drumming hoof beats were heard in the direction of the road, and seconds later two riders came thundering around the corner of the mansion. The Hart men and Web Steele recognized Reed Exley, slave overseer of the neighboring John Ruffin plantation, and one of the Ruffin slaves, a handsome young man named Mandrake.

David Hart mumbled, "The last person we need here right now is Exley."

Web agreed. As with most people in the Richmond area, he harbored a deep dislike for Exley, who was married to wealthy John Ruffin's oldest daughter, Elizabeth. Web was engaged to Ruffin's next-oldest daughter, Abby. While courting her for the past year-and-a-half, he had gotten to know Exley quite well...much to his sorrow.

At thirty-one, Reed Exley was three years older than Web. He was short, stocky, blond, and somewhat good-looking; he was also self-centered, greedy, and unprincipled. He had a mean, hair-trigger temper, shifty, ice-blue eyes, and a perpetual cocky smirk. His vile soul was exposed further by his vicious and cruel treatment of the Ruffin slaves. It was because of this treatment that Steele expected an all-out slave rebellion. There had been a few runaways in the past several months, but so far, no actual uprising.

It was Exley's job to oversee the slaves and to handle the buying and selling of them. Web, who had the same job on his father's plantation, was kind and compassionate with his slaves. His observation of Exley's merciless, inhuman handling of the Ruffin slaves had led him to discuss it on one occasion with Abby's widower father, but it had done no good. John Ruffin had a blind spot when it came to his son-in-law, and because Exley had never abused the slaves before his eyes, he refused to believe it ever happened. Even when Abby and her younger sister, Lynne, told their father of seeing Exley mistreat the slaves, he would not believe it.

Daniel Hart, who was courting Lynne Ruffin, also disliked Reed Exley. When he saw Exley and Mandrake ride up, he noticed that Exley was wearing a sidearm.

"Better get your head down, Reed!" called Jonas. "We've got a couple of slaves with their noses out of joint, and they've been doing some shooting."

Exley and Mandrake ran in and hunkered down. "Yeah, I heard it," said Reed. "I decided to come and see if I could help." As he spoke, he drew his gun, then looked at Jonas's bleeding shoulder. "You shot bad?"

"No. Mabel can fix me up once this is over."

"So what's going on?" queried Exley.

Jonas gave Exley a brief explanation, naming the two black men who were holding his daughter and son hostage.

Looking around at the others, Exley saw that the only weapon in the bunch was the revolver in Jonas's hand. "Well, why don't we get some more guns and rush 'em?"

"Web's about to try talking them out," said Jonas.

Exley gave Web a cold stare. "Talk?" he spat incredulously. "These beasts don't understand talk!" Then to Jonas, "They both have guns?"

"Yes."

"Where'd they get 'em?"

"I have no idea."

"I say let's lay our hands on some more guns and rush 'em."

"That's a good way to get Darrel and Melissa killed," Web said. "Dexter and Orman are desperate. Put your gun away, Reed, and let me handle this."

"Massa Jonas!" came Dexter's strained voice. "What's goin' on? Why's Reed Exley here?"

"He just came because he heard the shooting," Steele answered for Jonas.

"Yeah? Then why'd he bring that black man with him?"

Web knew Mandrake well. He smiled at him, then turned to Exley and said, "That's a good question. Why did you bring Mandrake along?"

A wicked grin spread over Exley's face as he set his icy eyes on Mandrake. In that brief moment, Steele saw a subtle and fleeting manifestation of the man's cruelty. Reed held his hard gaze on Mandrake and replied, "Simple, Webster. When I heard the shots, I figured it could be something like this. Mandrake, here, has shown a little too much starch to suit me. The other slaves sort of look to him as their leader. I suppose it's because he's young, full of fire, and has all those muscles. Anyway, I made him come along so if some of Jonas's beasts were gonna get disciplined for startin' trouble, he could see first-hand what happens to black boys who revolt against their white masters."

Trepidation showed on Mandrake's dark features. Daring not to look Reed Exley in the eye, he drew in a long, gravelly breath, passed a glance at Steele, and looked at the ground.

Suddenly a shot was heard inside the shed. Melissa Hart screamed. A harsh voice blared, "Nobody's hurt, Massa Jonas! I jus' shot through the roof! But Orman and I are tired of waitin' for you to let us go. We want those horses now! If'n we don't get 'em, somebody in dis shed is goin' to get hurt...an' it ain't me or Orman!"

"Jonas, you gonna do somethin'?" asked Reed Exley. "Or you just gonna sit here and let them animals kill your kids?"

Jonas licked his lips. "I've got to let Web see if he can talk them out. They like Web. Maybe he can do something with them."

"I doubt it," snarled Exley. "But so he talks 'em into lettin' your kids loose and throwin' their guns out. What you gonna do then?"

"I don't know," said Jonas. "Let's just cross one bridge at a time here. Most important thing is to get Melissa and Darrel out of there."

"Well, they oughtta be hanged or shot through the head in front of the rest of your slaves," grunted Exley. "If you don't make an example of 'em, the next time you whip one, you'll go through this kind of nonsense again."

"Dexter!" called Steele, unwilling to stretch the ordeal out any longer. "Can we talk?"

"We's listenin'."

Web Steele left his crouch and stood to his full height, exposing his empty hands. The Hart brothers set admiring eyes on him from their low position. Wealthy plantation owner Dudley Steele's handsome son stood three inches over six feet, with a muscular frame. He had thick, wavy black hair, matching well-trimmed mustache, medium-length sideburns, and coal-black eyes.

As Web was about to speak, Mabel Hart's high-pitched voice could be heard from the back porch of the mansion. "Jonas! Do something! They'll kill our children!"

"We are!" Jonas shouted back. "Just stay calm!"

"Dexter!" called Steele.

"Yassuh?"

"There is nothing to gain by doing harm to Melissa and Darrel. Let them come out, and we'll talk."

"Cain't do that, Massa Web! If'n we let the kids go, Massa Jonas will beat us again! 'Specially now that we done shot 'im. We ain't gonna have no mo' of those beatin's! We ain't lazy like he say. We works hard. But we cain't keep up the kind o' workin' he's puttin' on us."

"Dat's right, Massa Web!" came Orman's voice. "We knows about yo' slaves. Ain't none o' them gets treated like us."

"Well, I'm sure if you'll let Mr. Hart's children loose, he'll not beat you. His wound is not serious. I'm sure he'll not punish you for it, and will be more tolerant from now on."

"We wants to hear him say dat!" shouted Orman.

Steele looked down at Jonas Hart. "Well?"

Jonas's face flushed and his eyes had fire in them. "Web, I can't tell those two I'll be more tolerant! You can't expect me to just overlook this and tell them all is forgiven!"

"I think you're going to have to if you don't want to get those kids hurt...or killed," replied Steele.

"What's the matter with tellin' 'em everything's all right so they'll let the kids go...then blast 'em when they show their faces?" suggested Exley.

Web scowled at him. "You fool, Reed! There are more than thirty men in that crowd of slaves standing out there watching us. If we shoot Dexter and Orman, they just might decide to swarm in here and tear us apart."

"We got two guns," parried Exley.

"And how many bullets will you have after blasting Dexter and Orman?" clipped Steele. "Even if you could cut a few of them down, what about the rest? There'd still be enough of them to tear us limb from limb. You're not using your head, Reed."

Reed's temper flared. "They ain't gonna do no such thing! Even if they started for us, when they saw some of their black pals drop, they'd back off."

"You think so?"

"I know it."

Turning to the slave beside Exley, Steele asked, "What about it, Mandrake? Would they back off?"

Mandrake cleared his throat nervously. "Well, Massa Web, I cain't say fo' sure. If they's thinkin' straight, they'd prob'ly not come rushin' into a couple of blazin' guns. But seein' two of their own shot down after they had been tol' they was forgiven just might make 'em crazy-blind mad. If'n that was to happen, wouldn't be a white person left alive on this place."

Exley was livid. "Mandrake, you keep outta this! I don't want to hear another word outta you! You got that?"

Mandrake flicked a fearful glance at Steele, who glared at Exley and snapped, "I asked for his opinion, Reed! You had no right to jump him. Why do you have to be such an idiot?"

Exley bristled. His hot glare met Steele's. The message passed between them—a mute understanding of their mutual dislike.

Reed's teeth clamped together as he hissed, "I resent bein' called an idiot!"

"Then quit acting like one."

Steele looked down at Jonas and said, "Are you going to tell Dexter and Orman they're forgiven, and that you'll be more tolerant from now on?"

"Better do it, Pa," put in David. "Something's going to happen in that shed pretty soon if you don't."

Jonas pulled the bloody hand away from his wound and saw that the bleeding had stopped. Taking off his hat and throwing it angrily on the ground, he said in a hoarse half-whisper, "I can't let those two get away with this! If I do, others will be encouraged to rebel. I'll do anything to get Darrel and Melissa out of there safely, but after that, there has to be severe punishment."

"More beatings?" asked Steele.

"Yes! More beatings! They're not going to get away with this!"

"Pa," said David, "if you hadn't beaten them in the first place, we wouldn't be having this problem now. If you make it sound like everything is forgiven just to free Darrel and Melissa, then whip Dexter and Orman, that will really incite a rebellion. The best thing is for you to stand up right now and talk to them. Admit that you've been working them too hard, and that you were wrong to belt-whip them. You take any other course, and there'll be disaster."

Mabel's high-pitched voice pierced the air. "Jonas! What are you doing? Why are you taking so long?"

"I'm working on it!" Jonas shouted toward the house.

"Well, I say we rush 'em," interjected Reed. "Those black dogs deserve to die."

Mandrake licked his lips as anger welled up within him, but he did not set eyes on Exley.

"You're talking like an idiot again, Reed!" growled Steele. "You couldn't rush them fast enough to save those kids' lives."

"We'll do it my way," said Jonas. "I'll tell them they're forgiven. When Darrel and Melissa are safe and those beasts have thrown down their guns, we'll tie them to a tree and put the fear of God into them."

"Then I want no part in this," said Web, turning to walk away. He froze when another gunshot came from the shed.

Melissa's scream curdled the air and Mabel darted off the porch toward the shed, emitting a wordless wail. Darrel's voice was heard above his sister's scream, calling for his father to help them.

Web intercepted Mabel and guided her toward her husband and older sons hunkered behind the wagon.

David saw his wife coming a few steps behind Mabel, and shouted, "Chloe! Go back!"

Chloe Hart was frightened and did not heed David's command. Reaching the wagon, she dropped to her knees and threw herself into his arms, sobbing.

Dexter's desperate voice rang out from inside the shed, "Time's up! We want those horses right now!"

Jonas's ragged emotions flooded to the surface. "Dexter," he bawled, "I want my children out of there this instant!"

"No!" came the defiant reply. "You give us the horses, and like we already tol' you, we'll let Darrel and Melissa go when we think we're far enough away!"

"You'd never get far enough away!" boomed Hart. "You can't pull this kind of stuff on me and get away with it! You're not getting any horses! Now give it up! Let those kids out of there!"

"No! They're gonna get hurt if you don' do as we say!"

Web said, "Jonas, you've got to apologize for beating them and tell them you'll lighten their work load."

"I don't have to do any such thing."

Another plea came from Darrel, begging his father to help them.

"Jonas!" wailed Mabel. "What is wrong with you? Don't you care what happens to your children?"

"Of course I care, but nobody does this to Jonas Hart. They're not going to get away with it!"

David looked his father in the eye and said heatedly, "Pa, your pride is going to get Darrel and Melissa killed! Dexter and Orman trust Web. Why don't you just tell them you'll set them free right now, and let them ride out of here in Web's buggy with him? After this episode, they'll never be worth their salt around here any more. Let them go. We can get along without them."

"I paid good money for those two, David!" snapped Jonas. "They're not getting out of here! They're going to get what's coming to them!"

"I still say we rush 'em!" blurted Reed.

Ignoring Exley, Jonas looked toward the open window of the shed and bellowed, "Dexter! Orman! If you harm a hair of either one of my kids, you'll die! I'll kill you myself...personally!"

"We'd rather die than have to live like we've been livin'!" came Dexter's reply. "We've talked it over, Massa Jonas. If'n you don't let us ride out of here with Darrel and Melissa like we tol' you, den yo' gonna have to come in after us. We'll die, but so will yo' chillun!"

Mandrake glanced cautiously toward Reed, then said to Hart,

"Massa Jonas, they means what they's sayin'. B'lieve me. They is desperate, and they's gonna do what they's sayin' if'n you don' let 'em go."

Reed Exley cursed and slapped Mandrake's face. "You shut up!" he blared. "I said I didn't want to hear another word outta you!"

Mandrake's head whipped sideways from the blow. He took a step back, placing a hand to his smarting cheek.

Web wanted to knock Exley rolling, but the situation at the shed was about to explode. He could tell by the stubborn set to Jonas's jaw that the man was not going to give in. Mabel was whimpering, trembling with fear, and appeared on the verge of collapse. Glancing at the slaves gathered by the cabins, Web saw them watching intently and talking among themselves. Something had to be done, and it had to be done quickly.

Turning to Hart, he said, "Jonas, will you sell Dexter and Orman to me? Right now?"

"What? Why would you want to buy black devils like them?"

"David's right. After what's happened here today, neither of them will be worth their salt around this place any more. I know Dexter's not married, and I assume Orman isn't either."

"Right."

"I'll give you a thousand apiece."

"A thousand?" Jonas gasped. "Web, you know those two will bring a good eighteen hundred apiece at an auction."

"This isn't an auction, and you've got the lives of a son and daughter at stake. Time's running out. Just agree and I'll take them off your hands this minute. I'll be back with a check to cover payment within an hour."

Jonas rubbed his chin, pondering the offer.

David spoke up. "Pa, what are you waiting for? Tell the man he's got a deal!"

Jonas threw a scornful look at his oldest son, then said to Steele, "All right, Web. They're yours for a thousand apiece. Take them and get them out of my sight."

Mabel sobbed a sigh of relief.

"Dexter! Orman!" called Steele.

"Yassuh?"

"Do you trust me?"

"We does," said Dexter.

"Then you'll believe me when I tell you I've just made a deal with Jonas. He's going to sell both of you to me right here and now."

"He is? You mean we can ride outta here with you and be yo' slaves from now on?"

"That's right. I can't give him a check to pay for you until I get back home. He'll have to draw up the papers while I'm gone, and we'll close the deal later this afternoon. But you will have to conduct yourselves from this moment on as if you are my slaves. Do you understand?"

"Yassuh!" replied Dexter.

"Suits me jus' fine!" came Orman's lilting voice.

"All right. Now, how many guns do you have in there?"

"Two, Massa Web."

"You wouldn't lie to me?"

"No, suh!"

"All right, throw them both out the window."

There was a brief pause, then the two revolvers sailed out the open window.

"Oh, God bless you, Web!" Mabel said with a quaking voice.

Steele gave her a compassionate smile, then called toward the shed, "Fine! Now, open the door and let Darrel and Melissa come out."

The shed door swung open, and neither slave could be seen as first Melissa then her younger brother emerged. Sobbing, Mabel ran toward them and Jonas followed. Daniel was next, with David and Chloe behind him. Mary Ann had left the porch and was close by. She quickly joined the group.

Exley breathed a curse and mumbled something under his breath. Mandrake looked on with interest.

The faces of the two slaves were barely visible at the window as they observed the family embracing Darrel and Melissa. When Jonas was sure they were unhurt, he returned to Web's side. Web waited until the tight-knit group had passed the overturned wagon on its way to the mansion, then said, "All right, boys. I want you to come out now."

"Massa Web?"

"Yes, Dexter?"

"If'n we belongs to you now, then Massa Jonas cain't hurt us, right?"

"Right. Tell them, Jonas."

Hart shuddered and clenched his jaw, looking hard at Steele.

"You backing out now?" Steele half-whispered.

"I'd like to," came the heated reply, also in a half-whisper.

"You're a man of your word, Jonas. Answer Dexter's question."

Looking toward the dark faces at the window of the shed, Jonas said with sand in his voice, "Web and I have each other's word on the sale. I'm not going to harm his slaves."

"Come on," said Steele. "I'll take you to my father's plantation."

With fear evident in their faces, Dexter and Orman emerged slowly from the shed and walked cautiously toward the overturned wagon.

Jonas gripped his wounded shoulder once more and set burning eyes on the slaves. "You two better thank your lucky stars Web Steele happened along. Otherwise, you'd have gotten a beating like you've never seen in your worst nightmares. And if you had harmed my children, you'd have died at the end of a rope!"

"They still oughtta be strung up, Jonas!" thundered Reed Exley. "These two have more than over-stepped their bounds, and the way I see it, they deserve to die! When word gets out that they pulled this on you, there'll be more incidents just like it all over this county! Letting them get by with it isn't right. They need to pay for what they've done!" Even as he spoke, Exley whipped out his revolver, swung it on the slaves, and fired twice.

CHAPTER TWO

The first shot struck Orman at the base of his throat. He made a gagging sound, threw both hands to the wound, and pitched to the ground head-first. The second shot hit Dexter on the left side, just under the armpit. He stopped, stiffened, and teetered for an instant, then fell on his back.

In the same instant the shots were fired, Web Steele bolted toward Reed Exley and toppled him with a flying tackle, knocking the wind from Exley's lungs. Exley rolled on the ground gasping for breath as Steele leaped to his feet. Bending over, Web sank strong fingers into Reed's shirt and jerked him to a standing position. Cocking his right arm, Web unleashed a sledgehammer blow that connected with Exley's jaw. Exley's head whipped sideways and he landed on his back, unconscious.

Jonas Hart looked toward the others, who stood dumbfounded, and said, "Dan and David, you two stay here. The rest of you get inside the house."

Jonas turned about to see Web kneeling beside Dexter. Glancing at the unconscious Exley, Jonas set his attention on the group of male slaves coming across the field, carrying garden tools and clubs. There was anger in their eyes. A steel band of fear tightened around his heart.

Unaware of the angry slaves, Steele looked up at Jonas and said, "Orman's dead, Jonas. The slug Dexter took is in his left side, but it's not too deep. I don't think it pierced his lung. I'll get him into my buggy and take him to the doctor."

David and Daniel drew up as Jonas, eyes fixed on the approaching mob of over thirty black men, stammered, "I...I don't think you'll get the chance, Web. We've got real trouble brewing."

Steele stood and set his gaze toward the oncoming slaves as Jonas said to his sons, "Boys, run to the house and get the rifles."

"That would be foolish," Web said.

"Well, what do you suggest?" Jonas blurted, panic evident in his voice.

"You're going to have to talk your way out of this. You try using guns, and they'll kill all of us, including your family and servants."

Web quickly turned back to Dexter and knelt beside him. He pulled his large bandanna from his hip pocket, wadded it into a ball, opened Dexter's shirt, and stuffed the bandanna next to the wound, using it as a compress to stay the flow of blood. Dexter looked at him with glazed eyes and tried to smile.

"You just hold on, Dexter," Web told him. "I'm going to take you to my doctor in Richmond."

Gritting his teeth in pain, Dexter said, "Massa Web, no Richmon' doctor will work on a lowly slave."

"Mine will," Steele said.

Web caught sight of Reed Exley out of the corner of his eye. Exley was sitting up, holding his jaw. At that moment, the fierce-eyed slaves drew up. Cletus, a big man in his early fifties, was two steps ahead of the others. He carried a length of broken tree limb in one hand. His deep booming voice cut a swath across the yard as he blared, "We saw the whole thing, Massa Jonas! We aims to see that nuthin' like this ever happens again! Is both them slaves dead?"

"Orman is," Hart replied shakily. "Dexter took a slug in his side, but I think he'll be okay."

Cletus glanced at Dexter, then glared at Jonas. "De Good Book say vengeance belong to de Lord," he said cryptically, "but fo' dis one time, maybe it belong to us blackies."

The words sent a chill through Jonas. "Now, Cletus," he said with strain in his voice, "any violence will only bring trouble down on all of your heads. You remember the slave revolt over in South Hampton County nearly thirty years ago. Almost a hundred slaves were hanged. It won't be any different in 1860 than it was then, Cletus. They'll hang you just as quick today as they hanged those rebellious slaves then."

Cletus showed his white teeth in an angry grimace. "Yeah, I know. But I remind you, nearly sixty whites died befo' those slaves was hanged."

Stiffening, Jonas countered, "Do you think those slaves thought it was worth it when they felt the nooses around their necks?"

A young slave who stood close to Cletus cut in, "None of us slaves minds dyin' if'n it'll stop you rich white plantation owners from bein' cruel to our black brothuhs."

"If'n we don' get some satisfaction right now, I say we start bashin' heads!" shouted another.

Raising their clubs and garden tools over their heads and shaking them in a threatening manner, the others began shouting their agreement.

Jonas looked fearfully at his sons. David said in a low tone, "Pa, you'd best swallow your pride and beg their forgiveness."

Jonas's features hardened. "This is ridiculous!" he hissed. "I bought and paid for these beasts! Why should I have to kowtow to them?"

Web was close enough to hear the exchange. The slaves were still shouting, their clamor building to a fevered pitch. Having dealt with slaves all of his adult life, Web knew they had held off attacking for a reason. They really did not want to shed Hart family blood, but they did want the cruelty to stop. They knew that to wipe out the Hart family would only bring white men from all over the county with blood in their eyes. They would hang for sure.

Web thought of what the young slave had said only moments before. *We don' mind dyin' if'n it'll stop you rich white plantation owners from bein' cruel to our black brothuhs.* He knew the issue here was Jonas Hart's cruelty to his slaves. Orman was dead, and Dexter was seriously wounded as a result of the beating Jonas had given both of them earlier in the day. This, along with Jonas's past mistreatment of many of them, had them ready to shed blood unless they received assurance it would stop. Jonas was too hard-headed and blinded by his ego to see the true picture.

Realizing the danger of delay, Steele left Dexter's side, brushed past Jonas and his sons, and stood within three steps of Cletus. Shouting above the angry voices, he cried, "Cletus, let me talk to you! Quiet them down!"

Cletus raised his empty hand shoulder high, and the noise stopped. "All right, Massa Web," he said levelly, "I's listenin'."

Web motioned for Jonas to join them, then said, "Cletus, I want you to tell Master Jonas why you didn't just storm in here and start bashing heads after you saw Dexter and Orman shot down. All of you are mad enough to crack every white man's skull in sight. Why did you stop when you reached us? You've all got something in your hands that could maim or kill us."

Jonas stepped up beside Steele. David and Daniel were close on his heels.

Cletus ran his palm across his eyes and said, "We's plenty mad 'bout Massa Jonas beatin' Dexter and Orman dis mo'nin', Massa Web. An' we don' blame them fo' tryin' to get away, even if they had to threaten Darrel and Melissa. Bein' beat on fo' runnin' out o' stren'th is wicked an' vile."

Jonas was still holding his revolver. He raised his good arm and sleeved away the sweat on his brow, feeling the pressure from Cletus's hard gaze.

Cletus went on. "We didn't pick up dese tools an' clubs till that Reed Exley over there shot our brothuhs down. De only one we really wants to bash is him."

Exley was standing close to Mandrake by the wagon. Hearing Cletus's threat, he set his eyes on his revolver, which lay near Jonas and his sons. He knew it was useless to try to reach it. The slaves would be on him before he got halfway. His mind was racing. How would he escape them? Could he make a run for it and reach his horse in time?

"So heah's what we wants, Massa Jonas," continued Cletus. "If'n you will promise us there'll be no mo' beatin's, an' de work load will be made lighter, we won't do you an' yo' fam'ly no harm. We'll go on workin' fo' you within reason. We knows de consequences if'n we revolt against you. We also knows if'n we jis' ran away, we'd have to go way up north to make a livin', an' some of us wouldn' make it that far. So—to answer Massa Web's question—we didn' barge in here an' start knockin' heads 'cause we really don' wanna do that. We jis' wants to be treated with kindness and respec'."

"An' we want that white animal who shot Dexter and Orman!" spoke up one of the slaves.

Reed Exley bolted for his horse, commanding Mandrake to follow. A half-dozen slaves ran after them, but the two men were on their horses and galloping away before they could reach them. A couple of the slaves threw their clubs at them in frustration.

The rest of the slaves shouted their hatred for Exley, saying he should die for what he had done. Cletus quieted them, "It's too late, now. He's gone and there's no way we can catch 'im. White man's law would never judge him for killin' a black man, so we'll have to fo'git about 'im."

While the slaves grumbled at Cletus's words, the big man said to Jonas, "What's yo' decision, Massa Jonas? Does we git decent treatment with no beatin's?"

It went against Jonas Hart's grain to have his own chattel lay down demands to him, but he knew the powder keg he was sitting on if he pushed them any further. "Okay, Cletus. From now on, I won't demand as much work from each slave, and I won't use the belt on any of you unless you deliberately provoke me. Fair enough?"

The slaves looked at their leader in silence, waiting for his reaction. Rubbing his chin, Cletus said, "You won' consider a man or woman's lim'tations provokin' you delib'rately?"

Jonas hated to be put in this position, but the circumstances offered him no choice. "No," he said, clearing his throat. "I'll take those limitations into consideration."

"All right," nodded Cletus. "That's all we aks. We'll take Orman, now, and bury 'im."

"Pa," David interjected, "didn't you have something else you wanted to say to these men?"

Knowing what David meant, Jonas squared his jaw and clipped, "No. That's all." With that, he hastened toward Web Steele, who was once again at Dexter's side. While the slaves picked up Orman's lifeless form and carried it away, Jonas stood over the wounded slave and asked, "He gonna make it?"

"I think so," Web replied without looking up. "The bleeding has nearly stopped. I'm no doctor, but I'd say the slug is caught in his rib cage. It'll take surgery to get it out, but young and healthy as he is, he should be all right."

Jonas looked over his shoulder to make sure the other slaves were out of earshot. Satisfied they were, he said gratingly, "Too bad."

"What do you mean?"

"Too bad he didn't die like Orman, that's what I mean. After what he put my kids through, he deserves to die!"

"So you're not accepting any blame in this at all, I take it. The whipping you gave them this morning wasn't wrong?"

"Not at all!" boomed Hart. "They got what they had coming!"

David overheard and sucked in his breath. "Pa, I don't understand you. I thought you were finally seeing that you've been expecting too much from our slaves...that you've been working them too hard."

"I had to make it look that way to appease them, but those black devils are just putting on an act. They could work a lot longer and a lot harder, and they know it. I'll find a way to get more out of them!"

David scowled at his father. "Well, don't expect me to do it. I'll have nothing to do with working them to death."

Jonas swore and banged a fist into a palm. Wincing from the pain in his shoulder, he gruffed, "You're sounding more like a stinking northern abolitionist all the time, David, and I don't like it! As long as you draw pay on this plantation, you'll make those lazy black beasts work like I tell you to!"

Father and son were the same height, and they were now nose-to-nose. Mabel was watching from the back porch of the mansion. When she saw them arguing, she headed toward them.

Jaw jutted stubbornly, David rasped, "I will not be a part of working them till they drop! Do you hear me, Pa? I will not!"

"They're not going to drop!" Jonas bit back. "Can't you see? They're pulling the wool over your eyes! You'll work them exactly as I tell you!"

"No I won't!"

"Jonas! David! Stop it right now!" Mabel shouted. "There's no reason for you two to be arguing like this."

Jonas's face was flushed with anger. Turning to his wife, he said, "It's time he learned to obey my orders, Mabel. He's too soft on the slaves, and he's got to see that. If he'll work them like I say, they'll get used to it, and we won't have any more trouble from them."

"Well," she said, "maybe David's way is best. I don't think we'd have seen what we saw today if you had let David do his job the way he sees fit."

Jonas eyed his wife dully and said, "You watch after the affairs of the house, Mabel, and I'll take care of running the plantation. This is between David and me. You go back to the house, now."

David patted her arm and said quietly, "Go on, Ma. There's no reason for you to get wedged between Pa and me."

Mabel's lower lip quivered and tears misted her eyes. Patting her son's cheek, she gave Jonas a sharp glare and walked away.

Jonas watched her for a few seconds, then turned back to David and said, "I don't want to hear any more out of you. When I say you'll work the slaves hard for sixteen hours a day, I mean for you to do just that. Do you understand me?"

David's voice was measured as he said, "I understand, yes. But I will not be a part of working them till they drop."

"They aren't gonna drop!" cried Jonas. "And if they do, it'll be an act. Their Maker gave them strong bodies because He intended for them to be slaves. You're just too soft-headed to see that."

"God never intended for anybody to be slaves," David protested. "You'll never convince me any different. Every man has a right to be free."

Daniel Hart was standing a few feet away. He swallowed hard when he saw the fury in his father's features. Jonas's cheeks were mottled and his eyes had turned the color of slate. "You don't belong here any more, David!" he bellowed. "You're through! Do you hear me? Through!"

Daniel jumped between them, strain showing on his face. "Pa, you don't mean that! David's your own son!"

Ignoring him, Jonas looked past him to David and growled, "I mean it! Get off this plantation!"

"Suits me fine!" retorted David. "Get somebody else to do your dirty work."

"Get off this property, David!" bawled Jonas. "Take your wife and get out!"

"I will!" shouted David, turning and walking toward the mansion. Over his shoulder, he warned, "You better not push those slaves any further than you already have. What you saw today from Cletus and the others is only the tip of the iceberg."

"Shut up!" snapped the irate father. "I don't need any of your stinking Yankee abolitionist advice. Just pack up and get out!"

Web Steele moved past Jonas, carrying Dexter in his arms, heading for his buggy.

"Wait a minute, Web," said Jonas, hurrying to flank him. "If you're taking him into Richmond to the doctor, when will you be back with your check?"

Daniel moved up to Web's other side as he headed toward the buggy without breaking stride. Dexter's head lay against his chest, his eyes closed and his mouth set against the pain.

Without turning to look at Jonas, Steele said, "It may be tomorrow. I'll stay with Dexter till I'm sure he's going to be okay."

"But you said you'd pay me today," argued Jonas.

"I ought to make you collect the thousand for Orman from Exley," said Steele as they drew up to the buggy.

"Oh, no you don't!" said Jonas. "You gave me your word that you'd pay me a thousand apiece for them. It wasn't my fault Reed shot them."

"It wasn't my fault, either," sighed Steele as he gently placed Dexter on the seat. "But since I'm a man of my word, I'll pay you the two thousand as soon as I can bring it to you." Finding it difficult to put Dexter in a comfortable position on the buggy seat, he turned to the younger Hart and said, "Daniel, I could use your help. Would you mind riding along with me and holding onto Dexter?"

"I'd be glad to," smiled Daniel. "Would...would you give me a couple minutes to tell my brother good-bye?"

"Sure...but hurry."

Jonas glared at Daniel as he ran toward the house, then said to Steele, "You could have asked me if it's all right for Daniel to ride into town with you."

Web had had more than enough of Jonas Hart for one day, but he kept his voice unruffled as he said, "Daniel's an adult. I didn't know he had to ask your permission."

Jonas bit his tongue to check the retort that flashed into his mind.

While he kept Dexter from falling from the seat, Web said, "Jonas, you haven't asked for my advice, but I'm going to give it to you anyhow. You ought to reconsider your firing of David. Decisions made in the heat of passion are usually foolish ones. If you don't reverse it, it'll—"

"Like you said," interrupted Jonas, "I haven't asked for your advice. So keep it to yourself."

Inside the mansion, the family and the servants were gathered around David and Chloe in the large kitchen. The women were weeping. David had one arm around his wife and the other around his mother when Daniel entered the room.

"Oh, Dan," sobbed Mabel, "I can't stand this. Your father is acting like a stubborn fool!"

Daniel took hold of her hand and said, "I know, Ma, but there's nothing any of us can do about it." Looking at his brother, he asked, "Where will you go?"

"Beverly."

Daniel knew that Chloe's parents lived in the western Virginia town of Beverly. Harvey Trench owned a successful clothing store, and over the past two years had made several offers to his son-in-law, asking him to come work for him. "You going to take your father-in-law up on his offer?"

"Yes," nodded David. "I didn't tell you that when Chloe and I visited there three weeks ago, Dad Trench added more to his offer. He knows of my growing aversion toward slavery and offered to make me a partner in the business. I'm going to take him up on it."

"Can't blame you," said Daniel. "I'm sure you'll be much happier."

"What about you?" asked David. "Pa will probably want you to take my job."

"I'll tell him I'm just not overseer material," replied the younger brother. "I can't leave Ma and Pa, but I don't want the responsibility that you've had."

David smiled weakly and nodded.

Daniel quickly explained that he was going to ride to Richmond with Web and had to leave immediately. He embraced David and Chloe, saying he would try to come to Beverly soon and see them. Then he kissed his mother and hurried out of the house.

Web was waiting for Daniel in the buggy seat, supporting the wounded slave. Looking around for his father, Daniel asked, "Where'd Pa go?"

"Headed toward the slave shacks," replied Steele. "I tried to help him see that he was making a big mistake in letting David go, but he didn't appreciate my advice. Stomped off in that direction, muttering to himself."

With Daniel cradling Dexter in his arms, Web put the buggy in motion and headed down the shady lane to the road. He wanted to swing by the Ruffin place and tell Abby why he was late for their Saturday afternoon date, but he knew he had to get the wounded slave to the doctor in Richmond as soon as possible.

As the buggy rolled swiftly down the road toward town, Daniel said to the black man he held in his arms, "You'll be all right, Dexter. We'll have you to the doctor soon."

"Mm-hmm," responded Dexter, his pinched features revealing the pain he was experiencing. "I's glad Massa Web's doctuh will work on slaves. Lots of 'em won't."

"He'll have you fixed up good as new in no time," Web said. "When we get you to the Steele plantation, there are a couple of real pretty slave girls who'll be more than glad to nurse you back to health."

Dexter tried to smile. "Yassuh. I's jus' sorry I won't be able to work very good fo' a while, Massa Web."

"Don't you worry about it," said Web. "If Mr. Exley hadn't shot you, you'd be pulling your weight tomorrow."

"Dat's right," nodded Dexter. "No offense to Massa Daniel, heah, but I's glad to get away from de Hart plantation."

Daniel said to Web, "What are you going to do about Exley?"

"I haven't decided yet," replied Web. "I could take him to court for destroying what belonged to me, but I may just deal with him myself."

"Will Mr. Ruffin punish him?"

"Nope. By the time I get there, Exley will have John Ruffin believing that what he did was right. It always works that way. In Mr. Ruffin's eyes, Exley can do no wrong."

Daniel was quiet for a few seconds, then he said, "I wish you didn't face having Reed Exley for your brother-in-law."

"Me too," grinned Web, "but I'd put up with anything to marry Abby."

"Well, in about eight months, she'll be your wife."

"I can hardly wait." After a pause, Web asked, "When are you going to pop the question to Lynne?"

Daniel cleared his throat. "Well, I...uh...I haven't quite decided yet. Since we've only been courting for three months, I feel I should give it a little more time."

"You are going to ask her, though?"

"Oh, yes! I'm head-over-heels for Lynne. I've never met a girl who rang bells in my heart like she does."

"You're not hesitant because marrying her will make Reed Exley your brother-in-law too, are you?"

"Not in the least. I can't stomach the man, but as you say, I'd put up with anything to marry Lynne."

Reed Exley and Mandrake galloped for a mile after reaching the road, then slowed their horses to a walk. As they rode toward the Ruffin plantation, Exley said, "Now, Mandrake, I don't want you telling anybody about what you saw me do back there. I'll make my explanation to Master John, and nothing else will be necessary. I don't want the rest of the slaves to even know about it. So keep your mouth shut. Understand?"

Mandrake was feeling good about the big bruise on Exley's face. Deep inside, he was lauding Web Steele for putting it there. Aloud, he replied, "I undahstan', Massa Reed."

"I'm glad I took you along," said Exley. "You needed to see how I handled those two no-goods. If I'm crowded to it, I'll handle my slaves the same way. So you'd best remember what you saw today. If I get any kind of rebellion out of our slaves because of you, I'll not only shoot you, but I'll shoot them. Are you listening to what I'm saying?"

"Yassuh."

"Okay. So you'd better get the starch outta your pants and walk straight. If you show me any more resistance—even the slightest glimmer of it—I'll start by punishing Orchid for your sins."

Mandrake's mind ran to his beautiful wife. A cold chill washed over him. He would go crazy if Exley ever laid a hand on her.

"Am I getting the message across to you, black boy?" grunted Exley.

The deep hatred Mandrake felt toward Exley had grown this afternoon. He pictured himself strangling the life from the man. He knew Exley was capable of hurting or killing Orchid just to punish him. Keeping his eyes on the road ahead, he replied, "Yassuh. I got the message."

CHAPTER THREE

Beautiful Abby Ruffin sat on the long open porch of the Ruffin mansion, keeping a steady eye on the tree-lined lane that led to the road. Web Steele was late for their afternoon date, and it worried her. Web was always a little early for any and all engagements. Such deportment was indicative of his forceful and aggressive personality.

Abby had expected Web just about the time the sound of gunfire had erupted in the direction of the Steele plantation. She and her two sisters had been sewing baby clothes in the parlor when the firing began. Moments afterward, Reed and Mandrake rode at a gallop out of the yard. John Ruffin had entered the room to find his daughters collected at the window, watching Reed and the slave ride out.

Abby had expressed fear that the shots had come from the Steele plantation, but her father had calmed her quickly by saying the gunfire had come from much closer, perhaps from the neighboring Hart place. He explained to them that Reed had armed himself and was on his way to investigate.

The cool breeze that swept across the front of the mansion raised goose bumps on Abby's skin. Shuddering slightly, she lifted the shawl that lay beside her and wrapped it around her shoulders. The front door of the mansion opened and her two sisters joined her on the porch. Elizabeth, who was six months pregnant and weakened by her condition, sat down beside Abby and sighed. "No sign of him yet?"

"No," Abby sighed in return. "He should have been here forty minutes ago. It's not like Web to be late."

"Maybe he was on his way when those guns were fired and did like Reed," suggested Lynne. "Maybe he went to investigate."

Abby looked up at Lynne and smiled. "That's probably it, honey. I'm sure he'll be along pretty soon. I just hope he didn't get himself involved in some kind of trouble."

"I hope Reed didn't either," put in Elizabeth. "Papa seemed so sure the shots came from the Hart place. Reed is so brave and valiant. If there's a slave revolt at Hart's, he'll be right in the middle of it."

Abby felt her stomach flip. Reed Exley was anything but brave and valiant. He was arrogant and egotistical and wouldn't risk a fight unless he knew he had enough help around him to guarantee victory. Abby marveled at how blind her sister could be to what her no-good husband really was. She and Lynne exchanged furtive glances. Lynne didn't like Reed any more than Abby did.

At twenty-eight, Elizabeth was expecting her first child and had been experiencing difficulties since her third month. The family physician attributed the difficulties to her having her first baby so late in her twenties, but Abby and Lynne were certain Elizabeth's problems stemmed from the emotional stress Reed put on her. Of course Elizabeth would never admit to such a thing. Though Reed's mental cruelties kept her upset most of the time, Elizabeth did her best to conceal it. To hear her talk, Reed was a knight in shining armor.

Abby loved her older sister dearly, and wished she had shown better judgment in the man she picked for a husband. Of course, Papa John had done almost as much to ensure that Reed would become his son-in-law as Elizabeth had. Somehow, Reed had been able to wrap the old man around his little finger. The younger sisters had seen Reed for what he was the first time they met him. Their dear mother—God bless her memory—had seen through Reed, too, but her words of warning to John and Elizabeth had gone unheeded.

Elizabeth's hair was a mouse-brown, and she was quite plain. Abby did what she could to help her older sister, fixing her hair and helping her to use a little rouge on her face. With Abby's touch, Elizabeth was considered moderately pretty. She was tall and slender and, before she became pregnant, had very little shape to her figure.

Lynne, at twenty, was almost as tall as Elizabeth, but had a better figure and was more attractive. Her long hair was ash-blond, and she had the imagination and ability to style it in several different fashions. Her physical beauty and the bright spark of her personality had garnered many a would-be suitor. Lynne, however, was interested in only one man—Daniel Hart. She was living for the day when Daniel would ask her to be his wife.

Lynne moved around the bench where her sisters were and sat down on the edge of the porch. There was a worried look on her face as she said, "If Reed doesn't come back pretty soon, I'm going to ride over to the Hart place myself. I want to be sure Daniel is all right."

"I don't blame you, honey," smiled Abby. "If Web doesn't show up by just about the same time, I'm going with you."

"Might as well make it a threesome," spoke up Elizabeth. "I'm going, too."

"The two of us can do the investigating for you, sweetie," said Abby. "The one thing you don't need right now is excitement." She paused a few seconds, then added, "No sense in us getting all worked up over this situation yet. Let's give it at least another half hour."

Lynne agreed, letting her admiring gaze settle on the sister who was three years her senior. Lynne's heart carried an equal amount of love for both her sisters, but Abby had the edge on Elizabeth for admiration. Abby was the talented one of the three. She could sing and play the piano and the violin with the greatest of skill. She was bright, vivacious, warm, and compassionate. She was also the strongest of the Ruffin sisters. When their mother died almost two years ago, it was Abby who held her father and sisters together emotionally. She was the family's mainstay.

Lynne didn't mind admitting to herself that she also envied Abby for her striking beauty. Though Lynne knew she too was considered attractive, it was Abby whose elegant features turned the heads of men. Her sparkling eyes were the color of blue velvet, and her long auburn hair resembled the flame of a fiery sunset. Just under five-feet-three (some three to four inches shorter than her sisters) she carried an exquisite figure on a petite frame.

Though Abby had kept company with many young men from time to time, the only one she ever loved was the handsome, dashing son of Dudley Steele. Abby had fallen in love with Web when she was barely sixteen. Though they attended the same church and were often present at the same social functions, Web never seemed to notice her. Abby used to pray that he would notice her, and because he was five years older, she prayed that he wouldn't fall for another woman before it happened.

Abby's prayers were answered on December 4, 1858, when she was twenty-one. It was the day her mother was buried. People from miles around attended the funeral. It was at the graveside that Webster Steele set his eyes on Abby as she was comforting her father and sisters. He had known who she was for a long time, but on that day, he first took note that instead of looking at a mere girl, he was seeing a beautiful, mature young woman.

Web called on Abby a few days later and confessed that she had caught his eye at the graveside. A few weeks later, he also confessed that when she caught his eye, he fell in love with her. It was Abby's turn, then, to confess that she had fallen for him at sixteen, and had prayed that one day he would be hers. She was living now for the day they would be married.

Suddenly there was movement beneath the trees on the lane. Lynne jumped and cried, "It's a buggy! It must be Web."

Elizabeth remained seated, but Abby joined her younger sister at the edge of the porch, peering toward the horse and buggy that were winding along the lane in the dappled shade.

Seconds later, the buggy rounded the last curve, and they saw that the driver wore a stovepipe hat with bushy silver hair sticking out beneath the brim.

"Oh," said Abby, "it's Uncle Edmund."

"Well, girls," put in Elizabeth, "get ready to hear a lecture on politics, abolition, and how bad it's going to be if Abe Lincoln gets elected next month."

At sixty-six years of age, Edmund Ruffin was known in Virginia as the leading anti-abolitionist agitator in the state. A widower like his younger brother, John, Edmund lived comfortably off his two-thousand acre, eighty-slave plantation north of Richmond. When the slavery issue began to grow hot between politicians in the North and the

South, he had spent much time and money in an effort to persuade the southern states to secede from the Union and form a Confederate nation of their own.

Edmund was tall and slender like John, but as a badge of rebellion against the North, he wore his silver hair so long that it rested on his narrow shoulders and fell almost to the middle of his back. He was a grim man who never laughed and seldom smiled. The slavery issue consumed him. His hatred for the abolitionists and his desire to see the South break away from the North was all he ever thought or talked about.

Edmund swung his buggy onto the circular drive in front of the mansion and drew rein. Without smiling, he greeted his nieces, alighted, and tied the reins to one of the hitching posts that were provided for guests.

As he stepped onto the porch, Abby said, "To what do we owe this visit, Uncle?"

Edmund removed his hat, arched his bushy eyebrows, and replied, "Your father invited me for supper this evening. Didn't he tell you?"

"No," smiled Abby, "but it's nice to see you."

"I came early so as to spend some time with John," said Edmund. "Is he about?"

"He's in the library, Uncle Edmund," said Lynne. "You can go on in."

At that instant, Elizabeth stood and said excitedly, "Reed is here!"

Edmund looked on as the three sisters moved to the edge of the porch, eyes fixed on Reed Exley and Mandrake as they trotted up the lane toward the mansion. As they reined in near Edmund's buggy, Elizabeth called out, "Reed, we heard more shots after you left. Were they coming from the Hart place?"

"Yes," replied Exley, dismounting.

"What happened?"

"Just a minute, Elizabeth," Reed said tartly, "you can listen and learn while I talk to your father."

As always, Elizabeth tried not to show that her husband's curt mannerisms hurt her. Abby and Lynne exchanged glances, both wanting to slap Reed's mouth for the way he spoke to their sister.

Exley handed the reins to Mandrake, who remained mounted, and said something in a low tone. The handsome young slave nodded, then rode toward the barn, leading Exley's horse.

Edmund joined the women at the top of the steps as Reed began to mount them. "What's this about shots?" he asked.

"Come on in, Edmund," Exley clipped, shoving his way past the women and heading for the door. "You can listen also while I tell John."

Assuming John Ruffin to be in the library—where he spent a good deal of his time—Exley headed swiftly down the hall in that direction. Elizabeth's condition made it difficult for her to keep up. Her sisters stayed by her side, knowing it would be useless to ask Reed to slow down. Edmund walked ahead of them.

Abby called out, "Reed, did you happen to see Web on the road?"

"Not on the road," he replied over his shoulder, "but he was at the Hart place before I got there."

"Is he all right?"

"Yes."

"Is he still there?"

"I'm not sure, Abby." His tone was much kinder toward her than the one he had used on Elizabeth.

"What do you mean?" queried Abby.

"I mean, he may have taken a wounded slave into town to a doctor."

Satisfied that Web was in no danger, Abby told herself she would have to wait to learn any more from Reed.

Since there had been shots fired at the Hart place, Lynne was concerned about Daniel but refrained from asking Reed about him. Certainly he would have told her if anything had happened to Daniel.

Exley reached the door of the library and tapped lightly, saying, "John, may I see you? It's important."

"Come in," came John Ruffin's reply.

Exley opened the door and entered the library.

John was on his feet, holding a book in his hand. Concern was etched on his face as he asked, "Did you find out what the shooting was all about?"

"Yes, I did," nodded Exley, "and I want to tell you about it."

John looked past his son-in-law to see his daughters and Edmund filing through the door. Edmund had paused in the hall to allow the women to enter first.

"We want to hear it too, Papa," said Elizabeth, holding her midsection and making her way toward an overstuffed chair.

The sun had set and the western sky was a deep purple as Web Steele hauled his vehicle to a stop next to Edmund Ruffin's horse and buggy. He wondered what new avenue of attack on the abolitionists the old boy had come up with this time. It seemed he always had something new cooking over his flame of hatred for Northerners.

Web used the heavy knocker at the front door of the mansion, and it took only seconds for the butler to answer. Charles was in his late fifties, and like Uncle Edmund, never laughed and seldom smiled. Managing a weak grin, he said, "Good evening, Mr. Web. The family is just beginning their meal in the dining room."

"I'm sorry to arrive at such an inconvenient time, Charles," said Web, "but circumstances prevailed this afternoon. If I could just see Miss Abby for a moment, I—"

"Web!" came Abby's voice as she rushed into the entry way. "Come in, darling."

Web removed his hat and stepped in, allowing Charles to close the door. Charles quickly disappeared as Abby raised up on her tiptoes and planted a soft kiss on Web's lips.

Gripping his upper arms, she said, "Reed told us what happened at the Hart place. How awful! Did you take the wounded one to the doctor?"

"Yes, that's why I'm so late getting here. I...I'm sorry we missed our Saturday afternoon ride. I was just passing the Hart gate when the first shot was fired. There was nothing I could do but plunge in there and see if I could help."

"I understand," she said softly. "I'm just so thankful nothing happened to you."

"Did Reed tell your father about it?"

"Yes. He told all of us, including Uncle Edmund."

"Did he tell you that he shot the two slaves after they had thrown down their guns?"

Abby looked at Web with surprise. "I don't recall him saying they were unarmed when he shot them."

"That figures," Web said. "I wonder just how much truth you got."

"Well, if it's typical Reed Exley," she said, "the way he told it would be about half true."

"Did he tell you that before he opened fire on them, I had agreed to buy them from Jonas?"

"No."

"That figures, too."

"You mean Reed shot them, knowing they were to be your slaves?"

"Yes."

"And you're under obligation to pay Jonas even though one is dead and the other is wounded?"

"Since I'm a man of my word, I am, yes."

"Is the wounded one going to be all right?"

"Doc Simmons says he'll be fine, but it'll be about three months before he's able to do a good day's work."

"Well, I'm glad that you won't lose your money on him."

A stony look came over Web's black eyes. "I don't plan on losing the money on the dead one, either. Mr. Exley's going to pay me for killing him."

"Knowing him, that may be difficult."

"I have no doubt it will."

"I hope this doesn't cause a problem between you and Papa. You know how he is about Reed."

"I'll talk to Reed privately about it, honey," Web said quietly. "Your dad won't have to be involved. I don't expect it to come out of Ruffin money. It's going to come out of Reed's own pocket."

"I suppose what Reed told us about his heroics was a lie, too."

"Heroics?"

"Yes. The way he told it, the two slaves were holding Darrel and Melissa hostage in the tool shed and were threatening to kill them. It was his sharpshooting that dropped the slaves so the kids could escape."

Shaking his head, Web chuckled dryly, "Boy, is that a lie! Dexter and Orman had already let the kids go and thrown their guns out. On my word that I was buying them and Jonas wouldn't harm them, they came out of the shed. It was then that Exley shot them."

"Oh, my," Abby sighed. "He didn't tell it like that at all."

"Of course not. He's got to make himself look like the hero. Did he explain the bruise on his face?"

"He told us that you put it there. He said you were angry because he had handled a situation you couldn't take care of, so you hit him. I knew you probably hit him, but that it had to be for a different reason than that."

"When he opened fire on those two slaves, I tackled him to keep him from firing any more shots. I was so angry at him I punched him hard—and it felt real good, too."

"I've dreamed of belting him a few times myself," Abby snickered. "I'm sure it did feel good. Come on. I'll have Harriet set another place at the table. We've just begun eating."

"Oh, I'd better not," said Web. "You've got Uncle Edmund here. I don't want to barge in."

"You're not barging in," Abby assured him. "After all, you're practically family."

Folding her in his arms, he breathed, "Yeah! Isn't that the truth?"

After a long, tender kiss, Web said, "I *would* like to spend a little more time with you. You're sure it's all right if I stay for supper?"

"Of course," she giggled, taking him by the hand and leading him down the hallway toward the dining room.

They could hear Uncle Edmund ranting about the abolitionists as they drew near the door. He cut it short as the handsome young couple entered the room. Elizabeth and Lynne greeted Web warmly as Abby called toward the kitchen for Harriet to set an additional place at the table. Edmund saluted him without smiling, and Reed gave him a cold look. John—upset that Web had hit Reed—mumbled a less-than-enthusiastic welcome. Abby noticed it and flushed with anger.

The place was set, putting Web next to Abby and directly across from the Exleys. John sat at the head of the long table, and Edmund at the end. While food was passed and Web was loading his plate, Edmund picked up where he had left off. "Yes, sir," he said, "there's real trouble on the way. We're gonna have a fight between the North and the South as sure as shootin'. And I say, let it come."

"My sentiments exactly, Ed," nodded John. "I'm sick and tired of those pious northerners trying to make us feel guilty because we have slave labor. Just let them come down here and try to make a profit on cotton while at the same time paying all their workers. It can't be done."

"Best thing that can ever happen in this country is secession," grunted Edmund. "We don't need those yahoos butting into our business. That's why I'm voting for Abe Lincoln."

Everyone at the table seemed shocked. Web set curious eyes on Abby's uncle and said, "Pardon me, sir, but did I hear you right? I've heard you call Abe Lincoln 'that black Republican.' You're going to vote for him?"

"Of course," nodded Edmund.

"But I don't understand," said Web, picking up his fork while staring at the old man. "Why would you vote for a man you despise?"

"Simple," said Edmund, leaning on his elbows. "If Lincoln's elected, there's no doubt in my mind that South Carolina will pull out of the Union. They're poised on the edge of secession at this minute. All it'll take to push them over the edge is for Lincoln to be elected. When South Carolina secedes, the rest of the southern states will follow. We'll have our own government, our own president, and our own congress. We won't have to put up with those rooster-tail Yankees anymore. We can get on with our lives as God intended."

"That's something I've been thinking a lot about lately," Web said.

"What's that?"

"Whether God intended for one man to own another."

Reed looked at his future brother-in-law as if he had just turned green. "That's a fine thing for a southern plantation owner's son to say," he growled. "You're building a fortune by owning and working black people so you and Abby can get married, and you don't know if God intended for you to do it?"

"Of course God intended it," said Edmund. "He made 'em black, didn't He?"

"He made them black," replied Web, "but why do we take it to mean that He meant for white people to make chattel of them?"

"You'd better not let your father hear you talking this way, Web," spoke up John Ruffin. "He might not take to it very well."

"I've already talked to him about it," countered Web.

"Oh?" said John, looking surprised. "And how did he take it?"

"He's not upset. I haven't forsaken my family's age-old position on slavery. All I said was that I've been thinking a lot about it. Dad doesn't try to do my thinking for me. And there's one thing he and I absolutely agree on."

"What's that?" asked John.

"That since we own slaves, we will treat them like human beings. We keep in mind that they have limitations just like we do, and that they have feelings just like we do."

"Umm," put in Edmund. "That kind of thinking can get you into a lot of trouble. You start being soft with 'em, they'll take advantage of you. If they think they can pull the wool over your eyes, they'll act like they're sick when they're not, and they'll put on like they're just plumb tuckered out when there's plenty of work left in 'em."

"Yeah," interjected Exley. "You give 'em an inch and they'll take a mile. That's the problem Jonas Hart faced today because David has been too soft on those black beasts. Jonas tries to fix the problem by applying some discipline to a couple of real rebellious ones, and they take his kids hostage."

"I'm glad you brought the subject up, Reed," said Web, fixing the man with a hard stare. "I noticed that you turned tail and ran like a scared rabbit when that bunch of slaves decided they wanted to get their hands on you for murdering Orman. What you did could have gotten Jonas and his whole family killed, not to mention myself. I had to do some tall talking to get them calmed down."

"Wait a minute, Web," said John, pointing a finger at him. "It isn't exactly murder when two men are holding guns on a couple of innocent young people and a sharpshooter puts some hot lead in them."

"I agree, but Dexter and Orman were not holding guns on Darrel and Melissa when Reed shot them. They had let the kids go at my word that they would not be punished, and had thrown their guns out before they came through the door of the shed."

Abby smiled to herself.

John shot a glance at Reed, then looked back at Web and said, "You aren't telling it like Reed did."

"You have that correct, sir," nodded Web. "Reed's lying."

Exley stiffened in his chair and was about to speak when John beat him to it. "Wait a minute!" snapped John. "Why would Jonas just stand there and let you give them your word that they wouldn't be punished for what they'd done?"

"He did that because he had agreed to sell them to me for a thousand dollars apiece. The deal was clinched then and there, and Jonas himself told Dexter and Orman that as far as he was concerned, they belonged to me and would not be punished."

Looking at his son-in-law, John said, "Reed, this isn't the way you told it to us a little while ago."

"Aw, he's lying to make himself look good," Exley said crustily.

"Am I?" demanded Web. "Tell you what—you sit tight while I drive over to the Hart place and bring Jonas back with me. You can tell your story to Mr. Ruffin in front of Jonas. I could bring Daniel along as an extra witness, too."

Exley's face blanched. Abby elbowed Lynne, who was seated next to her. Lynne returned the gesture.

Elizabeth turned and faced her husband. Uncle Edmund looked on impassively.

John said, "Let's get to the bottom of this, Reed. As soon as we finish eating, let's have Web go bring both Daniel and Jonas." The very tone of John's voice showed that he believed Reed's version of the story and was eager to call Web's hand.

Reed knew that Jonas and Daniel would verify Web's words. He glanced at Elizabeth. She was watching him intently, her eyes question marks. His scalp tingled and he could feel cold sweat at his hairline.

Exley hated Web for exposing him as a liar. It would be a pleasure to kill him. Thoughts were racing through his mind. The family was looking on, and his father-in-law was waiting for him to agree to settle the matter. There was only one way to save face, and Exley took it Clearing his throat, he said, "John, I haven't exactly been up front about this. Actually, I shot those two black scum-buckets after they had thrown down their guns. But I had to. You know how word spreads in this county. By Web's buying them like he did, they were going to get away with their crime. If this got out to all the other slaves in the county, we would have a massive revolt on our hands. Others would try the same thing against their masters...including ours."

John Ruffin smiled, eyed his son-in-law warmly, and said, "Well, Reed, I wish you had told me the truth to begin with, but I can see why you reacted as you did. You're right. If those two had gotten away with their crime, it would give reason for slaves all over to try the same thing. That settles it for me. You did the right thing."

Anger was mounting steadily within Web Steele and it showed on his face. As always, Reed was able to manipulate Papa John into his way of thinking and make himself look good.

Abby sensed Web's rising anger and laid a hand on his forearm, squeezing it slightly. Web patted her hand and said to the plantation owner, "Mr. Ruffin, I realize I'm not part of this family yet, and I don't mean to cause trouble...but those two slaves had been belt-whipped by Jonas until they bled. According to David, their only offense was that they had been worked to the point of exhaustion, and when Jonas wanted more from them, they couldn't do it. This type of thing has been happening on the Hart plantation for quite some time. Dexter and Orman had simply come to the place where they couldn't stand it any longer. I understood this, and so did David. After going as far as they did to gain their freedom, it was apparent that Dexter and Orman would no longer fit in on the Hart plantation, so to avert a tragedy, I offered to buy them then and there. It would have worked, and everything would have been fine, if Reed hadn't shot them down."

John Ruffin was quite fond of Web Steele and was happy that Abby was going to bring him into the family. For Abby's sake, he wanted to keep peace. Smiling at Web, he said calmly, "I'm sure you were doing what you thought was best, Web, and I admire you for it. What's done is done, so why don't we just forget it and talk about other things?"

Web got a hold on his temper and nodded quietly. Turning to Reed , he said, "When supper's over, I want a word with you in private."

Exley had a cup of coffee in his hand, and was staring icily at Web over the rim. Web met his gaze and held it. After a long moment, Exley broke the spell and looked away.

CHAPTER FOUR

There was a brief lull in the conversation at the Ruffin table. Then Uncle Edmund launched into his condemnation of the "underground railroad" that was helping runaway slaves elude capture by their southern owners. Edmund lauded the Fugitive Slave Law that placed the full power of the federal government behind efforts to capture escaped slaves. He then began a verbal attack on the touring troupes that were traveling the North and performing a play based on Harriet Beecher Stowe's book, *Uncle Tom's Cabin*. The book, published eight years previously, was the ultimate piece of abolitionist propaganda. It personalized the scandal of slavery and pictured Southern society as evil. By 1860, the book had sold over a million copies.

Edmund's temper flared even more as he told how Mrs. Stowe's book had poisoned Northerners' minds with wickedly contrived rhetoric depicting the inhuman suffering of Uncle Tom, Eliza, and Little Eva at the hands of the vile slave overseer, Simon Legree. The play was having an even greater effect, tugging at the heartstrings of observers who had been previously unmoved by outspoken abolitionists. From that subject, Edmund took a bead on the upcoming presidential election, repeating his intention to vote for Abraham Lincoln.

When the meal was finished, Web leaned close to Abby and said, "Can we take a little stroll after I talk to Reed?"

"Sure," she smiled, "but try not to punch him again."

"That'll be up to him," he replied. Looking across the table, he said, "Reed, I'd like to have our little talk now."

John's face showed concern. "Web," he said cautiously, "you put one bruise on Reed today. I hope you're not planning to—"

"Smack him again?" cut in Steele. "Sir, Mr. Exley got himself punched today because he opened fire on two unarmed human beings. Unless he gets violent while we're having our little chat, he'll not feel my fist."

"Maybe you should have someone with you," suggested Edmund.

"No, sir," replied Web, shaking his head. "This is private business between Mr. Exley and myself." Rising, he said, "We can talk out on the front porch, Reed."

Elizabeth asked her husband what Web wanted to talk to him about. Pushing his chair back and rising to his feet, Reed said, "I have no idea, but I'm about to find out."

Under the gaze of everyone at the table, Web gestured for Exley to go ahead of him, then followed the shorter man down the hallway to the entry way and out onto the porch. Charles had fired two lanterns that hung on either side of the door. The combined light cast an orange glow on the porch.

When Web closed the door, Exley turned on him and snapped, "Okay, what's this private little talk supposed to be about?"

"The thousand dollars you owe me," Web replied bluntly.

"What are you talking about? I don't owe you any thousand dollars."

"You heard me make a deal with Jonas to pay him a thousand apiece for Dexter and Orman. You killed Orman, leaving me to pay for a dead slave. You owe me Orman's price. I want it, and I want it now. I mean to give Jonas that much of his money on my way home."

"I'll have to talk to John about it before I can pay you," rasped Exley. "He may not want Ruffin money going for a 'dead horse' as they say."

Steele's voice hit him like the flat of an ax. "I'm not talking about Ruffin money, I'm talking about Exley money. John Ruffin didn't kill Orman. You did."

"You're outta your mind!" Reed gusted. "I ain't payin' you nothin'!"

"You'll come up with the thousand right now or so help me, I'll hog-tie you and take you to the Hart place and plant you on the doorstep of Cletus's shack. You know who Cletus is, don't you?"

Exley's breathing was coming in short spurts. He burned Steele with fiery eyes, but did not reply.

"Don't look at me like that," warned Steele. "I mean what I say. Cletus will tear you limb from limb if you refuse."

Exley ran a dry tongue over equally dry lips. He studied Web's resolute face. Reed knew he would be at the mercy of the huge black slave and his black brothers this very night if he refused Web's demand. Exley was tough and good with his fists, but he knew he was no match for the powerful man who stood before him. Steele could back up his threat.

Resigning himself to the inevitable, Exley licked his lips again and said, "I don't have that much cash."

"A check will do. Make it to Jonas. The kind of pay you get, I have no doubt it will clear the bank. If it doesn't, then I'll take you for a little visit to see Cletus."

Exley opened the door, telling Steele he would return shortly. It took him less than five minutes to go to his and Elizabeth's quarters on the third floor of the mansion and return with a check made out to Jonas Hart for the correct amount. When Web folded it and placed it in his shirt pocket, Exley said, "You know, I'm really sorry that you're gonna become part of this family. Too bad Abby doesn't have better taste."

Steele regarded him coldly. "I don't like you, either. Now excuse me. I've got a date to take a walk with that woman who has such bad taste."

Moments later a pale moon looked down on Web Steele and Abby Ruffin as they walked arm-in-arm beneath the towering trees along the lane that led to the road. A slight breeze was blowing and leaves were fluttering to the ground around them. The air had a bite to it. Abby used her free hand to tug at the collar of her coat and said, "Did you have any success?"

Patting his shirt pocket, Web replied, "Yes'm. Your kind and sweet brother-in-law wrote out a check to Jonas Hart for a thousand dollars."

"In protest, of course."

"Of course."

Neither one spoke for a long moment, then Abby said, "Web, I'm worried."

"About what, sweetheart?"

"This secession talk. While you were on the porch with Reed, Uncle Edmund said he thinks there'll be bloodshed before it's settled...a lot of bloodshed. Civil war."

"Could be," nodded Web. "I sure hope not. An awful thing, civil war. So many families have people on both sides of the issue. Brothers will be shooting at brothers, cousins at cousins...even fathers and sons fighting on opposite sides. Horrible thing."

"Do you think Mr. Lincoln will be elected?"

"Hard to say, honey. Mr. Douglas has a lot of people behind him. And so do the men running on the other tickets. If Lincoln gets elected, it'll be by a small margin."

"Small or large, it won't make any difference. If he gets in the White House, it's going to light the fuse. At least Uncle Edmund seems sure of it."

"He's not the only one," mused Web. "Most of the political experts say the same thing."

Abby stopped, released her hold on his arm, and looked up at him in the pale light. "Oh, Web," she said with a shudder in her voice, "if war comes, you will have to fight, won't you?"

"I suppose so."

Tears filmed her eyes. "I...I can't bear the thought of you having to go into battle. If...if something happened to you, I—"

"Hey, wait a minute," Web said, taking her in his arms. "Let's not borrow trouble. Maybe the experts are wrong. Maybe there won't be a war, after all."

Abby tilted her face toward his. The tears spilled down her cheeks, turning silver in the moonlight. Web cupped her face in his hands and wiped her cheeks with his thumbs. Worry sharpened the rounded lines of her beautiful face. "I'm sorry," she said in a half-whisper. "It's just...that I love you. I can't bear the thought of watching you march off to some battlefield, knowing that...that you might never come back to me."

"I love you the same way, darling," Web said softly. "I hate the thought of such a thing, too. Let's just take our lives a day at a time and not let the possibility of war ruin our times together. Okay?"

Abby smiled and nodded. Sniffing, she said, "Okay."

They were standing where the trees were far apart and the silvery spray from the night sky was dancing in her hair and highlighting the rich loveliness of her features. Their eyes locked in a gaze of love, and an electric spark of emotion leaped between them.

Suddenly Abby's arms were about his neck, pulling his head down. Their lips molded in a velvet kiss that momentarily swept them from a care-filled world to a carefree paradise of love. Web held her tight for a few seconds, then kissed the tip of her nose and said, "We'd better get back. I've got to deliver this check to Jonas before he goes to bed."

Abby nodded and held tight to his arm as they headed down the lane toward the mansion.

Election day in 1860 was on Tuesday, November 6. The Republican candidate, Abraham Lincoln, was at his Springfield, Illinois, home that evening, awaiting the results. His family and a few friends sat in the parlor with him. A young neighbor boy had volunteered to be Mr. Lincoln's runner between the house and the telegraph office, which was only a short distance away.

By eight o'clock that night, the telegraph reported that Illinois, which had gone Democrat in the 1856 election, had gone Republican. Later, they learned that the neighboring state of Indiana had followed suit. Soon came a flood of Republican victories from other northern states. Before midnight, Pennsylvania—home of the present president, Democrat James Buchanan—fell into the Republican column.

Just after midnight the big news came that New York, the state with the largest electoral vote in the nation, had gone Republican. Abraham Lincoln's election was now certain.

The citizens of Springfield went wild. Bands played. There was dancing in the streets. Firecrackers were set off. The president-elect walked a few blocks with his family and friends to the Republican headquarters for a victory rally. The elated crowd sang to Mr. Lincoln, ending each song with cheers and applause. Among his well-wishers were people who had voted for his main rival, Northern Democrat Stephen Douglas, for Abraham Lincoln had failed to carry his own county.

Late in the afternoon on November 7, when the final returns were at last recorded, the electoral vote reflected with appalling accuracy the sectional split within the country. Lincoln had carried every free state except New Jersey, which divided its electoral vote evenly between Lincoln and Douglas. South of the Mason-Dixon line, Lincoln carried nothing. Many southern states had not even placed his name on the ballot.

Tennessean John Bell, the Whig candidate, had captured Virginia, Kentucky, and Tennessee. The rest of the South went solidly for Southern Democrat John Breckinridge. Lincoln, with 180 electoral votes, had won the majority and would be the next man in the White House.

The popular vote, however, showed the proverbial tightwire that the new man in the Oval Office would have to walk. The combined opposition outpolled Lincoln by almost a million votes. Even in the free states, his total majority was under 300,000. He would assume office with only a tenuous hold on the people of his own section of the country.

Arrayed against Lincoln were the seven states of the deep South, and there was little doubt that if secession came, the four states of the upper South would join them. No matter how the border states had voted, no one could predict which side they would take in the event of a Southern secession.

By December 1, the pendulum in the United States was swinging toward just such a secession. In a effort to keep it from happening, a committee of thirteen senators held an emergency meeting. Their mission: to reconcile the South and salvage the Union. Led by Senator John J. Crittenden of Kentucky, the committee put forth a proposal to reestablish the old Missouri Compromise line and extend it all the way to the Pacific coast, permitting slavery in the territories south of a fixed and permanent latitude. Along with this compromise to appease Southerners, the committee also attempted to mollify Northern sentiment by strengthening the Fugitive Slave Law, and to make both amendments unrepealable and unamendable for all time.

The special senate committee hoped to have the plan adopted by Congress and then put to a referendum. It was killed, however, by the Republicans in Congress, who opposed it bitterly.

Meanwhile, the South was reacting vigorously to the election of the despised "black Republican," Abraham Lincoln. Aging Edmund Ruffin, the leading secessionist provocateur, was traveling from city to city, holding rallies and giving loud, agitating speeches that whipped up Southern passions and patriotism. The flames of rebellion against the Union were being driven and enlarged by the winds of Ruffin's powerful, persuasive, and prolific words.

Dark, ominous clouds filled the sky over Richmond, Virginia, on December 12, 1860. A storm was on its way, sending a raw, biting wind through the town.

Christmas shoppers gripped their hats, bending their heads against the wind. In spite of the cold and the impending storm, the holiday season was in full swing. Shoppers greeted each other cheerfully on the streets and in the stores.

Up and down the main street of Richmond's business district, saddled horses tethered to hitch rails laid their ears back and turned their rumps windward, while those hitched to vehicles stomped their hooves and fought their bits. Naked trees swayed in the wind, their jagged branches resembling skeletal hands against the dull-gray sky.

Webster Steele and Abby Ruffin emerged from Poindexter's Dry Goods Store and moved briskly down the boardwalk. Web's arms were full of packages. Abby held onto her wide-brimmed hat and labored to keep up with him, taking two strides for every one of his.

"Hey, Goliath!" she said, squinting against the bite of the wind. "Slow down, will you? Not everyone's as long-legged as you!"

Grinning, Web eased his pace and replied, "Sorry. I forgot."

Nudging him playfully with an elbow, Abby said, "I hope you won't forget on our wedding day! After we're pronounced husband and wife, we're supposed to walk down the aisle and out the door *together.* It'll look sort of funny if you pass through the door ahead of me!"

Web laughed, his breath forming a small cloud in the frigid air. "Never fear, my love. I'll remember. When we're married, I'll stick so close to you, you'll think we're Siamese twins!"

A coldness swept over Abby that came from the thought that gripped her, and not from the icy wind. *Unless you have to put on a uniform and fight the Yankees.*

They greeted friends and acquaintances along the boardwalk and finally reached the spot where Web's horse and buggy waited at the rail. The animal snorted at the sight of him and bobbed its head. Leaving Abby on the walk, Web moved to the rear of the buggy, juggled the packages while he opened the lid of the box, and placed them inside. Returning to his beautiful bride-to-be, he smiled, took her gloved hand in his, and said, "Okay, Miss Ruffin, how about lunch?"

"I'd love it," she smiled in return. "Especially if it comes with a bucket or two of piping hot coffee. I think my blood is icing up!"

It was nearly one o'clock, and the lunch crowd was thinning out as the happy couple entered the welcomed warmth of the Blue Ridge Café. Ralph Talbot, the café's owner, greeted them from behind the counter and said, "What are we having today? A family reunion?"

Web stared at him quizzically. "What do you mean?"

Pointing across the room with his chin, Talbot said, "Over there."

Web and Abby followed the direction he was pointing and saw Daniel Hart and Lynne Ruffin seated at a table. Both were smiling at them. Daniel rose from his chair and motioned for Web and Abby to join them.

"We don't want to butt in," grinned Web.

"You're not butting in," replied Daniel. "We just got here ourselves and are about to order. We'd love to have you sit with us."

"Only if you let me pay the bill," Web insisted.

Grinning broadly, Daniel hunched his shoulders and said, "Far be it from me to pass up a free lunch."

Web helped Abby shed her coat and placed it on a wall peg nearby. He hung his own coat over it, then placed his hat on top. Web seated Abby, then sat down opposite her.

To her sister, Abby said, "You didn't tell me you were coming to town today."

"I didn't know it at the time Web picked you up," responded Lynne. "Daniel showed up about half an hour later and asked if I wanted to go Christmas shopping."

"What'd you buy me?" joked Web.

"Nothing," giggled Lynne. "You've been a bad boy."

Shrugging, Web said, "Can't argue with that, but I wish Abby hadn't tattled on me."

The foursome had a good laugh, then gave their order to the waitress.

While they drank steaming coffee, Daniel said to Web, "Lynne tells me that Dexter is doing all right."

"Sure is. He's not up to a full day's work yet, but he's doing fine." Web paused, then asked, "What do you hear from David and Chloe?"

Daniel's face went grim, and Lynne patted his hand tenderly. "Well, they won't send any mail to us because of Pa's anger toward them, but once in a while they get a letter to us through my Aunt Althea here in town. She's Ma's sister. Last we heard, which was about three weeks ago, they were doing fine. David's quite happy working with his father-in-law, and Chloe's glad to be close to her family. Chloe's the one who does the writing. She said there's a lot of talk in western Virginia about secession. Folks over there are eager to pull away from the Union."

"Same as here," Abby interjected glumly. "I'm so afraid there's going to be a civil war."

"Lynne tells me Uncle Edmund is eating fire over it," said Daniel.

"That's putting it mildly," said Abby. "Uncle Edmund should have been a preacher. He sure knows how to sway a crowd. He's been traveling all over the South, firing people up against the Union. He predicts that South Carolina will secede before the first of the new year."

"He really wants to see a war come, doesn't he?" said Daniel.

"Yes," nodded Abby. "In the worst way. As old as he is, he'll still be right there in the middle of it. He hates Yankees and everything they stand for. He'd probably be the happiest man in the world if he could fire the first shot."

"Well, I don't exactly hate Yankees," said Daniel, "but if war comes, I'll sure be willing to do my part."

Lynne blanched. Taking hold of Daniel's hand across the table, she whimpered, "I don't want you fighting in a war...any war. I can't stand the thought of you facing enemy guns and possibly getting killed."

"Lots of men go to war and come back, Lynne," Daniel replied, squeezing her hand. "If I have to go...will you wait for me? I mean...will you stay my girl even if other fellows come around?"

Tears filled Lynne's eyes. "Yes, Daniel. Yes, I'll always be your girl, and more than that if you want me."

"Maybe Abby and I should sit at another table," suggested Web.

"Oh, no," Daniel objected. "You two are family. Well, that is, Abby is. You will be pretty soon, Web. It's no secret that Lynne and I are very fond of each other. In fact, we've been just on the verge...that is, I've been just on the verge of telling her that I love her and want to ask for her hand in marriage once I get her father's permission."

"Oh, Daniel!" squealed Lynne, tears gushing. "I love you, too! And, yes, I'll marry you. Papa thinks the world of you. I know he'll give his blessing to our marriage."

"Well, Abby," sighed Web, "it looks like you and I just sat in on an engagement. Tentatively, I mean."

"Tentatively only until I can talk to Mr. Ruffin and buy a ring," laughed Daniel.

"It's as good as done, then," put in Abby. "Papa's already told me that he hopes you and Lynne will fall in love and get married. He really does think a lot of you, Daniel."

"I'm glad to hear that," said young Hart. "I'll be very proud to be related to the Ruffins. Mr. Ruffin is already like a second father to me, and I sure do love Elizabeth, and—" Daniel faltered in midsentence at the name that flashed into his mind.

Abby read it in his eyes and voiced the name for him. "Reed?"

"Yeah," he said dully. "Reed."

"Reed," echoed Web. "The original wart on the face of the human race."

Lynne snickered as she thumbed away her tears. "I agree with that a hundred percent."

"Let's talk about something else," put in Abby. "That topic will ruin my lunch."

The others agreed, and the subject was changed. When the meal was finished, Web and Abby excused themselves, saying they needed to get on with their shopping, and left the "engaged" couple to themselves.

Heads bent against the icy wind, they headed down the street toward Sarah Weatherby's Ladies' Ready-to-Wear Shop. "This is the last stop for today, isn't it?" Web asked.

"Right," responded Abby, holding onto his hand. "I'll have a little more shopping to do next week, but this is the last major thing."

Sarah Weatherby was middle-aged and gabby. She was talking a female customer's ear off when Web and Abby entered the store. She took time to smile and wave, but kept on talking. Web followed Abby to a pair of clothes racks and stood patiently while she began to examine dresses one by one.

Sarah's customer left, and the portly proprietor approached Web and Abby. "Hello, Abby. Something for yourself?"

Abby had the skirt of a dress stretched out so as to view its cut. "No," she replied. "It's for Elizabeth. Christmas present."

But Sarah wasn't listening. She was greeting Web. When Web and Sarah had exchanged a few friendly words, Sarah turned back to Abby and asked, "What did you say, dearie?"

Letting go of the dress and lifting another one, Abby responded, "I said I'm looking for a dress to give Elizabeth for Christmas."

"Oh," smiled Sarah. "I thought maybe you were coming in to order that wedding dress you'll be needing pretty soon. The wedding is still on for early June, isn't it?"

"Yes," Abby smiled in return, giving the man she loved a fleeting glance.

"My, I'm sure it's going to be a lavish wedding," sighed Sarah. "Just be sure you give me plenty of time to fit you and get the order in."

"I will," Abby assured her. Then a thought struck her. "By the way, Sarah, where do you have your wedding dresses made?"

"New York."

"I was afraid of that. What will we do if the Union splits up and Virginia sides with the South? Those New Yorkers won't want to do business with us 'troublesome Southerners.' "

"Ps-s-s-t!" said Sarah, laughing. "There ain't no civil war coming, honey. All this tough talk by the politicians on both sides is just so much hot air. Nobody can make me believe that either side wants to shed blood over this slavery issue. Once Mr. Lincoln takes office, the whole thing will cool off and soon die out. He says he wants the country united, and I believe he's got the wherewithal to bring it to pass."

"I wish I could agree with you, Sarah," spoke up Web, "but by the very fact that Mr. Lincoln was elected, the whole issue has become a lit fuse on a powder keg. Unless there's some kind of miracle that snuffs out the fuse, the North and the South are going to be at war."

Sarah bit her lip. Glancing at Abby, she said, "I don't mean no offense, honey, but if your Uncle Edmund would stay home and mind his own business, it would certainly help to snuff it out. He's doing more to bring on war than anybody else."

Abby did not reply. She would not speak against her father's brother, but Sarah had just voiced her own thoughts about Edmund Ruffin.

Noting Abby's silence, Sarah cleared her throat and said, "So you...ah...want to buy a dress for Elizabeth?"

"Yes," Abby nodded. Pointing to one that had struck her fancy, she said, "I like this one. I think it looks like her, don't you? It's her size."

Lifting the dress off the rack and holding it up to Abby, Sarah said, "It is Elizabeth to a T, honey. Would look good on you, too."

"I'll take it," smiled Abby.

As Sarah carried the hanger and dress toward the counter, she said, "Is Elizabeth doing all right, now? I knew she was having some trouble."

"She was pretty sick for a while," replied Abby, following her, "but she's doing a little better now. Still awfully weak."

"When's she due?"

"January fifteenth."

"Mmm. Just over a month."

"Yes. I want to give her the dress for Christmas. It'll be incentive after she's had the baby to get back to her previous size."

Taking the dress off the hanger and laying it on the counter, Sarah rolled a length of white wrapping paper from under the counter and cut it with a pair of scissors. "She shouldn't have too much trouble, slender as she is."

"A little more trouble than you might think," chuckled Abby. "She's put some flesh on her hips, and of course, there's always the task of getting the tummy back to size."

The dress was purchased and the young couple returned to the street and the cold wind. Turtling her head deep into the upturned collar of her coat, Abby looked up at Web and said, "I think it's colder now than when we started."

"Yeah, you're right," agreed Web.

Greeting a few more acquaintances along the way, Web and Abby soon arrived at the buggy. While Web was placing the package in the rear box, Abby's gaze strayed across the street. Parked in front of the general store was a Ruffin plantation wagon, which she recognized instantly. Sitting in the bed of the wagon amid boxes of supplies was Mandrake and his wife, Orchid. Wearing only their thin clothing, they huddled close and shivered against the cold. Orchid was pretty and smaller than Abby. Mandrake had his muscular arms wrapped around her, trying to make her as warm as possible. They were both looking down and had not noticed Web and Abby.

Web dropped the lid of the box and moved to help Abby into the buggy. She let him draw near, then pointed across the street and said, "That's the wagon Reed always uses to come into town for supplies. Look in the back."

Web could not believe his eyes. It was not normal for a plantation owner's slaves to be subjected to such severe weather without proper covering. He looked around for Exley, but there was no sign of him.

Abby saw Web's jaw muscles tighten as he growled, "So help me, one of these days I'm going to wring your brother-in-law's neck."

CHAPTER FIVE

Mandrake raised his head as Web and Abby halted halfway across the street, waiting for a carriage to pass. When he saw them clearly, he spoke to Orchid, and she looked up. Mandrake hopped over the tailgate, then helped his wife to the ground. As the white couple drew up, the slaves bowed their heads slightly and lowered their gaze.

"Hello, Mandrake...Orchid," said Abby.

Still looking down, Mandrake replied warmly, "Hello, Miz Abby. Good aftuhnoon, Massa Web."

"Hello, Miz Abby," echoed pretty Orchid. "Aftuhnoon, Massa Web."

"Hello to both of you," Web responded amiably.

Abby laid her hands on Orchid's shoulders and said softly, "Sweetie, I have told you before—you don't need to bow to me. And you can look me in the eye."

Orchid set her large eyes on her husband. Mandrake spoke for both of them. "Miz Abby, we loves you fo' bein' so kind to us, but we've agreed that we'd best do it anyhow. It's bettuh fo' us not to break the habit. If'n we got used to not bowin' and lookin' down in the presence of y'all white folks, we might fo'get at the wrong time with the wrong puhson."

Abby glanced at Web and said, "Might that wrong person be my brother-in-law?"

Fear etched its claw-marks on the features of both slaves. They looked at each other wide-eyed, then Mandrake nodded slowly. "Yaz'm."

"I thought so," Abby muttered.

"Did Exley bring you to town?" queried Steele.

"Yassuh," nodded Mandrake.

"Where is he?"

"At the Lamplighter Tavern."

"Where are your coats?"

"We don' got coats no mo'."

"What happened to them?"

Fear was still on Mandrake's face as he said, "I don' like to talk bad 'bout Massa Reed, Massa Web. Maybe it be bettuh if'n I don' answer you."

"You can answer him, Mandrake," Abby said.

"Yaz'm," he said, then looked at Web. "Well, suh, the las' month or so, Massa Reed has been treatin' me extra mean."

"By 'month or so,' do you mean since the incident at the Hart place when he shot Dexter and Orman?"

"Well, yassuh. It started right after that, and has got worse evuh since. He keeps findin' fault with my work, and blamin' me when somep'n gits broke...like tools. An' oncet it was the latch on the barn door...and then it was the handle on the watuh bucket. An' then... then this mo'nin' it was the winduh in the tool shed. I did'n break none o' them things, Massa Web. Hones' I did'n. I aks all the othuh slaves if'n it was them that broke that stuff, and ever' time, they tol' me they did'n do it. They ain' got no reason to lie to me, Massa Web. They knows that I would'n tell on 'em. It's like that stuff is gittin' broke jus' so's Massa Reed can punish me fo' it."

In spite of the cold, stinging wind, Web Steele's face went hot and turned crimson. Looking down at Abby, he grumbled, "Yeah, and I know who's been doing it." To Mandrake, he said, "So what about your coats?"

"Well, this mo'nin' jus' befo' noon, Massa Reed come to our shack and aks me if'n I know who broke the winduh in the tool shed. When I say I did'n' know, he call me a liar and slap my face. He say one of the slave chillun tol' him he seen me do it. When I aks him which one, he cuss me and say he don' have to tell me. Then he take my coat off the peg. Orchid was fixin' lunch. He grabbed a butcher knife off the cupboard and cut my coat to pieces. Orchid could'n he'p it, Massa Web. She started cryin'. Massa Reed tell her to shut up. She try, but she so scared she cain't stop. He grab her coat an' cut it to shreds, too."

Abby looked at the small black girl, barely nineteen years old, and said, "You poor dear."

"After Massa Reed cut up our coats," continued Mandrake, "he say we gonna ride into town wif him so's we can load the supplies in the wagon. He say to punish me fo' breakin' the winduh, me and Orchid both have to make the trip with no coats."

Steele ranged the length of the street with his angry gaze, looking toward the Lamplighter Tavern. Looking back at the slaves, he said, "I'm going to have a little talk with Mr. Exley, but first I'm taking you two over to the clothing store and buying you some new coats. Come on."

"Oh, no, we cain't, Massa Web," gasped Mandrake. "Massa Reed tol' us to stay with the wagon till he come back. If'n he should come while we was in the store, he'd really get mean."

Hearing the trepidation in Mandrake's voice, Web said, "All right. I understand." Peeling off his coat, he dropped it over Orchid's shoulders and added, "Miss Abby and I will be right back."

Abby was shedding her wrap, too. "Let Mandrake have Master Web's coat, Orchid. You take mine."

"Oh, Miz Abby," protested Orchid, "you keep yo' coat on. You'll catch yo' death."

"Don't argue, honey," Abby said firmly. "Just do as I say. We'll be back shortly."

The sharp knife-edges of the relentless wind stabbed at the couple as they hurried toward Stockton's Clothiers a half-block away. "Web," Abby said, her teeth chattering, "I don't know if you should get too rough with Reed. He's Papa's pet, and I don't want Papa getting it in for you. We are going to be married in a few months, and I—"

"Don't worry, sweetheart," Web cut in. "I'll not tarnish Papa John's image of me by bruising his pet son-in-law, but I am going to let Reed know what I think of him."

Ten minutes later, Web and Abby were back at the wagon, watching the slaves shoulder into their new coats.

"Massa Web," Mandrake said, emotion quaking his voice, "we don't know how to thank you fo' yo' kindness."

"You don't have to," smiled Steele. "It's thanks enough for me just to know you're warm. Now, Miss Abby is going to wait inside the general store while I go have a talk with Mr. Exley. You two get back in the wagon bed and see if you can't huddle down between the boxes and get out of this wind."

Orchid's comely face pinched, and she elbowed her husband, saying, "Go ahead an' tell 'im, honey."

"Tell me what?" Web asked.

Mandrake said nervously, "There's nothin' Massa Web can do 'bout it, Orchid."

"Tell 'im," she insisted. "Maybe while he's talkin' to Massa Reed, he can make 'im see how wrong he is if he goes through with it."

"But Orchid," argued Mandrake, "it ain't right fo' us to expec' Massa Web to handle our problems."

"What is Reed up to now?" Web asked.

Mandrake pulled nervously at an ear. "Well, he...he's threatnin' to sell one of us at the slave auction comin' up jus' aftuh Christmas."

"He what?" blurted Steele, scowling. "Why's he threatening to do that?"

"Jus' 'cause he knows I don' like 'im, Massa Web. He's tryin' to break my spirit."

"If he sells one of us," put in Orchid shakily, "we'll be separated forevuh!"

Putting an arm around Orchid's shoulder, Abby said, "Now, honey, don't you fret about that. Slaves who are married cannot be sold separately."

"No offense meant, Miz Abby," said Mandrake, "but they can."

"He's right, darlin'," said Web. "They can."

Abby's velvet-blue eyes widened. "Why, I've never heard of such a thing! It just can't be possible."

"Tell her about your marriage vows, Mandrake," said Web.

Looking Abby square in the eye for the first time, Mandrake said, "When we said our vows befo' that black preachuh two years ago, Miz Abby, yo' papa an' Massa Reed were both there. Massa John had tol' the preachuh to be sure to include the word *distance* in the vows."

"Distance?" said Abby. "What are you talking about?"

"You know that part where you white folk say, 'Til death do us part'?"

"Yes."

"We had to say, 'Til death or distance do us part.' "

Abby looked at Web. "Why hasn't my father ever told me about this?"

Shrugging, Web said, "He probably never thought it had anything to do with you, so why should he bother to tell you?"

"Whoever came up with such a preposterous thing?" she gasped.

"Probably whoever decided slave owners needed an ax to hold over their slaves' heads. If they get out of line, threaten them with selling their husband or wife."

The constant bite of the wind had reddened Abby's face, but her anger made it redder still. "Reed Exley!" she spat. "That low-down, dirty—"

"No cussing, now!" cut in Web.

"I wasn't going to. *Skunk* was the word I had in mind. Web, how could he be so cruel as to sell Mandrake or Orchid?"

"It's easy for him," said Web. "He's rotten to the core."

"Well, I'm not going to let him do it!"

"I wish there was some way you could stop it, darlin', but if Reed decided to do it, you'll be powerless to do anything about it."

"Then I'll have a talk with Papa."

"You and I both know that won't do any good. You're angry, Abby, and you're not thinking straight. Mandrake just said that it was your father who made sure *distance* was in the vows. You know Papa John will never reverse any decision Reed makes concerning the slaves. If Reed decides to sell Mandrake or Orchid, there'll be no stopping him."

Opening her eyes, Abby asked, "When you go over there to the tavern to talk to him, will you at least try to make him see how wicked it would be to separate them?"

"I can try, but Reed Exley will do whatever he wants."

"I'll appreciate it if you try," Abby said, sighing.

"We will too, Massa Web," said Mandrake.

"Yes," nodded Orchid. "We will, too."

"All right," said Web. "I'll be back as soon as I talk to Mr. Exley."

At the Lamplighter Tavern, Reed Exley hunched over a table, playing with an empty shot glass. There was a half-empty whiskey bottle on the table. The cold wind had driven many men off the streets, and the place was nearly full. The large room was clouded with smoke and rumbled with the garbled sound of voices, punctuated intermittently with an outburst of hollow laughter.

Exley's hat was pushed back on his head, leaving a shock of blond hair exposed and a matted clump of it dangling on his forehead. A black cigar was between his teeth and he puffed heavy clouds of smoke toward the ceiling while he waited for his friend, Bob Tally, to return to the table.

Tally was owner of the Lamplighter and had stopped by the table to chat several minutes earlier. Secession and the threat of civil war became the immediate topics of discussion. As they talked, Tally had asked Exley if he had ever seen an edition of the *North Star*, a Rochester, New York, newspaper owned and operated by Frederick Douglass, a black man who had run away from a southern plantation in 1842. Exley had heard of the paper but had never seen it. Excusing himself, Tally went to his office to fetch the latest edition.

Exley poured himself another shot of whiskey, removed the cigar from his mouth, and took a sip. Sticking the smoking cigar between his teeth again, he smiled to himself, thinking of Mandrake and Orchid outside, freezing in the cold.

Tally, a tall, slender man of sixty-five, drew up to the table with a folded newspaper in his hand. Sitting down, he flopped the paper on the table and opened it to the second page. Holding it up so Exley could see Frederick Douglass's picture, he said, "This's him. He always writes an editorial on this page. Look at the headline over the article."

Exley focused on the bold print and read it aloud, "Editor is Thief and Robber." Squinting against the smoke that was drifting into his eyes, he said, "What's he mean by that?"

"Let me read it to you. He says, 'I admit that I am a thief and a robber. Eighteen years ago I stole this head, these limbs, this body from my master, and ran off with them.' What do you think of that?"

Exley swore around the cigar and said, "Somebody oughtta go up there to Rochester and put that insolent smart-mouth in chains...drag him all the way back to the South behind a wild horse and nail his black hide to a barn wall."

Tally snickered. "Here's more of his black insolence. Old charcoal skin says, 'The other day a young Negro just coming into manhood asked me what he should do about white oppression against us colored folks. I gave him his answer in just one word: agitate!' Now, how does that tickle your spine, Reed?"

Exley jerked the cigar from his mouth, his face purple with rage. Swearing profusely, he banged a fist on the table, causing glass and bottle to jump, and roared, "If I had big-mouth Douglass on the Ruffin place for just one day, I'd teach him some manners!"

The circle of men at tables around them grew quiet, and eyes turned to view the man who had just made the loud outburst. Exley gave them a fleeting glance, then looked back at Tally and growled, quieter this time, "Give me Douglass for even one hour, and I'd make him think agitate! I'd put a whip to his back and beat him till he drowned in a pool of his own blood!"

A man at a nearby table said, "Hey, Reed! You talkin' about Frederick Douglass?"

"Yeah," nodded Exley. "His kind need to taste a little Southern hospitality for bein' a big black mouth!"

A rousing cheer went up as men raised bottles and glasses toward Exley, voicing their enthusiastic agreement.

With all the excitement, no one noticed Web Steele enter the tavern. Closing the door behind him, Steele peered through the smoke and picked out Exley in the crowded room. Listening to the tumult, he quickly picked up that Exley was the center of attention. He had evidently said something for all to hear, and they were in full agreement.

Moving aside into the shadows, Web unbuttoned his coat and waited to hear what Exley would say next.

Waving his smoking cigar, Exley said loudly, "I hate the black guts of every banjo-eyed African beast on this planet! If it weren't for the free labor we cotton producers get from 'em, I'd say put 'em all on leaky boats back to Africa!" After a loud outburst of voices agreeing with Exley's sentiments, he stood up, stuck the cigar back in his mouth, and gusted, "Tell you somethin' else, boys. Around the Ruffin place, those darkies don't get away with anything! I work 'em so hard, they don't have the strength left to sass-mouth. I also have my ways of handling 'em when they show that they're even thinkin' about gettin' stiff-necked on me. There won't be any slave revolts on the Ruffin plantation, I'll guarantee you. I keep 'em just plain scared all the time."

"That's the way to do it, Reed," spoke up the slave overseer of a local plantation. "Keep 'em scared."

"Guess you've all heard about that little shootin' incident Jonas Hart had back in October," said Exley. "Y'all noticed that right after that, Jonas's mealy-mouthed, soft-hearted, blackie-lovin' son David got himself fired and run outta the county! Jonas hired a hard-nosed overseer a couple weeks later, and they haven't had any of that kind of trouble since."

"That's right!" came an unidentified voice.

"And I'll tell you somethin' else, boys," said Exley. "That mealy-mouthed, soft-hearted, African-lovin' son of Dudley Steele is gonna learn the hard way that bein' tender and compassionate with those kinky-haired beasts ain't the way to go. It'll backfire on him sooner or later. Of course, he ain't got much sense. Only reason he's even got the overseer job is 'cause the old man knows he couldn't get a job anywhere else. Feels sorry for him."

As Exley was saying, "African-lovin' son of Dudley Steele," Web detached himself from the shadows. The men of Richmond knew Web Steele. Eyes in the crowd bulged and mouths gaped as patrons saw him through the clouds of smoke heading toward Exley, whose back was to him.

Exley wondered why no one was voicing agreement to his statement about Web. Chuckling, he said, "And what's more, Abby Ruffin is going to marry Webster because she feels sorry for him. She's gonna waste her life with that useless, no-good—"

Web had circled around Exley and stepped into view while the man was in midsentence. The shock of Steele's sudden appearance registered clear to the marrow, stealing Exley's breath. He felt his face burn.

"That useless, no-good what?" demanded Web.

A tic began to jump under Exley's left eye, and his face went ashen, replacing the deep-red of his embarrassment. He swallowed with difficulty, not only fearful of the whipping Web Steele might lay on him, but also of the shame he would have to bear if all these men were to watch it happen.

Web's voice was raw as he repeated, "That useless no-good *what*, mister? You were telling all these men that Abby was going to waste her life with some useless, no-good something, but you didn't tell them what the useless, no-good something is. Finish it."

There was a crypt-like silence in the smoky room.

Exley could feel the eyes of the crowd on him. His mind was racing. He wished Bob Tally would speak up and demand that there be no fighting in the place, but Tally was silently looking on with the rest of them.

Exley once again found himself in a corner. He dare not lose face with the men of Richmond, but it would come if he got whipped by Steele. He would also lose face if he backed down. His mind flashed back to the day Web showed him to be a liar in front of John Ruffin and the rest of the family. Steele would like to have worked Exley over then, but he refrained for one reason, and Exley knew what it was. Steele wanted to stay in the good graces of Papa John. Reed was going to have to gamble that Steele would not attack him now for the same reason he didn't do it before. It was a gamble, but he was in a corner and there was no other way out.

His heart banged his ribs as he looked Steele in the eye and retorted defiantly, "You want me to finish it? Okay. That useless, no-good, blackie lover."

Web knew what Exley was doing. He had taken a long moment to reflect on the situation before making his reply. He was gambling that Web would not batter him because it would upset Papa John. Had Exley known about Web's promise to Abby, he would have answered sooner.

Web was glad Exley had already embarrassed himself in front of the other men, but he decided Exley needed a little more embarrassment. He reached out and seized the front of Exley's shirt with his left hand and yanked him close. Exley's hat fell on the floor. Putting his nose within an inch of Exley's and fixing him with a hard stare, he hissed, "I'm in a jovial mood because it's Christmas time, bigmouth, so I won't bloody up Mr. Tally's place today. But you and I are going to have a private talk outside right now."

Making a half-turn and jerking Exley so hard his feet momentarily left the floor, Web dragged him, stumbling and groping for balance, toward the door. With his free hand, Steele pushed the door open, then saw the crowd about to follow. Pointing a stiff finger at them, he rasped, "I said private!"

The men got the message and eased back. Web shoved Exley through the doorway onto the boardwalk and slammed the door. The cold wind lanced them.

Reed was indeed embarrassed and was struggling against Web's powerful grip as he dragged him to the corner of the building. People on the street stared as Exley was forced into the six-foot space between the tavern and the next building.

Slamming the short, stocky man against the wall of the tavern, Steele said, "Now, we're going to have a little chat!"

"It's cold out here," complained Exley. "I want my coat and hat."

Steele let out a quick gust of irritation. "Aw, poor thing! It's cold out here, is it? Well, that's exactly what I want to talk to you about. Abby and I found Mandrake and Orchid sitting in the wagon in this freezing cold. When we asked them where their coats were, they were afraid to answer. Abby convinced them it was all right to tell us, and they finally did."

"Yeah? Well, you only heard their side of the story."

"I don't care about your side of it, Exley. You drove them into town like that, so I don't have to wonder where the fault lies."

"Oh, is that so? You're stickin' your nose in where it don't belong, Steele. It so happens that those two are under discipline."

"Because you broke a window and accused Mandrake of it?"

Exley was having a hard time breathing with Web twisting his shirt collar at his throat and pressing him hard against the wall. "That's a lie," he croaked.

"You and I both know better, so let's not waste time discussing it," said Web, pressing Exley against the wall a little harder. "Even if Mandrake did break the window, your making him and Orchid sit in that wagon with no protection in this cold is wicked and inhuman."

"Says you."

Web took a step back, jerked Exley toward him, then slammed him against the wall. His voice was menacing as he said, "I bought Mandrake and Orchid new coats, Exley, and I'm warning you—don't touch them."

"You got no business buyin' coats for another man's slaves," Reed countered.

"Yeah? Well how about Abby? I have an idea she'll make it her business to tell her father about finding Mandrake and Orchid freezing to death."

Suspecting by this time that Web wasn't going to beat him, Exley sneered, "She may tell Papa John about it, but it won't change a thing. I'll explain my side of things, and he'll agree that my discipline was proper."

Web knew the man was right. John Ruffin gave Exley a free hand with the slaves, and he would never believe Exley himself had broken the window. Web wanted to thrash him, but he had made Abby a promise.

The icy wind was knifing between the buildings, and Exley's teeth were chattering. "Let go of me," he demanded.

"Not until you promise me you'll let Mandrake and Orchid keep those coats and wear them."

"All right, all right, I promise. Now let me go."

Web released his hold, but did not step back. "You better not be lying to me."

The sneer returned to Exley's face. "You know what your problem is, Steele? You're just too soft. You've got as many slaves on your place as we do. You ought to have learned by now that the only way to handle slaves is to treat 'em like the animals they are. Keep 'em scared and discipline 'em hard when they get outta line."

"Too soft? Let me ask you something. In the three years you've been John's slave overseer, how many have run away?"

"Thirteen. So what?"

"It proves that you're too hard on them. We've never had even one slave run away from our plantation. They're fed and clothed well, and though we expect them to produce by working hard, they're still treated like human beings."

"Human beings! Bah! They're animals, I tell you. Nothin' but black-skinned animals."

Web was struggling to control his temper. His hands ached to pound Exley, but he had to keep his promise to Abby. He knew if he stayed much longer, he wouldn't be able to hold himself in check. "One other thing, Exley. What kind of animal are you for threatening to sell Mandrake or Orchid and tear them apart? Don't you have even one little speck of decency in that twisted brain of yours?" With a parting glare, Web turned and walked away.

"Get off my back, Steele!" Exley called after him. "What I do with the Ruffin slaves is none of your business!"

Web made his way down the street toward the general store, where Abby waited for him near the large front window. There was anxiety in her eyes.

Stepping up to him, Abby asked, "How'd it go?"

"We had a little talk."

"Is he angry?"

"You could say that."

Her eyes widened. "You...you didn't lose your temper and beat him up, did you?"

"Yes and no. Yes, I lost my temper. No, I didn't beat him up."

"Did you talk to him about his threat to sell Mandrake and Orchid?"

"Yes. He said whatever he does with the Ruffin slaves is none of my business."

"Do you think he'll really sell one of them?"

"Knowing Reed, it'll surprise me if he doesn't."

CHAPTER SIX

H uddled in the Ruffin wagon, Mandrake and Orchid watched Web Steele enter the general store. Pulling his wife close to him, Mandrake said wistfully, "I wish Massa Web was our massa."

"Me too," agreed Orchid. "He's such a kind and gentle man. I sho' is glad Miz Abby is marryin' him. It's Miz 'Lizbeth I feel sorry fo', bein' married to that mean Massa Reed. Sometimes I've seen him treat her so bad, she has cried and cried."

"I has, too," nodded Mandrake. "Only Massa John nevuh sees it. He nevuh sees anythin' bad that Massa Reed does."

"He's like the devil," said Orchid. "He's crafty and sly."

The cold wind whined around the wagon as neither one spoke for several minutes, then Orchid gripped Mandrake hard and said, "Oh, honey, what we gonna do if'n Massa Reed decide to sell one of us?"

"I don' know," replied Mandrake. "We jus' gotta hope and pray that he don' do it."

"But what if'n he does? I cain't stan' the thought of livin' without you. I...I'd rathuh be dead."

"Don't talk that way, Orchid," said Mandrake, hugging her tight.

Orchid was quiet for a moment, then she said, "Maybe we should run away."

Shaking his head vigorously, Mandrake said, "No, honey! Massa Reed would find us...and when he did—"

"Not if'n we had somebody like Massa Web to he'p us."

"Orchid, you gotta stop talkin' that way. We couldn' put a thing like that on Massa Web. Like I tol' you, we jis' gotta hope and pray that Massa Reed don' decide to sell one of us."

Orchid began sniffling.

Mandrake used one hand to stroke her cheek. "Aw, c'mon, now honey. Don' cry. Ever'thin' will be all right."

"But Massa Reed seems to hate you so. Why? You nevuh done nothin' to him."

"I know, honey, but he knows even though I obey 'im on the outside, I'm disobeyin' 'im on the inside. I try nevuh to show it, but somehow he knows."

"I think it also bothuhs him 'cause the othuh slaves look to you as a leaduh 'cause yo' strong in both yo' mind and body. Massa Reed mus' think you is some kind of threat."

"Well, it could be, honey, but—" Mandrake's words were cut off by the sight of Reed Exley coming up the street.

"What is it?" asked Orchid.

"It's him. Massa Reed. He's comin', and he looks real mad."

Snow was starting to fall from the low-hanging clouds as Exley drew up, eyes blazing. "You two are in real trouble! Do you hear me? *Real* trouble!"

Mandrake felt fire deep within him. He could take Exley's mistreatment of himself, but when the man turned his anger on Orchid, it was all he could do to keep from laying hands on him. Holding his voice steady, he said, "We stayed with the wagon jus' like you tol' us, Massa Reed. Why we in trouble?"

"You blabbed your big mouths off to Web Steele!" Exley blared. "Told him about me cuttin' your coats up this morning, and got him to buy you new ones. You're gonna be sorry, black boy!"

"We did'n' say nothin' to Massa Web. *He* aks *us* where our coats were. We did'n' wanna tell 'im nothin' 'bout it, Massa Reed, but Miz Abby say we should. But we did'n' aks Massa Web to buy us new ones. That was his idea. He did'n' like seein' us freezin'."

Exley swore angrily, reached over the side of the wagon, and seized Orchid by the arm. He yanked her over the edge and flung her to the ground. Mandrake tensed and fire flashed in his eyes. Instinctively, he started toward Exley.

Taking a step back, Exley reached into his coat pocket and pulled out a small caliber derringer. Mandrake froze with his body halfway over the side of the bed. Orchid gasped from where she lay on the ground.

Eyes wild, Exley waved the derringer in the black man's face and hissed, "Come on, Mandrake! You've wanted to lay hands on me for a long time, haven't you? Well, come on! Just give me an excuse. Nothing would make me happier than to put a bullet into that muddled black brain of yours."

People on the street were gawking, but no one made a move to intervene. What a white man did with his slaves was his own business.

Staring at the gun, Mandrake eased back into the wagon bed. Tiny snow crystals were sticking to his coal-black hair.

Holding the gun steadily on Mandrake, Exley glanced down at Orchid and said, "Take your coat off, girl."

"Massa Reed," pled Mandrake, "please don' do this to her!"

"Shut up!" snapped Reed. "She'll do what I tell her!"

Fear etched itself on Orchid's face as she fumbled with the buttons on her coat. When she finally removed the coat, a gust of wind hit her like a cold fist, taking her breath. With his free hand, Exley snatched the coat and threw it on the ground. Orchid whimpered, hugged herself for warmth, and put her back to the side of the wagon

Still holding the gun on Mandrake, Exley glared at him and said, "There's a can of kerosene in there, Mandrake. Grab it and climb out of the wagon."

Fumbling for the handle on the one-gallon can, Mandrake asked, "What you gonna do, Massa Reed?"

"Shut up! Climb outta there and take your coat off."

Under the threatening muzzle of the derringer, the black man obeyed. When his coat was off, Exley said, "Throw it down there next to Orchid's and pour some kerosene on them."

"Massa Reed, please," Mandrake pleaded. "Burn mine if'n you

want, but please don' burn Orchid's. She's cold. Please let her put it back on."

Exley swore, switched the derringer to his left hand, and cracked Mandrake on the jaw with his right, knocking him down.

Quivering from the cold, Orchid broke into tears.

Switching the gun to his right hand once more, Exley backhanded the girl across the mouth, railing, "Stop that stupid bawling!"

Mandrake scrambled to his feet with murder in his eyes.

Leveling the derringer at Mandrake's face, Exley yelled, "C'mon, black boy! Try me!"

"You got no call to hit my wife, Massa Reed. Leave her alone."

Exley showed mock surprise. "What's this I hear? Is the black scum of a slave daring to tell *me* what to do?"

Mandrake held his gaze, but did not speak.

"You just wait till I get you home, black scum. You're gonna be one sorry slave!"

Mandrake bristled and clenched his fists. Orchid saw that he was at the breaking point. "No, Mandrake!" she shouted. "Don't do it!"

The muscular slave looked at her, forced his emotions under control, took a deep breath, and said, "Don't worry, honey. I won't."

"Too bad," Exley chuckled. Reaching into his shirt pocket, he pulled out a wooden match and handed it to Mandrake. "Now, do as I tell you, boy. Soak those coats with kerosene and set 'em on fire."

Obeying reluctantly, Mandrake poured the liquid on the coats, then knelt down and struck the match against the side of the metal can. Cupping the flame in his hands against the wind, he touched it to the wet fabric. The coats caught fire, and the flames spread rapidly, fanned by the wind.

While in the general store, Abby had decided to make a few additional purchases. Web was carrying the string-tied bundles as he opened the door and let Abby pass through ahead of him. Looking over her head, he noticed that a small crowd had gathered on the street. Then he saw the wind-whipped smoke and the yellow flames on the ground. When he realized the fire was beside the Ruffin wagon and saw Exley and the two coatless slaves, he knew what was burning.

Handing Abby the bundles, Web said, "He's not getting away with this. If what I'm about to do tarnishes your father's image of me, then so be it."

Abby said something that was stolen away by the wind as Steele ran toward the scene.

Exley caught a glimpse of Web just before he drew up. Pivoting, Exley aimed the derringer at him and yelled, "Hold it, Steele!"

Web skidded to a halt. "Put the gun away, Reed. Man throws a gun on me, he'll wish he hadn't."

"Just butt out!" Exley screamed. "These slaves don't belong to you, and you got no business buying 'em coats! Now, get outta my sight!"

Web stepped within reach of Exley and extended an open palm. "Give—me—the gun."

Exley was so angry at Steele that his mind slipped over the edge of sound reason. His face went purple with rage. Shaking the derringer at Steele, he spouted, "I'm gonna kill you and do Abby a favor!"

Web moved with the swiftness of a panther. Grasping the gun arm, he gave it a savage twist and the derringer flew out of Exley's hand. Like a maddened beast, Exley wailed and swung the fist of his free hand at Web's face, connecting with his cheekbone.

The blow stung Web. He let go of Exley's arm in time to avoid a second punch and countered with a hard right to Exley's mouth. Exley staggered back a couple of steps. He swore at Steele, then lunged at him, bending low. His head caught Web in the stomach, driving him against the Ruffin wagon, barely missing Mandrake and Orchid, who clung to each other in the cold.

Abby hurried to the derringer and picked it up. Jamming it in her coat pocket, she moved back to within a few feet of the wagon.

The wagon shook with the impact as the two men slammed against it, and the two horses in the harness flinched and nickered nervously. With his head still low, Exley started to pull back. But he was too slow. Steele brought his knee up in a vicious thrust, catching Exley square on the nose.

The force of the blow snapped Exley's head back and dropped him on his backside. Blood appeared instantly, bubbling from his nostrils. Steele stood over him, spread-legged, waiting for him to get up.

Cursing violently, Exley sprayed blood and leaped to his feet. He charged like a wounded beast, swinging wildly. Web dodged Exley's fists and launched a combination of blows that found flesh and bone with bruising force. Exley backpedaled and slammed into the wagon. One blow had opened a cut above his right eye and blood began to seep down, obscuring his vision. He hung there wiping blood with the back of his hand, swaying on rubbery legs.

Abby knew the cut would need a doctor's attention. She found herself not caring how her father felt about this fight. Reed had it coming.

Steele moved in for the finish, lashing out with both fists. Exley countered weakly with his right while using his left arm as a shield. Web plowed through it and connected with a right cross. Reed Exley bounced off the wagon and hit the ground face-first. He was out cold.

Mandrake and Orchid tried not to show their elation.

The crowd looked on in silence as Steele knelt down and rolled Exley over. As Abby stepped close, he said, "This cut is going to need some stitches."

"I would say so."

Rifling through Exley's pockets, Web found a roll of money and said, "Mr. Exley doesn't know it, but he's going to buy new coats for Mandrake and Orchid."

Web took enough money to cover the cost of the coats and put the rest back in Exley's pocket. Handing the bills to Abby, he said, "If you'll go buy the coats, I'll take him to Doc McKinley. I know he's not the Exley's family doctor, but he's closest. I'll be back shortly."

Hoisting the limp figure over his shoulder, Steele moved down the street toward the doctor's office while Abby led the two slaves to Stockton's Clothiers.

Ten minutes later, Web entered Stockton's to find Mandrake and Orchid smiling and wearing their new coats. Mandrake said, "Thank you, Massa Web."

"Don't thank me," grinned Web, rubbing the bruise Exley had put on his cheekbone. "Thank Mr. Exley. He paid for them."

"Mm-hmm," nodded Mandrake, smiling furtively. "In more than one way."

"So what's Doc McKinley say?" queried Abby.

"He'll live," replied Web. "Doc says it'll take four or five stitches."

"He regain consciousness by the time you got him there?"

"Not completely. He didn't know what day it was. Well, let's get you and these two people home. Reed can drive himself in the wagon."

Darkness was falling and the snow was coming down harder as the buggy pulled up to the huge white mansion. Charles was in his overcoat, lighting the kerosene lanterns on the front porch.

Mandrake hopped off the buggy and helped Orchid down. As Web was stepping down to assist Abby from the buggy, Mandrake said, "Massa Web, since you gonna be in there fo' a while, I'll take yo' hoss and buggy and put 'em in the barn. Then they won't git covuhed with snow."

Web thanked him and guided Abby up the snow-covered porch steps as Mandrake led the horse away with Orchid by his side. Charles greeted Web and Abby as he finished lighting the last lantern, then followed them into the house. Pausing in the entry way and removing his hat, Web said, "Just a minute, Abby. I'm going to take my hat and coat back out on the porch and shake the snow off."

Charles said, "Don't bother, Mr. Web. Just give them to me. I'll take care of that little chore for you."

"Thank you," said Web, handing Charles his hat.

While Web was slipping out of his coat, Abby said, "Darling, I'm going up to my room for a moment. I'll be right back." Suddenly her hand flew to her mouth and she gasped, "Oh, the packages! We forgot to bring them in."

"I don't know why I didn't think of them," said Web.

"We've both got our minds on this little talk we're going to have with Papa," sighed Abby.

"I can fetch them for you, Miss Abby," volunteered Charles. "Are they in the box of Mr. Web's buggy?"

"Yes, thank you, Charles. You're a dear. Just put them over here in the closet. I'll pick them up later."

"Yes'm," nodded the butler, taking Web's coat.

Web helped Abby remove her coat as they walked together into the large receiving room. Coat in hand, she moved toward the winding staircase, saying, "Wait here, darling. I'll be right back."

"You really don't have to sit in on this," Web said. "I can talk to your father alone."

Shaking her head, she replied, "Huh-uh. It'll sit better if I'm there to back up your story."

Shrugging, Web smiled. "Okay. Can't argue with that."

With admiring eyes, he watched Abby mount the wide staircase. When she reached the top, she paused at the banister, smiled down at him, then hurried down the hallway. He marveled at how she made his heart leap. No other woman had ever affected him that way.

Web waited in the receiving room in the light of the large candle-bedecked chandelier that hung overhead. The grandfather clock that stood in a nearby corner chimed once. It was a quarter of six. Dinner was usually at seven-thirty at the Ruffin mansion. There would be ample time to have his talk with Papa John. He dreaded it, but it had to be done. He thought of Reed Exley and wondered how things were going at Doc McKinley's office.

Abby returned within five minutes, having smoothed her hair. Web met her at the bottom of the stairs and said, "How'd you get to be so beautiful?"

"I take lessons," she giggled.

"Are they expensive?" Web asked, giving her his arm.

"Very."

"Well, you're wasting the money. You couldn't *get* any prettier."

Smiling up at him, she chirped, "I think I'll keep you around. You're good for my ego."

They reached the library door and found it partially open. Sticking her head in, Abby saw her father in his favorite chair, reading by lantern light. "Hello, Papa," she said cheerfully. "May Web and I come in?"

"Of course!" said John, laying the book on a small table next to the chair and rising.

Abby hurried to him, kissed his cheek, and said, "I was able to find the perfect dress for Elizabeth."

"Wonderful!" he exclaimed, sending a broad grin toward his

future son-in-law. "She walk your legs off, Web?"

"Not quite, sir," Web replied, running a finger across his mustache.

"You were planning to stay for dinner, weren't you?"

"Of course he was," piped up Abby. "I invited him."

"Good," nodded Papa John, "because I did some inviting myself."

"Oh?" said Abby. "Who?"

"Well...Mr. and Mrs. Steele, for starters."

"Wonderful!" said Abby.

Web smiled his approval. His parents were well-acquainted with John Ruffin, but he wanted them to get to know each other even better.

"I figure," said Papa John, "that since Dudley and I are going to one day be grandfathers-in-law, we might as well start spending more time together."

Web and Abby laughed. Then Abby said, "Who else are we having for dinner, Papa?"

"The McLaurys."

"Oh, wonderful again!" said Abby. "We haven't had Reverend and Mrs. McLaury in some time."

"That's great," Web said. "It's almost like...an occasion."

"Well, it is sort of an occasion," replied Papa John. "Since Reverend McLaury is going to be the one to tie the knot between you two, seems to me he'll have a definite part in making Dudley and me grandfathers-in-law."

"Oh, Papa," said Abby, kissing his cheek again, "you're a sugar lump!"

John's face tinted slightly. Clearing his throat, he said, "The McLaurys couldn't make it by seven-thirty, so we're having dinner at eight." As he spoke, he noticed the purple bruise on Web's cheekbone, and squinted at it. "What happened, son? You run into a swinging door?"

"Uh...no, sir," responded Web, touching fingers to the bruise. "In fact, I want to talk to you about it."

"Oh?"

"Yes, sir. It has to do with an unpleasant incident that happened in town this afternoon."

Puzzlement showed on the older man's face. "All right. Want to sit down?"

"Sure," Web nodded, trying not to show his uneasiness.

John Ruffin sat in his favorite chair while Web and Abby took seats facing him. Wanting to get it over with quickly, Web said, "I got this bruise in a fight with Reed, Mr. Ruffin."

"Reed?" echoed John, stiffening. "What on earth did he hit you for?"

"Well, sir, this is what I want to expl—"

"You said 'fight' so I suppose you hit him back. Does he look worse than you?"

"Well, yes, sir. I left him with...uh...with Doc McKinley in town. He's—"

"Doc McKinley!" blurted Ruffin. "What on earth did you do to him?"

"Reed's not hurt bad, Papa," butted in Abby, keeping her voice low and level. "Please just let Web tell you what happened. I was there, so I can verify what he tells you."

"All right," said Papa John, frowning. "I'm listening."

The plantation owner listened intently as Web told him about finding Mandrake and Orchid sitting coatless in the back of the Ruffin wagon. Leaving nothing out, he told of the anger that grew within him while he was purchasing new coats for the slaves, and of how he then went to the tavern and dragged Exley outside for a confrontation. John paled as Web told of Reed's use of the derringer and of his ending up at the doctor's office in need of stitches. John was about to comment when Web told him of Exley's threat to sell Mandrake or Orchid and separate them forever.

Concluding, Web said, "Mr. Ruffin, in view of what I've just told you, and Abby has verified, I strongly suggest that you put a firm hand on Reed. He is quite short on temper, and in my opinion, he holds a strong dislike for all Negroes, including your own slaves."

John Ruffin adjusted his position in the chair, rubbed his slender chin, and said, "I really think you're misunderstanding Reed, son. He's a good boy, actually. Has a lot of excellent qualities."

Abby felt her stomach turn over.

Web wanted to say that he had never seen even *one* good quality in Reed Exley, that he was *not* a good boy, and that he *did* understand him, but he could not bring himself to put it that bluntly. "Well, sir," he said, "you have your opinion and I have mine. But I am suggesting that you watch him more closely. I'm concerned that he will eventually do something that will cause real problems with the slaves."

John Ruffin forced a weak smile and said in a placating tone, "Web, I appreciate your concern, but I don't think it's as serious as all that. You see, Reed hasn't been himself lately. Elizabeth's illness has played on his nerves. This pregnancy has been as hard on him as it's been on her. He loves Elizabeth so much that he can hardly think of anything else, you understand. With his nerves stretched to the limit, he's been much quicker to fly off the handle than usual."

Abby wondered how her father could be so blind.

"But, sir," said Web, "Reed's brutality with the slaves was going on long before Elizabeth got pregnant. Abby's been telling me about it for well over a year."

John glanced at his daughter, then looked at Web and said, "Son, you must remember that Abby's a woman...a very tender and compassionate woman. What looks to her like brutality is really just firm, wise discipline on Reed's part."

Leaning toward her father, Abby said levelly, "You can tell yourself that all you want, Papa, but I'm not blind and I'm not stupid. I know brutality when I see it. Reed has been brutal with your slaves almost from the day you gave him the job. Lynne has told you about incidents she has seen also, but you turn a deaf ear. Please listen to what Web is telling you. If Reed is allowed to proceed as he has been doing, sooner or later there's going to be some kind of tragedy."

Ruffin raised his hand, palm forward, and said with a chuckle, "Don't be such a worry wart, honey. Nothing's going to happen."

There was a tap at the half-open door. John looked up to see Charles peering at him. "Yes, Charles?"

"Pardon me, sir," said the butler, "but your brother is here. Should I have him wait in the parlor?"

"Of course not," replied Ruffin, "show him in. We're just chatting about trivial things."

Web and Abby exchanged glances and shook their heads.

Charles stepped back into the hall and seconds later, Edmund Ruffin appeared, his long silver hair dangling on his shoulders. "Hello, everybody," he said in his normal boisterous voice. "Charles insisted that I wasn't interrupting anything important."

"Of course not," John chuckled. "Sit down."

Edmund greeted Abby and Web and moved to a chair beside Abby. Excitement was evident in his eyes. Standing in front of the chair, he ran his gaze over the three faces and said, "I've got good news, and I just had to come over here and tell it."

"So what's the good news?" asked John.

"South Carolina's going to secede from the Union!"

John's jaw slacked. "Are you sure?"

"Absolutely. You know I stay in touch about these things. I received a telegram two hours ago from my good friend Dave Jamison in Columbia. He's the richest plantation owner in South Carolina and a leader in the state. There's going to be a convention in Columbia a week from today, and he has been chosen to preside over it. The one and only reason for the convention is so the government leaders of South Carolina can vote to take their state out of the Union. Delegates will be there from all the other southern states. Dave wants me to make a speech and stir them up to go home and lead their states to do the same."

"I have no doubt that you'll be quite persuasive, Edmund," said John, smiling. "You've said all along if South Carolina pulled out, the rest of the southern states would too."

"It's bound to bring on a war," Web said with conviction.

"I have no doubt that it will," Edmund said flatly. "And if this is what it takes to make those thick-headed Yankees leave our bread and butter alone, then I say let it come."

Abby's face lost its color as she turned and looked at the man she loved. She knew if war came, Web Steele would be in the thick of it.

CHAPTER SEVEN

Web and Abby went to the parlor, leaving the Ruffin brothers to discuss the details of the upcoming secession convention. Charles had built a fire in the fireplace and the room was warm and cozy. Closing the double doors behind them, they held hands as they crossed the room and stood close to the crackling, popping flames.

Two lanterns glowed softly in the room, and the flames from the fireplace cast dancing shadows on the walls. Those same shadows were on Abby's exquisite features as she turned to face Web, her eyes radiating her adoration.

Their lips fused together in a lingering kiss giving vent to the love they felt for each other. After a long moment, Abby rested her head against Web's muscular chest. She drew a shuddering breath and said, "Oh, darling, I can't bear the thought of you going into battle. If war comes, you'll be expected to enlist...and I know that's what you'll do."

"I'll have to," he breathed, pressing her head tighter to him with the palm of his hand. "As a loyal son of the South, I must...even though I'm struggling over this slavery business."

Lifting her head to look at him, she said, "It's really bothering you, isn't it?"

"Yeah. Especially when I see the kind of treatment Mandrake and Orchid receive from your brother-in-law. I know that other slaves are being mistreated in the same manner all over the South. It's inhuman, and it's dead-wrong."

"But there are lots of slave owners like you and your father who treat their slaves well."

"I know. But I'm still not sure it's right for one human being to own another."

"Well, since Reverend McLaury will be here for dinner, why don't you ask him about it? As far as I know, he has never broached the subject from the pulpit, but I'm sure he'd tell you his view. It would be good for him to express it with Papa and Uncle Edmund at the table."

"I don't know," said Web. "If Pastor McLaury views slavery as wrong, Papa John might take it quietly, but your uncle is liable to lose his temper and start a fight. You know how he is."

"I guess you're right. Maybe you should just ask if you can talk to him in private. At least then you'd know how a man of God views the issue."

"Okay. I'll do it that way. After dinner, I'll ask him if we can talk privately for a few minutes."

Hatred toward Web Steele burned hot in Reed Exley as he guided the heavy-laden wagon up the winding drive toward the Ruffin mansion. Cursing the falling snow, he noted the presence of Edmund Ruffin's horse and buggy in front of the house. He was happy to see that Web's buggy was not there. Moving past the mansion, he drove the wagon to the first slave shack and hollered, "Lenox!"

It took only a few seconds for the door to come open, casting a rectangle of yellow light on the snow-laden ground in front of the shack. "Yes, Massa Reed?" said the slave from the doorway.

"Come out here and take the wagon to the supply shed. Unload it and be sure to wipe the snow off the boxes."

"Yassuh," nodded Lenox, reaching for his hat and coat.

Exley slid from the wagon and walked gingerly through the snow toward the front of the mansion. His face was swollen from the beating Web had given him, and a small bandage covered the stitches over his right eye. It throbbed with pain.

He mounted the steps and crossed the porch. Pushing through the door, he slammed it behind him and moved across the entry way into the receiving area, scattering snow as he went.

Having heard the door slam, Charles emerged from the hall and said, "We're having guests for dinner, Mr. Reed. We won't be eating until eight o'clock. What happened to your face? May I take your coat?"

Without replying, Exley threw his hat on the floor, scattering more snow, and quickly removed his coat, dropping it before the butler could get a hand on it. "John in the library?" he snapped.

"Yes, sir," responded Charles, leaning over to pick up the hat and coat. As Exley headed down the hall, Charles called after him, "Miss Elizabeth isn't feeling well, Mr. Reed. I think you should go up and see her."

He was sure Exley heard what he said, but the man ignored him. At the same time, the parlor door came open. Web Steele looked at the snow on the floor and recognized Exley's hat and coat in Charles's hands. "Reed's back, eh?"

"Yes, sir," the butler replied with lack of emotion.

"Sounded like he slammed the door right through the frame."

"If it weren't so sturdily built, he would have, sir."

"Upset, eh?"

"To put it mildly," came the butler's dull answer.

Exley found the library door closed and burst through it without knocking. The Ruffin brothers were seated and in conversation, which broke off immediately as they turned and looked at the intruder.

Unruffled, John looked at Exley's bruised, swollen face and asked, "Are you all right, son?"

"I'm fine."

"Web told me about the altercation you two had," said Ruffin. "I hope you're not too badly cut."

"My cut will be fine," grunted Exley. He glanced at Edmund without greeting him, then looked back at John. "I want to talk to you, and I want to do it right now."

Gesturing toward a chair, John said, "Sit down."

"A *private* talk."

"Edmund's my brother," countered John. "We can talk in front of him."

Remaining on his feet, Exley rasped, "I don't know what Steele told you, but for no reason at all, he attacked me on the street there in town!"

"No reason at all?" echoed Ruffin.

"That's right! You should break up the relationship between him and Abby right now. The man is a troublemaker. If Abby marries him, she'll lead a miserable life. Hotheaded and violent as he is, he's liable to get mad at her some time and beat her up good. She tries not to show it, but I know she's afraid of him. He's got her intimidated."

John rubbed his chin. "Now, son, I've never seen any indication of anything like that."

"Of course not," huffed Exley. "Steele is not gonna let you see him for what he is. And poor little Abby...like I said, she tries not to show the fear she has of him. But, Papa John, I've seen enough to know that it's there. I don't know what kind of hold he's got on her, but she's terrified of him. I'm tellin' you, you've got to break that relationship off before they get married."

"I'll have a talk with Abby," said John. "She'll tell me if she has any reason to be afraid of Web. Now, he told me about the situation over Mandrake and Orchid's coats. Did you actually cut up their coats?"

"Yes I did. Mandrake has been a mule to handle lately, Papa John. I haven't told you about it because I didn't want to bother you with such matters, but he's showing rebellion and he's a leader among the slaves. I've applied discipline in order to correct his attitude. Cuttin' up their coats was part of that discipline."

"Well, I can't fault you for that," John said, "but making them sit in the back of the wagon exposed to the cold...they could catch pneumonia."

"Exposed to the cold? What do you mean?"

"I mean being out in this cold weather with no coats."

"Oh, so that's it. I see Mr. Steele forgot to tell you they were wrapped in blankets. The only time they were exposed to the cold was when I had them loading the supplies into the wagon at the general store. I didn't think a few minutes would hurt them."

"But why did you burn the coats Web bought them?"

"Why did *I* burn the coats? It wasn't me who burned them! It was Mandrake. Apparently he didn't like Steele stickin' his nose into Ruffin business any more than I did. I was in the general store talking to some friends, and all this coat business happened while I was in there. When I came out, here was Mandrake setting the coats on fire after pouring some kerosene on 'em from the supplies in the wagon. I was reprimanding Mandrake for burning the coats when big boy Steele came from out of nowhere and attacked me. I got in one good lick, but I don't fight dirty like he does, and—"

"Exley, you're a liar!" boomed Web Steele from the open door.

The Ruffin brothers looked up, and Exley's jaw dropped.

Abby followed Web as he stepped into the room.

Exley's open mouth began to frame a word, but Steele cut him off. "You weren't in the general store all that time. Why don't you tell the truth? You were in the Lamplighter Tavern drinking. You're the one who told Mandrake to burn the coats, and you threw a gun on him when he was ready to jump you for manhandling his wife. I didn't attack you and you know it. You pointed that derringer at me and I told you to hand it over. When you shook it in my face and threatened to kill me with it, I took it away from you. You swung first. I told you if a man throws a gun on me, he'll wish he hadn't. From the looks of you, I'll bet you wish you hadn't."

Exley framed another word, but Steele cut him off again. "Abby and I have been standing here since you told Mr. Ruffin that for no reason at all I attacked you today. Since that first lie, you've done nothing but pile more lies on top of it. Mandrake and Orchid did not have blankets, and you know it."

"And what's more," spoke up Abby, "Web doesn't have some strange hold over me, I am not intimidated by him, and I do not fear him. That is a concoction of your own wild imagination."

Pointing a stiff finger at Exley, Steele said tightly, "I'm going to say to you what I said to Mr. Ruffin. It is obvious that you have a strong dislike for all Negroes, including those slaves who live and work on this plantation. If he doesn't get a firm hand on you, you're going to cause some real problems with the slaves. And while I'm getting this off my chest, there's something else I want to say. Only a heartless fiend would separate a man and his wife like you've threatened to do to Mandrake and Orchid."

Exley turned to John Ruffin and growled, "I don't have to stand here and take this abuse!" With that, he whirled and headed for the door. He avoided Steele's hard glare as he passed him, but gave Abby a lingering, wanton look as he moved past her and out the door.

Abby burned the back of his head with flaming eyes.

John Ruffin sighed, rubbed the back of his neck, and stood up. Edmund, who had remained silent throughout the heated exchange, also rose to his feet.

John drew a deep breath and let it out through his nose as he moved slowly toward Web and Abby. To Web he said, "I wish you and Reed would get along. After all, when you and Abby marry, you'll be part of this family, just as Reed already is. You two are going to have to lay aside your differences and work at keeping peace in the family."

Web looked him in the eye, wondering if he was still blind to the truth. He and Abby had both showed Exley to be a liar, but John's last words made it sound as if he had not heard any of it.

Just then Lynne Ruffin and Daniel Hart appeared at the door, giving everyone in the library a cheerful greeting. Lynne had been at the Hart plantation all afternoon and had invited Daniel home for dinner, unaware that the Dudley Steeles and the McLaurys were coming. When she explained this to her father, John clapped a hand on Daniel's back and told him they could set another place at the table just as they were going to do for Uncle Edmund.

Abby suggested that she and Lynne look in on Harriet in the kitchen and see if she could use some help. They also needed to advise her of the two extra dinner guests.

The men sat down in the library. Edmund was eager to tell Daniel the news of South Carolina's upcoming secession from the Union.

Arriving in the kitchen, Abby and Lynne found Harriet busy preparing a lavish meal. Harriet informed them that Elizabeth had not been feeling well most of the day, and that she wasn't going to eat dinner with the family. Abby was concerned and decided to go check on her. When Lynne offered to go too, Abby suggested that she stay and help Harriet. Lynne agreed, asking Abby to give Elizabeth her love.

Climbing the stairs, Abby wondered if Reed had gone to the Exley quarters on the third floor. She doubted it. He was probably pouting. Usually when Reed pouted, he went off somewhere by himself. She hoped he had done so this time. At the moment, she would rather see Elizabeth alone.

Topping the stairs at the second floor, Abby thought about the salacious look Reed had given her while leaving the library. She was glad Web hadn't seen it, or there would have been more Exley blood shed. She thought of the many times Reed had made passes at her since he had married Elizabeth and moved into the mansion. Such incidents had become more frequent since Elizabeth's pregnancy.

Abby had scolded her brother-in-law each time, and each time Reed had laughed it off, saying he should have married Abby in the first place. Showing her temper, she had shamed him for talking that way. The last time it happened—just a week ago—she had told him angrily that she never would have married him under any circumstances.

Reaching the third floor and moving slowly down the hall, Abby's heart went out to her older sister. She could not fathom what Elizabeth had ever seen in the egotistical, self-centered Reed. Sooner or later he was going to break her heart.

Abby would never tell Elizabeth of Reed's advances toward her. It would serve no purpose. Reed would deny it and probably try to drive a wedge between the two sisters. Neither would she tell Web. That kind of trouble the family could do without. In a few more months, Abby would be married to Web and out of the Ruffin house. She would no longer be vulnerable to Reed's advances. For the sake of everyone involved, she could tolerate him a little longer.

Much to her relief, Abby entered the Exley quarters to find Elizabeth alone. Reed had not been there since arriving home.

Elizabeth was lying on her bed. She was pale and feeling weak. Abby filled her in on Uncle Edmund's news of South Carolina's upcoming secession, and they discussed the probability of war between the North and the South. Elizabeth showed deep concern that if war came, her husband would have to enlist in the military. Abby said she had the same fear about Web.

The two sisters talked for quite some time, then Abby kissed Elizabeth's forehead and said she would send Harriet up with a tray of food. Elizabeth thanked her for the visit and asked that she greet the Steeles and the McLaurys for her.

When Abby reached the second level and started down the winding staircase, everyone except Reed had gathered in the receiving area. Charles was taking coats, and there was much chatter as Edmund eagerly made his announcement of South Carolina's impending secession.

Web looked up and saw Abby descending the stairs. He smiled at her and said, "There you are, darling. How's Elizabeth?"

"She's not feeling very well, but at least she's going to try to eat a little."

When Abby reached the bottom of the stairs, Dudley and Cora Steele embraced her. Dudley planted a kiss on her cheek and said, "Just a few more months and you can call me Dad."

Smiling, Abby kissed him back and said, "I think I'll just start calling you that right now."

Dudley laughed, hugged her, and said, "Honey, you just go right ahead!"

Dudley Steele was two inches shorter than his son, but had the same build except for a slight paunch that was making itself more evident than he preferred. His thick head of hair was salt and peppered, and the lines at the corners of his eyes were deepening. Abby told herself that if Web were as handsome at fifty-seven as his father, she would have no complaints.

Web's mother was two years younger than his father. She stood five-feet-four, and in spite of a few wrinkles and silver streaks in her light-brown hair, was very attractive. She and Abby loved each other dearly, and were looking forward to an even closer relationship when Abby also became "Mrs. Steele."

Turning from her future in-laws, Abby welcomed the family's pastor and his wife. Benjamin McLaury did not fit the mold of a preacher. At forty-three, he was rawboned and muscular with a rugged, steely look in his blue eyes. Like Web Steele, he was square-jawed and every inch a man. There was compassion in him, as was needed for a man of his profession, but there was also the temperament of a man who would not avoid a fight. Standing straight-backed and six feet tall, he commanded respect from men and women alike.

Dorothy McLaury, quiet and reserved, was a perfect complement to her husband. She was about Abby's height and quite pretty. Though she would soon turn forty, no one would suspect it. She was often mistaken to be an older sister of her twenty-two-year-old daughter.

John Ruffin led the group into the dining room, where Harriet and Charles were ready to serve the meal. As everyone was gathering around the large table, Reed Exley appeared. The guests immediately noticed his bruised face and the bandage over his right eye, but nothing was said. Exley acted as if he looked normal.

Before Reed found a seat, Harriet said, "Mr. Exley, I have a tray of food made up for Elizabeth. Would you like to take it up to her?"

Looking surprised, Exley said, "Why isn't she coming down to dinner?"

The maid had little liking and less respect for Reed. Giving him a disdainful look, she said, "If you would take the time to look in on her occasionally, you would know how she was feeling. She's been doing poorly today and doesn't have the strength to leave her room."

Abby wanted to applaud Harriet. John Ruffin's face tinted slightly; he conveniently discovered lint on his dark suit coat and began brushing it off. Web nudged Abby and was nudged in return. Lynne and Daniel exchanged furtive glances, grinning at each other. The Steeles and the McLaurys looked at their plates, and Uncle Edmund was busy adjusting his chair to a choice position at the table.

Though angry at the lowly maid's insolence, Reed masked his feelings and said, "I've had a rough day myself, Harriet. How about you or Charles taking the tray up to Elizabeth? I'll look in on her later."

Harriet's face was like granite as she replied, "Very well, sir."

Web shoved his chair back and said, "I'll take it up to her, Harriet. You and Charles are going to have your hands full serving the meal, here."

"That would be appreciated, Mr. Web," nodded the maid, smiling. She gave Reed a sharp glare and said, "The tray is on the center counter in the kitchen."

Reed looked a bit uncomfortable as Web left the room, but was spared momentarily while Reverend McLaury prayed over the food.

As soon as McLaury said, "Amen," Edmund began talking about the secession convention in Columbia, South Carolina, and with his loud voice, dominated the conversation. Web returned and took his seat beside the woman he loved. Exley quickly looked the other way.

When Edmund paused a moment to eat, Daniel Hart spoke to John and asked if he could talk to him some time soon. John was nodding his assent when Edmund butted in and said, "You'll have to get it done before the seventeenth, Daniel—or wait until after John and I get back from the convention."

Feeling confident of the subject young Hart wanted to discuss with him, John asked, "Is it important, Daniel?"

"Quite important, sir."

"Is it something that can wait until Edmund and I return from the convention?"

"Well, perhaps it could, but I'd rather talk to you before you go."

Smiling, John said, "I think I can make it quick and easy for you."

Daniel met his gaze and swallowed hard. "You can, sir?"

"Mm-hmm. Right here in public. The answer is *yes*. You have my absolute blessing to take Lynne for your wife."

Everyone laughed—except for Reed Exley, who remained stone-faced. Lynne's eyes filled with tears as she took hold of Daniel's hand.

Daniel wiped a shaky palm over his brow and said, "Whew! You sure made that easy, sir."

"Yeah, a lot easier than you made it for me!" chuckled Web.

There was laughter again, but Reed said nothing about the time he had asked John for Elizabeth's hand in marriage.

Reverend McLaury leaned past his wife to look at Daniel and said, "You two have a date in mind?"

"We really haven't discussed it yet, sir. I just asked Lynne today. Come to think of it," he added, looking at Web and Abby, "it was sort of public when I did that, too."

"Well, let me know when you decide on a date and we'll make plans accordingly," said the preacher.

"We'll do it," nodded Daniel.

"Papa," said Abby, "I didn't know you were planning on going to the convention with Uncle Edmund."

"Well, I made that decision after you and Web left the library. I think I should go and lend my support. Besides, I've never taken the time to attend one of my brother's anti-abolition rallies. I've heard he's a right fiery speaker, and I want to be there when he makes his speech at the convention."

Web remembered that he was going to ask Pastor McLaury for an appointment. He was eager to find out what the man thought of slavery. He would ask him for the appointment in private after dinner.

Reed spoke up. "I'd like to go to the convention too, Uncle Edmund, but since John's going, I'll need to stay here and look after things."

"I understand," nodded Edmund, brushing the long hair from his face.

Exley broke into laughter, as if he had heard something funny.

"What are you laughing at, son?" asked John, speaking in a tender tone that made Abby's stomach turn.

"I was just thinkin'," replied Exley. "I'd love to see the look on ol' Abe Lincoln's face when he hears that South Carolina's finally gonna cut the dog's tail off!"

"He already knows it," said Edmund. "There are plenty of people in South Carolina, as well as the rest of the South, who are Lincoln lovers. They've gotten the news to Washington already, and you can be sure the president-elect has heard about it in Illinois."

Deviltry showed on Exley's puffy face as he said, "It'd be good if somebody put a bullet in ol' Abe's black Republican brain before he takes the oath of office. With him outta the picture, that war everybody's talkin' about could be averted. It'll be Lincoln's fault if the North and the South get into it."

Benjamin McLaury set hard eyes on Exley and said, "This slavery issue has been going on since Abraham Lincoln was teaching himself to read by firelight as a boy, Reed. If civil war comes, it'll not be his fault, nor the fault of any one man. Mr. Lincoln was elected by the abolitionists in the North, yes, but if somebody murdered him as you have so coldly suggested, they would simply put in another man with the same views."

Exley looked at his father-in-law, expecting support, but none came. John Ruffin was a true Southerner, but he would not advocate the murder of any man.

Edmund spoke up next. "Do I detect some abolitionist leaning in you, Reverend? I've never heard you preach, but I'm wondering if you're a true son of the South. Have you preached in behalf of slavery in your pulpit?"

"No, I haven't," replied McLaury quickly.

"Weren't you born in the South?"

"Yes, I was. Right here in Virginia."

"Then you've got to be for slavery."

McLaury's jaw jutted. "Who says ?"

"I did!"

"Now, gentlemen," cut in John Ruffin, "we're here to enjoy a nice meal together and be sociable. Let's not get into an argument."

"You used the word *gentlemen*, Mr. Ruffin," said Daniel. "Since they are gentlemen, certainly they can discuss this issue without arguing. I've had discussions with my brother about slavery. He's dead-set against it. In fact, he and my father had a severe falling out over it and he moved to western Virginia."

"Where in western Virginia?" Edmund asked.

"Over by Rich Mountain. Town called Beverly."

"Mmm," nodded Edmund. "Know right where it is. Held a rally at Philippi, which is near there, a couple of weeks ago. If your brother feels that way about slavery, why doesn't he move north?"

"There are a lot of people in the South who are against slavery, Mr. Ruffin," Daniel replied levelly. "A man doesn't have to cross the Mason-Dixon line just because he has his own opinion about the subject." Turning to McLaury, he said, "Since we are ladies and gentlemen here, Reverend, I'd like to know your opinion on it. What does the Bible say about slavery?"

"That's a good question," put in Web. "Dad and I have discussed it several times. I was going to talk to you about it in private, Reverend, but since the subject is on the table, how about telling us your opinion?"

"Yes," spoke up Dudley Steele. "I'd like to know, if war comes between the North and the South, whose side will God be on?"

CHAPTER EIGHT

Benjamin McLaury could feel the eyes of everyone at the table on him as he looked at Dudley Steele and said, "I'll be glad to discuss with you what Scripture says about slavery, but I'm not convinced that God will choose sides if there is a war. He loves all of His children, and there are believers on both sides. This is exactly why I haven't addressed the subject from the pulpit. There are people on both sides of the issue in my congregation, as most of you know. And as you will see, the Bible leans toward every man being a free man, but does not actually condemn slavery."

"So you haven't preached on it because it could divide the people of our church just as it is dividing the people of the North and the South?" asked Dudley.

"Basically, yes," nodded the pastor. "However, I do not shun controversy where the Bible is clear-cut and definitive. I'm willing to fight for what I believe. I have in the past, and will do so in the future." Looking at John Ruffin, he asked, "May I borrow a Bible, John?"

Abby jumped up, saying, "I'll get mine, Reverend."

While Abby was out of the room, Web said, "Reverend McLaury, you are a good judge of humanity, since humans are your business. Do you think either side in this North-South split is willing to go to war? Some are saying that in spite of all the war talk, neither side really wants to shed blood over it. They say America will simply become a divided nation."

"That kind of talk is ridiculous!" blared Edmund. "Of course we're willing to shed blood over it! I certainly am! It's time we sever ourselves from those pious snobs up north who condemn us slave owners. They won't take their noses out of our business until we shoot them off."

McLaury said to Web, "I agree with Edmund that there are people in the South who are willing to shed blood. Like him, some are even eager to do it. I don't think the Northerners will start a war over it. When war comes, it'll be initiated by Southerners."

"You say when war comes, Reverend," spoke up Cora Steele. "Are you actually expecting it to happen?"

"Yes. As Web said, some political leaders are saying America will simply become a divided nation. I don't think so. Once South Carolina secedes next week, the other Southern states will soon follow. When a confederacy of Southern states is created, there will be an immediate controversy over some Union real estate located south of the Mason-Dixon line. Like the forts off the coast of South Carolina. The South will say it's their property, and the North will balk. When the war starts, that's probably where it will happen. Mark my word, the South will fire the first shot."

"Amen!" gusted Edmund. "And I'll be there to see it happen!"

Abby returned and handed McLaury her Bible.

While thumbing his way to an Old Testament passage, McLaury said, "To keep this from getting too lengthy, let me simply state a few facts, then I'll read you some Scripture." When he had found the place he wanted, he shoved his plate aside and laid the open Bible before him. "The Hebrew word for slave is *evedh*. The Greek word is *doulos*. It is interesting that in our English Bible the word slave is only found twice, once in the Old Testament and once in the New Testament. Jeremiah 2 and Revelation 18. All the other times, the words *bond-servant, bondman,* or *bondwoman* are used...or even the word *servant*. Of course *servant* did not always mean *slave*. There are many instances in both Testaments when you find the term *hired servant*. This, of course, was a servant who was paid."

"So when we read the word *servant* in the Bible," spoke up Daniel, "it means *slave* unless we're told he or she was hired?"

"Correct," nodded McLaury. "In the Old Testament, God allowed slaves to be acquired in a number of ways. One was when Israel's enemies were taken as prisoners of war. This is found in Numbers 31. Another way was by gift, such as when Laban gave his daughter Leah a young woman named Zilpah for her handmaid. A handmaid was a slave."

"But not to be whipped and beaten into submission, right, Reverend?" spoke up Lynne.

"That's right, Lynne. Slaves among the Hebrews were more kindly treated than slaves among other nations, since Mosaic laws governed their treatment. Remember that Moses got his instructions from the Lord, and He would never advocate harsh treatment and cruelty by one human being to another."

Abby looked at Reed, hoping he was listening.

"This is what I wanted to read to all of you," said McLaury. "I said a moment ago that God allowed slaves to be acquired. In Leviticus 25, He made it clear that no Israelite was to own another Israelite. Listen to verse thirty-nine and a portion of verse forty: 'And if thy brother that dwelleth by thee be waxen poor, and be sold unto thee; thou shalt not compel him to serve as a bondservant: but as an hired servant.' We know that by the word brother, the Lord means another Israelite, because in verse forty-six, He speaks of 'your brethren the children of Israel.' "

"But what about owning slaves who were not Israelites?" queried John .

"God did allow that," nodded McLaury. "In verse forty-four, He says, 'Both thy bondmen, and thy bondmaids, which thou shalt have, shall be of the heathen that are round about you; of them shall ye buy bondmen and bondmaids.' "

"Aha!" gusted Edmund. "See there! We Southerners are in the right."

"Let me hasten to point out that three times in this chapter God warns against ruling with rigor," said McLaury. "The dictionary will tell you that *rigor* is 'severity.' Too often slave owners—in that day and today as well—tend to forget that their slaves are human beings, and treat them with severity."

"Maybe there wouldn't be such strong objection to slavery on the part of abolitionists if all slave owners were kind and caring to their slaves," said Dudley.

"I'm sure that would make a difference," nodded McLaury, "although there would still be opposition against one human being owning another one."

"Well, if God commanded it," spoke up Edmund, "how can anyone be against it?"

"God didn't command it in the sense of requiring or demanding it, Mr. Ruffin," replied McLaury. "Since slavery was a practice in Bible days, He allowed it. But in so doing, He laid down some restrictions on how slaves were to be treated."

Edmund seemed displeased.

"I said earlier," proceeded McLaury, "that God allowed slaves to be acquired in a number of ways. I mentioned that they could be taken as prisoners of war, and that they could be acquired as a gift. They were also acquired by birth as the offspring of slaves already possessed. Exodus 21:4 deals with that. In the very next chapter, we find that if a man stole something from another and was caught, the man from whom he stole could own him as a slave if he couldn't make restitution."

"Good enough for him," grunted Reed.

Ignoring Exley's comment, McLaury went on. "In Exodus 21, we learn that a person could volunteer to be someone's slave if they so chose. Which brings me to an important point. In the laws that God laid down concerning slaves, He set it up so they could gain their freedom in a number of ways. I won't take time to read them to you now, but you can find them in Exodus 21, Leviticus 25, and Deuteronomy 15. Now, let me show you something from Exodus 21, imbedded in the very context of slaves gaining their freedom. In verse two, God says, 'If thou buy an Hebrew servant, six years he shall serve: and in the seventh he shall go out free for nothing.' So God put a restriction on how long a Hebrew slave could be held as a slave. After six years, he was free. The next verse tells how the slave's wife can be freed.

"Sometimes a slave owner would decide he wanted to make a maidservant his wife, and he would betroth her to himself. If he changed his mind later and took another woman for his wife, the maidservant was to be set free. Verses ten and eleven say, 'If he take him another wife; her food, her raiment, and her duty of marriage, shall he not diminish. And if he do not these three unto her, then shall she go out free without money.' So you can see that the context here is slaves getting their freedom.

"Then notice verse twenty-three: 'And if any mischief follow, then thou shalt give life for life, eye for eye, tooth for tooth, hand for hand, foot for foot, burning for burning, wound for wound, stripe for stripe. And if a man smite the eye of his servant, or the eye of his maid, that it perish; he shall let him go free for his eye's sake. And if he smite out his manservant's tooth, or his maidenservant's tooth; he shall let him go free for his tooth's sake.' The context here is slavery, and slaves going free. Catch these words: Eye for eye, tooth for tooth. Now, the same words are used elsewhere in the Old Testament in a different context, but that does not nullify this one.

"Now watch a change in attitude on this eye for eye, tooth for tooth position by the Lord Himself in the New Testament." Flipping pages, McLaury found the passage he wanted. "Jesus said in Matthew 5:38, 'Ye have heard that it hath been said, An eye for an eye, and a tooth for a tooth: But I say unto you, That ye resist not evil: but whosoever shall smite thee on thy right cheek, turn to him the other also.' Down in verse forty-three, He said, 'Ye have heard that it hath been said, Thou shalt love thy neighbour, and hate thine enemy. But I say unto you, Love your enemies, bless them that curse you, do good to them that hate you, and pray for them which despitefully use you, and persecute you.' "

Reed Exley was squirming on his chair as McLaury ran his gaze in a quick sweep across the faces around the table and said, "Seems to me that since Jesus changed the eye for eye and tooth for tooth approach, and that it is found in a slavery context in Exodus 21, that His approach to slavery just might be different in the New Testament, also. Slavery did continue in New Testament times, but the love of Christ seemed to militate against its continued existence."

"You say *seemed* to, Reverend," said Edmund. "So the New Testament doesn't come right out and condemn slavery?"

"No, but I do think it leans toward all men being free, as I said a little while ago. Let me read something from Colossians 4. The servants spoken of here are not hired servants but slaves. Verse one: 'Masters, give unto your servants that which is just and equal; knowing that ye also have a Master in heaven.' In my mind, that which is just and equal would have to be wages. It seems to me that God is saying to abolish slavery and hire your slaves as paid workers."

"But it doesn't exactly say that," argued Edmund.

"I know," nodded the preacher. "That's why I haven't preached on this subject from the pulpit. However, it implies it. But let me show you some more." Wetting his thumb with his tongue, he flipped back a few pages, found the proper spot, and said, "Listen to this in Ephesians 6: 'Servants, be obedient to them that are your masters according to the flesh, with fear and trembling, in singleness of your heart, as unto Christ; not with eyeservice, as menpleasers; but as the servants of Christ, doing the will of God from the heart; with good will doing service, as to the Lord, and not to men: knowing that whatsoever good thing any man doeth, the same shall he receive of the Lord, whether he be bond or free.' So the servants Paul is writing about here are definitely slaves—bondmen."

"Can't argue with that," put in Web Steele, who was showing great interest.

"Now listen as Paul addresses the slave owners: 'And, ye masters, do the same things unto them, forbearing threatening: knowing that your Master also is in heaven; neither is there respect of persons with him.' Since there is no respect of persons with God, the slave and his owner are on the same level in God's eyes."

"Can't argue with that, either," grinned Web. "And...uh...that part about forbearing threatening—that means to refrain from threatening them, doesn't it, Reverend?"

"Exactly," nodded McLaury.

Web looked at the puffy-faced Exley. "You hear that?" Exley did not reply. John Ruffin ran his gaze between the two men, showing his discomfort over the strain between them.

Benjamin McLaury noticed this but did not let on. Instead, he said, "So it is clear that if a man has slaves, he should treat them kindly, remembering that he and his slaves are on the same level in the eyes of God." Turning pages again, he added, "Over here in Philippians 2:3, it says, 'Let nothing be done through strife or vainglory; but in lowliness of mind let each esteem other better than themselves.' I can see a man accomplishing this command when he compares himself to his employees, but it seems to me it would be extremely difficult to esteem a slave better than yourself. This is why I believe the Bible leans toward every man being a free man. But as I said, since it does not come right out and condemn slavery, I don't censure men such as yourselves for owning them."

"But you would censure us if we mistreated them, right?" said Web.

"Most assuredly," replied McLaury, "and so would God."

Again, Web threw a sharp glance at Exley. Then looking at the preacher, he said, "Thank you, Reverend, for being willing to discuss this with us. It's obvious that you've studied this issue thoroughly, and you have answered a lot of questions for me. I tend to agree with you that the Bible leans toward every man being a free man. However, since my father is a slave owner and he treats his slaves with kindness and compassion, I will not turn away from him. I also want to say here and now—if war comes between ourselves and the Yankees, I will fight for the South. The Northerners have no right to force abolition on us."

"That's the way I feel, too," spoke up Daniel Hart. "As a true son of the South, I'll fight for the South."

"I don't want any of our men to have to fight in a war," Cora Steele said with a pained expression.

"None of us do, Mrs. Steele," McLaury said in a tender tone, "but I'm afraid the bloody conflict is coming."

"Well, if it does," piped up Reed Exley, "I'll be the first to sign up in the Southern army. It will be my pleasure to help wipe the stinkin' Northerners off the map."

"Amen!" blurted Edmund , slapping a palm on the table top. "I say let's get on with it and stomp the Yankees into the dust!"

Charles and Harriet had waited in the kitchen until the discussion on slavery was finished, then carried the dessert to the table. While fresh apple pie was being consumed, the wind began to howl outside, pelting the windows of the mansion with snow and sleet. The storm was definitely getting worse.

Edmund announced that he would head for home right away. It was eleven miles to his place, and he wanted to get home before the storm became even more severe. Cora told her husband that she wanted to head for home, also. Daniel decided his parents would be worried about him if he was much later getting home. Web told his parents he wanted to spend a few minutes with Abby, then he would be right behind them.

When all the guests except Web were gone, Reed announced that he was going upstairs to look in on Elizabeth. John went to the library, Lynne to her room, and Web and Abby sought privacy in the parlor.

When the couple entered the parlor, they found that Charles had added logs to the fire. Abby sat down on the love seat that faced the fireplace while Web stirred the logs. Then he made his way to the love seat and sat beside her. They looked deep into each other's eyes for a long moment without speaking, then he took her into his arms and kissed her.

The kiss was long and lingering. Before their lips parted, Web felt moisture on his cheeks. Drawing back, he saw the tears spilling from Abby's eyes. The conversation at the dinner table had left her with the awful dread that war could not be avoided. She had suffered nightmares recently, dreaming of Web going off to war and never coming back. Each time, she had awakened with relief, knowing that it had been only a bad dream. She had dared to hope that the two sides would settle their differences peacefully. But now hope was an island, speedily succumbing to the tides of reality.

Clinging to him, Abby sobbed, "Oh, darling, I can't let you go to war! I can't! I just can't!"

Wrapping his arms around her once again, Web held her close. "I wish we weren't facing this awful thing, Abby," he said in a half-whisper, "but there it is, confronting us like a ferocious beast. All we can do is meet it head-on. I know you would not want me to run from the fight when it comes. I'll have to do my part, along with all the other able-bodied men of the South. Like it or not, we just have to accept what comes."

Sniffling, she said into his ear, "I...I'm sorry. Of course I wouldn't want you to play the coward and run from the war. It's just...it's just that I love you so much. I want us to have our lives together."

"And I love you very much too, sweetheart," sighed Web. "There's nothing I want more than to spend my life as your husband."

Trembling as she clung to him, Abby said, "Oh, Web, you have to make me a promise. You must promise to come back to me! If...if you didn't come back, I wouldn't want to live! You are my life, darling. You must promise to come back!"

Web Steele knew there were no guarantees when a man went into battle. Some would live through it, and others would die. But at the moment, the woman he loved needed something to cling to. She needed to hear him say it. Pulling back, he looked into her tear-filled eyes and said, "I promise, Abby. I promise that no matter how hot the battles, and no matter how long the war goes on, I'll come back to you."

After another kiss, Abby walked her man to the door, kissed him goodnight, and watched him vanish into the storm as he headed for the barn and his horse and buggy. She waited at the window until he drove away, then went upstairs to her room.

Reed Exley entered the bedroom to find his wife sitting up and reading a book by the light of the kerosene lantern on her bed stand. She had brushed her hair in anticipation of his appearance, and had applied some powder and rouge to make herself more presentable.

Elizabeth focused on his battered face as he shut the door and leaned against it. Closing the book and dropping it beside her, she asked, "What on earth happened to you?"

"Got into it with Web—and I don't want to talk about it."

"Okay," she shrugged. "Does Abby know about it?"

"Yeah. Why?"

"Well, she was up here earlier, and she didn't mention it."

"Why should she? She knew you'd see it when I came up here."

"Web brought my dinner tray up to me. He didn't say anything, either."

"Probably for the same reason," Reed said flatly. "You notice the bruise I put on his face?"

"Yes, but I didn't say anything about it. Of course, I didn't know you had put it there. What were you fighting about? Is that a cut above your eye?"

"I said I don't want to talk about it," he grunted, pulling away from the door.

As he approached the bed, she smiled weakly and asked, "Did you enjoy the discussion at dinner, honey? Harriet told me about it when she came up to get my tray."

"Aw, it was all right," he grunted. "The reverend seems to think God's sittin' up there in heaven frowning at us for owning slaves."

"Well, maybe He is. I've often wondered if it was right to own another human being."

Reed chuckled and said, "Elizabeth, those black animals aren't human beings. There isn't a thing wrong with us owning 'em. If we can own horses, we can own blackies."

Elizabeth didn't feel like arguing. Smiling up at him, she asked, "Don't I get a kiss?"

Mechanically, Reed leaned over and pecked her on the forehead. As he walked toward a chair, he said, "It's snowing pretty hard out."

Elizabeth did not comment. She only observed him with hurt in her eyes as he sat down and began to untie his shoes. After a few seconds she said in a tight voice, "Am I ever going to get a real kiss again?"

Reed pulled off both shoes before answering. "You probably will when you have the kid and look like your old self again."

Tears welled up in Elizabeth's eyes and her lower lip quivered as she said, "A woman can't give birth to a child without her body changing. I'm sorry that I'm big, but you had something to do with it, Reed. It's your baby. If you loved me enough, my appearance wouldn't matter."

Reed carried his shoes to the closet and tossed them on the floor. He took a moment to remind himself that he must feign love for Elizabeth. As long as he was married to her, he would be part heir to the plantation. One day he would come into a great deal of money. He secretly wished it was Abby he had married, but told himself that some day it would all work out. Somehow the time would come when Elizabeth would no longer be in the picture, and both Abby and a huge chunk of the inheritance would be his. Web Steele loomed large in his mind as a barrier between himself and Abby. I'll find a way to remove Mr. Steele from the picture, too, he thought.

Forcing himself, Reed walked back to the bed and sat down beside Elizabeth. He took her in his arms and kissed her passionately.

When he released her, he said, "I don't know what's the matter with me, Liz. I didn't mean what I said a minute ago. Forgive me?"

"Sure," she nodded, "if you'll kiss me like that one more time."

Reed forced himself to comply, and after the kiss he patted her shoulder and said, "You have my undying love, Liz."

The next morning, Reed Exley stepped out of the mansion after breakfast into the bright sunlight. The air was frosty, and nine inches of snow lay on the ground. The plantation's male slaves were already busy shoveling snow from the walks around the mansion and from the wide porch. Mandrake and a slave named Schyler were removing snow from in front of the mansion where the guests parked their vehicles.

As he stepped off the porch and headed toward the barn, Exley gave Mandrake a sidelong sneer. Plodding through the snow, he entered the barn and moved to a rear corner where a small cubicle was built beneath the hayloft. Turning the key in the padlock that held the door secure, he entered the tight space and removed a wicked-looking metal apparatus from a hook on the wall. There were two others just like it on the opposite wall.

Smiling to himself, he examined the apparatus, which he called his "Beast Collar." Made of heavy iron, the collar was constructed to lock around a victim's neck. Four prongs, eighteen inches in length, extended horizontally from the circular collar, or neck ring. The prongs were made with two upturned hooks on their tips, and prevented the slave who wore it from lying down. Its weight caused the head, neck, shoulders, and back to ache severely.

Stepping out of the cubicle, Exley leaned the collar against the wall and padlocked the door. Chuckling, he reached into his coat pocket and pulled out the derringer. Before breakfast, he had asked Abby if she knew what had happened to the gun. When she told him, Exley demanded that she return it. Reluctantly, she went to her room and returned with the gun. When Exley took it from her, he smiled and told her she was especially beautiful when she was angry. She had stomped away and refused to speak a word to him at breakfast.

Checking the chamber of the small pistol, Exley found that it was still loaded. Smiling to himself, he slid it back into his coat pocket, picked up the heavy collar, and left the barn. Trudging through the snow, he called to the men who were shoveling and told them all to gather around.

As the black men made a circle around him, their eyes showed fear at the sight of the "beast collar," which now lay at Exley's feet. Mandrake was on the outside of the circle. Fixing him with a cold glare, Exley snapped, "Mandrake, come here!" The owl-eyed slaves cleared a path for Mandrake.

"Take off your coat!" commanded Exley.

The young slave's face went rigid. "Massa Reed," he said, "you ain't got no call to make me wear that thing."

"I'll be the judge of that," clipped Exley. "Get that coat off!"

While Mandrake looked Exley square in the eye and unbuttoned his coat, Exley said, "Didn't I tell you yesterday I was gonna make you one sorry slave for tellin' me what to do?"

"Yes," mumbled Mandrake.

"Well, now's the time." Speaking to the others, Exley said, "I want every one of you to pay attention, here. This belligerent beast had the nerve to give me a command yesterday. Nobody with black skin tells me what to do! Do you all understand?"

There was a chorus of "Yassuhs."

Reaching into his pants pocket, Exley produced the small wrench that served as the key to the iron collar. Inserting it, he opened the collar and said to two of the slaves, "Dariel—Hector—pick it up and put it on Mandrake."

Dariel, who was a large man, bristled. He said in a deep basso, "Massa Reed, I cain't do it. Mandrake is my frien'. I cain't put no pain on 'im."

Exley's pale blue eyes took on a diabolic look. He whipped out the derringer and pointed it between Dariel's bushy brows and ground out his words. "Dariel, you do as I tell you this minute, or the rest of these blackies will bury you before sundown."

Dariel looked at Mandrake sadly, then bent over and picked up the collar by two of the prongs. Hector quickly took hold of the other prongs and helped Dariel guide the collar over Mandrake's head till it rested heavily on his neck and shoulders. Breathing hotly, Exley stepped up and used the wrench to lock the collar. When he was finished, he said, "This'll teach you, black boy. Now get back to work."

Dariel turned to Exley and said, "Massa Reed, I don' mean no disrespec', but if'n Mandrake don' wear his coat, he gonna catch his death."

Grinning wickedly, Reed replied, "That'd just be terrible, wouldn't it?" Wheeling, he trudged toward the mansion, then stopped, looked over his shoulder, and said, "Oh, well. Go ahead and put his coat on him."

Exley watched Dariel pick the coat up and put it on Mandrake. Scowling, he said, "All right. Now, all of you get back to work." After a few seconds of silence, he laughed, "Hope you have a miserable day, Mandrake. I guarantee you'll have a miserable night!"

CHAPTER NINE

The next morning, Elizabeth Exley was sitting in a chair by one of the bedroom windows, observing her husband down below as he gave work orders to a group of male slaves. The sky was cloudy, and it looked like it could start snowing again at any time.

There was a knock at the door, followed by her father's voice. "Elizabeth, may we come in?"

"Yes, Papa."

John Ruffin entered the room with Abby and Lynne on his heels. As they gathered around her, Abby said, "You look much better today. Harriet said you ate all your breakfast."

"Mm-hmm," smiled the expectant mother, adjusting her uncomfortable body on the chair. "I feel much better."

"We came up to tell you that we're going into town," said Papa John. "We'll probably be gone till late afternoon. Is there anything we can get you?"

"I could use some new rouge and face powder, Papa," she replied. "Abby and Lynne know what kind."

"We'll take care of it," Abby assured her. "Anything else?"

"Not that I can think of. My purse is over there in the top dresser drawer."

"That's all right, honey," said John. "I'll buy it for you."

"That's not necessary, Papa," protested Elizabeth. "You shouldn't have to pay for my needs."

"It's all right," he said with a wave of his hand. "You and Reed will be putting out plenty of money when my grandchild is born." Leaning down, he kissed her cheek. "See you later, honey. Papa loves you."

"And I love Papa," she chirped.

Abby and Lynne both kissed Elizabeth and followed their father toward the door. Just as John was about to pass into the hall, Elizabeth called out, "Papa?"

"Yes, honey?"

"Did you know that Mandrake is wearing one of the iron collars?"

"No, I didn't," replied John, walking toward her, puzzlement showing on his face.

Abby and Lynne hurried behind him and peered over his shoulders as he looked through the window at the collection of slaves just beyond the barn near the first row of shacks. The distance was only some forty yards, and the pain on Mandrake's face was quite evident. Reed was standing in front of Mandrake, making him remove his coat.

"I wonder what Mandrake could have done?" mumbled John. "Has to be a pretty serious offense before one of my slaves wears a collar."

"Not since Reed's been your overseer," said Abby, almost without thinking. "He's put them on several slaves since you gave him the job. You just haven't seen them."

John pulled away from the window and said, "Well, if Reed sees fit to use that degree of discipline, they must need it."

"I can tell you why Mandrake's wearing the collar," said Abby in a tone of disgust. "He's being punished for that incident in town day before yesterday."

"You mean that incident over the coats?"

"Yes."

"How can you be so sure that's what it is?"

"Didn't you just see Mandrake's coat coming off?"

"Well...yes."

"Your son-in-law delights in freezing your slaves' blood, Papa. I've tried to tell you before—he's cruel to them." Noticing the pained look on Elizabeth's face, Abby laid a hand on her shoulder and said, "I'm sorry, Sister, but it's true."

Elizabeth reached up and squeezed her sister's hand. "I know it appears that way sometimes, Abby, but Reed can be quite tender when he wants to."

"Oh. Guess I've never seen him want to."

"Abby," said John, standing tall and straight over her, "is Web's little feud with Reed turning you against him?"

"Not in the least, Papa," she replied, meeting his gaze without blinking. "Reed is doing that all by himself." Again, to Elizabeth she said, "I'm sorry, but that's the way it is."

Elizabeth squeezed Abby's hand once more and said, "I'm sorry, too. Everything will be all right once the baby's here. Reed's been under a great strain with me being sick."

Abby knew Elizabeth's sickness had nothing to do with her husband's meanness, but she said no more.

Lynne looked out the window again, and said, "Papa, certainly Reed shouldn't make Mandrake work out in the cold without his coat."

"Don't worry, Lynne," responded John, patting her shoulder. "Reed knows what he's doing. He won't let Mandrake work without the coat for very long. He doesn't want a sick slave on his hands. Come along, girls. We need to head for town."

When her father and sisters were gone, Elizabeth looked back down at her husband, standing in the snow with the slaves. A mixture of emotions stirred within her. She loved the man, but she hated him. When she first met him, Reed had swept her off her feet. He was handsome in his own way and could turn on the charm when he wanted to. Soon after they were married and Reed was made slave overseer by her father, it became evident that he had married her to get close to the Ruffin money. Elizabeth would not admit it to herself at first, but she finally faced the truth. Reed Exley was a greedy man.

When she announced to Reed that she was pregnant nearly seven months ago, what little affection he had been showing to her began to fade. Half of her loved him because he was the father of her unborn child, and that half needed his love and affection.

The other half despised the man because he had proven to be greedy, cold-hearted, and cruel. Abby's words had struck close to home, because Elizabeth had entertained the very same thoughts.

As she watched Reed treating young Mandrake cruelly, she wondered what could be done to stop him. At times Elizabeth was frightened by her husband. He was cool and calculating, and had a way of torturing her mentally without anyone else being aware of it. She was sure that the only reason he had not harmed her physically was because it would show, and John Ruffin would then see him for what he really was. She had often thought of talking to her father and baring her soul about her fear of Reed, but each time she had not gone through with it because she knew he would not accept it. He would dismiss it as a figment of her imagination and shame her for having such thoughts. Reed had his father-in-law totally blinded.

Elizabeth observed as one of the slaves drove a horse and buggy out of the barn and headed around toward the front of the mansion. This was the vehicle that would carry her father and sisters into Richmond.

She struggled to a standing position, waddled across the room to the bedstand, and picked up her book. Returning to the chair, she sat down and began to read.

The women and children watched from inside the shacks as Mandrake stood coatless, bearing the heavy collar on his neck and shoulders. His whole body was shivering. Orchid looked on with tears spilling down her cheeks.

Pacing back and forth in front of Mandrake and the gathering of male slaves, Reed noticed John Ruffin drive away from the mansion with Abby and Lynne beside him. He was lecturing the black men on the consequences of disobedience and the awful mistake Mandrake had made in daring to give him an order.

Mandrake felt the need to defend himself and boldly said, "Massa Reed, I wouldn' have spoke to you the way I did 'cept'n that you hit my wife fo' no reason."

"No reason!" blared Exley in a knife-keen tone. He stopped pacing and glared heatedly at Mandrake. "What do you mean, no reason? She was bawlin' her head off, and female bawlin' grates on my nerves!"

"She was cryin' 'cause she was scared and cold. You dragged her out of the wagon and throwed her on the ground. Then you made her take her coat off. Orchid couldn' he'p cryin'. That's when I said you had no call to hit her, an' I tol' you to leave her alone. Wouldn' you have gone to Miz 'Lizbeth's defense if'n a man had done to her what you done to Orchid? Ain' a man got a right to defend his wife?"

Face flushed beet-red, Exley screamed, "Black-scum slaves don't have any rights!" Even while the words were spewing from his mouth, he aimed a punch at Mandrake's jaw and knocked him down.

When the prongs on the backside of the collar stabbed into the snow, jerking his neck hard in the fall, Mandrake ejected a pained cry. Cursing like a madman, Exley railed at him to shut up and kicked him in the side.

Still at her window, Orchid broke into sobs. When she saw Exley kick Mandrake a second time, she bolted from the shack, stumbling through the snow.

Exley had kicked Mandrake a fourth time when he heard Orchid's voice screeching at him to stop. Breathing hard, he turned around to see her coming toward him, sobbing.

Unaware that Elizabeth was watching, Exley turned to meet Orchid, his eyes blazing. The slaves looked at each other, blinking, as Exley pointed at her and bellowed, "Get back in your shack, girl!"

Still stumbling toward Exley, Orchid ignored his command, screaming, "Don' kick 'im no mo', you filthy devil! Don' kick 'im no mo'!"

Exley swore and turned back to Mandrake, who was still lying on his back, holding his ribs. Orchid's use of the words "filthy devil" infuriated Exley. In retaliation, he kicked Mandrake in the face.

Orchid was on him like a wildcat, clawing and scratching. Exley fell and swung his arms to protect his face from Orchid's fingernails. "Get her off me!" he wailed. "Get her off me!"

Lenox, Schyler, and Hector seized the anger-crazed woman and pulled her off. "This won' do no good, Orchid," said Lenox as they held her tight.

She struggled against them, hissing, "Let me go! That filthy devil ain' gonna kick my man no mo'! I'll kill 'im!"

Mandrake was dazed by the blow from Exley's foot, but he was conscious enough to know what was happening. The ground seemed to be reeling beneath him as he tried to get up. The collar was a hindrance, and with his head spinning, he kept falling back in the snow.

Exley scrambled to his feet. Angrily sucking for air, he glared at Orchid and said to the slaves, "Let go of her!"

The men obeyed and backed away as Exley stood like a menacing beast, shoulders hunched, and roared, "Filthy devil, huh? You'll kill me, will you?"

Orchid's wrath had stolen away all her fear. Yelling wildly, she lunged at Exley, clawing at him. Sidestepping her, he struck her square in the face with his fist. She went down hard. Exley sent a swift kick into her side. The slaves were tense, eyeing each other as if trying to decide what to do.

Mandrake struggled to rise as Exley kicked Orchid again. He was drawing his foot back to kick her once more when he heard Elizabeth screaming at him to stop. He turned and looked at her as she leaned from her third floor window.

"Reed, stop it! You'll kill her!"

Pointing at her, he shouted back, "You shut up! I'll handle this my way!"

As he whipped around to resume his punishment, he found a huge dark form standing between him and Orchid, who was still on the ground. Dariel loomed over him. His features were grim and his deep voice steady as he said, "Massa Reed, I cain' let you hurt Orchid no mo'."

Exley looked him up and down, then whipped his derringer from his coat pocket. He took a step back to be out of Dariel's reach, aimed the small pistol at his face, and growled, "Try to stop me, Dariel, and I'll drop you where you stand!"

"Reed!" came Elizabeth's harried voice again. "Papa won't take it lightly if you kill Dariel! He paid a lot of money for him. Come in the house and cool down before you do something you'll be sorry for!"

Without looking her direction, Exley retorted, "I told you to shut up, Elizabeth. Get back in there and close that window. Now do as I tell you!"

Then to Dariel, Exley rasped, "I can kill you and get away with it, big black dog. The choice is yours. Get out of my way, or die! I'm gonna count to three. If you aren't outta my way, I'll drop you like a brain-shot bull."

"I ain't wantin' to die, Massa Reed," Dariel said levelly, "but it ain't right fo' you to treat Orchid like this. I'm askin' you to stop hurtin' her."

"You're gonna learn who's boss around here! If you're not clean outta my way by the time I count to three, you're a dead man." He paused for effect, and said loudly, "One...two...th—"

Reluctantly the huge man angled his body and backed away. Exley then saw that Orchid was still lying on the ground, but an elderly slave named Jedidiah had draped his frail body over her for protection. Mandrake was now on his feet, a bit glassy-eyed and unsteady, but preparing to go after Exley if he looked like he was going to hurt Orchid anymore.

Orchid was groaning in pain. Covering her as much as possible, the skinny old man braced himself, looked up at Exley and said, "Please, Massa Reed. Don' hu't her no mo'. If'n you gotta beat on somebody, beat on me."

For a moment it appeared that Exley would do just that. He drew a deep breath, then looked at Dariel and said, "You and Schyler take Orchid to her shack."

Speaking words of comfort to Orchid, Jedidiah rolled off of her, keeping his weary old eyes on Exley. While the two men picked Orchid up and carried her toward the shack, Mandrake started to follow.

"Hold it, Mandrake!" blared Exley, pointing the derringer at him. "You stay right here!"

Mandrake stopped and used his hands to support the heavy iron collar. He glowered at Exley, his body quivering from the cold.

As Jedidiah struggled to get up, Exley spat, "Stay right where you are, old man. I'm not through with you yet." Then to the others, he said, "You all have your work assignments. Get going."

Slowly the slaves began to move away. Scowling, Exley snapped, "Today! I want it done today!" Looking over their shoulders, they hastened their pace.

Exley slipped the derringer into his coat pocket, then reached under his coat and unbuckled his belt. Sliding it through the loops at his waist, he gripped the buckle and wound the belt around his hand twice, leaving the rest of it to dangle like a whip.

Standing over the old man, who was kneeling in the snow, Exley said, "So you want me to beat on you rather than Orchid, eh?"

A look of horror flashed over Jedidiah's wrinkled face.

Mandrake, still supporting the collar with his hands, took a step toward Exley, saying, "I'm askin' you not to hurt 'im, Massa Reed. All he done was try to protect Orchid. He didn' raise a hand against you. Besides, he's old and feeble. It ain't right fo' you to beat 'im."

Exley's mouth turned downward with irritation. "Did I hear you right, Mandrake? Are you correcting me?"

Before Mandrake could reply, Exley darted to him and lashed his face with the belt. The popping sound echoed among the mansion and the outbuildings. Mandrake staggered backward and fell. A large welt appeared on his face. Pulling the derringer from his coat, Exley pointed it at Mandrake and barked, "If you get up before I tell you to, I'll kill you!"

Elizabeth had closed the window against the cold, but remained there watching the scene below. She saw the slaves walk away at her husband's command, but noticed that while Reed was making a whip out of his belt, the slaves slipped around the corner of the barn. Two dark faces then appeared down low at the corner. No doubt the two "spies" were keeping the others informed of what was happening. She knew if Reed found out, he would be furious.

Elizabeth sucked in a quick breath and put her hand to her mouth when she saw Reed lash Mandrake across the face. Even with the window closed, she could hear the crack. She emitted a shrill whine and bit her forefinger when she saw Reed savagely lashing Jedidiah. The old man's hat had fallen off and he was in a fetal position in the snow, using his hands and arms to protect his head.

Elizabeth was so upset that her breath was coming in short, dry gasps. Suddenly she threw the window open and screamed, "Reed! Stop it! Stop it! How can you be so cruel?"

Exley had hit the old man several times when he heard Elizabeth's shrill voice. Pausing, he bellowed at her, "I told you to shut up!"

"But you'll kill him!"

"That's my business! You butt out!"

Elizabeth began to weep as Reed continued to whip the aging black man unmercifully. She could hear Jedidiah's pained cries each time the belt struck flesh. There was blood on his gnarled old hands and in his short-cropped silver hair.

As the belt continued its lashing, an unearthly wail came from the old man's lips. With a mounting panic, Elizabeth knew if Reed did not quit soon, Jedidiah would die.

Her mind went into a frenzy. She screamed at her husband to stop. Caught up in her passion, she leaned far out of the window—too far. Suddenly she felt the window sill press hard against her unborn baby, and then she was falling.

A helpless cry cut the cold morning air as she plummeted three stories to the ground.

Sitting obediently in the snow, Mandrake saw Elizabeth slip from the window and plunge to the ground. Exley had turned at the sound of the ear-splitting scream and watched his wife as she fell. But like an insane man, he kept lashing Jedidiah with the belt.

Adrenaline surged through Mandrake's body. Unable to contain himself any longer, he rose to his feet and charged Exley, hitting him with a flying tackle. Pain shot through his neck and shoulders because of the iron collar. Exley was momentarily stunned, but he quickly rolled over and scrambled to get up. When Exley was halfway on his feet, Mandrake landed a rock-hard fist to his jaw. Exley went down and lay still.

Mandrake was aware of the other slaves—men and women—rushing from the barn and the shacks as he reached into Exley's pocket for the wrench that would unlock the collar. Most of the slaves stopped to see about Jedidiah, while Orchid and Lenox drew up to Mandrake.

While Lenox helped Mandrake remove the collar, Orchid said shakily, "Oh, Mandrake, I'm 'fraid Miz 'Lizbeth is hurt bad."

"Me too," Mandrake said, his body numb from the cold. He ran toward Elizabeth and Orchid followed, slipping and stumbling in the snow. The rest of the slaves remained with Jedidiah, doing what they could to stop the flow of blood. Warily, they observed Exley, who was beginning to stir.

Mandrake knelt beside Elizabeth. She had hit the ground facing downward, but somehow had rolled onto her back. Blood was seeping from her nose and mouth and spreading on the lower part of her dress. She was hemorrhaging internally. She was barely conscious, and moaned incoherently, rolling her head slowly from side to side.

Looking up at Orchid, who stood over him wide-eyed and frightened, Mandrake said, "Run to the front door of the mansion and tell Charles what has happened. Harriet will need to make Miz 'Lizbeth comfortable while I ride into town and bring the doctuh. Hurry on, now. I'll carry her right behind you."

Orchid's face revealed her fear that Elizabeth would die. Without expressing it, she turned and ran toward the front of the mansion.

Gently Mandrake placed his hands under Elizabeth and said softly, "I'm gonna take you in the house, Miz 'Lizbeth. Harriet will take care of you while I ride into town and bring the doctuh."

Elizabeth did not respond. She had stopped moving her head and was no longer moaning. Were it not for the weak rise and fall of her breast, Mandrake would have thought she was dead. With his knees planted in the snow, the muscular slave hoisted her into his arms, cradling her like a baby. Her head and arms hung limply. Rising to his feet, Mandrake headed for the front of the big house.

He had taken only a few steps when he saw Reed Exley stumbling toward him with a few of the slaves following. Most of them were still collected around Jedidiah.

Mandrake was almost to the corner of the mansion when Exley's sharp voice bawled, "Mandrake! Stop right there!"

Mandrake stopped and looked at the wild-eyed man as he drew up with the derringer in his hand. He was angry and a muscle in his right cheek was twitching just below the eye. Mandrake wondered how long it would be before Exley went totally insane.

Exley glared at Mandrake and hissed, "You're in big trouble, black boy! You would dare lay a hand on me? And on top of that, you took the collar off without my permission. You are in big trouble!"

"Massa Reed," Mandrake said calmly, "you were beatin' on Jedidiah like a madman. I had to stop you. And I had to take the collar off so's I could come and take care of Miz 'Lizbeth. She's hurt bad. I'm takin' her in the house so's Harriet can tend to her while I ride into town and bring the doctuh." As he said this, Mandrake began moving toward the porch.

Exley hurried around in front of him, aimed the derringer at his head, and thundered, "Stop! Put her down!"

"Massa Reed, she's hurt bad. We gotta hurry and get her in the house."

The tic on Exley's cheek twitched rapidly as he shook the gun at Mandrake and growled, "Get your dirty black hands off her. I said put her down!"

Mandrake looked down at the woman in his arms and saw that she was no longer breathing. Her body was a lifeless weight. Tears filled his eyes. Looking at Exley, he said, "She's dead, Massa Reed. Miz 'Lizbeth is dead."

It was like the angry man had not heard what Mandrake said. Gritting his teeth, he hissed, "I told you to get your dirty black hands off her! Put—her—down!"

Slowly and gently, Mandrake placed Elizabeth's body on the snow. As Reed bent down beside her, the butler appeared on the porch. Harriet and Orchid were behind him. The servants had been working on the opposite side of the mansion and had not heard any of the disturbance.

Reed bent his face into a mask of grief as Charles came up behind him. Rising and trying desperately to produce tears, he said in a quivering voice, "Elizabeth is dead, Charles. She fell from the bedroom window up there. I don't know how it happened, or why she even had the window open. Would you carry her into the house?"

Harriet let out a whimper and covered her mouth.

"Yes, sir," nodded Charles, bending down to pick up the body. He struggled for a moment, then rose to a standing position. Mandrake wanted to help him, but knew he mustn't put his "dirty black hands" on Elizabeth.

"Thank you, Charles," said Reed, still putting on a show of grief. "Lay her on one of the couches in the parlor and cover her with a blanket. I'll be in later. Right now I have to have a talk with the slaves."

Charles moved unsteadily toward the porch with Harriet beside him. When they had vanished from view, Exley instantly lost his mask of grief and said, "All right, all of you, let's go see about Jedidiah."

All of the slaves gathered in a circle around the bloodied old man, where four black women were tending to him. Jedidiah was conscious, but lay quite still. Exley bent over him, made a quick examination, and standing erect, said, "Jedidiah will be all right. In a moment, some of you can carry him to his shack and wash him up. Once he's removed from this spot, I want you men to get your snow shovels and dispose of this bloody snow. When that's done, replace it with some of that snow behind the barn. Understand?"

There was a familiar chorus of "Yassuhs."

"All right. Now listen good. If any one of you ever breathes a word of what happened here today to anybody, I'll kill you! Master John will learn that Elizabeth fell from the window—nothing else. None of you saw anything. You did not see Miss Elizabeth leaning out of the window, nor did you hear her screaming. Nobody knows why she fell. Do you understand?"

Again came the chorus of fearful "Yassuhs."

"I mean what I say. If one word of what happened ever comes from one of you, I'll punish all of you, and I'll kill the one who told. Do you all understand?"

Knowing that Exley would carry out his threat, every slave assured him they would never tell what happened. If Master John, Miss Abby, or Miss Lynne should question them about it, they would not divulge the truth.

Reed was waiting in the parlor when John Ruffin and his daughters arrived home late that afternoon. Feigning grief once more, he met them at the door and solemnly told them that Elizabeth had fallen from the window and died.

The three of them were overcome with grief and clung to each other as they wept. Charles and Harriet came in to offer their sympathy. When the shock began to wear off, Exley said he had no idea why Elizabeth was leaning out the window. He could not figure out why she would even have it open on such a cold day. He told them he had questioned the slaves about it, but none of them had noticed her until she fell.

Elizabeth was buried with her unborn baby still in the womb on Sunday afternoon, December 16. People came from miles around to attend the funeral and offer their sympathy to the family. Web Steele was a strong pillar to John and Lynne, as well as to Abby. Though he detected a facade of grief on Reed's part, he offered his condolences. Exley only gave Steele a cold stare.

Edmund Ruffin stayed close by his brother throughout, and as they walked from the grave toward the waiting funeral coach, he asked John if he was still going with him to Columbia the next day. John hesitated, saying that he shouldn't leave Lynne and Abby so soon after their sister's death. But Edmund urged him to go, saying that it would help take his mind off his own grief. Abby had Web to lean on, and Lynne had Daniel. John discussed it with his daughters, and they both urged him to go, agreeing with Uncle Edmund that it would help ease his grief.

Feigning the role of a mourning husband, Reed remained beside the grave as everyone else walked slowly away. He laughed within himself. Now that Elizabeth was out of the way, he could pursue Abby—after a proper time of mourning, of course. He was sure Abby felt an attraction for him, but in respect for Elizabeth she had always put up a front. Things would be different now, he told himself.

There was one obstacle in his way, however: Webster Steele. Somehow Reed had to get Web out of Abby's life.

CHAPTER TEN

O n Monday morning, December 17, 1860, Edmund and John Ruffin boarded a train for Columbia, South Carolina, at the Richmond depot. Edmund was excited about the speech he was to give at the convention, and though John was not as enthusiastic about the secession as his brother, he was pleased that Edmund was considered a leader among the Southern patriots.

On the evening of that same day, Web Steele and Daniel Hart took the Ruffin sisters into Richmond for dinner at an expensive restaurant. They talked a lot about Elizabeth and what a bright light she had been in the Ruffin home when the girls were growing up. Abby and Lynne both shed a few tears as they revived old memories, some that hadn't been thought of in years.

When the discussion became too painful, Daniel brought up the pending war between the North and South. Lynne and Abby were soon on the verge of tears once more with the prospect of the men they loved having to enter the fight.

Web suggested they talk about their future, ignoring for the moment the war clouds that hung over their heads. Soon the conversation was lighter as the women brought up names they had considered for the children they would bear in the future. Web and Daniel suggested silly names just to keep the evening joyful.

During the frosty ride home in the Steele buggy, Lynne and Daniel were in the back seat, and Abby rode beside Web in the front seat as he handled the reins. Both couples were dressed warmly and were wrapped in buffalo-hide blankets.

When the lights of Richmond were behind them, Web turned so Lynne and Daniel could hear him and said, "I don't mean to freshen your grief again by talking about Elizabeth's death, but I have a strange feeling about it."

"You, too?" said Abby. "Lynne and I haven't been able to accept the story Reed is telling, either."

"When I heard it, there was an odd smell about it to me," put in Daniel. "Why would Elizabeth have the window open in the first place? Nobody opens a window this time of year unless there's a good reason."

"Certainly not to let the wintry air in, that's for sure," said Lynne.

"Elizabeth saw something outside that either frightened or excited her," Web said. "Something that had her attention enough that she wanted to hear what was going on, or something that she wanted to call out to someone below."

"Had to be," agreed Abby. "But Papa talked to some of the slaves, and they say they saw and heard nothing until Mandrake caught sight of her falling."

"I didn't tell you, honey," said Web, "but Saturday morning when I came to see you?"

"Yes?"

"Before I came to the house, I walked over to Mandrake and Orchid's shack. They were cordial as usual, but when I asked about the incident, they froze up. They tried not to show it, but they were scared to the bone. I didn't push it any further, but I've got a hunch Mr. Exley's holding an ax over their heads."

"Them and the other seventy-seven slaves," said Abby. "I asked Papa what he thought after he had talked to some of them, and he was willing to let the question die right there."

"Sure," said Lynne, "because if Reed is guilty of something, Papa really wouldn't want to know it."

"I know," said Abby, shaking her head. "And another thing—those scratches on Reed's face."

"Yeah, I noticed those at the funeral," interjected Daniel.

"Well, I asked him about them," Abby said. "He said it was none of my business how he got them. Later I asked Papa to question him. He refused, saying if Reed didn't want to tell me, I shouldn't pry."

Web sighed, shaking his head. "I love your father dearly, girls, you both know that. But I wonder if he'll ever see that snake-in-the-grass for what he is."

"It may take awhile," responded Lynne, "but I think the day will come."

"Really?"

"Yes. Do you remember that sermon Reverend McLaury preached, oh, about four months ago? The one about 'Be Sure Your Sin Will Find You Out'?"

"Sure do," said Web. "That was a powerful one."

"Well, my ex-brother-in-law isn't immune to God's laws. One day, sooner or later, his sin will catch up to him. When it does, Papa will finally see him for what he is."

"Your *ex*-brother-in-law?" said Daniel.

"Certainly," replied Lynne, tilting her head back to look at him in the dim starlight. "He was my brother-in-law when Elizabeth was alive, but he's not married to her any more, so he's no longer related to me."

"I guess we could say that's the only good thing about Elizabeth's passing, honey," sighed Abby. "Even though Reed's still slave overseer, at least he's not in the family any more."

"Hallelujah!" said Web.

"Amen!" agreed Daniel.

An hour later, Abby was in her bedroom brushing her hair and thinking about the sweet goodnight kiss she had received from Web before he and Daniel had driven away.

Clad in a dark-red silk robe, she looked at herself in the mirror and smiled. "Abby," she said to her reflection, "you are the luckiest woman in all the world. The handsomest, most charming, most wonderful man is in love with you, and you are going to become his wife. The Lord in heaven certainly has smiled down upon—"

Abby's soliloquy was interrupted by a knock on her door. Laying the hairbrush on the dresser, she went to the door and called, "Yes?"

"It's me," came Lynne's voice.

When the door swung open, Lynne gave her a wistful look and said, "I came to kiss you goodnight."

Abby cocked her head. "Sweetie, you kissed me goodnight ten minutes ago."

"I know, but I don't have Elizabeth to kiss goodnight anymore, so I've got to kiss you twice."

Abby's eyes moistened and she took Lynne into her arms. Together they cried for a few moments, then kissed each other goodnight.

Abby closed the door, wiped away her tears, and sat down once more in front of the dresser. Picking up the brush, she ran it through her long, thick auburn hair. There was another knock at the door. "Yes?"

"It's Harriet, Miss Abby," said the maid.

"Come on in."

"Just thought I'd check and see if you needed anything before I go to bed."

"Not a thing, Harriet. Thank you."

"All right, mum," nodded Harriet. "See you in the morning."

"See you in the morning," echoed Abby. "Goodnight."

Abby finished brushing her hair. It was full and beautiful, lying in swirls about her shoulders. Rising from the stool, she started to unbutton her robe when she heard a light tap at the door. *Charles?* she thought. *He never comes to tell me goodnight.*

"Yes?" she said through the door.

"It's Reed, Abby. I need to talk to you."

Abby felt a quick gust of irritation come over her. "I'm getting ready for bed."

"I'm really sorry to bother you, but it's important."

"Can't it wait till morning?"

"No. I have to talk to you now."

Abby sighed, buttoned her robe, and opened the door.

Without waiting for an invitation, Exley bowled past her into the room. She caught a whiff of liquor on his breath.

"Just a minute!" she snapped. "This is my bedroom. I did not invite you in here."

Exley ran his gaze over her and said, "You are one gorgeous woman, Abby."

Fire flashed in her eyes. "You said this was important, Reed. State your business and leave."

A lecherous leer curved his mouth. "You're irresistible with your hair down like that," he breathed, moving toward her.

Abby backed up, saying firmly, "Don't you touch me. I opened the door because you said it was important that we talk. All right, what is it?"

Still leering, Reed replied, "I was gonna wait a little longer beyond Elizabeth's passing before I came to you, but I can't wait. You're the most beautiful and desirable woman I've ever seen, and—"

"Get out of my room!"

Exley lunged for her, laying hold on her upper arms. Before she could free herself, he was kissing her. Revulsion sent a wave of nausea through her. Struggling against him, she finally broke free and sent a stinging slap across his face. "I said get out!"

"I'll go," Exley said quietly, "but I won't give up. I think deep down, you're attracted to me."

Abby's mouth bent down with loathing. "That's what you get for thinking when you're not used to it, Reed. I never gave you any reason to think that."

"How about the times I've made a pass at you, and you never even once told Elizabeth about it? Or Web, either? If you'd told him, I know he'd have been at my throat."

"I never told Elizabeth because it would have broken her heart. It most certainly was not because I enjoyed your passes or felt an attraction toward you. And as for Web, I didn't tell him because he would have pounded you senseless. There's been more than enough trouble between you and him already. I've been trying to keep some semblance of peace in the family."

"Well, some women just won't reveal their true feelings."

"I've just revealed them to you, mister. And while we're having this little talk, I want to tell you how angry I am for the way you treated my sister. Elizabeth loved you, Reed. I don't know why, but she did. You were not only wrong to make passes at me when you were married to her, but I saw many things you did to hurt her. You showed her little consideration, and as far as I could tell, you showed her no love at all."

"Don't you know why I didn't show her any love, Abby? Because I have always been in love with you. I would have made my play for you in the first place, but you were barely seventeen at the time. It wouldn't have set well with Papa John, and he might have run me off."

"So you married Elizabeth because your abominable greed couldn't wait to marry into Ruffin money!" Abby snapped. "Get out of here, right now! I'm in love with Web Steele, and I'm going to become his wife. If you ever make a pass at me again, I *will* tell Web."

Backing into the doorway, Exley grinned "I have to tell you, Abby, you are so beautiful when you're angry."

Exley took another backward step, which put him in the hall. The door banged shut in his face. Turning and walking toward the staircase that led to the third floor, he smiled to himself. He would win gorgeous Abby to himself once Web Steele was out of the picture.

Edmund and John Ruffin stood up to stretch their limbs when the train stopped in Wilmington, North Carolina. It was evening, and they had been on the train all day. Just before the train took on its Wilmington passengers, the conductor entered the car and announced that those passengers who were going to Columbia for the Secession Convention would need to get off the train and catch another one that was leaving for Charleston the next morning. The conductor explained that the convention had been driven out of Columbia because of an outbreak of smallpox. It would convene in Charleston on Wednesday morning, December 19, as planned.

The Ruffin brothers made the appropriate change of trains and arrived in Charleston just after sunrise on December 19. They were fortunate to find accommodations in a small, unheated room with two single beds in the Charleston Hotel.

The town was alive with enthusiastic Southern patriots. Cockades of South Carolina palmetto fronds were worn on every hat to symbolize the South's defiance of the Union. Bands played, and one parade followed another along the town's main streets to the loud cheers of thousands of "Southrons." Flags of many colors—except the Union's colors—were displayed everywhere. Merchants, bankers, and businessmen throughout Charleston lent themselves to the cause.

In addition to the South Carolina Convention delegates, the entire state government was on hand, along with many visiting dignitaries from all the other Southern states, including the governor of Florida, official representatives of Alabama and Mississippi, and one former United States attorney general.

In the hotel lobby, on the streets, and at St. Andrew's Hall where the Convention was held, Edmund Ruffin encountered scores of old friends and fellow "fire-eaters" who had been leaders in the battle to break up the Union. They were the cream of Southern society—bankers, lawyers, plantation owners, clergymen, judges, and newspaper publishers. To a man, they were delighted to meet Edmund's brother, and John was impressed with the confidence they all showed in his brother as champion of the fight for secession.

Edmund's friend and president of the Secession Convention, David Jamison, found him before time to start the proceedings and informed him that his speech would come just before the lunch break. Jamison welcomed John and gave him a seat of honor on the platform next to Edmund.

Edmund's fiery speech had the entire crowd whooping, shouting, and applauding. At times, he had to stop and wait for them to quiet down before he could proceed.

At the beginning of the afternoon session, Jamison told the excited crowd that the exact language of the South Carolina Ordinance of Secession was still being worked on in committee. Then he read a telegram from the governor of Alabama urging the convention delegates to let nothing delay them from seceding, adding that his state would not be far behind.

Jamison then explained that with secession, many important things remained to be settled. At the moment the Ordinance of Secession was adopted by all 169 delegates, South Carolina would cease to be bound by Union law, and a complete new code of law for the newborn Republic of South Carolina would have to be put together. South Carolina patriots had to be appointed to take over the functions previously performed by United States' government officials. There would have to be a new postal service, and customs agents would have to be appointed to handle incoming foreign travelers and foreign goods at Charleston's port.

Jamison then focused on a critical question. What would be done about United States properties inside the territorial limits of South Carolina? The most prominent of these were three federal military installations in Charleston Harbor: Fort Moultrie, Castle Pinckney, and Fort Sumter.

A resolution was passed instructing the newly established Committee on Foreign Relations to send three commissioners to Washington, D.C., to negotiate for the transfer of all such real estate to the new Republic of South Carolina.

By late afternoon, the committee preparing the Ordinance of Secession sent a representative to the platform in St. Andrew's Hall to inform David Jamison that they needed more time. Everyone in the hall was disappointed that the day ended without a formal declaration of secession.

Though the Convention convened at midmorning the next day, the Ordinance of Secession was not ready for a vote until one o'clock that afternoon. The product of the committee's anxious travail was read aloud from the platform by the committee chairman, and at a quarter past one, all 169 delegates voted to adopt the Ordinance as read. The document was then placed in the hands of South Carolina's attorney general for safekeeping. The public signing ceremony was scheduled to take place in Charleston's Institute Hall at seven o'clock that evening. The size of Institute Hall would allow a great number of Charleston's citizens to attend.

At seven, the Convention delegates filed through excited crowds of celebrants to the platform. The signing ceremony took a full two hours. When it was done, David Jamison gave his friend Edmund Ruffin ten minutes to make an impromptu speech, which brought on a thunderous roar of "Southron" patriotism.

Jamison then quieted the massive throng, held up the signed secession document and shouted, "I proclaim the Republic of South Carolina an independent commonwealth!"

The happy clamor that followed shook the hall.

Jamison then honored Edmund Ruffin by presenting him with the pen used to sign the Ordinance of Secession. This gesture was met with an enormous roar of approval, and the convention was adjourned.

When Edmund and John Ruffin took to their beds in the Charleston Hotel that night, they found it impossible to sleep. Church bells rang all night in celebration, cannons were fired hour after hour, military companies paraded, rifle salutes were fired, firecrackers were set off, and the milling crowds shouted.

On the train home the next morning, Edmund told John that he was going to watch closely the situation at the three Union forts in Charleston Harbor. He had a feeling the federal leaders in Washington were not going to give up their Southern real estate easily. The inevitable war just might start in Charleston Harbor, and if it did, Edmund Ruffin wanted to be there when it happened.

Word of South Carolina's bold break with the United States reached Richmond by telegraph in the middle of the afternoon on December 20. The news spread quickly through the city and into the rural areas.

That evening, Abby Ruffin was a dinner guest in the Dudley Steele home. While the Steeles, their son, and future daughter-in-law enjoyed a delicious meal of roast turkey and all the trimmings, they talked of secession and the threat of war.

"I'd like to know what's going on in the minds of President Buchanan and the rest of the government leaders in Washington right now," Cora said.

"And Abraham Lincoln in Illinois," put in Abby.

"Well, ladies," said Dudley after swallowing a mouthful of sweet potatoes, "you can bet Washington is a hot box right now. Neither the president nor the president-elect are happy about the news, I'm sure. Of course, Buchanan knows he won't have to worry about the big mess much longer. It'll be Lincoln's problem in a few more weeks. But I can tell you this much, those Northerners regard secession as a serious crime against the United States. I don't know how it can result in anything less than armed conflict."

"I don't either," said Web. "But I tend to agree with Reverend McLaury that it will be the South who fires the first shot."

Silence prevailed for a few seconds, then Abby said, "One thing for sure...if war does come, it will come before June. Which means our wedding will have to be postponed. Web will be off fighting who knows where come June."

Dudley shook his head. "Not necessarily, Abby. If there is a war, it'll be short-lived. Those hard-headed Northerners will learn quickly that we cannot be conquered nor dominated. A long war would be senseless."

Abby reached beside her and took hold of Web's hand. Sighing, she said, "I sure hope you're right, Dad."

On Saturday, December 22, Edmund Ruffin drove his buggy from the stable where he had left it near the depot in Richmond and headed for John's plantation to take him home. As they turned onto the road that led to the plantation, they found themselves following a surrey with three male occupants. To their surprise, the surrey left the road at the Ruffin lane and headed for the mansion.

The three well-dressed men were alighting from the surrey at one of the hitching posts when Edmund pulled his buggy to a halt at the front porch. John stepped to the ground, thanked his brother for taking him along to the convention, and bid him good-bye. As Edmund drove off, John moved toward the three men, holding his small suitcase. "Good afternoon, gentlemen," he said amiably. "I'm John Ruffin. May I help you?"

The one who seemed to be the leader introduced himself as Horatio Clements, and the others as Dean Faulkner and Wesley Denton, his business partners. They were slave traders from Harper's Ferry, and had an appointment with Mr. Reed Exley.

"Ah, yes," smiled Ruffin. "Reed must be going to do some buying or selling. He handles all of the slave business for me."

"Greetings, gentlemen!" came Exley's voice from the front door of the mansion. "Which one of you is Mr. Clements?"

Clements identified himself, then introduced Faulkner and Denton. Exley stepped off the porch and joined the group. He thanked Clements for his speedy reply by telegram, and for making the trip so soon.

"Had to," chuckled Clements. "The female you described sounds like exactly what I'm looking for."

"You selling one of the young girls, Reed?" inquired Ruffin.

"Yes," nodded Exley.

"Which one?"

"Orchid."

"Orchid? Aren't you selling Mandrake with her?"

"No, Papa John. I figure to sell Mandrake at the big auction in Richmond on the twenty-eighth."

"You're separating them?"

"Well, Mr. Clements isn't looking for any male slaves right now. He wants a young woman to mate with some of his choice men in order to produce the best-looking Negroes possible. I figure Orchid is perfect for what he wants, and I'll get you a good price for her. I haven't bothered you about the trouble I've been having with Mandrake lately, but he's been a real problem."

"I know about the coat incident that you and Web had some trouble over," said John.

"Well, there's a whole lot more you don't know, so I figured simply to get rid of him. When he's gone, the trouble will stop. He's developing into a leader, and I think he's dangerous."

"Rebellion?" asked Clements.

"Yeah...and other problems," Exley replied levelly.

Hunching his shoulders and heading for the porch, Ruffin said, "That's why I've got you, Reed. You're my man. Do with the slaves as you see fit. All I care is that we keep enough of them on hand and get our fair share of work out of them."

When John had entered the mansion, Exley said, "Well, gentlemen, let's go take a look at our fine specimen."

The sun was shining and the temperature had risen above what it had been for the past several days. The snow had begun to melt around late morning, and the ground was getting a bit sloppy.

While Exley led Clements and his partners toward the slave shacks, he laughed within himself. Orchid would now learn what a grave mistake she made when she attacked him. He wouldn't be able to tell her so in front of the slave traders, but Orchid was intelligent. She would figure it out. Threaten to kill Reed Exley, would she? Well, that opportunity was now gone. Within a matter of minutes, she would be on her way to Harper's Ferry.

Exley had assigned Mandrake an all-day job cutting firewood behind the barn. He wouldn't be around to make things difficult. Orchid would be gone before Mandrake came to the shack for the night. And when Mandrake learned she'd been sold to an unknown slave trader, he wouldn't need it spelled out for him, either. He'd know why, all right. Being separated from Orchid for the rest of his life was what he deserved. Sure, he'd stir up a fuss over it, but the fuss wouldn't last long. Mandrake himself was going on the block in less than a week.

A few slave women and their children were moving about the shacks when Exley and the three men drew up to the one occupied by Mandrake and Orchid. They stared at the small group of white men, wondering what was going on.

Knocking on the rickety door, Exley called, "Orchid! It's Master Reed. Come out here."

Presently the door came open a crack, then widened a bit more until two big eyes stared fearfully at Exley and the men who stood behind him.

"I want you out here right now," Exley said sternly. "There's someone who wants to see you."

Orchid swung the door wide enough to allow her slim figure to pass through, and moved into the warmth of the sunshine. Her features showed a combination of fear and distrust as Clements and his partners looked her over.

"Well, what do you think?" Reed asked Clements.

"Exactly what I've been looking for!" exclaimed Clements. Turning to his partners, he asked, "Don't you fellas agree?"

"Exactly, boss," nodded Faulkner.

"Couldn't do better anywhere, I'd say," put in Denton. "She has just the right amount of pigmentation, the right build, and she is a pretty one."

Orchid knew that Exley had put her up for sale. A look of horror flashed across her face. Her mouth went dry, and her heart drummed her ribs.

"I'll give you twelve hundred for her," offered Clements.

Exley chuckled. "You're kidding, of course."

"Not at all. She's perfect."

"No, I mean, you're kidding to be making such a low offer."

"Low?" gasped Clements. "Why, Mr. Exley, the average female her age goes for nine hundred, or at best a thousand. You know that."

"I also know that Orchid's not average. You said it yourself. She's perfect. And Mr. Denton said she's the right shade, has the right build, and that she's pretty. For what you want, I agree. She's perfect. I told Mr. Ruffin I'd get a good price for her, and you plenty well know she's worth a good price. Sixteen hundred."

"*Sixteen hundred?* Why, I've never paid that much for a female!"

Patting Orchid's shoulder, Exley said, "You can go on back inside. Mr. Clements has decided he doesn't want you."

"Now, wait a minute!" blurted the slave trader. "I...I'll give you fourteen hundred."

"Sixteen."

"Fifteen!"

"Sixteen," Exley held firm.

"Oh, all right," sighed Clements.

"Cash, like I told you in the telegram," said Exley.

"Yeah, sure, sure," said Clements, digging into his coat pocket for his wallet.

"I'll get you her papers at the house," Exley told him, smiling.

The shock that registered all the way to Orchid's marrow had stolen her breath. Terror and disbelief overwhelmed her. Working her mouth, she was finally able to speak. Shaking her head rapidly, she cried, "No! Massa Reed, you cain't do this." To Clements, she wailed, "I cain't be yo' slave, mistuh. I have a husbin. I cain't leave Mandrake!"

"Don't worry, little lady," chuckled Clements, handing a wad of bills to Exley. "I'll give you two or three husbands. You'll produce a lot of fine-looking slaves for me."

"No-o-o!" Orchid screamed as she plunged into the shack, slamming the door.

Exley jammed the money into his pocket and hit the door with his shoulder, causing it to swing open with a bang. The impact knocked Orchid down, and Exley quickly had a grip on her arms, dragging her back outside. Forcing her into the hands of the slave traders, Exley said, "Hold her. I'll get her coat."

Several female slaves looked on as their frightened children huddled close to their skirts.

"All right," Exley breathed heavily, "let's get her into your surrey. I'll run in and grab her papers, and you can be on your way."

Orchid dug her heels into the slushy snow, but to no avail. The three slave traders each had a hold on her, and she was being dragged away. Opening her mouth wide, she took a deep breath and screamed, "Mandra-a-a-ke! Mandra-a-a-ke!"

Freeing one hand, Denton clapped it over Orchid's mouth as she was about to scream again. Orchid found a finger, quickly had it between her teeth, and clamped down savagely. Denton let out a wild yelp and tried to jerk loose, but Orchid bit down harder and held on.

Exley saw movement in his peripheral vision. Turning, he saw an angry, muscular Mandrake charging like a wild bull from the direction of the barn.

CHAPTER ELEVEN

eed Exley stiffened when he saw Mandrake coming his direction full-speed, his whole countenance suffused with anger. He shoved his hand into his coat pocket, expecting to grip the derringer. Then he remembered that he had taken it out and laid it on a table in his quarters. The best he could do was try to stop the charging black man with a command.

Wesley Denton was howling with Orchid's teeth deep in his finger, and the other two slave traders were attempting to break her hold on him as Mandrake closed in. Exley leaped into his path and hollered, "Stop, Mandrake!"

The muscular slave rammed into Exley, knocking him rolling. Breaking stride only briefly, Mandrake caught up with the slave traders and drove a shoulder into Horatio Clements, sending him reeling in the melting snow. Gaining his balance, the angry husband turned on Dean Faulkner, striking him with a left and a right. Faulkner staggered backward, swearing.

Orchid let go of Denton's finger and pushed away from him, spitting blood. Mandrake went after him. Denton threw up his left arm in defense, but Mandrake batted the arm aside and landed a stiff right jab, followed by a roundhouse left. Denton went down hard.

Mandrake was turning about to see to Orchid when Exley and Faulkner both jumped him. The three men went down in a heap, rolling and thrashing about in the snow. Mandrake lashed out wildly, catching Exley on the mouth. Rising to his knees, he drew back a fist to strike Exley again. But before he could unleash the fist, Faulkner and Clements threw their bodies into him, knocking him flat. Exley's lip was split and numb as he swore at Mandrake and jumped in to help the two men subdue him.

Denton was shaking his head and struggling to get up. Orchid leaped on his back and began digging her fingernails into his face. Cursing her, Denton reached back, got a grip on her hair, and flipped her over his body. The breath was knocked from her as she slammed to the ground. Denton pounced on top of her and pinned her down.

When the three men were finally able to get Mandrake spread-eagled on the ground, Exley cast a glance toward the slave shacks and saw several of the slaves standing in a bunch, looking on. Shouting to them, he told them to go into the barn and bring leg and wrist irons.

Reluctantly, the slaves obeyed. Moments later, Mandrake was jerked to a standing position with his wrists and ankles in chains. Denton released Orchid, who dashed to Mandrake and threw her arms around him. "Oh, Mandrake, Massa Reed has sold me to these men! Don' let 'em take me! Please don' let 'em take me!"

Mandrake embraced her as best he could and set hate-filled eyes on Reed Exley. His nostrils flared. "You have no right to do this!"

Exley laughed. "I have all the right in the world, blackie! Orchid was Ruffin chattel. Master John has given me power to buy and sell his chattel. In my estimation, you two needed to be broken up. So I sold her." Wiping blood from his split lip, he added, "You deserve a good beatin' too, slave scum. But you're not gonna get one. In exactly six days I'm sellin' you at the auction in Richmond. Any marks on you would lower your price."

"No-o-o!" wailed Orchid, clinging to Mandrake with all her might.

"Put her in the surrey," Exley told Clements. "I'll go in the house, sign her papers, and bring them right out."

Orchid was pulled from her husband and dragged to the surrey, sobbing. Mandrake knew it was useless to try to follow. The chain between his ankles was very short. He could move only inches at a time. He watched as the slave traders put Orchid in the surrey, seating her between Faulkner and Denton.

Orchid continued to sob and cry for Mandrake while Exley was inside the mansion. After a few minutes, he emerged and handed the papers to Clements. Mandrake wept silent tears as the surrey drove away and disappeared among the trees.

With a look of triumph, Exley returned to Mandrake and chuckled, "Rebel against me, will you, black boy? I bet you're sorry, now. I'd put that neck ring back on you, but I want you lookin' fresh and fit as a fiddle when I put you on the block next Friday."

Mandrake kept his tear-filled eyes pinned on the spot where he had last seen the surrey.

Exley snapped, "Okay, slave scum, you can still cut wood with those chains on your wrists. Get back behind the barn and finish your job."

Leaving Mandrake to shuffle his way back to work, Exley walked toward the house, counting the money he had received from Clements. He stuffed two hundred dollars into his shirt pocket and smiled to himself. *The old man will never know the difference,* he thought. *He'll be happy thinkin' I got fourteen hundred for the little black wench.*

On Friday, December 28, Web Steele rolled his buggy to a halt at a hitching post beside the big barn in Richmond where the slave auction was being held. He had arrived an hour before sale time in order to look over the slaves as they were being brought in. He had orders from his father to buy one or two males if he could find good ones.

A few slave owners were already inside the barn, looking over what few Negroes were in the "pen" for observation. Web made his way across the barn floor, greeting the white men that he knew. After looking over the slaves in the pen, he stationed himself where he could get a look at the other slaves that would be brought in. He had been there about a quarter-hour when to his surprise, he saw Reed Exley appear at the door, leading Mandrake, who wore wrist chains.

Web could read the sorrow in Mandrake's eyes as he approached and asked, "You're not selling Mandrake, are you, Reed?"

"As a matter of fact, I am."

"Tell you what," Web said quickly, "you haven't registered him yet. I'll buy Mandrake and Orchid both from you right here. It'll save you the auctioneer's fee. I'll give you two thousand for Mandrake and twelve hundred for Orchid."

Reed laughed. "Orchid's gone, Steele. I sold her to a slave trader last Saturday."

"Who? Where'd he take her?"

"None of your business."

Web eyed him with naked aversion. "Since you were going to sell both of them, couldn't you at least have had the decency to sell them as a pair?"

"No, I couldn't."

"Exley, I've never known anything that called itself human to slither as low as you do. You're absolutely despicable."

Feeling safe with the crowd nearby, Exley grated, "Well, mister, let me tell you somethin'. I couldn't care less what you think of me. And let me tell you somethin' else—what I do with John Ruffin's slaves is none of your stinkin' business. So you're worried about Mandrake and Orchid being separated. You're afraid their feelings might be hurt. When you gonna wake up, big man? What's it gonna take to get it through that thick skull of yours that these blackies are nothin' but animals? Animals don't have feelings. Now, as for this animal in chains, here, he ain't for sale straight out. He's going on the block."

With that, Exley led the slave to the auctioneer's desk. Mandrake glanced over his shoulder at Steele, a look of hopelessness in his eyes.

Web took a seat in the makeshift bleachers among some of his friends, and soon the auction began. For over two hours Negroes were led from the pen to the block singly, in pairs, and in small family groups as the auctioneer sold them to the highest bidders. It soon became evident that the auctioneer was saving Mandrake for last because of his fine physique and evident strength. He would go for a high price.

None of the slaves that crossed the block gained Web's attention. His mind was fastened on young Mandrake.

Exley sat a few feet away, holding the wrist chains that had been on Mandrake. He purposely refrained from looking at Steele. Web's cutting words were burning within him, and his hatred for Steele was growing by the minute.

A young couple was led to the block, leaving Mandrake alone in the pen. One of the auctioneer's assistants removed Mandrake's coat and shirt. Moments later, when the stalwart young slave was ushered to the block, there were many favorable comments as the bidders admired his muscular body.

When the auctioneer was ready to start the bidding, he smiled, pointed at Mandrake, and said, "Take a look at this one, gentlemen! Your eyes will tell you that he can do the work of two men. Let's start the bidding at two thousand dollars."

Exley gloated as the bidding for Mandrake immediately went higher. He would get a good price, then alter the sales slip so he could pocket a nice bundle for himself. He'd done it many times before. John Ruffin was so trusting, he would never question Reed's honesty.

Exley was also feeling relief to get rid of Mandrake. Turning his head for a glimpse at Web, he grinned and thought, *You're next, big man! I'll be rid of you soon.*

As the price of Mandrake went higher and higher, Web looked at him with compassion. Mandrake's heart was broken at his loss of Orchid. When most of the bidders had dropped out, Web would enter the bidding.

Soon the bidding narrowed to two wealthy plantation owners. Web knew both of them. Harley Adams and Jack Wyatt loved to bid against each other. It happened at every auction.

They were countering each other ten dollars at a time, and the bid was up to $2,340.

"All right," said the auctioneer, "we have twenty-three forty! Do I hear fifty?"

"Twenty-three fifty!" called out Adams, lifting a hand.

"Twenty-three sixty!" countered Wyatt.

There was a pause. "Do I hear twenty-three hundred and seventy?" asked the auctioneer.

Exley was pleased with himself. For sure he was going to get a lot more than the two thousand Steele had offered him before the auction began. Besides, he didn't want the Steeles to own Mandrake.

Adams met the auctioneer's figure.

Wyatt quickly went to $2,380.

The men in the bleachers sat on the edge of their seats. Very few male slaves had ever gone for an amount edging up to $2,400.

"Twenty-three ninety!" said Adams.

"Twenty-four hundred!" responded Wyatt.

Slouching in his seat, Exley grinned wickedly. This was going better than he had expected.

Adams sighed and shook his head. He was through bidding.

The auctioneer said, "Going for twenty-four hundred dollars. Going once! Going twi—!"

"Twenty-five hundred!"

Mandrake's head came up.

The wicked smile drained from Exley's face.

Jack Wyatt turned and eyed Web Steele with disbelief.

The auctioneer said, "Twenty-five hundred is my highest bid. Do I hear twenty-six?"

Wyatt began shaking his head. Quickly Exley jumped to his feet and hurried to the auctioneer, saying in a low voice, "Don't let it stop here. I don't want Steele to buy him."

The auctioneer looked at him askance. "Mr. Exley, you put no restrictions on the sale of your slave when you signed him in. He must now go to the highest bidder, no matter who it is. Of course, you can make top bid and take him back home with you."

Exley cursed under his breath and walked away, mumbling to himself. His desire to be rid of Mandrake was stronger than his objection to having him bought by Web Steele.

"Do I hear twenty-six hundred?" repeated the auctioneer.

Steele looked at Wyatt, who shook his head again. The auction-eer saw it, and said, "Going for twenty-five hundred dollars. Going once. Going twice. Sold for twenty-five hundred!"

Mandrake's face showed the elation he felt as he watched Web Steele go to the desk and write out a check. Exley stood close by the desk and observed the transaction. He did not speak as Web stepped past him carrying Mandrake's papers, but quickly moved in to collect the twenty-five hundred, insisting he be paid in cash.

Mandrake had put his shirt on and was slipping into his coat when Web approached him. A wide smile exposed his white teeth as he said, "Massa Web, I'll make you glad you paid that much fo' me. Really I will. I'll work extry hard ever' day, an' I'll—"

"C'mon, my friend," cut in Web. "Let's go."

When Reed Exley swung his buggy from the lane toward the front of the Ruffin mansion, he was surprised to see the Steele buggy parked next to the porch with Mandrake seated in it alone. What was Web doing here? Surely he wasn't making a social call on Abby while leaving his newly purchased slave sitting outside.

Mandrake watched Exley drive by and head for the barn. He heaved a sigh of relief, knowing he would never have to knuckle under to the wicked man again. He was curious, however, why Web had driven to the Ruffin place instead of going straight home. When Web had turned off the road onto the Ruffin plantation, he had noticed the strange look on Mandrake's face. He reassured Mandrake that he need-ed to see Abby for just a few minutes, and would soon be taking him home.

Exley disappeared into the barn when Web came out of the house. Abby stood in the doorway, smiling. She waved at Mandrake, and he waved back, giving her his warm smile.

During the fifteen-minute drive between the Ruffin plantation and the Steele place, Web spoke to Mandrake of his anger toward Exley for selling Orchid. Though Mandrake was thrilled at now being owned by the Steeles, his sorrow over the loss of his beloved wife remained.

Web pulled the buggy to a halt at the porch of the Steele mansion. As a slave came to take the horse and buggy, Web said, "You can get out here, Mandrake. You're going inside with me."

Expecting to be taken immediately to his new quarters among the slave shacks, Mandrake blinked and said, "Yassuh, Massa Web."

Web was met by his parents as he entered the mansion. He made a quick explanation about purchasing Mandrake and told them of Exley's having sold Mandrake's wife to an unnamed slave trader. Cora spoke kind, comforting words to Mandrake, and Dudley Steele welcomed him as part of the Steele plantation. To give a slave such a welcome was unusual, but Dudley could see that his son had a special liking for Mandrake, and treated him accordingly.

Web then said, "Dad, I need to talk to you for a minute."

Dudley agreed. Cora said she would escort Mandrake to the library, where he could wait while father and son had their brief talk.

Mandrake was all eyes as he took in the lavish furniture, tapestries, and plush carpet while following Cora through the house to the massive library. While seated alone, he gawked at the hundreds of books that lined the long shelves of one entire wall, floor to ceiling. He thought Dudley Steele must own half the books in the world.

Presently Web appeared, still carrying Mandrake's papers, and sat down behind a large oak desk. Flattening the papers out on the desk top, Web set his dark eyes on the handsome young Negro and said, "Mandrake, I just explained to my father that the check I wrote for your purchase today was not a Steele Plantation check. It was my personal check."

Puzzlement showed on Mandrake's ebony features. He blinked and asked, "What does that mean, Massa Web?"

Picking up a pen and dipping it in the desk's inkwell, Web began writing on the papers before him. He had made a couple of notations and was signing his name at the bottom when he replied, "What it means, my friend, is that I personally bought you today. Dudley Steele owns all of the slaves on this plantation, but he does not own you. *I* own you."

Confused, Mandrake nervously pulled at an ear and said, "I guess I don' quite unduhstan', Massa Web."

Letting the ink dry, Web queried, "Would you like to get Orchid back?"

"Well, yassuh. Yas, of course! But how am I gonna do that? I don' know where she is."

"Do you know where Harper's Ferry is?"

"Yassuh. I been there a couple times."

"Think you can find it from here?"

Mandrake's heart was pounding. "Yassuh. I sho' can. Is Orchid at Harper's Ferry?"

"Yes. Those men who took Orchid are from Harper's Ferry. The man who bought her is Horatio Clements."

"How did you find out?"

"From Miss Abby. That's what I was doing when I was in the Ruffin house. She did a little searching in Reed's desk and found the record of Orchid's sale. There it was, plain as day."

"This Horatio Clements' place is right there at Harper's Ferry?"

"Right. I've heard of Clements. He's a ruthless and greedy man."

"Sort of like Reed Exley, huh?"

"Yeah," nodded Web, grinning. "A whole lot like Exley."

Squinting and tilting his head, Mandrake said, "Orchid's at Harper's Ferry, Massa Web, but...I's here. How do I get her back?"

"Well," said Web, "if it weren't Clements we were dealing with, I'd simply go there and offer the owner more than he had paid for her, buy her, and bring her back. But this wouldn't work with Clements. He didn't buy Orchid to use her as a slave."

"He didn'?"

"No. He intends to make her a breeder. The man is known for matching and mating the best-looking Negroes in order to produce even better-looking slaves."

Steele's words hit Mandrake like a battering ram. His eyes were round and hot, and his trembling fists were clenched. His voice quivered as he hissed, "It's that dirty Massa Reed's doing! He is the devil hisself!"

"I can't argue with that," responded Web.

"Massa Web, how am I gonna get Orchid back? She's got to be rescued befo'... befo'..."

"I know, Mandrake. I've just made it so you can go after her." Folding the documents before him and inserting them in an envelope, Web asked, "Do you know what manumission papers are, my friend?"

Mandrake looked at him questioningly and nodded.

Reaching across the desk, Web handed him the envelope and said, "That's what these are, Mandrake—your manumission papers. I told you that I bought you today. As your legal owner, I have just signed your release. Nobody owns you now. You are a free man. I'm going to give you a horse and provisions so you can ride to Harper's Ferry and find Orchid."

Tears filled the black man's eyes. He could not believe this was really happening. "Massa Web, yo' tellin' me that I's no longer a slave?"

"That's it exactly," grinned Steele. "You're your own man now. Be sure you carry those papers everywhere you go. You'll need them to prove you're a free man."

While Mandrake sleeved away his tears, Web said, "Now, be sure you understand, Mandrake. You will have to *steal* Orchid away from Clements. He bought her legally and paid for her. This is why I can't go along and help you. The law will consider it a crime. Do you understand?"

"Yassuh," nodded Mandrake, sniffing again. "I wouldn't break the law fo' no othuh reason 'ceptin' to get Orchid back."

"I know that. The *real* crime in all of this belongs to Exley and Clements. You'll have to hide out with Orchid until Clements gives up looking for her."

"Yassuh."

"And it'll be dangerous. If Clements catches you, he'll kill you."

"I unduhstan', Massa Web, but it's my only chance of gettin' Orchid back."

"I knew you wouldn't hesitate. I'll have the horse and the provisions ready before sunup in the morning. You can ride out at dawn."

"Yassuh," said Mandrake, smiling broadly. Then looking at the envelope in his hand, he blinked at fresh tears and choked, "Massa Web, there ain't no way I can thank you fo' makin' me a free man."

"You don't have to," smiled Steele. "It'll be thanks enough just to know that you and Orchid are back together and happy. Once Clements gives up the search, I want you to come by here and let me know that you're both all right. Okay?"

"How long do you think that'll be, Massa Web?"

"Probably not more than a week or two. Clements and his men won't have much time to spend on trying to hunt Orchid down."

"Well, then there's somethin' I want to say."

"Yes?"

"Since I's a free man, I can make my own choices, right?"

"Right."

"Then I choose to bring Orchid back here to the Steele plantation an' be yo' willin' slave fo' the rest of my days."

After swallowing the lump in his throat, Web said, "It might not work out that way. If we go into a civil war and the North wins, there'll be no more slavery in this country. We Southern plantation owners will have to hire all our labor."

"Then I'll be yo' hired han', Massa Web. I want to make a home fo' Orchid here, an' work fo' you the rest of my life whether it be as hired han' or willin' slave."

"That would make me very happy, Mandrake," said Web. "Let's plan on it."

"Yassuh!" exclaimed the black man. Then rubbing his chin, he said, "Massa Web, now that I's a free man, and 'specially since Massa Reed no longer have power over me, there's somethin' I want to tell you. It's about Miz 'Lizbeth's death, Massa Web. It was her husbin' who caused her to die. The reason she open the winduh was to holler at Massa Reed. He was beatin' on ol' Jedidiah with a belt. Miz 'Lizbeth was yellin' at him to stop when she lost her balance an' fell."

Web Steele ran a finger through his mustache and said, "Just as I thought. It *was* Reed's fault."

"Yassuh. None of us slaves ever tol' the truth 'bout it 'cause Massa Reed threaten us, an' we know'd he'd carry out his threat if'n we ever tol' on 'im."

"I appreciate you telling me this, Mandrake. It's important that we know the truth."

"I jus' hope he gits what's comin' to 'im," Mandrake said tightly.

"I do too." After a pause, Web said, "Tell you what, my friend. You can sleep here in the mansion tonight, and we'll get you on your way to Harper's Ferry before the sun is up."

Mandrake had never slept in a feather bed. Alone in one of the guest rooms that night, he nestled himself deep in the soft mattress and went to sleep thinking of Orchid.

The next morning Mandrake rode out before dawn, heading north. Avoiding towns and villages as much as possible, he stayed on course with only one thing in mind. He must find his wife and steal her from Horatio Clements.

Twice that first day he was accosted by white men who thought he was a runaway slave. They were eager to collect the reward money slave owners paid for the return of their chattel and were disappointed when Mandrake produced his manumission papers.

Late in the afternoon on the second day, Mandrake came upon beautiful Lake Anna. The sun was going down and he was tired, so he decided to make camp along the shore. There was a natural brush enclosure that would protect him from the night wind and also give him a measure of privacy. Web had provided him a warm bedroll.

Dismounting and giving the horse ample opportunity to graze on the tawny grass near the water's edge, Mandrake gathered enough twigs and sticks for a small fire. He was about to light the fire when he heard his horse nicker. Looking up, he saw two young white men walking toward him along the shore.

Harry Binder and Cletus Hicks were in their early twenties. They had scraggly beards and their dirty hair hung down over their ears beneath greasy hats. They approached the black man with their hands in their jacket pockets and a wicked gleam in their eyes.

Mandrake stood beside his pile of sticks, sensing trouble.

CHAPTER TWELVE

Horatio Clements and his men arrived at Harper's Ferry midday on December 29, having spent several days en route. Clements had stopped at plantations along the way taking orders for a new crop of his specially bred slaves who were coming of age.

Sitting in the back seat of the surrey with Dean Faulkner, Orchid rode in silence, pining for her husband. She had spoken very little during the entire trip.

The surrey skirted Harper's Ferry on the south edge of town and ran parallel with the Potomac River for about a mile. The Clements place was situated on the south bank of the river. The huge compound of unpainted frame buildings was surrounded by an eight-foot-high stockade fence, resembling a military fort.

A cold shudder ran through Orchid as they pulled up to the gate, which was manned by an armed guard. The guard swung the gate open and greeted the three men warmly. As he set curious eyes on Orchid, he grinned and said, "You did yourself right proud on this one, Mr. Clements."

"I think so, too," replied Clements, and drove the surrey through the gate.

The worm of dread that had been eating at Orchid's insides continued its gnawing as the surrey crossed the compound and drew up in front of a flat-roofed frame structure with a weathered sign over the door that read: Clinic. Unlike most slaves, Orchid had learned to read.

Hopping out, Clements said, "You fellas take the horse and surrey to the barn."

"Will do," nodded Denton.

Clements reached a hand toward Orchid and said, "This is where you get out."

Orchid's heart was pulsing in her throat. "Why do I have to go to a clinic?"

"Because I want Doc Tuttle to examine you, that's why," Clements said stiffly. "Come on."

Orchid's mouth was dry as she let Clements take her hand and help her from the surrey. She clenched her teeth, fighting the panic that wrapped itself around her.

Clements led her through the door of the clinic, which was a large one-room affair with a half-dozen cots, an examining table, and a medicine cabinet. In one corner stood four straight-backed chairs. Three of them were occupied by black women in various stages of pregnancy. All three turned their heads and stared at Orchid with lifeless, impassive eyes.

Standing over a woman on the examining table was a thin, elderly man in a white frock. His frail hands were pressing on her distended abdomen in an attempt to establish the position of the baby.

Dr. Henry Tuttle quickly finished his examination, informed the expectant mother that she would no doubt deliver within a week, and told her she could go. He then went to Horatio Clements like a puppy would hurry to his master. His back was bent and there was a gimp in his walk. Orchid figured he had to be in his late seventies.

Tilting his head back so as to view Orchid through the half-moon spectacles that rode the end of his narrow nose, he smiled and said, "Ah, Mr. Clements, you did bring us a pretty one this time, didn't you?"

"Mm-hmm," nodded Clements. "Give her a good going over and bring the report to my office when you're finished."

"It'll be a while. I've got these other three to examine first."

"Fine. Just let me know what you find."

"Yes, sir."

Orchid sat down with two of the women while Tuttle began examining the third. Neither one spoke to her, nor did they speak to each other.

Over an hour passed before Orchid was directed to lie down on the examining table. Aware that she was frightened, Dr. Tuttle kept up a steady chatter while he checked her over. He explained that he had been in practice in Leesburg for forty years when young doctors began opening offices in the town and taking his patients. He finally had to close his practice two years ago. Horatio Clements learned about it and offered him the job of taking care of his slaves.

When the examination was completed, Orchid was left alone in the clinic while Tuttle took his report to Clements. The room was chilly. She put her coat on, then made her way to a dirty, fly-specked window and looked out on the compound. The stockade fence loomed before her like a towering prison wall. To go over it would be impossible. The only way out was the gate. Somehow she had to get through the gate and escape...and she must do it before Clements put her with one of his black men.

The thought of such a horrible thing sent a chill down her spine. She must escape and make her way back to Richmond. She would go to the Steele plantation for help. Massa Web would do something so she could again be with Mandrake.

Orchid saw Clements and Dr. Tuttle emerge from one of the buildings across the compound. They were headed toward the clinic. Fear pushed her back from the window. A trembling hand went to her mouth, and she heard herself whimpering as she backtracked across the room. She heard the footsteps of the two men just before the door came open, and felt her mouth go dry.

Clements entered ahead of Tuttle, who gimped in behind him. Clements spotted Orchid braced against the back wall and moved toward her, saying, "Doc tells me you're in good physical condition, Orchid. That's good. Now come with me. I have a special room for you to stay in. After supper tonight, the man I have chosen to sire your first child will visit you."

The dreadful repulsion Orchid was feeling gave birth to blind panic. Her heart pumped so hard she could feel her eyes pulse. Shaking her head, she cried, "No!" and bolted, using the wall as a springboard. Clements grabbed for her as she shot past him, but missed. Tuttle made a weak effort to lay hold on her, but his reflexes were too ancient, and she was quickly out the door.

Once she was outside, Orchid looked toward the gate. Escape was the only thing on her mind. Two guards stood at the gate, chatting. A chilling fog of fear clouded her terrified brain. Suddenly she found herself running toward an open door in one of the buildings. She had to hide quickly. Clements's voice cut the air behind her as he shouted for her to stop.

Paying him no heed, she dashed for the open door. Just as she reached it, she glanced over her shoulder. Clements was running after her, and another white man had joined the chase. Orchid slammed the door, bolted it, then hurried down a hallway. Taking the first door she found open, she plunged through it and found herself in a large kitchen. Two pots of stew were cooking on the stove, and she could smell the aroma of bread coming from the oven.

There was a thunderous sound at the front of the building. Clements and the other man were trying to break the door open. Orchid dashed for a door a few feet away, pulled it open, and found herself staring at pantry shelves loaded with jars of food and sacks of flour and sugar.

Next she ran to a door at the rear of the kitchen that seemed to lead outside. She slid back the bolt and twisted the knob furiously, but it wouldn't budge. She heard the front door splinter open.

She was trapped. Suddenly her eyes fell on a butcher knife with an eight-inch blade that lay on the counter. Heavy footsteps were pounding down the hall as she picked up the knife and slipped it into her coat pocket. Seconds later Clements and Wesley Denton barged into the kitchen.

Clements's face was crimson with anger as he seized her arm roughly and snapped, "I want no more of this kind of thing, Orchid! There's nowhere to run, and the quicker you realize it, the better. I paid good money for you, and you're going to do as I say."

Orchid slid both hands into her coat pockets as Clements and Denton ushered her out of the kitchen. Her right hand closed around the handle of the knife. Somehow it comforted her. She didn't know how yet, but if she had her way, the knife was going to be her ticket to freedom.

The sun was lowering in the sky as Orchid was taken to a two-story building and led to a small room on the second floor. The furniture consisted of two wooden chairs, a rickety old bed, and a small table. On the table were wash basin, water pitcher, and a rusty kerosene lantern.

While Denton fired up the lantern, Clements said to Orchid, "Your supper will be brought to you about six o'clock. At eight, I'll bring you a nice gentleman friend."

Orchid stood next to the table as Clements and Denton stepped into the hall and closed the door. A key rattled in the lock, then their footsteps faded away.

The room was chilly. Deciding to leave her coat on, Orchid sat down on one of the chairs, buried her face in her hands, and wept, calling Mandrake's name over and over.

After crying for some time, Orchid used a towel that hung on a rack above the table to dry her face. She then walked to the room's single window, pulled back the worn, dusty curtains, and looked down on the compound. It was getting dark. An elderly black man was using a candle on a long stick to light the kerosene lanterns that hung on eight-foot poles about the grounds. Orchid guessed that the open area of the compound covered about one-and-a-half acres. The lanterns were far enough apart to leave wide, dark areas between them.

Huddling in her coat, the frightened young woman was looking at the building that housed the kitchen when the door came open, and a white man she had not seen before came out carrying a tray of food. She assumed it must be six o'clock, for he was heading her direction.

At the same moment, she heard doors opening and closing within her own building, and she saw black men and women emerging from other buildings. Many of the women were obviously pregnant. All of them were headed for a low-roofed frame structure attached to the building that housed the kitchen. Orchid told herself it had to be the dining hall.

She turned from the window when she heard a key rattle in the lock of her door. The door swung open and the man she had seen below stepped in, carrying the tray. He was young—probably no more than three or fours years older than she. He set the tray on the table and raised his face into the light of the lantern. Pushing his hat back, he said, "So you are Orchid."

Orchid nodded silently, noting that the young man strongly resembled Horatio Clements.

"I'm Harland Clements, Orchid," he said in a kind manner. "I'm the youngest son of your new master."

When Orchid did not reply, Harland looked down at the tray and said, "Here's your supper. The food is very good here. Father sees to that because he wants all of his breeders to be robust and healthy." Noticing that she was wearing her coat, he added, "I'm sorry about the chill in here. You'll only occupy this room tonight. There are plenty of covers on the bed, so you can make yourself warmer if you want to."

Orchid nodded, biting her lower lip. Her hands were in the coat pockets, and her right hand gripped the handle of the butcher knife.

There was a touch of compassion on Harland's young features as he said softly, "Orchid, I know you're frightened. It's always this way when the new ones come here. You're also very unhappy to be here. Right?"

Orchid nodded again.

"Let me give you a little advice. My father can get quite mean if he loses his temper. Don't fight this thing. It's going to happen in spite of the fact that you don't want it to. You seem to be a very nice young woman. And I might add, a very pretty one, too. I don't want to see anything bad happen to you. Please, just cooperate. Some Negro women my father has bought have defied him. They are no longer living. Do you understand what I'm saying?"

Orchid felt an icy chill in her stomach. She nodded again.

"And I should tell you this, too. The man my father is going to bring to you tonight can get quite short-tempered when the women he is to mate with show resistance. He has been known to become uncontrollably violent."

When she only stared at him, Harland took a step closer and asked, "Am I getting my message across, Orchid?"

"Yes," Orchid said, taking a step backward and tightening her grip on the knife.

"Good," he smiled. "That's good. I'll be here early in the morning to take you to your permanent quarters. There's a fireplace to keep you warm. You'll like it. Okay?"

Defiance was abounding within her, but disguising it, she said, "Yes."

"Good. Very good," Harland said, heading for the open door. Pausing with his hand on the knob, he added, "Hope you enjoy your supper." With that, he moved out and closed the door. The lock rattled, and the sound of his footsteps faded away. Orchid pulled her hands from her coat pockets, clenched her fists, and squeezed her eyes shut, fear and rage merging into one seething groan.

Just after eight o'clock the lock rattled again and the door swung open. Orchid was seated on one of the wooden chairs next to the table. She rose to her feet and pushed her hands into her coat pockets as Horatio Clements came in, followed by a massive black man. He stood a head taller than Clements (who was six feet tall) and had shoulders so wide, they almost touched the door frame on each side.

A strange, almost electric sensation surged through Orchid. Her blood went cold and her heart beat wildly, sending a weak, watery feeling to her knees.

The mountain of a man moved up beside Clements, who said, "Orchid, this is Theodore. I'm going to leave him with you now. He'll return to his quarters later."

Theodore smiled and said in a deep, guttural voice, "Hello, Orchid."

The terrified woman thought of what Harland Clements had told her about Theodore being short-tempered and violent when he met resistance. He was not wearing a coat. The shirt that covered his upper body pressed tight against a powerful, muscular frame. She knew if he was of a mind to do it, he could kill her. "H-hello," she said, fearing the consequences if she did not reply to his greeting.

Clements looked down at the food on the tray and said tartly, "Orchid, you haven't touched your supper. Now, we can't have this. If you're going to make my investment in you worthwhile, you must eat the food we give you. It will be the same when you eat in the dining hall with the rest of the Negroes."

"I...I jus' wasn't hungry," she said weakly.

"Well, hungry or not, when we give you food, you're to eat it. Do you understand?"

Nodding slowly, she replied, "Yassuh."

"All right," grunted Clements. He handed the skeleton key to Theodore, and said, "Be sure to lock her in when you go."

"Yes, Massa Horatio," nodded Theodore. He waited till Clements was in the hall, then closed the door and locked it. Turning about, he pocketed the key and set his eyes on Orchid. The yellow glow of the lantern cast shadows in the hollows of his face, giving him a hellish, diabolical appearance.

Theodore took a step toward Orchid, moistening his heavy lips, and said in his deep basso, "If you're thinkin' 'bout puttin' up a fight, Orchid, you'd best forget it."

Orchid's fingers tightened around the handle of the knife in her coat pocket. Never had she experienced such fear. Her heart began to pound like a mad thing in her chest.

She thought of Mandrake, telling herself that unless she escaped this awful place, she would never see him again. The knife was her only hope. Maybe she wouldn't make it, but she would rather die than give in to this giant.

"Let's get your coat off," said Theodore, moving toward her.

Orchid could hardly breathe. Theodore's hands were reaching toward the buttons on her coat when she whipped out the knife and plunged it with all her might into his belly, just above his belt buckle. It went in, full haft.

Theodore groaned, his eyes bulging, his mouth gaping with shock. Acting on instinct, Orchid yanked the knife out and rammed the blade in again, higher up this time. The knife buried itself in Theodore chest.

Orchid wanted to jerk it out and stab him again, but the handle slipped from her grasp as Theodore stumbled away from her and fell heavily on the table, knocking it over. Pitcher and basin went flying. The lantern hit the floor, shattering the glass chimney and spilling kerosene. Instantly the flame found it.

Theodore lay on his back, struggling to remove the knife from his chest. Orchid knew the door key was in his pocket. She had to have it to escape. Fire was rapidly spreading over the dry floor.

In desperation, Orchid grasped a chair and brought it down savagely on Theodore's head. The blow stunned him, and his hands fell away from the knife. Theodore's eyes rolled back in their sockets so only the whites showed. He coughed once, spewing blood, then his crimson teeth showed in a grimace of death. Knowing she may have to use the knife again, Orchid yanked it from his chest and searched his pocket for the key. It took only seconds to produce it.

The fire had reached the bed and flames were licking their way up the bedspread. A cloud of smoke pressed against the ceiling and would soon fill the entire room.

Orchid could hear loud voices coming from the compound as she coughed and unlocked the door. Peering into the hall, she saw that a lone lantern burned halfway toward the rear of the building. It was enough for her to see that there was a door at the other end of the hall, which she assumed led to a staircase outside, identical to the one she had mounted at the front when forced into the building. There was no one yet in sight.

She had enough presence of mind to reason that if she locked the door, it would lead them to believe that both she and Theodore were still inside. The more people occupied with the fire, the better her chances of escape.

Just as she turned the key in the lock, Orchid heard footsteps on the front stairs and the sound of excited voices. Thrusting the key in a coat pocket, she held the knife and ran toward the rear of the building. When she passed through the door, she found that it did lead to a landing and stairs that went all the way to the ground.

It was pitch dark, but she found her way to the bottom and headed along the side of the building toward the dimly lit compound. More people were running toward the burning building.

Keeping to the shadows, Orchid made her way along the edge of the compound toward the gate. She was determined to make good her escape. As she neared the gate, she paused in the shadows and looked back across the compound. A large crowd of Negroes, sprinkled with a few whites, was gathered at the blazing building. The fire had the attention of everyone. Men were dashing to the spot with buckets in hand, and the crowd was forming a bucket brigade from the water trough some forty yards away.

Orchid turned toward the gate. Two guards stood together, looking at the blaze. As Orchid inched closer, she heard one guard say to the other, "You stay here. I'll go help fight the fire."

The lone guard watched his friend hurry toward the burning building and was unaware that a small, dark form was moving up behind him. When the knife was plunged into his back, he let out a loud cry, but the sound was swallowed up in the clamor on the compound, and no one heard it.

The guard lay on the ground, moaning, the knife burning like a red-hot iron. He raised up to see a woman fumbling with the heavy latch on the gate. Determined to stop her, he struggled to his knees and pulled his revolver from its holster.

Suddenly the gate was open and the woman was dashing to freedom. The guard fired. He heard a pained cry and saw her stagger against the gate frame, then disappear. The guard stumbled to the gate and was able to make out the woman's form weaving toward the bank of the Potomac River. When she reached it, there was a slight pause, then a distinct splash.

CHAPTER THIRTEEN

Mandrake's muscles tensed as Harry Binder and Cletus Hicks drew up. Both of the unkempt young men had smirks on their faces. Hicks, who was tall and slender, said, "Hello, boy. What's your name?"

"Mandrake," replied the black man levelly, distrust showing in his eyes.

Hicks read it. Looking at his short, thick-bodied partner, he said, "S'pose this African boy has a last name, Harry?"

"Well, if he don't," chuckled Binder, "he's got to be a runaway slave. We could pick us up a right handsome reward if that's the case."

"Yeah," replied Hicks, casting an appreciative glance at Mandrake's horse. Looking back at Mandrake, he asked, "You steal that horse and run away, boy?"

"No. I have manumission papers. The horse is a gift from the man who used to own me."

The dirty, long-haired men exchanged glances and laughed.

"You believe that, Clete?"

"Naw. You cain't trust a black-skinned African. I say he either produces them papers or we take him to the law and let them find out where he run away from."

Without a word, Mandrake walked to the horse, opened a saddlebag, and pulled out the envelope that held his manumission papers. Removing the papers, he unfolded them and held them up so Binder and Hicks could see them. "You satisfied now?" asked Mandrake. "I's as much a free man as either one o' you."

The two men looked at each other, nodding.

"Okay," chuckled Hicks, "so you ain't no runaway slave. But me and Harry really do need us a good horse. We'll just take that one."

Mandrake bristled. While replacing the papers in the envelope, he retorted, "You won' be doin' anythin' of the kind."

The stocky Binder's features hardened. He stepped close to Mandrake and growled, "Who's to stop us? You think you can handle both of us, boy?"

Mandrake countered, "I'm on an important trip, an' I gotta get where I'm goin' soon as possible." He wheeled and returned to the animal, placing the envelope back in the saddlebag.

Suddenly a strong arm was around Mandrake's neck, clamping it in a scissor-lock. Harry Binder bore down hard on Mandrake's throat, choking him. At the same time, Hicks grabbed Mandrake's ankles and they carried him toward the lake. He twisted and squirmed, but both men were strong, and he couldn't break free.

Binder and Hicks waded into the lake, heading for deep water. They were going to drown him.

In desperation, Mandrake made an abrupt twist of his upper body and grabbed for Binder's head. It worked. Binder lost his grip, stumbled, and went to the bottom in four feet of icy water. Hicks then lost his hold on Mandrake's ankles, stumbling slightly himself. Mandrake went to the floor of the lake, quickly righted himself, and stood up. When he rose out of the water, Hicks was waiting for him. But Mandrake dodged Hicks's haymaker and countered with a hard right to the jaw. Hicks went down just as Binder jumped on Mandrake's back. The impact sent both of them into the water.

Mandrake bobbed up first and gained his footing. When Binder surfaced, the angry black man unleashed two rapid blows to his face, sending Binder back down again. Mandrake felt a fist strike him in the right kidney, sending a streamer of pain through his body. He spun around, ducked a second punch, and lashed back with one of his own. Hicks flopped backward from the impact, and at the same time, Mandrake heard Binder come out of the water behind him, gagging and choking.

In one fluid motion, Mandrake whirled and punched Binder again, sending him under the surface. He quickly spun around, expecting Hicks to be on him again, but was surprised to see him dashing for the shore. Fearful that Hicks was going after his horse, Mandrake ran after him and tackled him just as they reached the shoreline.

Both men came to their feet. Hicks swore at Mandrake and swung at him. Mandrake ducked and answered back with three rapid, forceful blows. Hicks staggered back, trying to keep his footing. But Mandrake was after him like an angry beast and cracked him with two more hard blows. Hicks went to his knees, then sprawled forward on the sand.

Mandrake stood over him for a few seconds, breathing heavily. He looked toward the lake, expecting another assault from Binder, but there was no sign of him. Perhaps he had hightailed it while Mandrake had been occupied with Hicks. Mandrake made his way to his campsite, mounted the horse, and rode northward along the shore. His mind went to Orchid. Nothing was going to stop him from finding her and taking her away from the vile man who had bought her.

Mandrake rode at a steady trot all night and reached the north edge of Lake Anna just before dawn. He decided to hole up during the daylight hours and ride at night. It would take him longer to cover the miles to Harper's Ferry, but he didn't need any more confrontations.

Just before sunrise, Mandrake found an abandoned barn and took his horse inside. After eating some cold biscuits and beef jerky provided by Web Steele, he lay down and slept.

That night he traveled again, stopping to water the horse periodically and allowing it to graze a bit. At dawn, he found a secluded spot beside a small creek just south of Warrenton. He ground-reined the horse so it could get to the creek for water and munch on the tawny winter grass. He had been asleep about two hours when he was awakened by a sharp male voice shouting, "Hey, black boy, wake up!"

Mandrake came awake instantly and sat up. Blinking against the bright Virginia sunlight, he could see a tall man standing over him with a cocked revolver in his hand. A badge pinned to the man's waist-length coat read: Sheriff, Louisa County, Virginia.

"Come on, get up!" barked Sheriff Ned Langley.

Mandrake rose to his feet and looked around at the half-circle of armed men who faced him. A half-dozen black muzzles were trained on him. Mandrake then saw Cletus Hicks astride a horse in the background.

"You're under arrest for the murder of Harry Binder," Langley said gruffly.

Mandrake was taken to Louisa and locked up in jail. His manumission papers were confiscated by a deputy and locked in the safe at the sheriff's office.

During the ride to town, Mandrake did not speak a word in his defense. Hicks had told Sheriff Langley that the newly freed Negro had assaulted him for no reason, leaving him lying on the shore of Lake Anna with a broken jaw. Harry Binder had come on the scene just as Mandrake was leaving, and tried to stop him. The ex-slave overwhelmed Binder, dragged him into the lake, and drowned him.

Mandrake knew that free or not, he didn't stand a chance. He was black. No one would believe the true story.

After locking Mandrake's cell, Langley pressed his face close to the bars and told him that because he was a free man, he would be entitled to a trial. The trial would be held in about six weeks when the circuit judge showed up in Louisa. Then laughing as he walked away, the sheriff told him the trial would only be a formality; Cletus's testimony would put a rope around Mandrake's neck.

During the next six weeks, Mandrake languished in the cell, yearning for Orchid and wishing he could get a message to Web Steele. Massa Web would believe Mandrake's story and come to his rescue; but there was no way to contact him.

One day in early February, 1861, Sheriff Langley told Mandrake that the circuit judge had taken ill and would not be able to come to

Louisa until he recovered. There was no way to know when that might be.

Late in the afternoon several days later, Mandrake was lying on his bunk thinking of Orchid. He feared that by now she had been forced to mate with one of Horatio Clements's choice black males. He was fighting tears when the jail door banged open and two deputies came dragging a white man down the narrow corridor, followed by the sheriff.

Langley unlocked the door to Mandrake's cell and pulled it open, saying, "Got some company for you, black boy. No sense putting him in another cell. That'd just mean two to keep clean."

The new prisoner was thrown into the cell and landed on the floor in a heap. Langley locked the door and walked away with his men.

Mandrake left his bunk and helped his new cell mate to the bunk on the opposite side of the barred cubicle. The man had been beaten severely. His lips were cut and there were bruises all over his face.

Sitting up on the bunk, he dabbed at the cuts on his mouth and said, "Thank you, my friend."

"Looks like they done work you over good," remarked Mandrake.

"Yeah. You might say that."

"What'd you do?"

"Killed a man."

"Murder?"

"Yep."

"Oh," nodded Mandrake. "The man you killed do somethin' bad to you?"

"Not to me. He beat up a friend of mine and crippled him for life. I was just takin' out vengeance for my friend."

"I see."

Extending his hand, the bruised man said, "Name's Jess—Jess Dorman."

Meeting the hand with a solid grip, Mandrake said, "Glad to meet you, Jess."

When their hands parted, Dorman asked, "What's your name?"

Mandrake had a sudden thought. Now that he had been freed by Web Steele and was no longer a slave, he needed a last name. It took only seconds for him to reply, "Mandrake Steele."

"You a runaway slave?"

"No!" Mandrake replied. "I was a slave, but my massa set me free."

"So what are you in here for?"

"Same thing as you."

"Murder?"

"Yassuh."

"Who'd you murder?"

"Nobody. I killed a white man in self-defense."

"How'd it happen?"

"You sure you wants to hear it? It's a long story."

Scooting back on his bunk so he could lean against the wall, Dorman said, "Sure. Ain't got nothin' else to do. I'd like to hear it."

Mandrake took a half hour to tell his story, beginning with Reed Exley's treatment of Orchid and himself. He explained how and why Exley sold Orchid to Horatio Clements, then described how Web Steele had bought him and set him free so he could go after her. Finally he told how he had been attacked and forced to defend himself, resulting in the apparent accidental drowning of the man he was now accused of murdering.

When the story was finished, Dorman shook his head and said, "Well, even though it was self-defense, Mandrake, you'll die just as dead when you hit the end of your rope as I will when I hit mine."

"Yassuh," Mandrake said, bowing his head, "but that's not the wo'st part of all this. The wo'st is what Orchid's facin' at Harper's Ferry. I don' want to hang, Jess, but more'n anythin' I don' want my wife sufferin' what she's sufferin'."

Dorman was quiet for a moment, then he said, "I haven't told you much about myself, Mandrake. I'm no angel, believe me. I've been in trouble with the law plenty of times. And...ah...I've broken outta jail before."

Mandrake's heavy eyebrows arched. "You have?"

"Yeah. Three times. Neither one of us is gonna hang. Let me think on it a while, and I'll figure a way to bust both of us outta here."

Just before midnight the following day, young deputy sheriff Alvin Sparks was seated in the office alone. He had come on duty at eleven o'clock, checked on his two prisoners, and returned to the office for the night. He had a newspaper spread out on the desk and was reading of the heated battle in Congress over slavery.

In the small cell block behind the office, Jess Dorman whispered through the darkness, "It's been nearly an hour since he was in here, Mandrake. That oughtta be enough time. You ready?"

Unable to see his cell mate in the pitch black, Mandrake sat up on his bunk, took a deep breath, and said, "Yassuh. Let's git this thin' over with. I's got to head fo' Harper's Ferry."

"Be sure to hit him plenty hard."

"Don' worry, Jess. I'll put 'im out."

Rolling to his knees on the bunk, Dorman stuck his forefinger down his throat, gagged, and began giving up what was left in his stomach from supper.

Mandrake shouted toward the office door, "Deputy! Hey, deputy! We gots trouble in here!"

The office door came open and Deputy Sparks appeared, carrying a lighted lantern. Dorman kept gagging and heaving as Sparks hurried to the cell door and asked Mandrake, "What's the matter with him?"

"I don' know," replied Mandrake, looking worried, "but he's really sick. Must've been somethin' in the food that disagreed with 'im."

"Well, you aren't sick, and you ate the same stuff he did."

"Yassuh, but he was tellin' me befo' supper that he gots a stomach problem. If'n somethin' ain' done, he could die."

Sparks set the lantern on the floor, pulled the key from his belt, and began to unlock the door. "Let me take a look at him. Doc Smithers don't appreciate bein' called out in the middle of the night if it isn't a matter of life and death."

Sparks drew his revolver from its holster, pointed it through the bars at Mandrake, and said, "Get over there against the far wall."

When Mandrake had obeyed, Sparks swung the door open and entered the cell. He was trying to keep one eye on Mandrake while leaning over Dorman, but for a brief instant, he put his full attention on the sick man. Mandrake moved with the swiftness of a cougar and chopped the deputy behind the ear.

Sparks crumpled to the floor, then tried vainly to rise, knowing he was in trouble. Mandrake bent over and struck him savagely on the jaw. Sparks collapsed and lay still.

Dorman had been careful not to soil his clothing. Leaping from the bunk and wiping his mouth, he said, "Good job, pal! Let's go!"

Leaving the deputy locked in the cell, the two men hastened to the street and ran down the block. Finding a dark spot between two buildings, they slipped into the shadows, breathing hard.

"Okay," gasped Dorman, "this is where we part company. Like I told you, I'm headin' for Ohio. It's been good knowin' you."

"Same here," responded Mandrake. "Thanks fo' helpin' me break out."

"I was helpin' me as much as I was you. Hope you get your wife outta there."

"Thanks," said Mandrake, then wheeled and darted across the street.

Moments later, Mandrake was out of town, heading due north for Harper's Ferry, which he knew was some ninety miles away. Without his papers, he would have to be very careful.

For two days and nights, Mandrake worked his way northward, staying clear of towns and villages. He kept to the brush on the farm land as much as possible, and though he hated to do it, he stole food from farmers' storm cellars at night. On the morning of the third day, he skirted a cotton plantation by bending low and darting between clumps of bushes and huge oak trees. While halting to catch his breath, he saw the slaves working among the buildings. The sight made him feel a warm spot deep inside toward Web Steele. Massa Web had set him free. He thought of Orchid at that awful place near Harper's Ferry and longed for the day they could be together on the Steele plantation, willingly serving the man who had paid such a high price to free him.

Unaware that he was being watched, Mandrake moved furtively another hundred yards or so and found that he was approaching the Rappahannock River. He would follow the bank till he found a safe spot to cross. Maybe there would even be a bridge.

He drew within twenty yards of the river bank, moving slowly through dense brush. He was about to come to a small clearing when two men in their mid-twenties suddenly appeared, aiming shotguns directly at him.

"Hold it right there, blackie!" shouted the taller one.

Mandrake froze.

The short man, who had a cocky look to him, ran up and said, "Where you from, boy?"

The other one hastened to flank his companion. Keeping his eyes on Mandrake, he said, "Hughey, looks like we've got us a runaway. I'll bet there's a plantation owner somewhere south of here who'd pay a handsome sum to get him back."

"Maybe, but I'll tell you what, Bobby. My pa might like to keep him for himself."

Mandrake felt as if a spear of ice had pierced his chest. "I...I used to be a slave," he said cautiously, "but I was set free by Massa Web Steele down by Richmon'."

"Oh?" said Hughey. Keeping the shotgun trained on Mandrake, he held out his free hand and clipped, "Let me see your papers."

Mandrake swallowed hard. "I...I don' got 'em no mo'."

"What happened to them?" asked Bobby.

Mandrake didn't dare tell them the truth. Sheriff Langley might be willing to give a reward for getting him back. "I...uh...I lost 'em," he said weakly.

"Humpf! Likely story," said Hughey. "Let's take you to see my pa. He's always looking for black boys built like you."

"Wait a minute, Hughey," cut in Bobby. "Your pa won't pay us anything for him. We could make some money if—"

"Shut up!" snapped Hughey. "If this black boy was old or skinny or something like that, we'd try to make some money on him. But even with his coat on, I can tell this African has what it takes to do a real day's work."

Mandrake was taken at gunpoint to the very plantation he had been skirting. Wealthy owner Todd Morrison emerged from the mansion at his son's call and smiled broadly when he set his eyes on Mandrake. Looking him up and down, Morrison asked, "Where'd you come from, boy?"

"I was a slave on the John Ruffin plantation down by Richmon', suh," answered Mandrake. "Then his slave foreman—"

"He any kin to Edmund Ruffin?" cut in Morrison.

"His brother, suh."

"I see. You said you *were* a slave on the John Ruffin plantation?"

"Yassuh," nodded Mandrake. "But I'm a free man now."

"You have papers to prove it?"

"Nossuh. I did have, but I lost 'em."

"Lost them?" repeated Morrison, his face displaying his disbelief. "You know what, boy? I think you're lyin'. I'd bet my last dollar you're a runaway."

"Nossuh," said Mandrake, shaking his head. "I's tellin' you the truth. Like I started to tell you, Massa John's slave foreman sold my wife to a man in Harper's Ferry fo' a breeder, then took me to the auction in Richmon'. Massa Web Steele bought me, give me my manumission papers and a horse, and tol' me to find Orchid and take her away from that place. My papers was in the saddlebags, but somebody stole the horse and I lost 'em."

Todd Morrison smiled to himself. He figured the story was probably true, but seldom did a man get a chance to lay hold on a Negro like the one who was standing before him. Turning to Hughey, he said, "Son, keep your shotgun trained on this boy. Don't let him take a step."

Mandrake felt the pressure of the shotgun's twin bores as he watched Morrison walk part way across the yard and hail a passing slave. He commanded the black man to go to a shed and bring a pair of leg irons, then returned and said with a smile, "Looks like we picked us up a nice piece of chattel for free, Hughey. Just in case he gets any ideas about running, we'll hobble him good."

"Please, massa," said Mandrake, his face pained. "I needs to get to Harper's Ferry an' save my wife. Please don' do this!"

Morrison sneered. "You don't really expect me to believe that cock-and-bull story, do you? You're my slave now, and I don't want to hear any more about it."

Despair washed over Mandrake like a cold ocean wave. As long as he was kept in leg irons, there would be no hope of escape. Somehow, some way, he had to convince the plantation owner to trust him and remove the irons. When he did, Orchid's husband would resume his relentless journey to Harper's Ferry.

CHAPTER FOURTEEN

The North and the South passed the point of no return in early February 1861 when secessionist delegates met in Montgomery, Alabama. Six other Southern states followed South Carolina in seceding from the Union to form the Confederate States of America. Virginia, North Carolina, Tennessee, and Arkansas were making plans to join them.

On February 8 the Provisional Constitution of the Confederate States of America was adopted. Each state was declared sovereign and independent, and the charter guaranteed the right to own slaves anywhere within the bounds of the Confederacy.

Jefferson Davis of Vicksburg, Mississippi, who had been a U.S. senator prior to secession, was appointed president of the Confederate States, and on February 18 he took the oath of office and gave a dynamic and stirring inaugural address.

Two weeks later another inaugural address was heard that was just as dynamic and stirring. On March 4 Abraham Lincoln became president of the United States. In his speech, Lincoln rejected any prospect for negotiation concerning the three federal forts in Charleston Harbor: Moultrie, Sumter, and Castle Pinckney. They were Union property, and they would stay Union property. When word came of Lincoln's refusal to even consider negotiation over the forts, Southern tempers flared.

At the same time, tension was building between separatists and Union loyalists in Delaware, Maryland, Kentucky, and Missouri. West of the Mississippi River, all of the organized territories had spoken out in opposition to slavery and were favoring their admission to the Union as free states. This prospect further angered leaders in the Southern movement and added impetus toward open hostilities. The roiling tide of anti-Union sentiment was cresting in the South by the last days of March.

Ominous clouds of war were gathering.

There was a private war raging in the twisted soul of Reed Exley. Desiring free rein to pursue Abby Ruffin, Exley was searching for a way to remove Web Steele from the picture. He had to do it in a manner that would not implicate himself and that would allow him to look good in Abby's eyes.

One night in early April, Exley was sitting alone at a table at the Lamplighter Tavern in Richmond. While periodically pouring whiskey into a shot glass and downing it, he worked at coming up with a foolproof plan.

In a far corner of the tavern, a painted-up woman was singing a jovial song beside an upright piano played by a silver-haired man in striped shirt and arm garters. The patrons on that side of the place were attentive to the songstress. Those on Exley's side were engaged in quiet conversation.

Exley had been there about half an hour when a shabbily dressed man came in and sat at the table next to him. Reed gave him a casual glance as the man ordered a glass and bottle from the waiter. Some ten minutes later, another shabbily dressed man came in. The new man ran his gaze to the bar, and noting that it was jam-packed, looked around for an empty table. Seeing that all the tables were occupied, he began making his way toward the two tables that were each occupied by only one man. Exley was relieved when the man drew up to the table next to him and asked his neighbor if he could use some company. He was immediately asked to sit down.

Exley overheard the new man introduce himself as Wilbur Yates from a small town in southern Virginia. He had come to Richmond in search of a job. The other man, Exley learned, was Hec Wheeler. Like

Yates, Wheeler was down on his luck. He was passing through Virginia from Tennessee, on his way to Carlisle, Pennsylvania. His brother John owned a carriage business in Carlisle, and Hec was hoping John would give him a job.

The two men confided in each other that they were getting low on cash, then the conversation turned to the strife between the North and the South. While they were agreeing that if war came, they would fight on the Confederate side, Exley's evil plan was quickly taking shape.

Rising from his chair, Exley stood over the next table and said, "Excuse me, gentlemen. I couldn't help overhearing your conversation. My name is Reed Exley. I'm slave overseer on the John Ruffin plantation just outside of town, and I perceive that you could both use a little cash in your pockets."

Yates and Wheeler stood and introduced themselves to Exley, asking him to join them. They knew by the cut of his clothes that Exley was well-to-do.

As they sat down, Yates said, "You're right about our pockets being short on cash, Mr. Exley. What do you have in mind?"

"Well, I want to play a little joke on a friend of mine, but I need some help. It'll take a day or so to set it up, so here's what I'll do. I'll put you both up in a nice hotel and pay for your meals while you're here, and I'll give you each fifty dollars for helping me. How does that sound?"

Wheeler had carrot-red hair and a face that always looked like it was sunburned. Smiling, he replied, "Sounds great to me, Mr. Exley. Exactly what is this joke?"

"I'll come to the hotel tomorrow after I get things set up. I'll explain it to you then."

Exley took the two men to the Virginia Hotel, which was only a half-block from the tavern, and got them each a room. They could eat at the hotel's restaurant and charge the meals to their rooms. Telling them he would see them some time the next day, he left the happy men to enjoy a good night's rest.

The next morning, Exley positioned himself at one of the windows in his bedroom on the third floor of the Ruffin mansion. The window allowed a view of the lane that came from the road. Abby was expecting Web to come and pick her up so they could spend the morning together in town. Exley wanted to intercept Steele before he entered the house.

It was exactly nine-thirty when Exley caught sight of the buggy coming up the lane. He dashed down the two flights of stairs and was on the porch as Web drove up.

Webster Steele alighted from the buggy, wondering why Exley was standing there almost smiling at him. As he mounted the porch steps, Exley stood between him and the door and said, "Web, I've been wanting to talk to you. I know you're here to take Abby to town and won't have time to see me now, but how about late this evening? We could have a drink at the Lamplighter."

"You know I don't drink, Reed."

"You could have some coffee. They've got good coffee at the Lamplighter."

"How would you know? Seems to me you always smell like whiskey when you come from there. Besides, you and I don't have anything to talk about."

As he spoke, Web started to walk around Exley, but the shorter man laid a gentle hand on his arm and said, "Please, Web. I really do need to talk some things over with you." Feigning a sheepish look, he added, "I've been...well, I've been wrong about some things. I need to get them off my chest. How about it?"

Web was skeptical, but in case the man had actually undergone a change of heart, it would make things much better within the family if they could patch up their differences. "Okay," he nodded. "What time do you want to meet?"

"How's ten o'clock?"

"A bit late, but I guess that'd be all right."

"Good!" exclaimed Exley, showing relief. "See you at the Lamplighter at ten tonight."

Elated that his plan was working well so far, Exley left the porch and headed toward the back of the mansion. He waited in one of the sheds until Web and Abby had driven away, then hitched his wagon to a horse and headed for town.

Meeting with Wheeler and Yates in the privacy of Wheeler's room, Exley found them eager to get on with the joke. They thought it was grand being in on it while getting paid, too.

Exley told them he wanted to make his friend, Web Steele, think he was helping to thwart a robbery. He explained that Steele was the gallant hero type, and without a doubt would fall for it. After they staged the "robbery" and Steele had been suckered in, they would laugh and tell him it was all a joke.

Exley carefully laid out the robbery plan to Yates and Wheeler, then went over the details several times to make sure they knew exactly what to do. Telling them to meet him in front of the Lamplighter at nine o'clock so they could do a little practice before Web showed up, Exley left the hotel and hurried to a small house three blocks from the town's main thoroughfare. He was glad to see that a lantern was still burning in the parlor window.

Stepping onto the creaky porch, he knocked on the door. He heard muffled footsteps, and the door swung open. A short, stout man of fifty squinted at him and said, "Reed? That you? Don't have my specs on."

"Sure is, Stan. You busy?"

Stan Frye laughed, flinging the door open, and said, "You know an old bachelor is just like a housewife, Reed. There's always somethin' to keep me busy. But come on in. I was just cleanin' out some drawers in the bedroom. They can wait."

Frye closed the door and asked, "You want some coffee? I can heat some up real quick-like."

"Sure. While it's heatin' up, I can tell you why I stopped by."

Reed Exley would leave no stone unturned. He must make sure his scheme against Web Steele was air-tight. He was certain Stan Frye would be willing to help him.

A few years before, Stan's older brother Arnie had been a successful slave auctioneer in Richmond. One day Arnie had hitched a mule he had just purchased to his wagon and had gone to town to do some business at one of the banks on Richmond's main street. When he climbed into the wagon to head for home, the mule refused to budge.

Arnie Frye, like his brother Stan, was known for being short-tempered. People on the street were looking on as he stood before the mule, cursing it and lashing it mercilessly in the face with a whip. Just then Web Steele came out of a nearby barber shop. When he saw what was going on, he moved in and shouted for Arnie to stop. Already aflame with anger, Arnie turned the whip on Web.

Web defended himself with his fists and unintentionally broke Arnie's jaw. The doctors were unable to set the fracture correctly, and Arnie was hardly able to talk after that. He lost his job as an auctioneer. He took his wife and moved to Roanoke, where he was given a job as a stable keeper by an old friend. The pay was quite small compared to what he had made as an auctioneer, and his wife left him.

Arnie turned to the bottle. He soon became a drunken sot, and even lost the stable job. Things went from bad to worse, and finally Arnie drank himself to death.

Web had never known what happened to Arnie, but nonetheless Stan blamed Web for it all and held a bitter grudge. Reed Exley had few friends, but Stan was one of them. He had often shared with Exley his smoldering hatred toward Steele. Stan was prime material for aiding Exley in his scheme.

As they sat down at the kitchen table, Exley complained that Steele had done him wrong and needed to be punished. Frye was immediately interested, and was soon happily involved in the scheme. Vengeance would be sweet.

While they sipped their coffee, Exley carefully instructed Frye, emphasizing that timing was of utmost importance. When Frye was able to repeat his part of the plan perfectly, Exley said, "Be sure that you're in the Lamplighter by eight o'clock. I'll come in about twenty after. Don't come near me. I don't want anyone to be able to say they saw us talkin' in there. Understand?"

"Got it," nodded Frye.

"Okay. Be sure you join up with some friends as soon as you get there."

"No problem."

"Good. I'll leave the tavern a little before nine to do a short rehearsal with Wheeler and Yates and return within fifteen or twenty minutes. Just in case Steele should show up a bit early, be sure you're on the street by nine thirty. Tell your friends you need to get some fresh air, and that you'll be back shortly. I'll keep an eye on you. Once you're outside, hide in the shadows till you see me come out of the tavern. I'll be at the door watchin' for Steele and move out to meet him when he pulls up. While I'm talkin' to him, you slip back inside. Stay with your friends till everybody in the place learns that there's trouble out on the street. When you come out with them, give the police the story I've gone over with you."

"Will do."

"Remember—you'll have to tell the story again in court. You've got to tell it exactly the same on the witness stand."

"Don't worry. I'll keep the story straight." Laughing wickedly, he added, "I can't wait to see that dirty skunk Steele get what's comin' to him."

There was little traffic on Richmond's main thoroughfare and only a few people were on the boardwalks when Web Steele pulled up and parked his buggy in front of the Lamplighter Tavern at five minutes before ten. Web had pondered just what Reed Exley might have to say. Perhaps he was going to apologize for the times he had done Web wrong. Would he also admit his guilt in Elizabeth's death? Web doubted the man would go that far.

As he was tying the reins to a hitching post, Web saw Exley emerge from the tavern. By the light of the street lamps, he could see a wide smile on his face.

Knowing that his two accomplices were watching from the dark space between the tavern and the next building, Exley approached his victim amiably and said, "Web, I sure appreciate your meeting with me. It's time to bury the hatchet."

"Well, I'm glad you feel that way," Steele said warily. "Even though Elizabeth's gone, Papa John still considers you a part of the family. And since I'm marrying into the family shortly, you and I need to do what we can to get along."

Exley made it sound like he was in full agreement with Web as he waited for a wide break between people on the boardwalk and vehicles moving along the street. The break came quickly. Exley gave his accomplices the preset signal by raising his coat collar and saying, "Let's go inside, Web. The air's a bit nippy tonight."

Steele and Exley were almost to the door of the tavern when a cry came from between the buildings, "Help! I'm being robbed!" followed by the sounds of a scuffle.

Exley, relieved that no one else was on the street to hear it, looked that direction and said, "Sounds like somebody's in trouble, Web!"

True to form, Web Steele said, "C'mon!" and made a dash for the ten-foot-wide space between the buildings.

Making sure to stay a few steps behind Steele as they ran, Reed pulled a length of lead pipe from his coat pocket. There was an alley at the rear of the buildings with a lantern burning on a pole. By the dim light, Steele could see two men on the ground scuffling. Just as he drew close, Exley cracked him on the back of the head with the heavy pipe. When his accomplices heard the blow and saw Steele go down, they stopped scuffling and leaped to their feet, staring wide-eyed at Exley.

"Hey, what's goin' on?" gasped Yates. "What'd you do that for?"

"That's no way to treat a friend!" Wheeler said accusingly.

While Steele lay unconscious on the ground, Exley slipped the pipe back into his coat pocket and pulled a hunting knife from its sheath on his belt. Moving close to Yates, he said, "This was no joke to begin with, pal," and in a swift, violent move, drove the knife into Yates's heart.

Wheeler's mouth flew open in shock. He felt he was in a nightmare standing transfixed, unable to move.

Yates collapsed to the ground, dead, with the knife protruding from his chest. Exley pulled the lead pipe from his coat pocket, moved close to Wheeler, and said, "Hec, I planned it exactly this way. I killed Wilbur and not you because you're by far the smartest. Cooperate with me and you won't get into trouble."

The light from the lantern in the alley revealed Wheeler's terror-stricken features. The usual redness of his skin had faded to an ashen-gray. Swallowing hard, he struggled for a moment to locate his voice, then stammered, "Wh-what do you want fr-from me?"

Pointing toward Web's crumpled form, Exley said, "This man is my worst enemy. He's done me wrong a hundred times. I had to trick him to get him here, but finally I can have my revenge."

Licking his lips, Wheeler said, "Y-your worst enemy?"

"Yeah. He's rotten to the core. Will you help me?"

"Well, I...I..."

"It'll be worth a lot of money for you if you do."

Wheeler scrubbed a shaky hand across his mouth. "Money?"

"Yeah. A generous sum. Will you do it?"

"Wh-what do you want me t-to do?"

"I hit Steele plenty hard. He'll be out for a few minutes. Before he comes to, I'm gonna put this sheath on his belt to make it look like he was carryin' the knife. Then we'll call the police. I'll give them the story. You just back me up. We'll tell them that you and I were standin' on the boardwalk in front of the tavern when we heard this call for help from back here. We ran back to investigate and came on the scene just as Steele was plungin' the knife into Yates's chest. Got it? You just back up whatever I say."

"Just go along with whatever you say?"

"Right. You'll have to testify to it in court, too. But I'll make it worth your trouble, Hec. I'll give you a thousand dollars if you'll help me."

"A thousand dollars!" gulped Wheeler.

"That's right. You'll get five hundred tomorrow, and five hundred after you testify at the trial. How about it?"

Wheeler quickly appraised the situation. He hardly knew Wilbur Yates...and besides, there was no way he could bring the man back to life by refusing to help Exley. He had never even seen a thousand dollars in his whole life. Exley was a scary man, and he was still holding the lead pipe. Why not go along with him? Nodding, he said, "Okay, Mr. Exley. I'll help you."

"Good!" said Exley. "This is your lucky day, wouldn't you agree, Hec?"

"Sure," said Hec, nervously wringing his hands. "My lucky day."

Exley had stolen the hunting knife and sheath from a local gun shop while the proprietor was in a back room looking for extra ammunition for his derringer. There was no way the knife could be traced to him. Working fast, he placed the sheath on Web's belt, then told Hec to go shout for the police.

Before obeying, Hec said, "There's somethin' I don't understand, Mr. Exley."

"What's that?"

"Well, if you wanted to get back at this Steele fella, why didn't you just put the knife in his chest?"

Exley grinned. "I have my reasons, pal. I want his woman, too. She's sorta been down on me, but I'm gonna make ol' Reed Exley look like a saint in the courtroom, and my act will draw her to me like a magnet when Steele goes to prison...or maybe the gallows."

Web Steele's head was throbbing when he came to and heard voices all around him. Opening his eyes, he saw where he was, then remembered running into the dark space between the buildings to help a robbery victim.

"He's comin' around," said a familiar voice.

Several lanterns sat on the ground to give light on the scene. Web focused on the face of Richmond's chief of police, Frank Crabbe. Steele and Crabbe had been acquaintances ever since Crabbe had joined the force some ten years before. Leaning over Steele, he said, "Webster, I never would've guessed you could do such a thing."

Sitting up, Steele winced, rubbed the back of his head, and looked at the policemen who surrounded him. He was aware of a large knot on the back of his skull, and that it was bleeding.

Looking at Crabbe, Web said, "You never would've guessed that I could do what?"

"Murder a man," the chief replied flatly.

"What are you talking about?"

Crabbe shifted his position, giving Steele a clear view of Reed Exley and Hec Wheeler, who stood behind him. Pointing with his head, he said, "Mr. Exley told us how he and his friend were chatting on the boardwalk in front of the tavern when they heard a cry for help coming from back here. When they ran between the buildings, they saw you drive your knife into this man's chest."

Following Crabbe's finger, Web saw the corpse a few feet away with the knife still buried in its chest. Crabbe was waiting for the coroner to arrive before disturbing the body.

The truth came home to Web Steele like a punch to the solar plexus. Reed Exley had set him up. The whole thing about wanting to talk was a farce. Exley no doubt had both men working with him, then stabbed one of them to death in a wickedly devised scheme to frame him.

"They're lying, Frank," said Web.

"That won't work, Steele!" Exley snapped. "That's your knife that's stuck in him."

Web looked at Crabbe and said, "He's lying, Frank. I've never seen that knife before."

"Well, I'd say it would fit that sheath on your belt perfectly," countered Crabbe.

Web found the sheath on his belt and lanced the smirking Exley with hot eyes. Then he said to Crabbe, "The truth is, Frank, that Exley lured me to the tavern tonight, saying he wanted to make amends for the trouble he has made for me. Then he tricked me into running to help some poor victim who was supposedly being robbed. This 'friend' of his was scuffling with the poor guy who's now dead. Exley hit me over the head with something, then he or this other man stabbed him. While I was unconscious, they put the sheath on my belt."

Exley pulled the pipe from his coat pocket and waved it at Steele. "This is what I hit you with, you murderer! Only it was just after you had rammed your knife into that man's chest. As I told Chief Crabbe, I always carry this piece of pipe with me when I come into town at night...for my own protection. Good thing I was carryin' it tonight, or you might have gotten away."

Web struggled to his feet and stood swaying while he used his handkerchief to stay the trickle of blood from the cut on his head. To Crabbe he said, "Exley wouldn't know the truth if it slapped him in the face. It happened like I told you, Frank. You've got to believe me."

Shrugging his shoulders, Crabbe replied, "Whether I believe you or not isn't important, Web. It's what the jury believes that matters."

Then pointing to Stan Frye, who stood with the group of policemen, he said, "This is the man they're liable to believe."

Peering at Frye, Steele asked, "What do you have to do with this, Stan?"

"Plenty," responded Frye. "I've been at the Lamplighter since about eight o'clock. I came outside to get some fresh air around nine thirty, and I saw you and that dead man over there standin' at the corner of the buildin' and goin' at each other real angry-like. I could tell from what was said that the two of you had had some kind of serious disagreement previously and that you'd come into town tonight to settle it. I figured it was none of my business, so I went back into the tavern. Looks like you wore that knife into town to do that poor man in. You did a good job of it."

Web looked at Crabbe and said with strained voice, "Frank, I'm telling you, this whole thing is a crock of lies!"

"You're the one that's lyin', mister!" spoke up Hec Wheeler. "The jury will believe Mr. Frye here, and they'll believe me and Mr. Exley, because we're tellin' the truth."

Taking hold of Steele's upper arm, Crabbe said, "You're under arrest, Web, for the murder of this man we'll identify when the coroner arrives. Take him to the jail, men."

"Frank, you're making a mistake. I'm telling you this is Exley's setup."

"We'll let the jury decide. Right now, you're being booked for murder."

Setting fiery eyes on Exley, Web said, "You won't get away with this."

Exley shrugged, cocked his head, and said, "Web, I'm not tryin' to get away with anything. Hec and I saw you murder that poor man. We had to call the law on you."

To Crabbe, Web said, "Will you see that somebody let's my parents know about this? They'll be expecting me home soon."

"I'll send a man out right away," nodded the chief.

"Tell him to have Dad let Abby Ruffin know too, will you?"

"I'll see that it's done," Crabbe assured him. "But understand— none of them can visit you till morning."

The sun was barely up the next day when Web Steele heard the door to the cell block swing open. Presently a guard appeared at his cell and said, "You've got a passel of visitors wanting to see you, Steele. Only other prisoner we've got right now is the fella next to you. He's sleeping off a drunk, so I guess he won't mind a crowd in here. You want to see them all at one time?"

"Sure," nodded Web.

The guard disappeared, and seconds later Abby Ruffin was the first to come running into the cell block. Tears were on her cheeks as she pressed herself up to the bars and choked, "Oh, Web! This just can't be happening. It's...it's like a bad dream."

Web reached through the bars and embraced her. "It's Reed's doing, honey," he said. "He set the whole thing up. Even murdered that poor man just to get back at me."

Web looked up to see his parents, Lynne Ruffin, Daniel Hart, and the family attorney, Thomas Bean. Abby moved aside so the others could approach Web. Cora embraced her son, speaking words of encouragement, followed by Lynne and Daniel. Then father and son gripped hands.

Dudley Steele said, "I brought Thomas with me, Web. He'll take your case and see that justice is done."

Bean stepped forward and shook Web's hand. "This whole thing is preposterous, Web," he said with anger in his voice. "I'll do everything in my power to see that you're cleared."

"I know you will," replied Web.

Everyone wanted to hear Web's side of the story. Abby stepped close and held his hand through the bars as he told of Reed's treachery. While the group talked with Web, Thomas Bean went to Chief Crabbe's office. He returned an hour later, informing Web that his trial was set for Monday, April 15, at ten o'clock in the morning. This gave Bean nearly two weeks to work on Web's defense. He asked that the others give him some time with Web so they could talk. They all assured Web of their full support. Last to leave was Abby, who spoke words of love and kissed him soundly through the bars.

CHAPTER FIFTEEN

In late November of 1860, President James Buchanan assigned ex-West Point instructor Major Robert Anderson to head up the Union forces at Forts Moultrie, Sumter, and Castle Pinckney in Charleston Harbor. Secession was a genuine threat, and Buchanan wanted the federal forts in the best of hands.

When South Carolina seceded from the Union on December 20, Anderson knew that he and his men were in a dangerous position, just a stone's throw from the very spot where the secession had taken place. The major knew war was now inevitable. He also knew that neither President Buchanan nor President Abraham Lincoln, when he took office, would negotiate a sale of the three forts to the Southerners. It was Anderson's job to defend the federal positions the best he could.

As the days passed after South Carolina's secession, Anderson had a growing concern over his vulnerability in the harbor. He had only sixty soldiers to man all three forts. Anderson's main base, Fort Moultrie, on big Sullivan's Island, commanded the northern entrance to Charleston Harbor. It was vulnerable to land attack from the rear. Fort Castle Pinckney, lying less than a mile off the coast of Charleston, was poorly armed, and unless subsidized with more men and arms, would fall quickly in an attack.

Clearly the most advantageous place for Anderson to make a stand was Fort Sumter, located on a small island a little over three miles from Charleston. Although hasty efforts to strengthen Fort Sumter were still underway, the major's predecessor had laid in enough supplies to last sixty men several months. Sumter's guns could answer any attack by closing the harbor to Southern shipping to and from Charleston.

When Anderson sent a message to Secretary of War John B. Floyd asking for more men, he was turned down. Floyd believed the forts were in no danger.

Concerned for the lives of his men, Anderson decided to gather them all in one place to face the attack he was sure would come. They would take their stand in Fort Sumter. Keeping his plans quiet, the major and his men spent all Christmas Day packing movable goods in Forts Moultrie and Castle Pinckney. A cold, hard rain postponed the transfer to Sumter that night, but the next night the soldiers ferried their gear to Sumter, and no one in Charleston was aware of it until dawn on December 27.

That morning the people in Charleston saw smoke rising across the harbor waters from the wooden gun carriages that Anderson and his men had set afire at Moultrie and Castle Pinckney to deny the Southerners use of the cannons. It was not until noon, however, that they realized that Fort Sumter was now fully garrisoned. *The Stars and Stripes were being raised on the mast atop the ramparts.*

Major Robert Anderson's message was clear. Fort Sumter was a federal installation in enemy territory, from which the United States would not retreat.

During the next three months, Major Anderson and his men lived on the supplies that had been laid up in the fort while Southern leaders attempted to bring about a diplomatic surrender of Sumter. It was to no avail. Washington would not budge. When Abraham Lincoln became president the first week in March 1861, he immediately tried to get supplies through to Anderson and his men. This infuriated the Southerners. They blocked the boat carrying the supplies, denying it entrance to the harbor.

This move by the Federals prompted President Jefferson Davis to immediately contact his commander at Charleston, a handsome, dapper Louisiana Frenchman named Pierre G.T. Beauregard. The brigadier general was ordered to begin building up his artillery on the islands around the harbor.

Beauregard worked feverishly to comply with President Davis's orders. By early April he had brought overwhelming firepower to bear on Fort Sumter, including eight-inch, long-range columbiad cannons, eight-inch high-trajectory howitzers, twenty-four and forty-two pounders, smoothbores that fired thirty-two-pound balls, and squat, wide-mouthed ten-inch mortars designed expressly to crumble fort walls. Beauregard had well over five thousand men stationed in his various fortifications, ranging in age from boys in their mid-teens to silver-haired oldsters in their late sixties. A few would man the guns, while the others stood by to storm Fort Sumter if the general deemed it necessary.

As recruits continued to arrive from all over the South, they were given a rousing welcome by the citizens of Charleston and the thousands of loyal Southerners gathered in the city.

Among those who arrived at the Charleston dock on April 9 was Edmund Ruffin. Three ferries were carrying the recruits to the islands, assigned by Confederate captains George S. James and Stephen D. Lee. Ruffin approached one of the captains, introduced himself, and asked to be ferried to wherever General Beauregard was stationed. Captain James was delighted to meet the man who was known as the "father of secession," and gave him a warm handshake. He informed Ruffin that General Beauregard had set up his headquarters at Fort Johnson, which was located on James Island, and that the general would welcome him with open arms.

Ruffin said he was sure the impending war would start in Charleston Harbor, and that he wanted to be there for the occasion. He had never met General Beauregard, but earnestly desired to do so.

When the ferries were loaded with new recruits, the men were delivered to the various islands. The ferry occupied by the two captains and Edmund Ruffin let fifty-four men off at Fort Moultrie, then cut across the harbor of James Island. Ruffin's long gray hair whipped in the breeze as the captains escorted him inside Fort Johnson. They introduced him to several uniformed men as they made their way to the upper level of the fort where the Charleston Harbor commander had his temporary office.

The office door stood open as the three men drew up. Captain James rapped on the door frame and said, "General Beauregard, sir, we have a very distinguished guest who would like to see you."

"Well, bring him in," came a resonant voice.

Edmund Ruffin entered the stone-walled room, which had been used in days gone by as the fort commander's office. Beauregard was standing behind his desk, and two other officers got up from their chairs to meet Captains James and Lee and their guest.

When Beauregard saw the old man, he smiled and said, "You gentlemen don't need to introduce this great Southerner to me. I've seen his pictures in the newspapers." Rounding the desk, the tall, stately general extended his hand. "Mr. Edmund Ruffin. I am more than pleased to make your acquaintance."

"Thank you, general," smiled Ruffin, "likewise, I'm sure."

By Beauregard's mature features and the deep-set lines of his face, Ruffin knew he had to be in his fifties. The man was strikingly handsome, with a thick head of jet-black hair and a heavy mustache that drooped at the corners of his mouth. Ruffin wondered that there was not some gray mingled in the black of his hair and mustache.

When the two men had shaken hands, Beauregard gestured toward his other two officers and said, "Mr. Ruffin, I would like you to meet Colonel Jim Chesnut and Colonel James Chisholm."

Both Chesnut and Chisholm had also seen Ruffin's picture in the papers. They shook hands with him, expressing their appreciation for his courage and determination in leading the South to break with the North.

Additional chairs were produced, and when all were seated, Beauregard asked, "To what do we owe this visit, Mr. Ruffin?"

Ruffin smiled. "Well, sir, as I told Captain James and Captain Lee, with all this military buildup, it sure looks to me like things are going to come to a head between our Confederate forces here in the harbor and those few foolhardy men out there in Fort Sumter. I figure the war's going to start right here, and I want to be on the scene when it happens."

"You're probably right," nodded the general, "but as of yet, President Davis and his cabinet have not given me the command to launch an attack. There's one man in the cabinet who's holding things up."

"Who is that?"

"The secretary of state."

Ruffin lifted his bushy silver eyebrows. "What's Robert Toombs got against us attacking Sumter?"

Beauregard toyed nervously with his mustache. "He's warning that if we fire upon Major Anderson and the men in Sumter, we'll inaugurate a civil war greater than any the world has ever seen."

"He could be right, sir," spoke up Captain James. "I'm a true and loyal son of the South, and I hate the thought of burying thousands upon thousands of our men. I'm just fearful that it's going to be bloodier than any of us have imagined. I believe Mr. Lincoln senses it, too. When he sent that supply ship down here for the men in Sumter, he was very careful to point out that there were no weapons aboard and no reinforcements. He doesn't want war."

"If Lincoln doesn't want war, why did he refuse to negotiate with us on the sale of these forts?" spat Ruffin.

"Seems to me," put in Colonel Chesnut, "Lincoln wants his forts sitting here in our harbor with their guns pointed at us, and at the same time he wants us to act like there's no problem between the Union and the Confederacy."

"Yeah," agreed Ruffin. "The situation's a little lopsided, I'd say." Then turning to Beauregard, he said, "General, it's my understanding that the cabinet needs only a majority vote to authorize an attack on Sumter. Why doesn't President Davis just bypass Toombs and give the order?"

"I don't know," replied Beauregard. "It's not for me to know how politicians think. All I can do is sit here and wait for my orders."

Ruffin quietly accepted the answer, then asked, "Who is this Major Robert Anderson the Union's put in charge of Sumter?"

"Well, this is the irony of all ironies," said the general, scratching at an ear. "Major Anderson was my artillery instructor at West Point twenty-three years ago. He and I became close friends after I graduated, and have been all these years. We went on a hunting trip together in the Smokies a year ago last fall. He's only a few years older than me, and we've got a lot of interests in common." The general paused to swallow a lump that had risen in his throat, then added with a quiver in his voice, "Now...now all of a sudden, we're enemies."

Captain Lee leaned forward in his chair and said softly, "General, sir, does President Davis know of your past friendship with Major Anderson?"

"No. He has no reason to be aware of it."

"When the order is given to fire the first shot, will he expect you to be the one to do it?"

"No. I have already been instructed *not* to be the one to yank the lanyard. I am to give the order to the man I choose, but Davis feels that the man to start the war should not be the officer in charge of this operation."

There was a tap at the open door. Beauregard looked up to see one of the enlisted men silhouetted against the growing darkness outside. "Yes?" he said.

"General, I'm here to advise you that the meal will be served in twenty minutes."

"Thank you, Wilson. Tell the cooks we have a guest who will be dining with us this evening. We'll need an extra setting at the officers' table."

"Yes, sir," said the soldier, and was gone.

Then to Ruffin, Beauregard said, "If you want to stick around until my orders come, Mr. Ruffin, you're more than welcome. We've got some spare cots. You can sleep in the officers' quarters with us."

A broad smile spread over Edmund Ruffin's weathered face. "I'll just take you up on that offer, sir."

On Wednesday, April 10, 1861, General Pierre G.T. Beauregard was standing on the eastern tip of James Island with Edmund Ruffin shortly after they had eaten lunch in the fort. Both men were discussing the impending conflict when they saw a rowboat coming from the mainland.

Beauregard lifted his hat, ran fingers through his hair, and sighed shakily, "I've got a feeling this boat may be bringing me my orders from the president."

The rowboat pulled up to the shore with four men aboard, each handling an oar. One man stepped out and hurried to Beauregard with an envelope in his hand, saying it was a telegram from Montgomery, Alabama. The general signed for it and noticed his four officers hastening toward him from the fort as the messenger was returning to the boat.

Beauregard opened the envelope and read the message silently. Ruffin saw his features tighten and lose color. At that moment, officers Chesnut, Chisholm, Lee, and James drew up, anticipation showing on their faces.

When Beauregard looked at them with dismal eyes, Colonel Chesnut asked cautiously, "Are those your orders, sir?"

The general nodded solemnly. "Yes. Directly from the secretary of war. I am to draw up a written surrender ultimatum and have it delivered to Major Anderson. Fort Sumter is to be evacuated within a short time after Anderson has the document of surrender in his hands. Secretary Walker is leaving the length of that short time to me. If Major Anderson refuses for any reason, or he and his men do not leave Fort Sumter by the deadline, we are to open fire on their position with all our artillery batteries."

Captain James glanced toward Sumter and asked, "Do you think the major will surrender and evacuate without a fight, sir?"

General Beauregard's face was gray and stony. "I know the man well, Captain," he replied evenly. "He will not surrender and evacuate without a fight."

James looked around at the others, then set his gaze on Beauregard and said with furrowed brow, "Once we fire on Sumter, sir, there'll be no turning back. We'll be at war with the Union."

Beauregard nodded and looked wistfully in the direction of Fort Sumter.

The officers exchanged glances, then Colonel Chisholm said, "General..."

Beauregard brought his head around slowly, "Yes, Colonel?"

"It...it's Major Anderson you're concerned about, isn't it?"

Beauregard brushed a hand over his mustache and replied with feeling, "I'm concerned first and foremost about commencing a war that will scar this great country of ours in a way that it may never recover, Colonel. And yes, I am concerned about bombarding the very fortress where stands one of the best friends I have ever had—a man I love and admire."

"Well, sir," said Chisholm clearing his throat, "if you want to find some reason to go ashore, as one of your officers, I will take the orders and fulfill them."

Beauregard laid a hand on Chisholm's shoulder and said, "I appreciate your offer, but these orders were sent to me. President Davis put me in command of this operation, and I cannot allow my personal feelings to cloud my thinking. Secretary of War Walker has laid out my orders. I must obey them to the letter."

"How long will you give Major Anderson to evacuate, sir?" queried Colonel Chesnut.

"I don't know yet. I'll have to work on it." Turning toward the fort with a sigh, the general said, "I'll be in my office if you need me, gentlemen."

The five men stood and watched Beauregard until he vanished inside Fort Johnson's walls, then Captain Lee said, "It would be a mighty hard thing to give the order to unleash all our firepower on one of your best friends."

The other officers were nodding their agreement when Edmund Ruffin spoke up. "That's just part of the price of war, gentlemen. But war must come. Those Yankees couldn't keep their big noses out of our business. Well, now they're going to pay for it. I say the quicker we fire that first shot, the better. We'll teach those Yankee dogs a lesson they won't forget!"

The men at Fort Johnson saw very little of their commander until ten o'clock the next morning. At that time, he gathered all of them in the exercise area at the center of the fort and explained his orders from Secretary Walker. He informed them that he had drawn up a written surrender ultimatum to be delivered to Major Anderson. The ultimatum demanded that the Union soldiers lay down their arms and evacuate the fort by four o'clock that afternoon. If they refused or delayed beyond that time, they would be fired upon from every direction.

Beauregard then spoke to Captain James. "Take two men with you in one of the rowboats and convey this message to the other artillery installations. Tell them about my ultimatum to Major Anderson and to be on the alert at four o'clock. If the signal gun is fired from here on James Island, they are to begin bombardment within one minute."

"And what if...well, sir, if there should be some kind of unforeseen delay? What then?"

"Tell them to stay on the alert until they hear differently, even if they have no contact from us until tomorrow. If and when we fire the signal gun from here, they are to follow with bombardment as ordered."

"Yes, sir," responded James, and with a snappy salute, he approached two soldiers he knew well and told them to follow him.

Turning to Chesnut, the general said, "Colonel, you will take the ultimatum to Major Anderson. I have it in my office. Take Colonel Chisholm and Captain Lee with you"

"Yes, sir. Ah...sir?"

"Yes?"

"Is there any personal message you want me to give to Major Anderson?"

"No," replied Beauregard, slowly shaking his head. "All that—" he cleared his throat—"all that needs to be said is in the ultimatum."

Chesnut quickly appointed two soldiers to man a rowboat and be ready to shove off in five minutes. As they rowed away from the shore moments later, General Beauregard stood like a statue atop one of the ramparts and watched them. In the boat, Captain Lee looked back at the general and said to the others, "I wouldn't want to be in his shoes right now."

When the rowboat touched shore on the small island that bore Fort Sumter, a half-dozen armed soldiers were waiting to meet it. A number of men observed the scene from inside the stone walls.

Chesnut stood up in the boat and said to the Union soldiers, "I am Colonel James Chesnut, army of the Confederacy. I have a written message from General Pierre Gustave Toutant Beauregard that I am to deliver personally to Major Robert Anderson."

"You may come ashore," a young lieutenant informed him.

"I also have Colonel James Chisholm and Captain Stephen Lee with me," said Chesnut. "May they come ashore, also?"

"Permission granted," nodded the lieutenant.

The three Confederate officers were escorted inside the fort and presented to Major Anderson, who was at a crude desk in his makeshift office on the first level, next to the barracks.

Anderson rose and greeted the Southerners with a polite nod. He was a tall, slender man in his late fifties. His hair was dark, but on the sides had turned silver-gray. The deep lines in his face and the bags beneath his eyes showed the strain he was bearing.

Chairs were brought in and Anderson invited the Confederates to be seated. Several Union soldiers waited just outside the closed door. Though his comrades sat down, Chesnut remained on his feet, as did Anderson. The colonel produced an envelope from inside his coat and extended it to the major, saying, "I have a written message for you, sir, from General Beauregard."

Anderson's face was grim as he accepted the envelope and said, "Please be seated, Colonel." Easing onto his own chair, he fixed weary eyes on Chesnut and asked, "How is my old friend, Pierre?"

"His health is fine, sir, but at the moment, he is bearing a heavy load."

Anderson closed his eyes, then opened them slowly, acknowledging that he understood. Asking the men to excuse him, he opened the envelope and silently read the ultimatum. When he finished, he folded the paper, and said, "I will have to discuss this with my officers. You gentlemen wait here."

Anderson left the door open behind him as he departed from the office. He was gone less than ten minutes. Returning to his chair, he ran his tired gaze over the faces of the Confederate officers and said solemnly, "My officers have agreed with me, gentlemen. We reject General Beauregard's ultimatum. We refuse to evacuate the fort."

While the Southerners exchanged heavy glances, Anderson took a sheet of paper and an envelope out of a small box on top of the desk and said, "I will put it in writing for the general."

When the response had been written and placed in the envelope, the major placed it in Chesnut's hand and said, "I will walk you gentlemen to your boat."

As they approached the Confederate boat, Anderson asked, "Colonel Chesnut, will General Beauregard open his batteries without further notice to me?"

"It is my understanding, sir, that the only notice you will get will be the signal shot from Fort Johnson. Exactly one minute after that, the batteries are to open up full force."

Nodding slowly, Anderson said, "Then I shall await the first shot at four o'clock, Colonel." After a brief pause, he added quietly, "If you do not batter us to pieces, we shall be starved out in a few days."

Returning to Fort Johnson, the officers met with Beauregard and gave him Anderson's note. After the general had read it, Chesnut said, "Sir, just before we left him, Major Anderson said something that I think might have been a hint."

"And what was that?" queried the general.

"He said that if we didn't batter them to pieces, they'd be starved out in a few days. You know him, sir. Do you think it was a hint that if we didn't fire on them, they'd have to give up shortly anyway because they'll be out of food?"

"I'm not sure, but it's worth giving it a little time. I'll wire Secretary Walker, explain the situation, and see if he'll grant us a few days to starve them out."

Immediately a wire was sent to Montgomery with Beauregard's request. Hours passed with no response. While eager Confederate soldiers waited at the battery installations, four o'clock came and went. Finally, just after midnight on April 12, the message from the secretary of war arrived. Walker replied that he did not desire to bombard Fort Sumter if it could be avoided, and if Major Anderson would state the date when he would evacuate, Beauregard could hold his fire.

The general went to his office and by lantern light composed another message. Handing the envelope to Chesnut, he said, "Colonel, I want you to take this message to Sumter immediately. I'm on touchy ground, now, with the powers that be in Montgomery, so this has to be the final message to Major Anderson. I am giving you the authority to act on the spot according to the major's response. If you're satisfied with it, then you speak for me in making the arrangements for a quick and smooth evacuation on the date he has chosen. If, however, you are not satisfied with his response, you also speak for me in refusing his terms."

"If the latter should be the case, sir," said Chesnut, "am I then to give warning as to when bombardment will start?"

Beauregard paused briefly before replying, "That is exactly what you will do."

The other officers and Edmund Ruffin were standing close by. Ruffin observed as Beauregard assigned Chisholm and Lee to go along with Chesnut once again. Eager to be in on as much of the action as possible, Ruffin stepped up to Beauregard and said, "General, would you mind if I went with them?"

"I don't see any reason you can't," replied Beauregard. Then to Chesnut he said, "You don't mind, do you, Colonel?"

"It's fine with me. Let's be going."

Again, two soldiers were employed to do the rowing, and the boat glided through the dark waters of Charleston Harbor toward Fort Sumter.

It was nearly 1:00 A.M. when the envoys were met at the shoreline by several Union guards. When Chesnut explained their purpose, they were led to the dining area next to the kitchen and seated at one of the tables. A sleepy-eyed Anderson entered five minutes later and greeted them courteously. When he had read Beauregard's message, he left the Southerners, saying he would get his officers out of bed and discuss a response with them.

When Anderson had not returned after nearly two hours, the Confederate officers began to murmur amongst themselves. Ruffin saw their agitation and said, "Gentlemen, I realize I'm not part of the official party here, but for what it's worth, I think our Major Anderson is stalling. Seems to me we need to call his hand."

"I agree," said Chesnut. "It's time he gave us an answer. I'll go put his feet to the fire."

Chesnut left the dining hall and headed for Anderson's office. The officers were just wrapping up their discussion when the impatient

Colonel Chesnut interrupted them. It was shortly after 3:00 A.M. when Anderson handed Chesnut his response in writing.

The major followed Chesnut back to the dining hall and stood by as the colonel read the response aloud to the others. The message was that Anderson would evacuate the fort on April 15, holding his fire in the meantime unless fired upon, or unless he detected some act of hostile intent that would endanger his men or the fort. Further, his agreement to hold fire might be altered if he received other instructions from his superiors, or if somehow a Union boat could get through to him with additional supplies.

When Chesnut finished reading the response to his companions, they could tell he was unhappy.

Pulling a pad of paper and a pencil from his coat, the colonel said, "Major, this is unacceptable. I have been authorized by General Beauregard to—"

"Why is it unacceptable?" cut in Anderson.

"You're allowing yourself too many ways out," Chesnut replied tartly. "I have been authorized by General Beauregard to advise you that your response is indeed unacceptable. If you will give me a moment, I will write out a formal declaration."

When Chesnut had finished writing, he said, "I will read it to you, Major, then it is yours to keep."

Holding the paper to the lantern light, Colonel Chesnut read, "By authority of General Pierre G.T. Beauregard, commander of Confederate military operations at Charleston Harbor, I have the honor of notifying you that we will open fire with all of our batteries on Fort Sumter in one hour. Signed, James Chesnut, Colonel, Army of the Confederacy."

At 3:30, Anderson escorted the Confederates back to their boat and shook hands with each one. As they climbed into the small craft, he said, "If we never meet in this world again, gentlemen, God grant that we may meet in the next."

The bells of St. Michael's Church in Charleston were chiming 4:00 A.M. as Chesnut's party rowed up to James Island. General Beauregard and Captain James met them as they climbed from the boat. When Colonel Chesnut announced Anderson's response, the general took it silently. As the officers and Edmund Ruffin moved back into the fort, Beauregard finally spoke. "Captain James, prepare the twenty-four pounder. I want the shell to arch over Sumter and strike water on the other side. The artillery that follows will do proper damage."

At precisely 4:30, there was a slight hint of dawn on the watery eastern horizon. Every man in Fort Johnson stood near the big twenty-four-pound cannon in a semicircle. There was electricity in the air. Their hearts beat with anticipation.

Captain James stood beside the cannon and said to Beauregard, "The gun is ready to fire, sir. It is aimed and elevated to send the ball over Fort Sumter and strike water on its opposite side, as you commanded."

Beauregard swallowed hard. "All right. Fire it, Captain."

James's face paled in the dim light. "*Me*, sir?"

"Yes. It's four-thirty. Yank the lanyard."

The captain trembled as he said, "General Beauregard, sir, I do not mean to be insubordinate, but I keep thinking of what your secretary of state said: *If we fire upon Major Anderson and the men in Sumter, we'll inaugurate a civil war greater than any the world has ever seen.* Please, sir. I respectfully request that I be relieved of the duty of pulling the lanyard. I...I just can't fire the first shot of the war."

The general's features showed no anger. "All right, Captain," he replied softly.

No one in the group said a word or moved a muscle. Beauregard gave his mustache a quick stroke, and turned toward Edmund Ruffin. "Mr. Ruffin," he said briskly, "you have fought harder for secession from the Union and independence for the South than any man I know. Would you like to be the man to fire the first shot of the war?"

Without hesitation, the old man stepped forward and snapped, "Yes, sir! I'll be glad to do it."

Ruffin had been around big guns before. He knew exactly what to do. With every eye on him, he took hold of the lanyard and jerked it. The deep-throated roar of the cannon echoed across the harbor as the fiery signal shell arced high into the lightening sky, sailed over Fort Sumter, and struck the water. Within sixty seconds, the harbor was alive with booming cannons and bright, yellow-red flashes of fire.

Now no one could stem the tide of war. America was out of control.

CHAPTER SIXTEEN

At a quarter of ten on Monday morning, April 15, 1861, a crowd was gathering in the main courtroom at the Henrico County courthouse in Richmond, Virginia. The topic of discussion was General Beauregard's attack on Fort Sumter on Friday, and General Anderson's surrender on Saturday afternoon. The Confederate guns had fired 3,341 projectiles at Fort Sumter during thirty-three hours of bombardment. All the barracks were in ruins and the main gate was destroyed. The outer walls had been blasted heavily. Incredibly, the Confederate artillery had injured only four Union soldiers and had killed none. The Confederates also had only four men injured by return fire, all at Fort Moultrie. Major Anderson and his men had evacuated the Sumter garrison at four o'clock on Sunday afternoon while thousands of Southerners looked on from Charleston's wharf, and General Beauregard observed from a boat in the harbor.

The rumble of voices in the courtroom carried one common thought: The time for words and accusations between Northerners and Southerners had run out. There was no doubt the Union would retaliate for the attack on Fort Sumter. Now, instead of talk, there would be fire, smoke, blood, and death. The dreaded war between the states was a grim reality.

As Abby Ruffin and her father entered the courtroom, they were discussing the newspaper article they had read just that morning, which named Edmund Ruffin as the man who had fired the first shot at Charleston Harbor. Though John and his daughter were loyal Southerners, neither was happy about Edmund's deed.

Abby insisted that they sit on the front row so she could be near the table where Web Steele would sit with attorney Thomas Bean. Directly behind John and Abby came Dudley and Cora Steele. Their faces showed the strain they were feeling over the commencement of the war, but even more, their concern over Web's fate. Daniel Hart and Lynne Ruffin followed them. Lynne's eyes were puffy from weeping. Daniel was going to enlist in the Confederate army, and though Lynne understood why, she feared for his life.

John Ruffin sat on Abby's right, Cora Steele on her left. They looked at each other tenderly and joined hands. Next to Cora was Dudley, and beside him were Lynne and Daniel.

Stan Frye had arrived early and was seated with some of the men he had been drinking with in the Lamplighter Tavern the night Wilbur Yates was murdered. Reed Exley came in with Hec Wheeler and sat on the front row across the aisle. Abby burned Exley with a hot glare when their eyes met. Exley had told her that very morning that he was sorry he had to testify against Web, but he was only doing his civic duty. He would have to take the stand and tell the truth. Web had murdered a man, and he would have to suffer the consequences. Men who committed murder had to be dealt with to the fullest extent of the law.

Knowing who the real murderer was, Abby had wanted to slap his smug face, but she had refrained. It would have accomplished nothing except to make her feel good. She hated Reed Exley. He had wickedly connived the murder and framed Web. Even if Web were acquitted, Exley would still never pay for his crime.

Abby felt a wave of anxiety as Web was led by a deputy from a side door to the table, followed by Bean. The attorney had already told Web and the family that he was concerned about the outcome. The case against Web was tight, and the prosecutor was pushing for the death penalty. If the jury convicted Web, Bean would plead for a sentence of life imprisonment based on Web's clean record up until the night of the murder.

As Web sat down at the table, he set his worried but loving gaze on Abby. Tears brimmed her dark-blue eyes as she forced a smile.

At precisely ten o'clock, Henrico County Judge William B. Tenant took his place at the bench and brought the court to order. While the charges against Webster Steele were being read, Reed Exley let his gaze stray past Hec Wheeler to the captivating redhead. She was the most beautiful woman he had ever seen. He told himself that after the little speech he was going to make on Web's behalf, Abby would look upon him more favorably. Once Web was either dead or locked up for life, in time she would forget him. She would be lonely. Reed Exley would be there to fill that loneliness and take her in his arms. One day in the not-too-distant future, lovely Abby would be his.

Stan Frye was first to take the witness stand. He gave his false testimony under oath without blinking an eye. As he related the story exactly the way he had told it to police chief Frank Crabbe, Web Steele felt something cold slide next to his spine. Reed Exley had done an expert job of coaching. Could Stan Frye really hate him enough to do this to him? Sure he had broken Arnie's jaw, but it was while trying to stop him from abusing a defenseless animal. Web thought of Stan's brother, wondering where he had gone. He hadn't seen Arnie around town for a long time.

Attorney Thomas Bean did his best in cross-examination to trip Frye up, but Exley had him well-schooled. Bean's attempt proved fruitless. As Frye left the witness stand, Abby tried to read the faces of the jurors. Sensing that the men of the jury were moved at Frye's testimony only increased her anxiety.

Hec Wheeler was next on the stand. He explained that he was on his way to Carlisle, Pennsylvania, in hopes of getting a job with his brother, who owned a carriage business there. He then testified that he saw Web Steele take the life of Wilbur Yates in cold blood. Thomas Bean's attempt to break Wheeler's story was as futile as it had been with Stan Frye.

Next, Reed Exley graphically told his version of the story, which made Yates's murder appear to have been coldly premeditated. He pictured Web Steele as a heartless man who had it in for the victim and lured him to a dark alley where he took his life. Thomas Bean tried to break Exley under stiff cross-examination, but Exley was too good a liar. Again, Bean was unsuccessful.

When Exley left the stand, the mood of the spectators was definitely against Web Steele. Web felt it and feared the jury was probably leaning the same way. Web was then called to the stand to give his side of the story. Though he denied committing the murder and showed the feasibility of Exley's setup, it did not impress the twelve men who sat on the jury. They were honest men who were trying to withhold judgment until they had heard all the evidence, but the testimonies of Frye and Wheeler and Exley's ability to capture their imaginations and evoke sympathy for the victim had left an indelible mark.

It took the jury only twenty minutes to return after retiring to a side room for deliberations. When the judge asked for the verdict, the jury foreman replied that they had found Webster Steele guilty as charged.

A cold hand clawed at Abby Ruffin's heart at the foreman's words, and she broke into heartrending sobs. Lynne tried to comfort her as Dudley Steele held Cora, who also wept uncontrollably. The judge banged the gavel and called for order. Abby saw Web looking at her as she fought to bring her emotions under control. His face was ashen and his eyes were filled with despair.

When order was restored, Thomas Bean stood and asked if he could address the judge. Judge Tenant granted his request and listened intently as Bean reminded him that Webster Steele had never before had a brush with the law. Based on his past record, Bean pled for the sentence to be life in prison rather than execution.

Tension was high in the courtroom as Bean sat down. Judge Tenant commanded the defendant to rise and approach the bench for sentencing. Before Steele and his attorney could leave their chairs, Reed Exley stood up and said, "Your honor, would you allow me to say a few words before you pass sentence? I realize this is a bit abnormal, but I respectfully request that you allow me to address you before these spectators and the court."

Judge Tenant was visibly annoyed at the interruption, but replied, "All right, Mr. Exley. You may speak your piece. But I caution you—be brief."

All eyes in the courtroom were fixed on Exley as he told of having known Webster Steele for several years. He concurred with Bean's statement that until his arrest, Steele had been a model citizen. Exley went on to explain that he and Steele had experienced some differences between them, but that he still respected and admired him.

John Ruffin sat with folded arms, feeling deep appreciation toward Reed for what he was trying to do. Abby glanced at her father, saw the look in his eyes, and read his thoughts. Her hatred for Exley only increased.

"And so, your honor," concluded the eloquent liar and murderer, "I ask you to show leniency to Mr. Steele. If you were of a mind to pass the death sentence on him, I implore you to make it life imprisonment instead. Mr. Steele made an awful mistake when he took the life of Wilbur Yates, and I think he realizes that now. During his years in prison, he could be an influence for good to his fellow inmates. Thank you for allowing me to speak on his behalf."

As he walked back to his seat, Exley glanced hopefully at Abby, whose gaze locked with his. Her scathing look made him shudder. He wondered why she hadn't appreciated what he had just done.

The judge then called Webster Steele to stand before the bench. Web felt as though he was in a nightmare from which he couldn't wake up as he stepped to the bench with Thomas Bean at his side.

Judge Tenant looked Web in the eye and said, "Mr. Steele, you have been duly tried in this court of law and found guilty of murdering Wilbur Yates in cold blood. Do you have anything to say before I pass sentence on you?"

"Yes," nodded Web. "The testimonies you heard from Mr. Frye, Mr. Wheeler, and Mr. Exley were nothing but well-planned lies. I did not kill Wilbur Yates. What has happened in this courtroom today is a travesty and a total miscarriage of justice. Reed Exley contrived this whole thing, and there is no doubt in my mind that he put the knife in Wilbur Yates. He only asked you just now to show lenience to me to make himself look good to all these people."

The judge waited a few seconds, then asked, "Is that all you wish to say, Mr. Steele?"

"Yes."

"All right," said Judge Tenant, clearing his throat. "Weighing the fact of your spotless record before this incident, I hereby sentence you to life imprisonment in the Virginia state penal facility at Lynchburg. You will be transported there tomorrow to begin your sentence." With that, the judge banged the gavel and pronounced the court dismissed.

Several of Web's friends tarried in the courtroom while Abby and his parents embraced him. While Abby and Cora clung to him, Web looked at John Ruffin and asked, "Do you think I'm guilty, Mr. Ruffin?"

John's face crimsoned. He looked at Abby, then at Web and said weakly, "I...uh...I must accept the verdict of the jury." Abby gave her father a cold, unbelieving stare. Unable to bear it, he turned and headed for the door, where he was met by Reed Exley.

The deputy stepped in and said, "Mr. Steele, I have to take you back to the jail now."

Thomas Bean laid a hand on Web's shoulder and said, "I'm sorry I couldn't get you acquitted."

"I'm not blaming you," replied Steele. "Exley had this thing too well planned. It's my own fault for believing him when he said he wanted to make amends."

"He'll get his, Web," spoke up Dudley. "Sooner or later, he'll pay for what he's done to you."

"Yes," nodded Abby. "And the sooner the better."

Dudley turned to the deputy and asked, "What time will my son be leaving for Lynchburg tomorrow?"

"I'll be taking him by train, sir. It leaves at ten o'clock in the morning."

Suddenly Cora burst into tears and wrapped her arms around Web. He tried to comfort her, saying that maybe after a few years they would consider letting him out on parole for good behavior. Dudley embraced Web, saying they would be at the depot in the morning to see him off. Lynne and Daniel expressed their sorrow at the miscarriage of justice, and walked away with the Steeles.

Weeping, Abby flung herself at Web, holding him tight. Web wrapped his arms around her and said, "I love you, darling. I will always love you."

"And I will always love you," Abby sobbed. "I know it's a hundred miles from here to Lynchburg, but I'll come and visit you often. I promise."

"Listen to me, Abby," said Web, gripping her shoulders. "We're at war now. Soon it won't be safe for anyone to be traveling. I don't know when the fighting will begin, but it will come. Most of our leaders don't think the war will last very long, so please—don't try to come until the war's over and it's safe to travel. Promise?"

Abby thought on his words for a long moment, then nodded. "All right. I'll do as you say."

The deputy took hold of Web's arm, said, "Let's go, Mr. Steele," and led him away.

With grief and anger churning deep within her, Abby left the courthouse and found her father waiting outside in the buggy. When he saw her coming, he stepped out and offered his hand to help her up. "I can get in by myself, thank you!" she blazed.

John Ruffin felt the wall between his daughter and himself as he drove down the street. Abby stared straight ahead, biting her lip to keep from bursting into tears. Finally John said, "Honey, I know this has been a terrible blow for you. It grieves me to see you so upset and unhappy."

Abby maintained her stiffness, staring and saying nothing.

"Now, Abby, you must face the facts. With Web behind bars—"

"I must face the facts! What about you facing the facts? Reed is the murderer, not Web. Nobody's as slick and slimy as your little pet snake. Even when Satan slithered into the Garden of Eden and beguiled Eve, he was no more scaly-bellied than Reed Exley!"

"The jury found Web guilty," John said defensively.

"Yes!" she spat. "Because Exley's as cunning as the devil himself. If you weren't so blind, you'd see him for what he is."

"Now Abby, you—"

"Just let me finish! Let's see if I'm right. You started to say that with Web behind bars for life, I should find another man, right?"

"Well, I—"

"Come on, Papa! That's what you were going to say, wasn't it?"

John Ruffin cleared his throat. "Well...yes. Yes, I was."

"And you were going to suggest that I consider making your pet snake that man, weren't you?"

"Honey, you shouldn't call Reed—"

"I'm calling him what he is, Papa! Come on. You were going to suggest that I make a stab at striking it up with Reed, weren't you?"

"Well, yes. I feel like since he's already part of the family and—"

"Well, you can forget it! Don't you ever even hint at it again!"

John Ruffin took a deep breath and let it out slowly through pursed lips. "All right," he breathed.

"And I'm going to tell you something else, Papa. When I visited Web in jail a few days ago, he told me that Mandrake gave him the lowdown on why Elizabeth had her window open, and why she fell."

"Oh?"

"While we were in town that day, Reed was beating unmercifully on old Jedidiah. Elizabeth opened her window and screamed at Reed to stop. He yelled back at her to shut up and kept beating Jedidiah. Elizabeth was so upset—she kept shouting at Reed and lost her balance. Reed threatened the slaves not to tell you or anyone else what had happened. Your little pet is the one who caused my sister to die."

"Now, Abby, it's only Mandrake's word against Reed's."

"I know, and you'll take Reed's word every time. How can you be so blind?"

John Ruffin did not answer, but even he had to admit to the beginning of some doubts about Reed Exley. No more was said between father and daughter the rest of the way home.

That night Abby lay in her bed shedding hot tears. Her spirit broken, she hugged her pillow and said, "Why, God? Why have you allowed such an injustice to happen to Web, and to me? We love each other, and You gave us that love. I don't understand. How can You let Reed get away with this? You know he's the one who killed that man, so why is Web going to prison? Why are we being torn apart?"

After tossing and turning for hours, Abby finally got out of bed, fired a lantern, and sat at her desk. Taking out a slip of paper, she took pen in hand and began to write a note to the man she loved.

The next morning, Abby rode into town with Dudley and Cora Steele. Daniel Hart had picked up Lynne in a buggy, and they were waiting on the platform at the depot when Abby and the Steeles arrived. As people milled about, they talked of the blow Web's conviction had dealt them.

Soon they saw a police wagon draw up, carrying Web and the deputy who was to escort him to Lynchburg. The prisoner wore handcuffs. As lawman and prisoner came onto the platform, Abby rushed to Web and embraced him. Looking down at her tenderly, he asked, "Have you heard about Stan Frye?"

"No," she replied, shaking her head.

"He died last night about nine o'clock. Chief Crabbe told me about it this morning—said it was heart failure. Frye was at the Lamplighter last night, drinking hard and celebrating my conviction. Witnesses in the place said he suddenly clutched his chest and keeled over. He was dead within minutes."

Dudley Steele pulled at an ear and remarked, "I would like to say he got what he deserved, but I know it's not right for me to feel that way. The Lord says vengeance is His."

"That's right," said Daniel, "but seems to me the Lord must've decided to call Stan to account real quick. Exley and Wheeler will get theirs in due time."

"I hate to butt in, folks," said the deputy, "but you'd best be making your parting remarks to Mr. Steele. I've got to get him on the train shortly."

It was five minutes before departure time when all but Abby had said their good-byes. The Steeles sat in their buggy near the platform, as did Daniel and Lynne, giving Web and Abby a few minutes alone.

Web looped his cuffed hands over Abby's head and folded her into his arms. They kissed tenderly several times, then held each other for a long moment. The engine's whistle blew, and the deputy said, "I'm sorry, Mr. Steele, but we've got to get on board."

The sorrowful couple kissed again, then handed each other envelopes. Abby was deeply touched that Web had also written a note to her. She stood on the platform and through a wall of tears, watched the train pull out of the depot. When it had vanished from sight, she opened the envelope and wiped tears as she read:

My Darling Abby,

What I am about to say, I could not do in person. I had to put it in writing. I love you with everything that is in me, and your happiness is my greatest concern. That is why I must tell you that I release you from all promises. It is not right that you should live a life of visiting me periodically in prison. You deserve better than that. You have a right to happiness and a normal life. So I am asking you to forget me and find someone else.

To do this breaks my heart, but it is the only right thing for you. For the rest of my life, there will never be a day when you are out of my thoughts.

Love always, Web

Holding the note close to her breast, Abby Ruffin wept and whispered, "Never, my darling. I will never even consider another man. You will always be the only one I love."

Aboard the train, Web Steele sat next to the window with the deputy at his side. Richmond had just passed from view when he pulled the envelope from his pocket and took out the neatly folded slip of paper.

My Dearest Web,

I am writing this at three o'clock in the morning of the day they will take you away from me.

Words sometimes fall short of conveying what is really in the heart. Such is the case at this moment. I can only say, my darling, that I love you more than I could ever tell you, and I always will.

As you have requested, I will not try to visit you until the war is over. But you will see me just as soon as it is safe once again to travel!

What R.E. has done to you is a tragedy, and I pray that he will pay for it. I feel so sick at heart for what you must endure in that prison because of his wickedness. I know you well, Web Steele, and if I am correct, you will begin thinking about me going through life with you behind bars. You will have thoughts about telling me to find happiness by cutting you out of my life and finding someone else. When those thoughts come, dismiss them immediately.

I will never want anyone but you. Never. You will always be the only one I love. That is my solemn promise. I mean it with all my heart and soul. I love you desperately.

Your Abby

The deputy turned and looked at Web Steele as he clutched Abby's note in one hand, covered his eyes with the other, and wept.

CHAPTER SEVENTEEN

During the month of March, Mandrake Steele wore leg irons at all times on the Todd Morrison plantation. He was sick at heart for Orchid's sake, assuming that she had been forced to mate with one of Horatio Clements's choice Negroes. Yet he was determined to run for Harper's Ferry and steal Orchid from Clements once his leg irons were removed.

On the night of March 21, two male slaves had run away from the plantation because of the cruel treatment they had been receiving from Morrison and his two sons, especially Clifford, who was his father's slave overseer. Aided by men from neighboring plantations, Clifford had gone after the runaways and caught them in the next county before noon the following day.

They were brought back to the plantation and whipped brutally by Clifford while the rest of the slaves were forced to watch. During the beating, three slaves jumped Clifford, took his whip, and turned it on him. Todd Morrison heard the ruckus, came running with a revolver, and shot the three slaves.

From that incident on, Clifford wore a revolver at all times, making sure the other slaves understood that he would use it if there was any more trouble.

Mandrake played the part of the model slave. While the days passed into weeks, he acted as if he were intimidated by Clifford's new hard-line approach, and said things to make the Morrisons think he would be afraid to ever try running away.

Since the day he had been forced to become a slave for the Morrisons, Mandrake had bunked in a small, windowless shack with three other men. When he told them his story, they sympathized with him and said they would help him escape once his leg irons were removed.

Then came the escape of the two slaves on March 21.

When the escapees were beaten and the slaves who tried to stop the beatings were killed, Mandrake's roommates changed their minds about helping him escape. To make matters worse, the following day Clifford started locking the slaves in their shacks at nightfall.

Mandrake knew his only chance of escape was at night. He would have to overpower Clifford and render him unconscious when he came to padlock the door of his shack. He would take Clifford's revolver and dash to the corral while the other slaves in his shack ran to the house to report what had happened. Even if they still wanted to help him, they couldn't do it without incriminating themselves. Mandrake did not want to get them in trouble, so he would make the move on his own without telling them ahead of time, and expect them to act accordingly.

Timing would be of the essence. When he got to the corral, he must take a horse for himself and scatter the rest of the horses into the open fields. Since it would be dark, it would take the Morrisons till daybreak to gather the horses. This would give him a good head start. They would know he was headed for Harper's Ferry. He needed enough time to get to Clements's place, break Orchid free, and be gone before either Morrison or Clements could catch them.

The whole thing was a long shot, but Mandrake felt he had no choice but to try it. He must try to get Orchid back no matter the risks. The first glimmer of hope that his scheme might work came on Saturday, April 13—Clifford rewarded Mandrake's good behavior by removing his shackles.

News of the attack on Fort Sumter came to the Morrison plantation the next day. The country was now in a civil war. Mandrake knew this could complicate things for him. The Morrisons talked about the military buildup that would take place in both the North and the

South. People would be on the alert. The fifty miles that lay between Morrison's plantation and Harper's Ferry would be more difficult than ever to travel.

Clifford left the plantation on April 15, adding a further complication. The nightly lockup of the slaves would be done by Todd Morrison and his younger son, Hughey. Mandrake doubted he could overpower two men. He would have to wait until Clifford returned in two weeks.

On the afternoon of April 29, Clifford came riding in on horseback and was greeted by the family in the yard. That night, when Clifford came alone to lock the slaves in their shacks, Mandrake looked to make sure he was still wearing his revolver. He had to have that gun. It would give him the edge he needed to steal Orchid away from Horatio Clements.

The next night Mandrake put his plan into action. He surprised Clifford, knocking him unconscious with a heavy stick, and took his gun. His roommates were also surprised, but told him they would wait till Clifford started coming to before they alerted the family.

Mandrake selected a horse, scattered the rest, and raced away bareback into the night. He rode the back country toward Harper's Ferry, and though he was on horseback, the going was slow. He arrived at the edge of Harper's Ferry on Saturday morning, May 4. The town was a beehive of activity. Mandrake wondered if it had something to do with the war. While he was trying to figure out how to find Clements's place, he saw an elderly black couple emerging from town on foot, moving his direction.

Leaving the stolen horse in the brush, he approached the couple and asked what was going on in town. They explained that Harper's Ferry had been made the induction center for Virginia men to join the Confederate army. Hundreds were arriving every day. Mandrake then asked for directions to the Clements place, and was told to simply follow the Potomac River northwestward and he would come to it. He couldn't miss it, for it was the only place surrounded by a high stockade fence.

Shortly afterward, Mandrake was hunkered in a ditch across the road from Clements's gate. The horse was secured in a deep gully nearby. His heart fluttered as he thought of being so close to Orchid, who had to be somewhere inside the formidable fence.

Observing the coming and going of white men at the gate, Mandrake told himself he would have to wait till Horatio Clements came out, get the drop on him, and with the revolver held to his head, force him to command the guards at the gate to send Orchid out. He would then hold Clements as a hostage until the three of them were a long way from Harper's Ferry. Once he felt he and Orchid were safe, he would leave Clements and they would head for Richmond.

It was early afternoon when Horatio Clements appeared. He was riding in a wagon, sitting next to Dean Faulkner, who held the reins. The gate closed behind them, and the wagon headed toward town. Mandrake hopped on the horse and followed at a safe distance.

The sun was slanting toward the hills to the west when Clements and Faulkner drove out of Harper's Ferry with a load of supplies under a tarp in the bed of the wagon. They rounded a bend in the road that was skirted by a steep, brush-covered embankment. Both men had belted down a few drinks. They were laughing and joking when suddenly they heard a heavy thud behind them.

Mandrake had jumped into the wagon bed from the embankment and was holding a cocked revolver on them, his eyes bulging.

"Stop the wagon!" snapped the black man.

Clements and Faulkner both recognized Mandrake immediately. Their faces paled as Faulkner pulled rein, halting the wagon.

Waving the gun at Faulkner, Mandrake said, "Get out."

"Wh-what are you gonna do?" stammered Faulkner.

"I'm gonna kill you if'n you don' get out!" rasped Mandrake.

The man obeyed quickly, fear framing his features as he touched ground. Mandrake pressed the muzzle of the gun against the back of Clements's head. "Now drive, mistuh. No fast moves, or this gun'll go off."

With shaky hands, Clements took the reins, saying, "Th-this isn't going to do you any good, blackie. There's something you need to—"

"Shut up and drive!"

Clements made sure the horses eased forward slowly, then held them at a steady walk. Holding the revolver firmly against Clements's head, Mandrake said, "We gonna pull up in fron' of the gate at yo' place, and you gonna tell yo' guards to sen' my wife out. If'n they don' do it, I'll kill you."

"I...I can't tell them to send her out," replied Clements. "We don't have her anymore."

"Liar!" boomed Mandrake. "You jus' wanna keep her fo'—"

"No! I'm telling you the truth."

"Then where is she?"

"She...she's dead."

The words hit Mandrake like a blow to the chest. "Stop the wagon!" he commanded.

Clements drew rein and the wagon rolled to a stop. If Clements was telling the truth, Mandrake's life was pointless. Orchid was all he had lived for. Pressing the muzzle hard against the man's skull, he breathed through clenched teeth, "Yo' lyin'!"

"No," said Clements, his mouth dry. "I...I put her with one of my choice men the very first night, but somehow she had gotten her hands on a butcher knife. She stabbed the man to death and made her way to the gate. There was only one guard at the gate, and she drove the knife into his back and let herself out. The guard told us this before he died. He was able to draw his gun and fire just as she passed through the gate. He hit her, but she kept going. He groped his way to the gate in time to see her staggering toward the river. She reached the bank and fell in. He heard the loud splash."

"This cain't be!" cried Mandrake.

"I'm sorry, but it's true," Clements said with a quiver in his voice. "The next morning we followed a trail of blood to the edge of the river. It left no doubt that she fell in. She's dead, boy."

Mandrake shook his head, refusing to believe it. "Yo' lyin' so's I'll go 'way and you can keep her to have slave babies. I know what yo' doin'."

"I...I understand why you'd think so, but I'm telling you the truth."

"How do I know yo' tellin' me the truth?" demanded Mandrake.

Cold sweat was a sheen on Horatio Clements's face. His breathing was ragged as he answered without the slightest turn of his head, "Go back and ask Faulkner. Is he following us?"

"He's a ways back, but he's comin'," replied Mandrake. "But how do I know you two didn' cook this story up?"

"Why would we do that? How would we know that you would ever show up? Think, boy."

Mandrake realized there would be no reason for Clements and his men to make up such a story. They had no one to answer to concerning Orchid. The chance that her husband would ever find where she had been taken was remote. Certainly Reed Exley would never tell him.

"All right," said Mandrake after a brief pause. "Tu'n the wagon 'round."

When they met up with Dean Faulkner, Mandrake asked him where Orchid was. When he got the same story about her escape and death, he knew it was true. His heart became heavy as lead.

Mandrake's grief clawed his insides as he made Faulkner drive the wagon to the spot near where he had stashed his horse. Leaping from the wagon, he told them to drive on, and dashed into the brush. He watched to make sure they kept going, then hopped on the horse and rode hard for the hills with tears streaming down his face.

When darkness fell, Mandrake was in a low-lying gulch ten miles southwest of Harper's Ferry. Dismounting, he prostrated himself on the ground and gave full vent to his grief. After weeping hard for some time, he sat up, wiped his face with a sleeve, and let his mind travel to the man responsible for Orchid's death. He felt the flame of vengeance burning in him.

Mandrake would return to the Ruffin plantation and kill Reed Exley. Nothing else mattered. With Orchid gone, he didn't care what happened to him. He had only one thing to live for now—to make Reed Exley pay with his life for what he did to Orchid.

On the morning of May 5, Reed Exley emerged from John Ruffin's library, where they had discussed Exley's desire to enlist in the Confederate army. He wanted to kill Yankees and do his part to bring the war to a quick end. Ruffin, being a loyal Southerner, agreed. He would hire an older man to take Reed's place temporarily. The experts were saying in the newspapers that the conflict would be short-lived. Once the Northerners realized they could not dominate the Southerners, nor take away their right to own slaves, it would all be over. Exley would tie up a few loose ends and board the train for Harper's Ferry in a couple of days.

Exley had delayed paying Hec Wheeler the second half of the thousand dollars he owed him, and Hec was becoming difficult about it. He wanted to be on his way to Pennsylvania, especially with the war developing. Exley hated the thought of parting with another five hundred dollars. Now that he had used Wheeler to help him frame Web Steele, he decided to simply kill him and keep the money. Wheeler would die the night before Exley left for Harper's Ferry to enlist.

Exley went out onto the front porch of the mansion and found Charles talking to a young man who wanted to see Abby. Now that Web was in prison, the young man hoped Abby would agree to spending time with him. The butler explained that Miss Abby was seeing no one. She was still in love with Web and had made it clear that she always would be.

Exley waited till the young man drove away in his buggy, then chuckled, "I figured this would happen."

"There was no doubt in my mind that it would," commented Charles. "Miss Abby is the most beautiful young woman in this county. Now that it appears she is available, they're going to be beating down the door. This is the fourth one I've turned away since Mr. Web has been gone."

"Really? Well, just keep turning them away, Charles."

"I will, sir. Miss Abby told me she made Mr. Web a promise that she would love only him for the rest of her life."

Leaving the porch and heading for the barn, Exley said to himself, *We'll see about that, Miss Abby.*

Daniel Hart hauled his buggy to a halt at the hitching post in front of the Ruffin mansion just as Reed Exley was driving away from the barn. Exley looked at him but did not greet him.

Young Hart mounted the steps beneath the great white pillars and rattled the big brass knocker. Lynne Ruffin had been watching for him from her bedroom window and opened the door.

Daniel looked around to make sure no one was watching, then took her in his arms and kissed her. There were tears in Lynne's eyes as she said, "I hope you understand, darling, why I can't come to the depot to see you off. I just couldn't bear watching that train pull away."

"I understand. This isn't easy for me either, but I have to go."

"I know you do," she said with a tremor in her voice. "All loyal young Southern men must rally to the call. I just hope the experts are right, and this war will be over in a few months."

"Me, too," sighed Daniel. "I want us to be married and spend the rest of our lives together."

They embraced and kissed again.

Daniel cupped Lynne's pretty face in his hands, thumbed away the tears, and half-whispered, "I love you, sweetheart. You take care of yourself."

"I will," she sniffed. "And you take care of yourself. I couldn't stand it if something happened to you."

"I'll be fine. You'll see me coming down the lane before you know it."

Lynne walked Daniel to his buggy, where they kissed again. As he climbed aboard, he said, "Tell your sister I'll be thinking of her. What a horrible thing she's going through."

"I'll tell her," nodded Lynne, her eyes glistening with tears.

They exchanged "I love yous" again, and Daniel put the horse to a trot. Lynne stood and watched the buggy roll up the lane. Just before he passed from view, Daniel leaned out from the cab and waved. Lynne waved back, broke into sobs, and ran into the house.

On the morning of May 7, the birds were singing in the trees while the Ruffin slaves worked around the yard and the corral. The slaves were watching Reed Exley talking to Master John on the front porch of the mansion. A horse and buggy waited at one of the hitching posts. The slaves smiled at each other furtively, happy that Exley was leaving. Old Jedidiah whispered to a slave next to him, "I sure hopes theuh's a Yankee bullet waitin' fo' 'im."

"Yeah, me too," whispered the other slave. "Nuthin' would make me happier than to git the good news dat Massa Reed done lef' dis worl' an' wen' to his reward."

"I's not too shuah it'll be a reward," said Jedidiah.

The slave chuckled softly. "You knows what I means, Jedidiah. When he faces de Lord, he'll git what's comin' to 'im."

On the porch, John looked toward the open door of the house and said, "Reed, you did tell Abby what time we were leaving for town, didn't you?"

"Yes."

"Well, I don't understand why she's not down here to tell you good-bye."

Exley shrugged, pleased that John wanted Abby and Reed to get together. He hadn't said so, but Exley knew the desire was there.

Perturbed at Abby, John called toward the door, "Charles! Go up to Miss Abby's room and tell her Mr. Reed and I are leaving. He has to catch his train."

"Never mind, Papa John," Exley said. "I'll just run up to her room and tell her good-bye."

"Better make it snappy! That train doesn't wait for anybody."

"I'll be right back."

Moments later, Exley tapped on Abby's door. She opened it and gave him a bland look.

"Abby," he said, smiling, "aren't you going to tell me good-bye?"

"Good-bye!" she snapped, swinging the door to slam it.

Exley checked the swing of the door, and said, "I'm going away to fight in the war. Don't I at least deserve a good-bye kiss?"

As he spoke, he seized her and planted a hard kiss on her lips. When he released her, she slapped him across the face with both hands. Exley grabbed her wrists.

"Let—go—of me," she hissed.

Savoring the kiss, he grinned and obeyed. Abby held him with a hard glare and wiped her mouth with a sleeve. Exley was about to speak when John's voice came from the bottom of the stairs, "Reed, you'd better hurry! You'll miss your train."

Backing toward the door, Exley smiled and said, "At least you'll remember that kiss for a while."

"Yes!" she spat. "It takes a long time to get the taste of venom out of your mouth."

Exley stopped halfway out the door and his smile vanished. Giving Abby a malevolent look, he wheeled and hurried down the hall.

When he reached the bottom of the stairs, he smiled at John and said, "She kissed me good-bye."

"Really?" gasped John, smiling as he followed. "Wonderful!"

"It sure was, Papa John," laughed Reed, hoping John would not notice the redness of his smarting cheeks.

John drove the buggy, snapping the reins to push the horse into a fast trot.

When they were about halfway to Richmond, the road took a curve around a marshy area that was surrounded by a number of large oak trees. Exley glanced at the spot near a huge oak that stood in tall grass. Grinning to himself, he knew the body of Hec Wheeler lay in two inches of water at the base of the oak.

The night before, Exley had gone to the hotel and taken Wheeler to the hotel bar for a drink. While at the bar, he told Wheeler that he had come to give him the second five hundred dollars but had forgotten to pick the money up off his dresser after changing clothes. He would take Wheeler with him right then to the plantation, and give him the money and a horse to ride to Pennsylvania.

Hec expressed his appreciation, saying this way he could head out from Richmond at sunrise. He was eager to get to Carlisle and see his brother.

When Exley's buggy had reached the spot near the huge oak, Hec felt a cold blade thrust into his side. Exley stopped the buggy, stabbed him twice more, then dragged the body into the tall grass and left it for the snakes and water creatures to feed on.

The Ruffin buggy was out of sight when there was a stirring in the tall grass at the base of the huge oak. The cold water had helped stay the flow of Hec Wheeler's blood. After being unconscious all night, he had finally come to just after sunrise. It had taken him all this time to gain enough strength to begin crawling toward the road.

CHAPTER EIGHTEEN

Webster Steele had been in the prison near Lynchburg for less than a week when he happened to push against the bars that covered the small window in the rear of his cell. It was a warm day, and he had to work hard to free the glassed framework so he could get some fresh air. While trying to force the framework open, he gripped the bars for leverage and found them loose.

The bars were imbedded in rotting wood. The window frame was apparently directly below a leak in the roof and many years of rain and melting snow had taken their toll. Gripping the bars and pulling hard on them, he found a great deal of play. He decided a man could work at it and finally free the bars from the wood.

The window overlooked the exercise yard, which was surrounded by an eight-foot wall. At the far corner of the wall stood a platform some fifteen feet high where armed guards watched over the prison compound. Steele knew if he was to work the bars loose and crawl through the window, it would take a miracle to ever make it across the yard and over the wall to freedom. Even if he made his escape at night, the entire place was dimly-lit with kerosene lanterns. The guards on the platform could see a man moving in the yard.

As impossible as it seemed, Web sat on his bunk day after day and tried to figure a way of escape. Every time he read Abby's note, the determination to break out grew stronger. Web thought of Reed Exley running loose when *he* should be the one in prison. Only one person could clear him of the trumped-up charge—Hec Wheeler. Web would have to break out of prison, find Wheeler, and persuade him to tell the truth.

Web thought of Wheeler on the witness stand. He had said he was on his way to Carlisle, Pennsylvania, to work for his brother who had a carriage business there. He remembered that the brother's name was John—the same as Abby's father. Carlisle was no doubt a small town. Finding a John Wheeler who owned a carriage works would be easy. Once Web got his hands on Hec, he'd scare him into telling the truth.

Every day, while there was noise and activity in the prison, Web worked the bars a little looser. Somehow he would find a way to escape. The cells in his cell block housed only one inmate apiece. Web's cell was a small cubicle six feet wide and eight feet long, and was on the second floor. The kitchen was directly below him.

Word came to the prison of skirmishes taking place in northern Virginia between Union and Confederate troops, but as of the first of May, there had been no big battles.

As tension over the war increased, the prisoners grew restless. At meals and during exercise time, there was much talk about what would happen to them if the Yankees took Virginia. Locked up in the prison, they would be sitting ducks.

On the morning of May 6, Web was sitting with five other men at a table in the mess hall, eating breakfast. Keeping their voices low, they discussed their precarious position if the Yankees decided to get rid of over two hundred Southerners cooped up within the prison walls.

A beefy man named Hugo Bond was sitting directly across from Web. Looking at the men around him, he grunted, "All those stinkin' Yankees would have to do is set this tinderbox on fire. We'd all burn to death in a matter of minutes."

"Yeah," chimed in another inmate, "Hugo's right. We'd be goners in a hurry."

"I been listenin' to some of the other guys," spoke up another. "There's talk about rushin' the guards when they least expect it and makin' a break for it."

"That could still get some of us killed," said Web. "There's always that platform—I've never seen less than two guards up there. They could cut a bunch of us down while we're trying to escape."

"Most of us would make it," said Hugo. "I guess we'll just have to decide if we're willin' to play the odds."

"Bein' shot down would be better'n burnin' up," put in a skinny little man named Ollie.

Next to Ollie sat a slow-minded, heavy-set man named Harold. Setting his dull gaze on Ollie, he asked, "If the Yankees shot a cannon-ball in here, would it set the place on fire, Ollie?"

"Sure would," nodded Ollie, letting his eyes roam to the walls, beams, and ceiling. "This whole prison is constructed of wood—*old* wood—and it's dry too. Once a fire started anyplace in here, it would go up fast."

"If that happened," said Harold, "would the guards let us out? Or would we be left in here to burn?"

"We're supposed to be too dangerous to live in society," remarked Hugo. "Maybe they'd just let us burn. What do you think, Web?"

"Well, I can't say for sure. No doubt the guards would try to keep us under control so we didn't run away, but I have a hard time believing they'd just save their own skins and let us die."

"I agree," said Ollie. "These guards are human. Surely they'd take us out with them."

Ollie and Harold worked as janitors in the prison. That night they were mopping the floor in the large kitchen while a guard watched them. After a while the guard left, saying he would meet them at the end of the hall when they were finished and take them to their cells.

It was late, and the other prisoners were bedded down for the night. They were about to finish up when Harold said, "Ollie, I been thinkin'. If them Yankees was to set the place on fire, and even if the guards let us go outside the walls with 'em, them Yankees would be out there in the bushes waitin' to shoot us down when we came out the gate."

"I hadn't thought about that," said Ollie, "but I think you're right. They'd shoot all of us."

Harold squeezed his mop out over a bucket of dirty water and said, "You really think Web's right...I mean that the guards would take us out with 'em if the prison was burnin'?"

"Yes."

"Then we oughtta make our break right now, before them Yankees come."

Ollie looked at him thoughtfully and said, "Right now?"

"Sure. There's lots more of us inmates than there are guards. Dark as it is out there right now, some of us could get away. And even for those who didn't, whatever happened would be better than what's gonna happen if them Yankees come."

Ollie grinned. "You know, Harold, I think you're smarter than a lot of guys around here give you credit for."

Harold returned the grin and said, "No better place to start a fire than right where we stand."

"I agree. Let's do it. There are two cans of kerosene underneath the cupboard. We'll pour it all over the room, even on the walls. Once it's burning good, we'll go running down the hall, screaming that the place is on fire. It'll be too late to do anything but let all the prisoners out of their cells and take us out of here in a hurry."

In his cell, Web was just drifting off to sleep when loud shouts met his ears. He jerked awake and sat up on his cot. The smell of smoke assaulted his nostrils, and there was a bright yellow light showing through his window.

Dashing to the window, he saw that the building was on fire directly beneath him. The kitchen was ablaze. He saw guards running about the exercise yard, attempting to corral the inmates as other guards were letting them out of their cells. There were no guards on the platform.

There would never be a better time to make good his escape. While he was hastening into his clothes, he heard inmates coughing and shouting along the corridor. The floor was hot on the bottoms of his bare feet. His cell would be on fire within minutes. He slipped his shoes on, tied them quickly, and went to the window. It took only seconds to finish ripping the bars from the rotten wood.

Pushing himself through the window, Web dropped to the ground. In the midst of all the excitement, no one noticed him dart to a shadowed corner, grip the edge of the eight-foot wall, work his way over the top, and drop to the ground below. Moments later, he stopped to catch his breath on top of a hill, and looked back. Hugo was right. The old prison was a tinderbox. It was going up in flames fast.

As he bounded down the other side of the hill, Web had one goal in mind—get to Carlisle and find Hec Wheeler.

It was mid-afternoon on May 7 when Charles answered the sound of the knocker. Opening the door, he saw Dudley and Cora Steele standing with three well-dressed men.

"Good afternoon," said Charles, showing a faint smile.

"Good afternoon, Charles," said Dudley. Gesturing toward the three men, he said, "This is Judge William Tenant, Dr. Donald Adams, and our family attorney, Thomas Bean. We have some wonderful news for Miss Abby. Is she here?"

"Yes, sir," nodded Charles, opening the door all the way. "Please come in."

The maid was in the large receiving area, looking on with curiosity. Charles turned to her and said, "Harriet, will you fetch Miss Abby from her room while I make these people comfortable in the parlor? Mr. Steele says they have some good news for her."

"Might as well bring in John and Miss Lynne if they're around," Dudley said. "They'll be happy to hear our news, too."

Moments later, John Ruffin eased onto a couch between his two eager-eyed daughters and said to Web's father, "So what's this good news, Dudley?"

"I haven't told it yet, John," said Steele, who was the only one standing. "It'll mean most to Abby, but I wanted you and Lynne to hear it, too."

Cora sat in an overstuffed chair next to Abby, and was already dabbing at her eyes with a hanky.

Dudley took a deep breath, eyes sparkling, and said, "Web has been cleared of the murder charge and will be coming home!"

Lynne shrieked with joy, and Abby gasped and threw her hands to her mouth, wide-eyed.

"I'll let Dr. Adams tell you the rest of the story," said Dudley, and took a chair next to Cora.

Dr. Donald Adams was a prominent physician in Richmond, and though the Ruffins did not know him, they knew his reputation. He was in his early fifties and had a compassionate look about him. Easing forth in his chair, he set his eyes on Abby and said, "A man named Hec Wheeler was brought into my office this morning by a couple of men who found him on the side of the road between here and town. Wheeler had been stabbed three times and left for dead in one of the marshy areas. He was in bad shape, and at first I didn't think I could save him. He overheard me tell my nurse that I was afraid he was going to die. The knife, miraculously, had not penetrated any vital organs, but I thought he would hemorrhage to death before I could do surgery."

"Did he tell you who stabbed him?" asked John.

"Not at first. He stayed pretty mum until he heard me say he was probably going to die. He began to weep and told me there was something he had to confess before he died. He wanted to tell it to Judge Tenant. I had sent for another doctor to help me with the surgery, so I told Wheeler if we could get the judge there before the doctor arrived, he could get whatever was bothering him off his chest. It just so happened that when my nurse found Judge Tenant, he was in his chambers and was free to come. He arrived at my office before the other doctor, so I let Wheeler talk."

"And did he ever talk!" cut in Judge Tenant. "He told me, first, that it was Reed Exley who had stabbed him and left him in the marsh. This happened last night, and in the dark, Reed thought Wheeler was dead."

John Ruffin's features went white.

The judge continued. "He went on to confess that he had lied on the witness stand because Exley had paid him to go along with his story. Exley, not Web Steele, stabbed Wilbur Yates. The whole thing—including Stan Frye's testimony—had been contrived to frame Web."

Abby burst into tears, saying, "Oh, thank God! Thank God! My darling Web will be coming home to me!"

While Cora and Lynne hugged Abby, John sat pale-faced and said, "Judge, maybe this Wheeler is lying. Maybe, for some reason, he has it in for Reed. You can't convict Reed on the statement of a dying man."

"*I* can't," said Judge Tenant, "but I believe a jury will. If Wheeler had died today and wasn't around to testify, getting a conviction would have been more difficult. But he's alive to tell a jury his story. While the doctors were doing the surgery, I sent for Mr. Bean and the Steeles. The wounds weren't as bad as Dr. Adams had thought. The hemorrhaging was stopped quite easily, and when Wheeler was able to talk again, Dr. Adams told him he was going to live. Wheeler was relieved, but he still stuck by his story, knowing that it will nail him for perjury and accessory to murder. I guarantee you, the jury will buy that."

Dr. Adams said, "I told Wheeler that Web's parents and his attorney were there, but that since he was so weak, he didn't have to see them. He insisted that I let them in the room."

"We just came from there, John," said Dudley. "Wheeler told the whole story again to us."

Ruffin looked sick. "So what about Reed? He left this morning to enlist in the army."

"I know," nodded Judge Tenant. "Wheeler knew it. Exley had told someone in the hotel bar last night that he was leaving for Harper's Ferry this morning to enlist. He told it right in front of Wheeler."

"Will he be brought back for trial?"

The judge shook his head. "Not until the war is over."

"Why not?" asked Abby. "He's guilty as sin."

"I know," said Judge Tenant, "but since Wheeler didn't die, and it will be Exley's word against Wheeler's in the next trial, the army will keep him until the war is over. I wired the induction center at Harper's Ferry as soon as we were through talking to Wheeler, and got an answer right back. With this war coming on, the Confederate army needs every man it can get. Exley hadn't even shown up at the induction center yet, but when he does, they'll take him in the army and we can't touch him till the war's over."

Abby was now holding Cora's hand. Brushing a lock of auburn hair from her eyes, she asked, "So when will Web be released, Judge Tenant?"

"I'm not sure. I sent a wire to the prison superintendent right after I received the response from the induction center. I waited a few minutes for an answer, but none came, so we'll have to wait till we hear back. I'm sure they'll release him immediately on my word that he was framed."

"Will you let us know as soon as you hear?" asked Dudley. "We'll all want to be at the depot when he comes home."

Tears were spilling down Abby's cheeks again. "And what a reception he's going to get!" she exclaimed.

Cora, who was also crying again, nodded her agreement.

Abby let go of Cora's hand and wiped the moisture from her cheeks. "Mr. Reed Exley is going to get a real reception the day he returns, too. I want to be there and see his face when he's arrested."

John blinked and ran splayed fingers through his graying hair. Turning to Abby, he said, "Honey, I owe you an apology. You've tried to open my eyes to Reed, but I wouldn't let you. I'm sorry."

Abby wrapped her arms around his neck, hugged him tight, and said, "I accept your apology, Papa. I'm sorry it took all of this to open your eyes, but at least now you know the truth."

Judge Tenant assured both families that he would advise them as soon as he knew when Web would be arriving home. With that, he, the doctor, and the attorney headed back to town.

The Steeles stayed long enough to discuss the welcome all of them would give Web. When the details of the reception were agreed upon, Cora said, "The only dark thought I have now is that my boy will soon be enlisting in the army. He'll still be away from us."

"Yes, dear," said Dudley, "but at least he won't be locked up in a dingy old prison cell for the rest of his life. When the war's over, he'll come home to us. He and Abby can be married and live happily ever after, as they say in the fairy tales."

"Yes," sighed Abby. "Happily ever after."

"Daniel and me, too," chirped Lynne.

Abby hugged her. "Yes, sweetie. You and Daniel, too."

When noon came the next day without any word from Judge Tenant, Dudley Steele said to his wife, "This waiting is getting on my nerves. I'm going to ride into town and see what's going on."

"I'm sure the judge will contact us as soon as he has any word, dear. There's no need for you to make the ride."

"I *have* to. There's no reason for it to take so long to get a message through from Lynchburg."

Cora followed her husband to the entry way of the mansion. When Dudley opened the door, they both saw a buggy pulling up to the porch.

"Here's the judge, now," Cora said cheerfully. "I wonder who that is with him."

"Don't know. Never saw him before."

Judge Tenant's face was ashen-gray as he mounted the porch steps with the tall, slender man in top hat beside him. The stranger made Dudley think of Abraham Lincoln. The pallor of Tenant's features told the Steeles that something was wrong. Cora laid a hand on her husband's arm.

"Hello, Judge," said Dudley cautiously. "Any word about when our boy will be coming home?"

Tenant cleared his throat. His voice had a somber tone as he replied, "I'm afraid I have some bad news, Mr. Steele. This is Clarence Netherling of the Virginia state penal system. May we go inside and talk?"

"Of course," responded Dudley, his brow furrowed as he glanced down at his wife.

Cora's eyes showed fearful uncertainty when she met Dudley's glance. Together they led the two men into the parlor. When everyone was seated, the judge said, "Mr. and Mrs. Steele, this...uh...this is a very difficult thing to do. I—"

"What is it, Judge Tenant?" cut in Dudley. "Has something happened to Web?"

"Yes," nodded Tenant. "I received a wire early this morning from the superintendent of the prison. He told me that Mr. Netherling here would be coming to my quarters at eleven o'clock, and would have news for me concerning your son. Mr. Netherling's office is in Richmond. I'll let him tell you what has happened."

Netherling was visibly uneasy as he began by saying, "Mr. and Mrs. Steele, there was a fire last night at the Lynchburg prison. It was a bad one. In fact, the entire place burned to the ground."

Cora began to tremble. She knew what was coming next. Seated beside her husband on a love seat, she leaned against him, drew a shuddering breath and gasped, "Oh, no! Please don't tell us our boy died in that fire!"

Dudley's arm went around Cora as he silently waited for Netherling's reply.

For a brief moment the room was quiet as a crypt. Then Netherling said falteringly, "Yes, ma'am. I'm sorry."

Cora went to pieces, sobbing incoherently while Dudley held her in his arms. She wailed for several minutes, then settled into a subdued sobbing with her face buried against her husband's chest.

Proceeding, the rail-thin man said, "The fire started in the prison kitchen, directly beneath your son's cell. The buildings were constructed totally of wood and the fire spread quickly. The guards worked feverishly, attempting to get all the prisoners out, but by the time they worked their way to the second floor, the area above the kitchen was totally ablaze."

Netherling choked up for a moment, then said, "We have accounted for all the prisoners. Your son and four other men on the second floor perished in the fire. I am so sorry to have to bring you this bad news, especially since Judge Tenant informed me that your son has been cleared of the very charges that sent him to the prison."

Dudley fought against the hatred welling up inside him toward Reed Exley. He desperately wanted the man to pay for his crimes.

Dudley stayed with Cora for a long time after the two men had gone, doing everything he could to comfort her while his own heart was filled with grief. When it seemed that she had gained control of herself, he said, "Honey, it's only right that Abby should know about Web as soon as possible. I wish she could be spared, especially because of the happiness she had just yesterday, but she has a right to know that he's...he's gone."

"Yes," nodded Cora, her face pale, "but I want to go with you. I don't want to be here alone...and Abby was practically our daughter-in-law. The two of us should break the news to her together."

"All right, if you're sure you're up to it."

She nodded, holding back the tears.

"Something else, honey," said Dudley. "Maybe we should go into town and see if Reverend McLaury will go along with us. He should be advised of Web's death, and he can be a strength to Abby in a way that we can't."

"Yes, let's do that. Abby's going to need all the help she can get."

An hour later, the Steeles and Benjamin McLaury were welcomed into the Ruffin mansion by Charles, who seated them in the parlor. Then Charles went to fetch John and Lynne, who were conveniently together in the library. When Charles advised them that Abby was upstairs in her room, Reverend McLaury told him to leave it that way. They needed to see John and Lynne first, and would like to have Charles and Harriet present also.

When the four people had collected in the parlor with McLaury and the Steeles, the pastor sadly informed them of Web's death. Lynne took it hardest, breaking down and sobbing, "Oh, poor Abby! My poor, poor Abby!"

Cora folded Lynne in her arms, speaking soothing words. Lynne suddenly stopped crying and said, "Oh, Mrs. Steele, I'm sorry. What a horrible thing for you, too. Web was your only son! I'm so sorry." Looking at Dudley, she cried, "And for you, Mr. Steele. How terrible for you to lose Web. He was such a fine man. I was going to be so proud to have him for a brother-in-law."

Cora continued to hold her while John offered his sympathy to Web's parents. Harriet and Charles then gave their condolences, telling the Steeles what a fine young man their son had been.

When Lynne had settled down, the preacher said, "Mr. Ruffin, I think it's time to let Abby know. Would you like me to break it to her?"

John bit hard on his lower lip. "Yes, Reverend. I think that would be best. Rather than call her down here to tell her, let's go to her room. The Steeles and Lynne and I will go up with you. She'll need all of us when you break it to her."

"Harriet and I will give Miss Abby our sympathy once she's over the initial shock, Mr. John," said Charles.

"Thank you," John said, forcing a weak smile for his servants.

When they reached the top of the stairs, Reverend McLaury moved out in front and led the others quietly down the hall. His heart was pounding, knowing what he had to do. When he reached the spot, he took a deep breath, let it out slowly, and tapped on Abby's door.

CHAPTER NINETEEN

eb Steele ran hard through the night until he reached the west
bank of the James River north of Lynchburg. Exhausted, he lay
in the tall grass and tried to sleep, but he was too keyed up. His
mind was racing. How could he get a message to Abby and his parents? Had the prison officials thought he died in the fire? What would
he do if Hec Wheeler had not shown up in Carlisle? His brother
would have no idea where to find him. Without Wheeler to force into
telling the truth, Web would be right back where he started.

At dawn, the fugitive was up and running again, heading due
north. As he pressed on, he considered taking a horse from some farmer's
field or corral and bringing it back once he had Wheeler in hand. If he
stayed afoot, it was going to take a long time to get to his destination.

By midmorning, Web was growing weak from hunger. He was
staying in the back country just in case some of the prisoners had escaped
during the fire and local authorities had been wired to be on the alert. He
spotted a small farmhouse and barn up ahead. Maybe there would be a
root cellar where he could get some fruits and vegetables. And maybe
they had a horse to spare that they wouldn't miss for a while.

It turned out better than he expected. The root cellar was there,
and he was stuffing himself with raw potatoes when the farmer happened on to him. When Web explained his situation, the farmer

believed him and put him on a horse with provisions in a gunny sack.

On May 12, Web had reached the northern tip of the Blue Ridge Mountains and was riding through the forest just west of Manassas Junction when suddenly a half-dozen men on horseback came out of nowhere and blocked his path. Two of them were in gray uniforms. Both appeared to be officers, though Web could not identify the markings on their collars. Were these the uniforms of the newly formed Confederate army?

The older man in uniform, who was about forty, nudged his horse toward Steele, and was quickly followed by the younger officer. The other four laid their muskets across their saddles and looked on with keen interest.

Web's heart thudded his ribs. Could the authorities have been alerted this far north about the fire and his escape?

"Good morning," said the older officer. "I'm Captain Philip Carney, Confederate Army. This gentleman in the uniform behind me is Lieutenant Chet Foster. These other men are new recruits and have not been supplied as yet with uniforms. Might I ask your name and where you're from?"

Web knew by their casual manner that these men did not suspect him of being an escapee from the Lynchburg prison. Smiling, he said, "My name is Webster Steele, Captain. I'm from down by Richmond. My father owns a large plantation there. I'm his slave overseer."

Carney's features were relaxed. "I see. A home-grown South'n boy, eh?"

"Yes, sir." Web was glad the prison had not made the inmates wear marked clothing.

Adjusting his position in the saddle, Carney said, "I judge by the direction you're heading that you're not on your way to Harper's Ferry."

Noting the change in tone of Carney's voice, Web said, "No, sir. I'm headed for Carlisle, Pennsylvania. Have to see a man there about some very important personal business."

The captain's jaw jutted and he frowned. "You do know there's a war on, don't you?"

"Yes, sir."

"Then as a loyal South'n boy, you should be aiming for Harper's Ferry. That's the induction center for all Virginia men."

Acting as if he already knew that, Web said, "Before the war started, sir, I made plans to join up if it happened. And I still plan to do it, just as soon as I clear up this important personal matter."

Carney's eyes went stony. "Well now, Mr. Steele," he said, with an edge to his voice, "all of us have had to set aside important personal business in order to prepare ourselves to fight the Union. Every able-bodied man is expected to join the army. You look plenty able-bodied to me. Man refuses to jump in and make ready for the big conflict that's coming is looked upon with a high degree of scorn. You following my drift?"

Web knew he was cornered. If he rode away, saying his personal business came before the well-being of the Confederacy, they would probably shoot him off the horse. He had no choice. Clearing himself of the murder charge would have to wait. Returning to Abby would have to wait, too.

"Yes, sir," nodded Web. "I understand what you're saying. My personal business can wait."

"That's what I like to hear," smiled the captain. "It just so happens that Lieutenant Foster is going to be riding to Harper's Ferry yet today. It's only thirty miles from here. You can ride along with him. If you need to wire the folks back home, you can do that at the induction center."

"Thank you, sir," said Web. As they rode toward the army facility at Manassas Gap, Web told himself there was no way he could send a wire home. The telegraph operator in Richmond no doubt knew of Web's prison sentence. It had been written up in the local newspaper. If the operator received a telegram from Web Steele, the authorities would be after him.

There was nothing he could do to let Abby and his parents know where he was. He had learned while in the prison that mail service had been disrupted by the Yankees and that finding men to carry the mail was becoming impossible. Several skirmishes had taken place when Confederate soldiers had come upon Federals who were attempting to stop the mail from going through. Writing letters home was out.

Abby and his parents would just have to wait till the war was over to know that he was alive and well. He hoped the experts were right about the war lasting only a few months.

On the night of May 12, elderly slave Jedidiah was about to put out the lantern and go to bed in his tiny shack on the Ruffin plantation. He was humming an old hymn while sitting on his only chair and pulling off his socks when he heard a faint tap at the door.

"Who's dat?" he asked.

"Mandrake!" came a hoarse whisper through the cracks in the door.

Jedidiah hobbled to the door and pulled it open. The yellow light from the lantern showed him the weary face of his dear friend. "Well, Mandrake, boy, come in!" he said jubilantly. "Whut you doin' heah?"

"I'm here to kill 'im, Jedidiah," Mandrake said as he stepped inside.

Closing the door, the old man asked, "Yo' heah to kill who?"

"That heartless animal Reed Exley, that's who! I figured since he treated you so mean, you'd hide me in yo' shack till mo'nin' so's I can watch fo' 'im and shoot 'im down."

Jedidiah noticed the revolver under Mandrake's belt. Rubbing the back of his neck, he said, "We all heahed 'bout Massa Web buyin' you and sendin' you off to fin' Orchid. Did you fin' her?"

Mandrake's face grew solemn. "No, I didn'. She's...she's dead."

"Daid! How?"

"It's a long story."

"Well, sit down and tell me 'bout it," said Jedidiah, gesturing toward the chair.

While the old man eased down on the edge of the bed, Mandrake sat on the chair. With his emotions running high, Mandrake told of the obstacles he faced in getting to Harper's Ferry, then of learning from Horatio Clements that Orchid was dead. He told how Orchid had stabbed the man she was supposed to mate with and even stabbed the guard at the gate in a valiant attempt to escape.

When Jedidiah heard that Orchid had been shot and had fallen into the Potomac River, he wept and said, "None of this would've happen', Mandrake, if'n dat dirty Reed Exley hadn' sold her to dat no-count Clements man."

"Yes, an' that's why I come back. That filthy devil's gonna die, and I'm the one who's gonna kill 'im!"

"If you did dat, dey'd hang you, Mandrake!"

"I don' care. With Orchid gone, I don' got nothin' to live fo'. All I wan' is to see Exley dead!"

"Well, you ain' gonna be killin' him any time soon," came Jedidiah's toneless reply. "He ain' heah. He wen' off to fight in de war."

"What! When'd he leave?"

" 'Zactly a week ago."

Mandrake stared into space for a long moment.

"Whut you thinkin'?" asked Jedidiah.

"I'm thinkin' that all Virginia men have to join up in the army at the 'duction center in Harper's Ferry. If I go to the 'duction place, they'll know where they sent 'im. Once I fin' that out, I'll go there and kill 'im."

"You gonna leave right away?"

"I need to rest a couple days. Gettin' down here with all the war stuff goin' on's been rough. Can I stay here in yo' shack?"

"Sho' nuff, but ain' you gonna let Massa John or Miz Abby an' Miz Lynne know yo' heah?"

"It's best that I don't, Jedidiah. They'd jus' try to stop me. Massa John would, anyway. You know how he loves that low-down skunk. I'll jus' stay in here so's none of the other slaves sees me, and leave in the dark when I go."

"Whatevuh you say," nodded Jedidiah. He rubbed his hands together nervously and dropped his eyes to the floor.

Mandrake eyed him with speculation and said, "You worried 'bout somethin'?"

"Well," the old man said with a sigh, "you wouldn' call it worry. I guess you'd call it dreadin'."

"You dreadin' somethin'?"

Still looking at the floor, Jedidiah responded shakily, "Dreadin' whut I gotta tell you now."

"Tell me what?"

Raising his eyes to meet Mandrake's gaze, he said, "Dat somebody else you lubs a whole lot is daid."

Mandrake saw tears film the old man's eyes but did not venture to ask who he was talking about.

"I's talkin' 'bout Massa Web." As he said it, tears spilled down his wrinkled cheeks.

Mandrake's heart seemed to stand still. He couldn't believe his ears. It took him a moment to find his voice. "Massa Web? How? When?"

Jedidiah explained that John Ruffin had told the slaves about Web's death so they would understand why Abby was in a deep state of grief. He told how Exley had framed Web for murdering Wilbur Yates and of Web's subsequent imprisonment and death in the fire. Jedidiah followed that sad information with the news that after being stabbed and left for dead by Exley, Hec Wheeler had come clean and cleared Web of the murder charge.

Mandrake lay on the floor of Jedidiah's shack that night, weeping silently over the loss of the man who had set him free. When he thought of Reed Exley, the name seemed to burn into his mind. To Mandrake, Exley was the scum of the earth and needed to be removed. Mandrake was determined to hunt him down...or die in the attempt.

CHAPTER TWENTY

On April 15, 1861—three days after the bombardment of Fort Sumter by Confederate troops—President Abraham Lincoln seized the opportunity to act without congressional encumbrance and called for seventy-five thousand men to join the Union militia and punish the Confederacy. Lincoln declared war on the Southerners, not only for their attack on Fort Sumter, but because the seven seceded Southern states had opposed and obstructed the laws of the United States.

In his campaign for military volunteers, Lincoln appealed to all loyal citizens of the Union to favor, facilitate, and aid in the vastly important effort to maintain the honor, the integrity, and the very existence of the Union. He made it clear that only by military force could they correct the wrongs of the Confederacy already too long endured by the federal government.

Lincoln gave the Southern military forces twenty days to disband and disperse. The implication was that if they did so, they would be forgiven; if they did not, his intention to "correct the wrongs of the Confederacy" would be fulfilled.

The president's bold stand stirred great enthusiasm throughout the North. In every city, town, village, and hamlet, young men turned out in large numbers to enlist, and Lincoln quickly exceeded the quota of militiamen he had wanted.

When the message came to Confederate President Jefferson Davis in Montgomery, he bristled with anger. A message quickly went to the newspapers of the South from Davis, quoting Lincoln's "bold, brash, and naked" threat, stirring up the Southern people to unite and make ready to meet that threat head-on.

Southerners of every class gave vent to their long-festering rage at the Northerners, who would dare try to force abolition on them and take away their states' rights. The Confederate enlistment drive, which had been moving nominally since early March, suddenly boiled over. Eager young men all over the South stormed the recruiting offices, ready to fight the Yankees when they invaded sacred Southern land.

Just two days after Lincoln issued his threat, a state convention was held in Richmond. The delegates passed an ordinance of secession.

On April 18, a Virginia military unit moved swiftly to take the federal arsenal at Harper's Ferry. The small Union garrison there decided to make for friendly territory and let the Confederates have the arsenal. To put up a fight when outnumbered more than ten to one would have been suicide. They retreated hastily across the Potomac River to Hagerstown, Maryland. When the Virginians marched into the arsenal, they found to their delight five thousand rifles and a healthy supply of ammunition.

After the secession of Virginia, both sides marked time. Neither had their men trained, and neither was ready to go into full-scale battle. In both the North and South, thousands of women went to work making uniforms. Progress was slow, but little by little recruits were supplied with uniforms while being trained.

Though the Confederacy was conscious that it could never muster the numerical or material strength of the North, it had a spirit and a will to fight. The South would be on the defensive. It rested its hope of victory not on conquest of the North, but in wearing down the Yankee will to fight.

The North, on the other hand, would be the aggressor. Its military objective was to invade and conquer the South, thus meting out retribution for its crimes against the United States. When the objective was accomplished, the Southern states would then be under federal jurisdiction once again, and slavery would be abolished.

On April 29, Jefferson Davis delivered to the Confederate Congress a powerful and emotional speech that stirred Southern patriotism to an even greater degree. The movement toward full secession of the Southern states moved forward rapidly. On May 1, the Tennessee legislature passed a military alliance with the Confederacy, though the popular vote to formally decide the issue would not come until June 8. Secession for Tennessee was a foregone conclusion.

Arkansas left the Union on May 6, and when North Carolina followed on May 20, the eleven-state Confederacy was complete.

Since Virginia was in a strategic position bordering the North, it was apparent to President Davis and the Confederate Congress that the heavy fighting would begin on Virginia soil. Davis and the Congress, encouraged by Virginia's zeal for battle, opened negotiations to move the Confederate capital from small, remote Montgomery to the larger and more accessible city of Richmond. The transfer was completed when President Davis and his staff arrived in Richmond on May 29. Now just a hundred miles separated the two capitals—Washington D.C., and Richmond, Virginia. Both sides went to work to secure their respective centers of government.

As the month of June came in 1861, and both sides were busy enlisting and training troops, the prime geographical region of concern was western Virginia, which did not become known as West Virginia until its entry into the Union as a state in 1863. Politically the Northern hold on that area was of major psychological importance, since the people of that region had remained loyal to the Union despite the secession of their state.

To Abraham Lincoln and the federal government, western Virginia was a strategic spot that had to be kept intact with its natural neighbors, Union states Ohio and Pennsylvania. The state governments of both Ohio and Pennsylvania looked upon western Virginia as a battleground on which to halt the Southern advance. Strategically, that region was viewed by both the Union and the Confederacy as a key position which could be used as a base for strikes deep into enemy territory.

In mid-May, the governor of Ohio put pressure on President Lincoln to order an invasion of western Virginia on the grounds that it was necessary not only to deny the use of the area to the Confederates, but to support the Union sympathizers there. The U.S. military commander of that district, General George B. McClellan, agreed that some sort of campaign was warranted.

At the time, the Confederates were disrupting trains of the Baltimore and Ohio Railroad in western Virginia, so it took little effort by Ohio's governor to persuade Lincoln to order McClellan to take prompt action.

The troublesome Confederates were bivouacked at the small town of Philippi. On June 2, McClellan dispatched a small force toward Philippi with instructions to drive off the Confederate forces and protect the railroad. On the night of June 3, an attack was launched on the Rebel camp at Philippi. The Southerners were totally unprepared, failing to even have sentries on patrol. In a minor skirmish, a few men were wounded on both sides, but the Confederates made a hasty retreat southward to the town of Beverly, located at the northern base of Rich Mountain.

The relatively easy rout gave General McClellan and his men an overwhelming air of confidence. Laughing about how fast the Rebels ran from Philippi, the federals dubbed the incident "The Philippi Races." It was apparent to the Union troops that the Confederates did not have the resolve to fight, and that the war would soon be over.

General Robert E. Lee, a native Virginian, had been appointed by President Davis as commander-in-chief of the Confederate forces on April 23. As a result of the incident at Philippi, Lee sent twenty-five hundred troops to Beverly under the command of Brigadier General Robert S. Garnett, a forty-one-year-old Virginian who was known as a dedicated family man. Garnett had served in the Mexican-American conflict with gallantry and, as a strict military disciplinarian, was considered one of the brightest officers in the old Regular Army.

Private Webster Steele had been assigned to Garnett's command upon enlistment and had been undergoing training at Harper's Ferry until General Lee dispatched the unit to Beverly. They arrived at Beverly on June 19 and set up camp between the town and the northern base of Rich Mountain.

When General McClellan's scouts reported the large number of Confederate troops that had marched into Beverly, McClellan moved toward the area, leading some fifteen thousand men to join with the small force already at Philippi.

In response to the large Union deployment, General Lee ordered an additional thirty-five hundred troops who had been training near Winchester, Virginia, to march to Beverly and join Garnett. Lee realized his regiments at Rich Mountain were still greatly outnumbered, but he had no more trained recruits that he could spare. Fear of Union attack on Richmond caused him to keep a large number of prepared men there, and another large unit had to stay at Manassas Junction to protect the vital center of the Manassas Gap Railroad.

On the morning of June 28, Private Steele was working with two other enlisted men to stabilize a twenty-four pounder cannon at the edge of the dense timber on top of Rich Mountain. The three men were sweating in the hot sun as they blocked the cannon's wheels with heavy rocks to keep it from moving when fired.

When they had finished, Web stepped behind the cannon and sighted along the barrel, eyeing the open field of grass and small trees that spread over the sharp slope on the east side of the mountain. "This ought to be about right," he said to his companions. Then running his gaze toward the dozen other cannons of like size lined across the crest of the mountain southward, he added, "Looks like we've got the entire open area covered. When those Yankees come over that grassy ridge down there and see these big guns trained on them, they just might decide to do a little backtracking."

Worry showed on the freckled face of young Private Dooley Carson. "Wish we had twice as many cannons up here," he drawled, sleeving away sweat from his brow. "From what General Garnett told us, we're gonna be grossly outnumbered."

Dooley was barely eighteen years old, spoke slowly with a heavy Southern accent, and carried an easy smile. Web had liked him from the moment they met at Harper's Ferry.

"Well, I'm glad our troops from Winchester are gonna get here before McClellan arrives with his big bunch," put in twenty-one-year-old Leroy Sheldon. "At least we can get well-fortified on top of this mountain before the blue-bellies get here."

While Sheldon spoke, all three of them looked toward the path that wound its way down the north end of the mountain. General

Garnett had ordered his troops to set up camp amid the heavy timber on top of Rich Mountain. They would meet the enemy from the edge of the timber with all the fire power they could muster. Being above the Union troops would give them an advantage. Horses and mules pulled heavily loaded wagons and carts up the path, their coats shining with sweat. Some of the wagons were reaching the crest and heading for the cannons. They carried gun powder and cannonballs.

Dooley Carson moved into the shade of the trees and lifted a large canteen off the stub of a broken limb. Looking back at his partners, he called, "Hey, you Rebels want a drink?"

Steele and Sheldon looked over their shoulders at him and nodded. Carson uncorked the canteen, took a long pull, and handed it to Sheldon. While Sheldon was drinking, Web said, "Maybe these boys will have word for us about the troops from Winchester."

"Hope so," said Carson. "I'll feel a lot better when those Winchester Rebels are on top of this mountain with us."

"Won't we all?" grinned Web as he took the canteen from Leroy.

Dooley noticed there was dust on the pants of his new gray uniform. Brushing it off, he said, "Sure don't want to soil this uniform. Some Southern belle worked hard to make it."

Web was corking the canteen when the lead ammunition wagon hauled up and stopped. The mules blew as the driver set the brake and said, "Brung you boys somethin' to shoot at them blue-bellies when they come."

While the three men helped the driver unload the heavy canisters of gun powder and some sixty cannonballs, he informed them that the troops from Winchester had been spotted by one of General Garnett's scouts and would arrive within an hour. Word was that they were being led by a twenty-nine-year-old colonel named John Pegram, a graduate of West Point. Pegram had experience in fighting Indians on the western frontier.

It was nearly eleven o'clock when Colonel Pegram and his troops arrived at the base of Rich Mountain. General Garnett met them and explained to Pegram that he would be dividing the forces into two units within a couple of days. The second unit would be the largest. The Confederate scouts were reporting that General McClellan was leading his large force toward the Grafton-Philippi area to meet up with the small brigade camped there.

Acting on this information, Garnett planned to take forty-seven hundred men to Laurel Mountain, just north of Rich Mountain, and try to cripple the Yankee army by hitting them from atop the mountain. The thirteen hundred men on Rich Mountain would have to take on whatever smaller unit McClellan sent their way. Pegram would command the Rich Mountain men.

Pegram's troops then climbed to the top of Rich Mountain where they set up camp until the forces would be divided within a couple of days. The entire brigade of six thousand men was assembled in the open grassy area on Rich Mountain's east side where the tall, slender general addressed them and explained his plan.

An hour after the men had been dismissed, Web was cleaning his army-issue Springfield rifled musket in front of his tent while talking with Dooley Carson. Dooley had his right shoe off and was rubbing a sore toe.

"I think it's marvelous that Abby would be so dedicated to you that she'd promise never to consider another man," said Dooley. "Seems to me that with you in prison for the rest of your life—as she thought would be your lot—she'd want to find another man, get married, and live a normal life."

Web grinned. "You'd have to know Abby to understand. When the Lord made her, He threw away the mold. What she wrote in that note was no idle promise."

"But she may think you died in that prison fire. Maybe she'll feel that her promise can be broken since you're dead."

"Nope," said Web, shaking his head. "When this war is over and I go home, she'll still be single and unattached. Her love for me is pure, and her heart is true. She'll never love another man any more than if she died, I'd ever love another woman."

"I sure hope when I fall in love, it'll be with a girl like Abby."

Dooley was silently wondering if such a girl really existed. Maybe even now, Abby Ruffin was seeing other men. Maybe his friend was in for a shock and a broken heart when he returned home.

While Dooley was putting his shoe back on, he watched as Web picked up his bayonet and attached it to the musket. A cold shiver ran down his spine as he shuddered aloud, "Web, I don't know if I can do it."

"What's that?"

"Fight hand-to-hand with a bayonet. The idea of cold Yankee steel in my body makes my knees go weak."

Web grinned and said, "It's not supposed to be Yankee steel in your body, my friend, but Rebel steel in a Yankee body."

Dooley ran shaky fingers through his mop of sand-colored hair. "I know, but maybe those blue-bellies have been trained better than us."

"Man has to have a positive attitude," said Web. "You can't go into battle thinking you're going to die. You have to—"

"Web Steele!" came the sound of an astonished voice.

Web looked up to see Daniel Hart rushing toward him. Laying the rifle down, he stood up and met Daniel's hand in a warm handshake.

Daniel's features showed the shock he was feeling as he blurted, "Web, how'd you get out of prison?" He quickly covered his mouth as he realized what he had just said.

"It's all right, Daniel," chuckled Web. "He's a close friend and knows about my being in prison. Dooley Carson, meet Daniel Hart."

Carson and Hart shook hands, then Web told Daniel the whole story.

Daniel shook his head and said, "Web, from what you've told me, the authorities for sure think you died in the fire."

"That's pretty much the way I see it," nodded Web.

"Then that's what they've reported to Abby and everybody back home."

"If our assumption is correct, it sure is."

"Poor Abby! This has to be awful for her. And for your ma and pa, too."

"I know, but there's no way I can get a message through to them. No soldier is allowed to send anything personal on the telegraph, and as you probably know, the mail service is no longer operating."

"I guess there's nothing you can do about it till this war is over and you can go home."

"That's about it," replied Web. He then explained to Dooley Carson that Daniel was engaged to Abby's sister, Lynne.

Dooley asked Daniel if Lynne was as good-looking as Abby. Daniel grinned at Web and assured Dooley that Lynne was even more beautiful than Abby.

Web laughed, "Well, I guess that's one thing we're in disagreement on!" Then he said, "So you came over with Colonel Pegram from Winchester."

"Yeah," Daniel nodded. His face took on a solemn look and he said, "There's somebody else you know who came with me."

"Oh? Who?"

"Reed Exley."

The distaste Web felt at the sound of the name showed on his face.

Daniel chortled, "Seems like good fortune just follows you around, Web."

"Sure!" exclaimed Dooley. "He met up with me, didn't he? And what's more, he drew me as one of his two assistants to man his cannon."

"So you're a cannon master, Web?" Daniel asked.

"He sure is," cut in Dooley. "Web took to it during training at Harper's Ferry like a duck takes to water. He can aim a cannon and hit a bull between the eyes at four hundred yards!"

"Well, let's hope it's Yankee bulls he hits this time," laughed Daniel. Clearing his throat, he said, "This is some coincidence, Web."

"What do you mean?"

"I'm in the artillery too. Trained on twenty-four pounders."

"You don't say," responded Web with a broad grin. "That's the size of my gun. You a cannon master?"

"Naw, I'm not that good at aiming one...but I'm pretty fast at getting one loaded."

"I suppose you'll be assigned to Laurel Mountain with General Garnett," said Web.

"I assume so," replied Daniel. "Sure wish I could work with you."

"Well," chuckled Dooley, "if wishes were horses, beggars would ride. Web had a dozen or more men wantin' to be on his team, but me and a fella named Leroy got the assignment."

"Guess I was born under a crooked star," groaned Hart. "Nothing like that ever happens to me." After a brief pause, he said, "I'd better get back to my outfit. Nice to meet you, Dooley. Hope to see you around, future brother-in-law."

As Daniel started to walk away, Web called after him, "Daniel!"

Halting, young Hart made a half-turn. "Yes?"

"When the battle comes, you watch yourself, y'hear?"

"Yep. You too, okay?"

"Okay."

Just after breakfast the following morning, General Garnett worked with Colonel Pegram on his plan to divide up the troops. Since the Confederate scouts reported that Union General McClellan and his giant force were still several miles to the north, Garnett decided the move to Laurel Mountain would not need to be made until Monday, July 1.

Late that afternoon, the sky clouded up and rain began to fall. It was coming down heavily when Daniel Hart appeared at the tent occupied by Web Steele and his two companions. Dripping wet, he announced to Web that an opening had come up for a helper at one of the cannons on Rich Mountain. He would be working with a cannon master named Private Ed Cahill. Web was pleased to learn it. He laughed, saying they would be neighbors. Web's gun was first in the line at the north end. Cahill's gun was the very next one. Daniel stayed until the rain began to let up about half an hour before suppertime. As he was about to leave the tent, he told Web that Reed Exley had been appointed as a runner between General Garnett and Colonel Pegram once Garnett was situated on Laurel Mountain.

Web asked if Daniel had told Exley about him being out of prison and in uniform on Rich Mountain. Daniel said he had not. He was hoping that in the crowd of six thousand men, Web would not have to meet up with his hated enemy.

The next morning Web and his crew were at their cannon, making sure the powder was dry, when another ammunition wagon pulled up. They were given additional powder and cannonballs. At the same time, Lieutenant Floyd Courtman, who was in charge of artillery on Rich Mountain, rode up on a bay gelding and told Steele he wanted to meet with all the cannon masters immediately at his tent. Web left Carson and Sheldon to help unload the wagon and followed Courtman.

When the brief meeting was over, Web headed back through the timber toward his cannon. He was some forty yards from the timber's edge when suddenly a short, stocky form stepped out from behind a tree, blocking his path.

"Well, well, well," sneered Reed Exley, waggling his head. "Look who's here."

Drawing up within arm's reach, Web said, "Get out of my way."

"Or what? You'll batter me with those fists of yours? Do you know the trouble you can get into for striking a fellow soldier?"

"So what do you want?"

"I want to know how you broke out of prison."

"You going to turn me in?"

Exley laughed, rubbed the back of his neck, and replied, "Not till the war's over. Since the South needs every man it can get, Garnett wouldn't do anything about it right now. But you can count on it—when the last shot is fired, I'll see that you're back behind bars faster than a hummingbird can flap its wings."

"We both know who ought to be behind bars," Web said heatedly.

Looking around in the dappled shade of the trees to make sure no one was near, Exley remarked tartly, "Yeah, but you and I are the only ones who know."

"Not really," Web countered. "Hec Wheeler knows, and so does Abby."

Exley ignored Web's reference to Wheeler, but his straw-colored eyebrows arched at the mention of Abby. "Oh? And how is that? She wasn't there that night I killed that stupid drifter."

"She didn't have to be. She just knows you, that's all."

A mocking grin curved Exley's mouth as he said insolently, "She sure does know me. In fact, she knows me a lot better since I got you out of the picture."

"And just what do you mean by that?"

"Exactly what it sounds like. She knows her dead sister is out of the way now, and since you are too, she threw herself at me. You were only second choice, Steele. Abby really wanted me all the time. Those lips of hers are mighty sweet, aren't they?"

"Don't give me that poppycock, Exley. You've never kissed those lips."

"Oh, yes I have. You should've seen the kiss she gave me the day I left for Harper's Ferry. Said she'd be waitin' for me to come back, too. You're out of her life forever, Steele. Forever. When this war's over and I go home, she'll be waitin' for me with open arms and eager lips."

"You're lying. I know Abby and I know how she feels about you. She hates your guts almost as much as I do." Moving toward him, Web clipped, "This conversation is over."

When Web saw that Exley wasn't going to move, he slammed him in the chest with his shoulder, knocking him flat on his back.

With the wind knocked out of him, Exley rolled over, sucking for air and swearing between gasps. Looking at Web Steele's broad back as he strode toward the open area, he gasped in a half-whisper, "You ain't...ever gonna see Abby...again, Steele. I'll find a way...to put a bullet in you...before the battle on this...mountain...is over. Ha! Who'll know the difference? Confederate bullets look just like Yankee bullets."

CHAPTER TWENTY-ONE

On Monday, July 1, 1861, General Robert Garnett moved forty-seven hundred of his troops to Laurel Mountain, leaving the planned thirteen hundred on Rich Mountain with Colonel John Pegram in charge. When the Laurel Mountain position was fortified, Garnett kept Reed Exley busy riding back and forth between the mountains with messages.

During the next few days, the Confederates on both mountains waited nervously for McClellan to arrive and the battle to begin.

General George McClellan had moved his troops slowly toward the Philippi-Beverly area while gaining information about the Confederate strongholds on Laurel and Rich Mountains. Having left behind some fifty-four hundred men to guard the line of the Baltimore and Ohio Railroad, McClellan arrived at Philippi with over fourteen thousand troops late in the day on July 9.

McClellan divided his force into four brigades under Brigadier Generals Thomas Morris, Newton Schleich, William Rosecrans, and Colonel Robert McCook. His scouts had not seen the actual move of General Garnett and his troops to Laurel Mountain on July 1, and erroneously reported that the bulk of the Confederates were on Rich Mountain.

Acting on this information, McClellan set up his plan. He was aware that General Garnett and Colonel Pegram were each in charge on a mountain, but assumed that Garnett was with the larger force on the one farther to the south. He would use July 10 to march troops south to the town of Beverly, and to learn all he could about the terrain of both mountains by talking to local Union sympathizers. Once he knew the layout of the mountains, he would have his artillery set up at their bases under cover of darkness on July 10. At dawn on the eleventh, the cannons would cut loose on both mountains, softening them up for the infantry attack that would follow.

According to his plan, two columns would advance at the same time. General Thomas Morris would move on Laurel Mountain and McClellan would lead the other three brigades against Rich Mountain.

At three o'clock on the afternoon of July 10, the Union troops halted at the edge of Beverly and prepared to set up camp. General William Rosecrans took two officers and rode into town. Reaching Main Street, they began to ask people about the terrain of Rich and Laurel Mountains. One old timer advised Rosecrans to go to the Trench Clothing Store next door to the Beverly Bank and talk to young David Hart. David, he explained, was an enthusiastic hiker and had climbed all over both mountains. He was also a Union sympathizer.

Moments later, General Rosecrans, who was a stately man of forty, entered the clothing store alone while his officers waited on the street. A tall, slender young man came from a counter at the back of the store, smiled when he saw the blue uniform, and said, "Good afternoon, sir. I'm David Hart. How may I help you?"

The general introduced himself and explained his purpose for coming into the store. David was eager to help the Union cause. He offered to close the store early and go with Rosecrans to give a description of both Laurel and Rich mountains to General McClellan.

Rosecrans gladly accepted the offer, and within fifteen minutes, David was sitting in General McClellan's tent on the outskirts of Beverly giving the general a description of both mountains, telling him of the most frequently used paths, and which sides were easiest to climb.

When Hart finished and had answered several questions, McClellan said, "I appreciate your help, David. It has been of the utmost value. I do want to ask you something, though."

"What's that, sir?"

McClellan stroked his heavy mustache and queried, "Why aren't you in a blue uniform?"

"I'd love to be in the Union army, General McClellan, but circumstances are standing in my way. You see, I'm a business partner with my father-in-law at the clothing store, and he had a stroke a few months ago and can't work. If I joined the army, the store wouldn't make it. My wife and mother-in-law can run it for awhile, but not for an extended time. Without the store, the family would soon be destitute. I have no choice but to stay here and take care of it."

"I understand," smiled McClellan. "You've been a great help to the Northern cause in this matter, and I thank you."

General Rosecrans asked David, "Are you a native Virginian?"

"Yes, sir. My father owns a cotton plantation over by Richmond. That's where I was born and raised."

"A cotton plantation?" said McClellan, surprised. "Your father no doubt is in sympathy with the Confederacy then?"

"Yes, sir. He and I don't get along very well."

"You have any brothers in the Rebel army?"

"I only have one who would be old enough. But I have little contact with the family, and I don't know whether Daniel has joined the Confederate army or not. I kind of think Pa might keep him home to help with the plantation."

McClellan nodded and rose to his feet. David followed suit, and so did the brigade leaders. "Thank you again, David," said the general. "You've been a real help."

Scratching at an ear, David said, "Sir, I think I can be of even more help."

"How's that?"

"I assume by what you've said that you will attack Rich Mountain from the east side, since it's not nearly as steep as the west side."

"That's right," nodded McClellan.

"Well, sir, since your scouts have told you the larger number of Confederates are on Rich Mountain, wouldn't it be good to hit them from the west, also?"

"Yes it would, but if it's as steep on that side as you say, climbing it with artillery would be impossible."

"Artillery would be out for sure," said David, "but men on foot could do it, and it would probably take the Rebels by surprise. I know a path up the west side near the north end. It's quite obscure, but if you want me to lead a detachment of men up that way, I would be happy to do it."

McClellan stroked his mustache thoughtfully. After a moment, he said, "I like the surprise idea, David, but most of my men aren't experienced in warfare. Since we're going to launch the attack at dawn tomorrow, they'd have to make the climb in the dark. I'd need them to be at the top so when our artillery finished its bombardment on the east side, they'd be ready to hit the Rebels from the west. If somehow the Rebels found out our men were coming up the west side, they'd be sitting ducks."

General Rosecrans said, "Excuse me, sir. I know it would be risky, but the unexpected sally from the west side could mean the difference between success or failure in this battle, especially since we have no idea how many troops are on Rich Mountain."

McClellan nodded slowly. "Yes, I wish we knew how many troops Garnett has." After a pause, he said, "I believe you're right, though. The element of surprise could make the difference. All right, we'll take the risk. General Rosecrans, you take your task force of nineteen hundred men and let David lead you up the west side of the mountain." Turning to Hart, he asked, "David, how long will it take that many men to make the climb up your obscure path?"

"I'd say about an hour, sir."

"And you're willing to take this risk of your own life?"

"Yes, sir. Since I can't be in your army, I'd sure like to do my part in this battle. If we can whip the Confederates here, maybe it'll be enough to make them give it up and lay down their arms. Maybe the war will start and end right here on Rich Mountain."

"The battle could get hot, son," McClellan said. "You know how to use a musket? We'll supply you with one if you do."

"Yes, sir. My brother and I have done a lot of hunting together. Pa has several Springfield muskets on the place."

"You don't mind using it if you're forced into a fight?"

"I've never killed a human being, sir, but war is war. I'll use it if I have to."

"All right," smiled the general. "Be here at three-thirty in the morning. You and General Rosecrans will lead his brigade up the mountain at four o'clock."

Just before dawn on the morning of July 11, 1861, Private Webster Steele stood at his cannon with Dooley Carson and Leroy Sheldon. They could barely make each other out in the dark. Heavy clouds had covered the sky during the night, and the scent of rain was in the air.

"Gonna be fun tryin' to kill Yankees in a downpour," mused Sheldon. "Be hard to see 'em."

"It'll be raining on us, too," said Web. "We'll be just as hard to see. Hardest thing is going to be keeping our powder dry."

"So what'll we do if it gets wet and we can't fire the cannon?" asked Dooley.

"Use our rifles," replied Web. "And if that powder gets wet, we'll have to use our bayonets."

Dooley shuddered. "Bayonets—I just don't think I can face bayonets."

"You may have to," said Sheldon. "If our powder gets wet, Yankee powder will be just as wet. This whole battle could be won or lost with bayonets, musket butts, and fists."

"You'll be all right, Dooley," said Web. "When a man gets his back to the wall, he can do a lot of things he didn't think he could."

"Hey!" came a hoarse whisper from the darkness to their right. "You guys ready for the fight?"

It was Daniel Hart. As his vague form drew up, Web said, "Yeah, we're ready. Just show me a bunch of Yankees, and I'll send them a cannonball for breakfast."

"You really think they'll come today?" asked Daniel.

"Colonel Pegram is convinced they will," Web said. "Of course he's going by the messages that have been coming from General

Garnett." When Web thought about who was delivering those messages, his stomach turned over.

The sound of hooves on dewy grass met their ears. Seconds later, Lieutenant Floyd Courtman rode up in the obscure gloom and said, "Colonel Pegram just got a report from one of our scouts that the blue-bellies are setting up artillery at the base of the mountain right in front of you. Military custom is to commence firing at dawn. We're going to beat them to it. Private Steele, I've given orders to the other cannon masters along the line to lob some balls over the edge and drop them down on top of their artillery. As you know, it's three hundred yards to the trees along the edge of the mountain at the bottom of that open field in front of you. I figure they have to be about fifty yards away from the base of the mountain to get their cannonballs up here. The slope makes the edge at the top about thirty yards inside the base line, so set your gun's range accordingly."

"Yes, sir," said Steele.

"I'll ride along the line and give orders for each gun to fire," Courtman continued. "Be ready in fifteen minutes. Load fast and fire two more shots at will. Maybe we can cut some of their fire power before they're ready to bombard us."

"We'll be ready, sir," Web assured him.

As the lieutenant rode back along the line, Daniel said, "Well, that answers my question. This is the day. I'd better get back to my cannon."

"Take care, Daniel."

"Will do. Nobody but me is going to marry the prettiest Ruffin sister."

"You've got that wrong again," Web chuckled. "I'm marrying the prettiest one."

Daniel walked away in the darkness, saying over his shoulder, "I think you need spectacles, old man!"

Web bent over the side of his cannon, placed the fingers of his left hand along the face of the range-finder, and turned the crank until the needle was on the proper mark. The muzzle of the cannon was now raised to the precise level for lobbing shells the distance Lieutenant Courtman had requested.

"You sure you've got it right?" asked Leroy.

"Are you kidding? I can aim this gun blindfolded."

"I guess that's almost what you did."

Web and Leroy could hear Dooley's heavy, unsteady breathing. Web found him in the gloom and put an arm around his shoulder. His body was trembling.

"Hey, c'mon now," Web said. "Leroy and I need you. You're our powder man. It won't do Leroy any good to drop balls down the muzzle and work the ramrod unless there's powder in the magazine. And I sure can't fire the thing unless both of you do your job."

Dooley swallowed hard. "Okay, Web. I'm sorry. It's just that—"

"I know, kid. Leroy and I are just as scared as you are. We're just better at covering it up."

"Really?"

"Yes, sir. Right, Leroy?"

"I'm probably more scared than the two of you put together," Leroy said. "My stomach is in my throat and my heart is in my stomach."

"Well, they say the waiting for battle is worse than the battle itself," said Web. "If that's true, our jitters are about to ease off."

At a quarter of five, a dull gray light appeared in the heavy clouds of the eastern sky. Leroy stood beside the cannon with two pyramids of cannonballs at his feet. The long ramrod leaned against the wheel that was blocked with rocks. Dooley, feeling better to know that his partners were also scared, was at the magazine with a full canister at his feet and the powder scoop in his hand. Web, allowing himself a private moment to think of Abby, had his hand on the lanyard. The gun was loaded and ready to fire.

"Get ready, boys," said Web, looking along the line to his right.

Lieutenant Floyd Courtman could be seen at the far end, astride his mount, and every cannon crew was on the alert.

Web tightened his grip on the lanyard when Courtman moved forward and the first cannon roared. Number two cannon fired five seconds later, and one by one the others followed suit. When Ed Cahill's cannon boomed, Web tensed. Five seconds later, Courtman was adjacent and commanded Web to fire. He jerked the lanyard and quickly covered his ears as the big gun roared. As soon as the sharp sound rode away across the airwaves, Dooley was packing powder in the magazine and Leroy was picking up a cannonball.

At the same instant number one gun let loose with its second shot, the sound of artillery was heard from below. Suddenly the east side of Rich Mountain was alive with whistling shells, explosions, and the roar of Confederate cannons along the line.

Realizing that the Yankees were firing back, Lieutenant Courtman rode along the line, shouting for the cannon crews to keep firing.

As the light in the heavy clouds grew brighter, the men at the cannons noticed a great number of footmen in gray uniforms collected behind them to the far left in the thick shadows of the dense forest. Colonel Pegram was with them. Everyone knew the artillery bombardment would last only for a while, then blue-uniformed soldiers would be coming up the path and across the open fields in front of them.

Most of the Union shells were landing short of the cannon line, digging small craters in the grass. However, two of them struck near cannons one and two, throwing dirt and rocks all over the crews and slowing them down momentarily. A third Yankee shell came down at the cannon just the other side of Cahill's and blew all three men into eternity.

Web turned to look when the shell hit, and was thankful it had not taken out Cahill's crew, which included Daniel Hart. He jerked the lanyard for the seventh time, covered his ears, then waited for Dooley and Leroy to reload. The clouds overhead were darkening and beginning to spit rain.

Just after he had fired shot number eight, Web noticed a horseman gallop up the path at the north end of the mountain and skid to a halt at the edge of the trees where Colonel Pegram was standing. It was Exley.

While Dooley was loading the magazine again, Web shouted above the thunder of cannons and shells, "Still scared, kid?"

"Yes!" nodded young Carson. "But I'm too busy to let it bother me!"

"Good! Then just keep busy!"

As Exley slid from the saddle, Colonel Pegram stepped up to meet him.

"Colonel!" Exley gasped excitedly. "General Garnett sent me to tell you that their morning started with a skirmish with the Yankees halfway up Laurel Mountain. It didn't last long, but two of our men captured a wounded Union sergeant. Before he would give the Yankee any medical help, General Garnett demanded to know the positions of all their brigades. Seems McClellan guessed that the larger number of our forces were situated here on Rich Mountain, so he sent the bulk of his troops against you. I had to ride hard to get past a huge bunch of them positioning themselves to come up the path. You already know they've got heavy artillery along the base of the mountain on the east side, but the Union sergeant also told General Garnett that there's a unit of about nineteen hundred men coming up behind you on the west! The general wanted you to know about it as soon as I could get here so you could prepare for them."

"Thank you," nodded Pegram. "I'll get right to work on it. Are you to return to Laurel?"

"The general wants to know if I got through, if possible, but he told me if it looked too dangerous to ride past the Yankee lines, I'd best stay here with you."

Exley had lied about having to ride hard past Union soldiers to make it up the mountain. He figured they would be coming up the path at some stage of the battle, but it appeared the bulk of them were going to attack from the east side once the artillery bombardment ceased. His lie would let him stay on Rich Mountain so he could get close to Web Steele when the land battle began and put a bullet in him.

"So you think it's too dangerous?" asked Pegram.

"Yes, sir," Exley lied again. "If I tried it, I'd be a dead man."

"Okay. Do this for me. Ride to Lieutenant Courtman at the far end of the cannon line and tell him about the Yankee unit that's coming up the west side. Better stay in the timber for protection. Those Union shells are hitting close to the cannons. Tell Courtman I'll send some men to help protect the backs of the men on the cannons while I send more to meet the blue-bellies head-on."

"Yes, sir," said Exley, mounting his horse.

"When you've done that," said the colonel, "come back here and you can join one of the units for the battle that's coming."

Exley nodded tightly and gouged the horse's sides. As he worked his way along the edge of the open area just inside the timber, he set hard eyes on Web Steele. The big guns continued to thunder and Union cannonballs were hitting dangerously close to Web's end of the line.

At a quarter of five that morning, General William Rosecrans and his brigade were slowly winding their way up the west side of Rich Mountain, following David Hart. Men kept stumbling and cursing in the long line. At the head of the column, General Rosecrans was on Hart's heels. "Sure smells like rain," he said, projecting his voice so Hart could hear him above the sound of hundreds of feet tramping on dirt and small rocks.

"Wouldn't surprise me if it came a downpour any minute," David said over his shoulder. "That would make this fight we're about to get into a whole lot harder, wouldn't it?"

"Yes. I don't fancy having to carry out this bloody chore in the midst of a rainstorm. How much farther to the top?"

"Not too far, now. Another ten minutes or so."

"Good. We'll push into the woods once we're on top and wait till dawn. Then I'll send a couple of men to scout out the Reb camp and where they positioned themselves. I've been thinking, Hart..."

"Yes, sir?"

"Maybe you ought to get us on top, then head back down. Once we're close to the enemy, we won't need you any—"

The general's words were cut off by the thunder of big guns, firing about five seconds apart. Stiffening, he lifted his face toward the crest of the mountain and said, "Looks like the battle's started. Those have to be Confederate guns."

"Too close to be ours," David said.

There was a buzzing amongst the men in the column as they discussed the sudden sound of cannons.

"Hold up a minute, Hart," commanded Rosecrans. Turning to the closest men behind him, he said, "Sheffield...Manley..."

"Yes, sir," came the two voices in unison.

"Let Hart take you up to the top while we wait here. See what you can learn about what's happening. Don't take too long. If there's a chance we can be even more of a surprise, I want to know it."

"C'mon," David said to the two soldiers. "Stay close on my heels." Within seconds they had disappeared in the thick gloom."

The general told the men to pass the word along that they would halt while a reconnaissance mission was being carried out.

The Confederate cannons continued to roar for several minutes, then suddenly the distinct sound of exploding cannonballs met their ears. "Our artillery is answering back," Rosecrans said to the men just behind him. "Looks like we've got us a good fight going already."

The unseen battle raged as the Yankees waited for Hart, Sheffield, and Manley to return. The fierce discharges of artillery and the thunder of shells were incessant as the heavy-laden sky began to lighten.

Nearly a half hour had passed when the reconnaissance team became visible among the trees above them. Breathing hard as they descended the rugged path, they soon drew up, with Sheffield saying, "General, the Rebs are thick in the woods up there. We couldn't get close enough to the artillery to see how many cannons they have, but it sounds like they've got quite a few. They've got their horses and mules in a rope corral maybe sixty yards from this side of the mountain."

"We could make out their tents just past the corral, sir," said Manley. "Can't tell how many. They stretch out quite a ways. We could only see so far. The forest is quite thick up there."

The general spoke to Sheffield. "When you say the Rebs are thick up there, how are they situated?"

"Hard to tell how they're spread out over the mountain, sir, but at this end, we could tell there's a big bunch of them huddled and waiting for the ground battle."

"Can we get this unit on top without being spotted, you think?"

"If we stay low and deep in the woods, I think so, sir. Probably be best if we go up behind the rope corral. Once we're up there and get more light, we can make our surprise move."

Rosecrans looked skyward. "We're not going to get a whole lot of light the way it looks up there, but I think we'll wait till we get more than we have right now. We need to be able to see what we're doing. Once we reach the ridge, we'll go the rest of the way on our bellies."

It was beginning to rain.

Just after the break of dawn that same morning, a muscular black man waited at the parlor window inside the David Hart home in Beverly. His heart quickened when he saw Chloe Hart returning on the run, holding her skirts calf-high. The thunder of the artillery battle going on at nearby Rich Mountain made the house tremble.

When Chloe stepped up on the porch, the black man moved through the door to meet her. Breathing hard, she said, "Like I thought, Mandrake, I didn't have to climb the path on Laurel very far till Rebel sentries told me to halt and identify myself. I told them I was a resident of Beverly, and that I had heard that Private Reed Exley was attached to Colonel Pegram's unit. The information the enlistment office in Harper's Ferry gave you is correct. He is."

"Good!" exclaimed Mandrake. "So you tol' the sentries you heard Exley's wife had died...that Miz 'Lizbeth was a good frien' of yours, and that you wanted to talk to Exley to fin' out if'n it was true?"

"Yes," nodded Chloe. "And I appreciate your telling me about Elizabeth's death. She and I were good friends." Her face took on a look of granite as she added, "I despised that husband of hers from the day I met him, but I despise him more since you told me he caused her death...and Orchid's...and Web Steele's, too. Poor Abby."

"Jus' 'bout ever'body who knows that rat despises 'im, Miz Chloe. Did the sentries tell you which mountain he's on?"

"He's a messenger between General Garnett on Laurel Mountain and Colonel Pegram on Rich Mountain. He's back and forth on horse-back."

"Are the sentries gonna tell Exley you want to see 'im?"

"They said they would whenever they got a chance, but who knows if that'll happen now that the fighting has started."

"Yo' right. Guess the only choice I got is to sneak my way on top o' one of them mountains and try to get close enough to shoot 'im."

Chloe looked down at the revolver under Mandrake's belt. "I...I guess I have to look at this as war, right? I mean, it's not murder. David and I are on the Union side. If I'm helping you to take out a Confederate soldier during a battle, it's the way of war, isn't it?"

Mandrake smiled. "Yaz'm. You jus' keep that in mind, Miz Chloe. This is war, all right." Turning toward the edge of the porch, he said, "I'll jus' leave my horse out back with yo's, Miz Chloe, if that's all right. I can sneak up a mountain better bein' on foot."

"Of course," replied Chloe, reaching out and patting his arm. "I'll see you when you get back."

"Thank you, ma'am. An' if I don' come back, it's all right, too. My chances of killin' Exley and gettin' away without bein' shot is purty slim. But don' grieve fo' me if'n it happens. With Orchid gone, I got nuthin' to live fo' anyway."

With that, Mandrake was off, hurrying toward the road that ran between Laurel and Rich Mountains. He had hardly reached the road when he saw a rider in gray galloping toward him from the direction of Laurel Mountain.

Mandrake plunged into the brush alongside the road and ducked down. When the rider thundered by, Mandrake's jaw went slack and his eyes bulged. The rider was Reed Exley!

The hammering of the battle on Rich Mountain was heavy in Mandrake's ears. Exley was headed there, and the vengeful black man would follow.

CHAPTER TWENTY-TWO

The incessant roar of artillery vexed the cloudy morning as the battle raged.

The rain was still at the spitting stage two hours after the Confederate batteries had first unleashed their barrage on the Yankees at the east base of Rich Mountain. Two other cannon crews along the line had been hit. Three men lay sprawled on the wet grass, and the other three had been taken to the camp in the woods for medical attention.

Web Steele and his crew were keeping the barrel of their cannon hot as they continued to lob shells over the edge of the mountain. Web could tell there weren't as many Union cannons firing as there had been at the beginning, but the fusillade was still plenty heavy.

The thunder of artillery rolled across the top of the mountain, punctuated continually with the shriek of shells, followed by deafening explosions and the horrid humming of their dangerous fragments. Four times, shells had landed close to Steele and his crew, but so far they had escaped being hit.

The moist air was filled with the flash of fire from cannon muzzles and shell explosions, and wreaths of smoke drifted with the morning breeze. At one point, Web caught sight of Reed Exley galloping back to where Colonel Pegram and his infantry waited for the land battle that was sure to come. Leroy Sheldon pulled the ramrod from the barrel of the cannon and yelled, "Ready!"

Web jerked the lanyard while keeping his eyes on Exley, and spit.

Suddenly a Yankee shell screamed over their heads and exploded as it struck the trees behind them. Wood and shrapnel went every direction as a flash of fire sent up billows of smoke.

"That one just about took my cap off!" shouted Dooley Carson.

"Better duck next time!" Web shouted back.

While his men were reloading, Web saw Lieutenant Floyd Courtman riding hard along the rear of the cannon line. Suddenly a Yankee shell whined shrilly and struck some ten or twelve feet ahead of his mount. The concussion rocked the area, and shattered bits of cannonball struck horse and rider. The animal took it in the face and peeled over head-first. Courtman sailed forward and landed like a rag doll on the smoking spot where the shell had hit. He was directly behind Ed Cahill's cannon, a distance of about sixty feet.

Cahill yanked his lanyard and shouted at Daniel Hart to see about Courtman. Daniel wheeled and ran toward the fallen officer. Just as he knelt beside him, a shell slammed Cahill's cannon, blowing Cahill and his other helper to fragments.

The concussion slammed Dooley against his cannon and staggered Web. Sheldon was leaning over his diminishing stack of cannonballs and barely felt the shock.

Just as Web righted himself, Dooley rolled against the big gun and looked at the carnage around Cahill's broken cannon. The sight pulled a wail of terror from his mouth. His whole body shook as he looked on with fists clenched. He stood there, wailing over and over in a paroxysm of blind horror. Quickly, Web grabbed his shoulder, spun him around and slapped him. The wailing stopped instantly. Dooley's bulging eyes focused on Steele as his hand went to the burning spot on his cheek.

Grasping both shoulders hard, Web said, "Get a grip on yourself, Dooley!"

The freckle-faced youth blinked and went limp. Looking at Sheldon, Web said, "Talk to him, Leroy. I've got to check on the lieutenant."

Dashing to Daniel Hart and the unconscious Courtman, Web found Daniel weeping. Courtman had taken shrapnel in his chest, arms, and face. Though he was bleeding and his shirt was tattered, none of the metal pieces seemed to have gone deep enough to threaten his life.

Tears streamed down Daniel's face as he sobbed, "Why was I spared, Web? If that shell had hit ten seconds sooner, I'd have been killed, too!"

Web saw Courtman's horse lying on the ground, neighing in pain. To Daniel he said, "I'll carry him back to the camp. Take my musket and put that horse out of its misery, will you?"

As young Hart was rising to his feet, wiping tears, Web turned and shouted, "Leroy! You and Dooley fire the cannon where I've got it aimed! I'll be back in a few minutes!"

Suddenly there was an eruption of gunfire deep in the woods to the west. Web looked that way and said, "Daniel, now that those Yankees have topped the mountain back there, it won't be safe for the lieutenant in the camp. There's no place really safe, so let's just lay him here next to his horse."

Running to his cannon, which Leroy had just fired, Web snatched up his musket and raced for the wounded horse. Aiming the gun at its head, he cocked the hammer and squeezed the trigger. Rushing back to Daniel, he said, "Go help my guys reload. I'll be there in a minute."

Web carried Lieutenant Courtman to the dead horse and laid him as close to the animal's back as possible. Courtman was starting to come around, but Web couldn't wait. He had to get back to his gun. He would get help for the lieutenant as soon as possible.

He was halfway back to the cannon when the sky seemed to open up and a torrent of rain came down. When he reached Daniel and his men, he cried, "We'll keep firing until it's impossible! Dooley, are you all right?"

"I'm okay, Web," replied Dooley, blinking rain from his eyes. "Thanks for popping me one. I needed it."

Web was about to tell Daniel to go back and see to Lieutenant Courtman when it suddenly struck him that there was no more artillery fire coming from the Union guns. "They've given up already on firing their cannons," he said to the others. "I've an idea we'll see infantry any second."

The musketry was going strong in the timber. Web and his companions looked back that way, then their heads jerked around as shouts met their ears from the east ridge. Hundreds of Yankees were emerging from the trees and running onto the open field. They looked like ants coming out of a giant anthill.

Turning to Sheldon, Web asked, "Is the gun loaded?"

"Ready to fire!"

Wiping rain from his eyes, Web stepped to his big gun. As he turned the crank to lower the muzzle, he heard three of the cannons along the line open up. The shells screamed down the grassy slope. None of them reached the front line of men-in-blue, but their explosions sent many of them scattering.

When he had the range-finder at the right spot, Web yanked the lanyard. The twenty-four pounder belched fire and smoke as it roared. Seconds later, the shell dropped into the front line and blew Yankee soldiers in every direction.

The three men beside him let out a whoop.

"Quick!" said Steele. "Load it again before the rain douses the powder."

As Sheldon and Carson hopped to it, Web turned to Hart and said, "Go check on the lieutenant, will you? Maybe the rain has revived him. See what you can do to stop the bleeding."

Daniel was turning to go when there were wild shouts and whoops coming from the south end of the mountain. Through the falling rain, they saw countless blue uniforms swarming out of the timber. Just as abruptly, musket fire came from the forest to the west, and the Yankees began to fall. Men-in-gray charged at them, and the land battle was under way.

At the same time, their attention was drawn to the north, where Union soldiers were sallying up the path by the hundreds. Again, Confederate muskets opened fire. The Battle of Rich Mountain was in full force.

Daniel said, "Web, I don't have a gun. My musket went up when my cannon was hit."

"Use the lieutenant's revolver. Get down beside that horse and do everything you can to protect him."

Daniel ran toward the fallen officer. Returning to his cannon, Web turned the crank to meet the front line of Yankees, which was getting closer, and fired. The shell whined down the slope and landed in the middle of a tight-knit bunch.

Dooley said, "Web, the rain's gotten into the magazine—we can't fire the gun any more!"

A swarm of Confederate infantrymen bowled out of the timber behind Web and his men, running past them to meet the oncoming charge.

"Okay, boys!" he cried. "We're down to our muskets now! Do all you can to keep your powder dry."

The cannon crew had dug out a spot next to the big gun when they were stabilizing it. Dashing into it, they flattened out. While Web was reloading his musket, Dooley said, "None of 'em are in rifle range yet!"

"They will be soon. Be ready!"

All across the top of Rich Mountain, the thundering roll of musketry was deafening. Shouts, loud commands, and screams of dying men were barely heard in the din.

Soon the rain let up, but the fighting only intensified. Within an hour, there was no rain at all, but the sky remained cloudy and threatening.

The battle raged. Soon there was a long line of infantrymen stretched out on both sides of Web and his partners. Web kept an eye on Daniel and the lieutenant, but so far no one had gotten near them. Also of concern was Dooley. He was firing and reloading as fast as he could, but his face was showing the strain. Web knew that even if Dooley held himself together under gunfire, it was liable to change quickly if the fight got down to bayonets.

Blue-white smoke drifted across Rich Mountain like a heavy fog. The acrid smell of burnt gunpowder hung in the air.

From his prone position with Carson on his right and Sheldon on his left, Web brought down three Yankees with five shots. Bullets were chewing ground all around them and whizzing over their heads like angry hornets. More Yankees were coming over the eastern edge of the mountain.

Leroy had just fired a shot and was reloading when a bullet hissed and struck him between the eyes. He fell back, dead. Dooley saw it and began to sob.

"Nothing we can do for him, kid," Web said levelly. "Don't panic. You've got to keep firing."

Leroy had often spoken of a girl named Bonnie Sue. She was waiting for him back home in eastern Virginia. Web wondered how long it would be before Bonnie Sue would learn that the man she was waiting for was dead. His mind flashed to Abby. No doubt she thought he had died in the fire. God willing, he thought, I'll go home to her someday when this is over.

When the rain stopped, David Hart was in the woods with a Yankee corporal named Jimmy Dyer. General Rosecrans had assigned Dyer to stay with David and do what he could to keep him alive. The general didn't want the death of a civilian on his conscience if it could be avoided.

Packing the musket he had been issued, David was crawling with Dyer toward the edge of the woods on the east side. Gunfire was all around them.

When they reached a spot about twenty yards from the open field, they beheld the raging, bloody battle with awe. Presently, Dyer focused on two men in gray who were lying low behind a dead horse not more than sixty feet from the edge of the trees. One man was flat on his back. The other was up on one elbow with his back toward the woods, tending to him.

"Looks like we got one Reb taking care of another," Dyer said in a low voice. "Since it's my job to kill Southerners, this one gets it right now." As he spoke, the corporal cocked his musket and took aim.

"You're not going to shoot him in the back, are you?" asked David, feeling his stomach go cold.

"What do you want me to do? Shake hands with him?"

"No, but it's hard for me to see a man get shot in the back."

"Bet he'd do it to me," said Dyer, and squeezed the trigger.

The Confederate soldier spasmed at the impact of the bullet, arching his back. His cap fell off as he rolled over, exposing his face. David focused on the familiar features in choked-off silence. His hands palsied as he threw them to his cheeks. He found his voice and scrambled to his feet, gasping, "It's my brother! It's my brother! You shot my brother!"

Stunned at what he was hearing, Dyer leaped up as David bolted out of the trees, crying, "Daniel! Daniel!"

Bullets were splitting the air all around. Dyer darted to the edge of the timber and shouted, "Hart, come back here!"

At that instant, a Yankee bullet struck Dyer in the heart. The impact knocked him down. His right foot trembled for a few seconds before he died.

Daniel looked up with languid eyes as David knelt beside him. Lieutenant Courtman had been conscious earlier, but had passed out again shortly before Daniel was shot.

"Daniel!" sobbed David, noting that the bullet had passed through his brother's body and exited his chest. Blood was spreading over the front of his sweaty shirt.

Daniel gritted his teeth in pain, set his dull eyes on David and worked his jaw, trying to speak.

"Daniel! Oh, Daniel, I'm so sorry! I didn't know it was you!" cried David.

Daniel licked his lips, worked his jaw again, and mumbled softly, "I...I didn't know you had joined the Union army, David. Many...many brothers will kill each other in this war."

"No, Daniel! It wasn't me who shot you! It was—Daniel! Daniel!"

Daniel's eyes stared vacantly into space. His breathing had stopped.

David held Daniel in his arms and wailed, "I didn't kill you! I didn't kill you! Daniel, don't die thinking I shot you!"

Web fired a shot and lay on his side to reload his musket. Bullets were flying all around. Through the blue-white smoke, he saw David Hart holding Daniel next to the dead horse. Shocked to see David, Web shouted, "David! Get down! Get down!"

But David did not hear him for the thunder of the gunfire and the sound of his own wailing.

Laying his musket down, Web shouted above the din to Dooley, "I'll be right back!"

Dooley started to ask where he was going, but Web was already darting away. Diving flat as he reached the spot, Steele took one look at Daniel's vacant eyes and knew he was gone. David's face was dirty and streaked with tears. He stopped wailing when he recognized his old friend and shuddered, "Web, Daniel's dead. He thought I shot him. I didn't, Web! I didn't shoot him!"

"What are you doing here, David?" asked Steele. "You're not in uniform!"

"I only led a unit of Yankees up the back side of the mountain, Web. I'm not in the army."

Taking hold of David's arm, Web said, "C'mon, let's get you back into the trees. You'll be safer there."

"Not without Daniel!" David shouted.

There wasn't time to argue. "All right. Pick him up. But hurry."

The shock David was feeling had sapped his strength. Web took the limp form from him and said, "Head for the trees!"

David staggered ahead of Web, noting the body of Corporal Dyer as he passed. Once they were deep in the timber, Web laid Daniel's body down beside a fallen tree and said, "David, get down next to the tree and stay there till this battle is over."

Just as he was about to head back to his post, Web looked up to see a lone Yankee soldier taking aim at him from behind a tree. He dived for the ground in the nick of time as the bullet whizzed over his head. Rolling over and gaining his feet, he saw the Yankee charging at him with his bayonet. Web feinted as if he would leap to the right, then quickly moved left as the man-in-blue sailed past him. The Yankee cursed, pivoted quickly, and came at him again. Web spotted a broken tree limb about five feet in length lying near his feet. He snatched it up, sidestepped the charging enemy again, and cracked him on the back of the head.

The Yankee stumbled and fell. Web grabbed the musket from the man's hands and rammed the bayonet through his heart. Dashing back to David, Web told him again to stay put, and ran to his post.

The battle raged on. By three in the afternoon, Web, Dooley, Wiley Chance, and Billy Bob Hankins had moved back into the edge of the timber and were firing from a shallow draw. Dead men in blue and gray were scattered all over the open field and in the deep shade of the forest.

While Web and his companions were defending their position, Exley crept through the timber, carrying a Navy Colt .45 he had taken from a dead Union officer. He had spotted Web in the shallow draw only moments before. When he was within fifty feet to the rear of them, he wriggled into the midst of a stand of heavy brush and waited. When his opportunity came, Web would get a bullet in the back.

Steele, Carson, Chance, and Hankins had been firing from the draw for over an hour when Chance noticed six Yankees bolt from the trees to their far right, muskets blazing. He had just loaded his own gun. Swinging it on them, he fired and shouted to his companions.

One of the charging Yankees went down, but so did Chance with two slugs in his chest. Billy Bob Hankins took a bullet in the midsection, but was able to fire and drop one of the men-in-blue before he fell.

Angry bullets buzzed by Steele and Carson, one of them coming so close to Steele's right ear that he felt its hot breath. Both of them pivoted to meet the four Yankees who were coming on the run, bayonets gleaming. Dooley Carson focused on the hungry bayonets and his whole body seemed to freeze.

Web fired his gun and braced himself for the onslaught. His bullet took out one Yankee, who fell flat on his face. The other three had blood in their eyes. Two went for Steele, leaving the other one to take out Carson.

Suddenly Dooley found his courage and shot one of the two men bearing down on Web. Then he swung his bayonet on the

Yankee coming at him, but the man dodged it and rammed his sharp blade into Dooley's left side. Dooley cried out and fell when the man jerked the bayonet out. He was about to finish Dooley off when he saw that his partner was in trouble. Steele had knocked him down with the butt of his musket and was about to plunge his bayonet into him.

Carson's man wheeled and bolted toward Web, bayonet poised for his back. Dooley cried, "Web! Look out!"

Web spun around to meet his attacker, parrying the bayonet thrust with his musket. Both men fought for survival, bayonets and musket butts swinging.

Gripping his bleeding side, Dooley struggled to his feet, eyes fixed on the other Yankee, who was getting up with musket in hand. Web's back was toward him, and the resolve in his eyes was obvious. He would end the fight by plunging his bayonet into the Rebel's back. The determined Yankee was moving toward Web, bayonet thrust forward. Ignoring his pain, Dooley dashed past the two combatants and threw himself between Web and the deadly bayonet.

Web had just killed the other Yankee and was turning about when he saw the cold steel of the Union bayonet being rammed full-haft into Dooley's chest. He knew what the freckle-faced kid had done. Moving quickly, Web thrust his bayonet into the Yankee's throat. The man emitted a gurgling scream and collapsed.

Dooley fell with the bayonet still buried in him. Breathing hard and oblivious to the roar of the battle around him, Steele dropped his gun, took hold of the Yankee musket, and pulled the bayonet from Dooley's chest. Tears gushed from Web's eyes as he knelt beside Dooley's lifeless form.

In the midst of the fire, smoke, and thunder of the battle, Mandrake crawled through the dense forest, his black skin blending with the deep shadows. His heart was pounding. Only moments before, good fortune had smiled upon him. He knew the odds of finding Reed Exley amid the battle were slim, but he had only one purpose left in life. Even the heavy rain that had fallen earlier, obscuring visibility on top of the mountain, had not deterred him. The search went on even though he knew that a stray bullet might find him at any moment, or some soldier on either side might mistake him for the enemy and gun him down.

Then, just moments before, Mandrake had spotted Exley. He was alone, working his way amongst the trees as if he had some destination in mind. Mandrake followed, but was forced into hiding when a small unit of Rebel soldiers came charging his way. When they were gone, Mandrake took up the pursuit again, but had lost sight of Exley.

Crawling persistently with the revolver in his hand, Mandrake maintained a set course, aiming the same direction Exley had gone. He would find him and kill him, or lose his own life in the attempt.

Mandrake was inching his way through the timber near the edge of the open field, where most of the battle was concentrated, when his attention was drawn to a hand-to-hand battle taking place in a shallow draw some thirty yards ahead. At first, he could not believe what his eyes were telling him. One of the fighting Rebels looked exactly like Web Steele. But it couldn't be! Massa Web was dead.

To get a better view, Mandrake crawled closer and positioned himself in a stand of heavy brush. The gunfire all around him was deafening as once again he set his gaze on the nearby fight and the man who so strongly resembled Web Steele.

Cold chills went all over him. It was Web! He had not died in the prison fire as Jedidiah had mistakenly told him! *Massa Web is alive!* The shock paralyzed the black man. He wanted to rush in and help his friend, but he could not make himself move.

Mandrake watched as Steele and a boyish Rebel were engaged in a life-and-death struggle with two Yankees. Just then he saw movement in the clump of brush next to him. He peered through the maze of thin branches and saw the form of a man. The man raised up, exposing his gray-capped head. Though Mandrake was lying below him, and a bit to his rear, he recognized Reed Exley.

The deafening sound of battle assaulted Exley's ears as he hunkered in the clump of brush and watched the hand-to-hand battle. He hoped the Yankees would kill Web and save him the trouble. He would like the pleasure of sending the hated man into eternity, but the main thing was to see him dead and out of the way. Exley would then have Abby for himself.

Exley was disappointed when the last of the Yankees in the draw went down. Web Steele was still alive. Swearing under his breath as Web knelt beside the young Rebel who had taken a bayonet for him, Exley eased back the hammer of his revolver. Steele's broad back was conveniently turned toward him.

Quickly Exley raised his head above the top of the bushes and looked around. The battle was still going strong all over the mountain, but no one was looking his direction. He would shoot Steele and let them think a Yankee did it. Exley grinned and drew a careful bead at a spot between Web's shoulder blades. His heart pounded with excitement as he took a deep breath, held it, and placed his forefinger on the trigger.

Web knelt over Dooley and said with quivering lips, "You took the thing you feared most to save my life. God bless you, Dooley. You're a hero, my friend—a real hero."

Though the sound of muskets continued on the open field, Web's attention was abruptly captured by the discharge of a handgun behind him. He whipped around to see a black man rising to his feet beside a stand of brush, holding a smoking revolver. He was stunned to see a Negro on the mountain at all, but when he recognized Mandrake, he was doubly stunned. He thumbed away tears and rose to his feet, so caught up in seeing Mandrake that he forgot the danger.

Suddenly two Union soldiers burst from the woods off to Mandrake's left, firing at Web Steele. One bullet hissed past Web's hip, but the other one struck him in the right leg.

Mandrake spun around. Cocking his revolver, he raised it and fired, hitting the Yankee closest to him. When the other one veered his direction with a wild yell, aiming his bayonet at him, Mandrake snapped back the hammer and shot him point-blank in the heart.

Mandrake ran to Web and found him in a half-sitting position, gripping his wounded leg above the knee. Blood was running between his fingers.

"Massa Web!" gasped Mandrake. "Is it bad?"

Gritting his teeth, Web replied, "I think the slug hit the bone and broke it, but I'll live. What are you doing here?"

"I came to find Reed Exley and kill him, Massa Web," said the muscular black man. "C'mon. Let me he'p you get back in the woods, where it'll be a li'l safer."

"You came up on this mountain to kill Reed Exley?"

"Yassuh," said Mandrake, picking Steele up in his arms, "an' I done it, too."

"You did?"

"Yassuh," Mandrake responded, carrying his wounded friend toward the thick stand of brush where Web had first spotted him.

"When?" queried Steele, still gripping the wounded leg.

"Jus' befo' you saw me. Exley was hidin' right here in these bushes, and was 'bout to shoot you in the back when I saw 'im."

Mandrake placed Web on the ground beside the heavy bush where Reed Exley's body lay half-supported by branches. His legs were still hung up inside the bush, but his torso was bent chest-up, with his head touching the ground. Web could see that Exley had been shot through the head from behind at close range. The cocked Navy Colt was still in Exley's right hand.

"That's twice my life has been saved today, Mandrake," Web told him with a quiver in his voice. "Thank you."

"No need to thank me, Massa Web," the black man said humbly. "As I tol' you, I was gonna kill him anyway. 'Course when I seen that he was aimin' to shoot you, it made it even easier. Now, let's see 'bout stoppin' this bleedin' in yo' leg."

Mandrake used a dead Yankee's belt to make a tourniquet, then tore up the man's shirt to use as a bandage. While he did, he asked Web how he escaped the prison fire and ended up in uniform on top of Rich Mountain. After Web had explained it all, Mandrake described what he had been told by Jedidiah, which confirmed that everyone at home thought he had died in the fire. Web was elated to learn of Hec Wheeler's confession, and that he had been cleared of the murder charge.

As the sun lowered toward the west, the sounds of battle began to dwindle. Web asked Mandrake why he was so intent on killing Exley that he would follow him all the way to Rich Mountain. Mandrake wept and told him of Orchid's death at Harper's Ferry, saying that without her, life had no meaning. The only thing he lived for from the moment Horatio Clements informed him of Orchid's death was to kill the man responsible.

Gritting his teeth in pain, Web asked, "So what now?"

Mandrake's eyes misted. "Well, Massa Web, I'd have somethin' to live fo' if'n you'd let me be yo' willin' slave."

"First thing we've got to do is get out of this situation alive," groaned Steele. "Then we'll make our plans. One thing, though..."

"Yassuh?"

"How about if we call you my servant instead of my slave, and I pay you wages?"

"I'll leave that up to you, Massa Web. I jus' wan' to serve you an' Miz Abby fo' the res' o' my days. An' don' you worry none. I'll get both of us off this here mountain so's we can get you an' that beautiful lady back togethuh."

CHAPTER TWENTY-THREE

As the sun went down over Rich Mountain, the fighting began to diminish. By dusk, no more gunfire could be heard.

Colonel John Pegram knew that he and his troops were hopelessly outnumbered. They would never survive another day of battling General George McClellan's forces. Though the gallant Confederates had killed and wounded a great number of the enemy, they had sustained the greater losses.

Even before it was completely dark, Pegram had wagons on the move, picking up as many wounded Rebels as possible. They would slip off the mountain under cover of darkness and join General Robert Garnett at Laurel Mountain.

Lieutenant Floyd Courtman was picked up still alive, along with David Hart, who insisted on taking Daniel's body with him. Though Hart had aided the Union, they would allow him to return to his home in Beverly unmolested because his brother had died fighting as a Confederate soldier.

Some time later, another wagon picked up Private Webster Steele. Mandrake refused to leave Web and was allowed to go along. They gathered some other wounded men, and made it off Rich Mountain without being detected by Union soldiers.

Concerned for the lives of his wounded men, Pegram immediately sent the wagons southeastward to the town of Mt. Meridian on the Shenandoah River. The colonel knew Mt. Meridian had a small hospital. Union sympathizers were scarce in the town. His wounded men would be welcomed and given proper medical attention.

During the night ride to Mt. Meridian, Web—with his faithful servant beside him—was able to learn from one of the wagon drivers that David Hart had been allowed to go home to Beverly and take Daniel's body with him. Web wondered if David would attempt to let his parents and Lynne Ruffin know of Daniel's death. There was no telling how long it might be before the Confederate government would be able to advise families of those killed or wounded in action. Web's heart went out to Lynne. The news of Daniel's death—whenever it reached her—would hit her hard. It would be tough on Daniel's parents also. Web hoped that somehow Daniel's death would draw David and his parents back together.

Unable to sleep because of the jostling of the wagon and the pain, Web leaned on Mandrake's shoulder and thought about Abby. Was he wounded bad enough that the army would discharge him? Or would they patch him up and send him back into the war? How long would the war last? When would he see Abby again? These were questions no one could answer.

Colonel Pegram found Laurel Mountain virtually inaccessible because of the great number of Union troops in the area. Not knowing how the battle had gone at Laurel Mountain, nor having any way to communicate with General Garnett, Pegram had no choice but to pull what was left of his unit out of the region before dawn. He hated to leave his dead men on top of the mountain, but he had no choice. To stay till morning and face McClellan's huge force would produce only more dead men.

At dawn on July 12, General William Rosecrans found that the Confederate troops had abandoned their position on Rich Mountain without alerting his weary men on night guard duty. The enemy's whereabouts could not be discovered.

On Laurel Mountain, General Garnett's scouts soon reported the situation. Learning that Pegram had taken his men and fled into the night, Garnett knew his position was desperate. He had suffered the loss of many men in the previous day's battle. The decision was made to abandon Laurel Mountain immediately.

They had been off the mountain for only a short time, marching hastily northeastward, when General McClellan learned of it. Quickly he sent Brigadier General Thomas Morris and his brigade in pursuit.

The next morning Morris's brigade caught up with Garnett and his troops at Carrick's Ford on the Cheat River, some thirty miles from Rich Mountain. The Confederates fought hard, but lack of ammunition left them vulnerable. In the brief encounter that took place, General Garnett was shot and killed.

Because Garnett was the first Civil War general to be killed in action, and because of the way the Union army had put the Confederates to flight, the Battle of Rich Mountain constituted a victory for the federal forces. General McClellan was summoned to Washington by President Lincoln and commissioned as Supreme Commander of the Union Army.

Northern newspapers took advantage of the Union victory to heap indignities on the South, which gave Northern citizens something to cheer about. It also gave them the elated notion that the Confederates were unable to withstand Union military might, and with the war movement getting into full swing, the Confederacy would soon be defeated.

However, on July 21, the Union army suffered a much worse defeat in a bloody battle on Bull Run Creek near Manassas Junction. The Bull Run rout changed the tune of Northern newspapers, which admitted in print that it was going to be a long war, after all.

Private Webster Steele was treated at the Mt. Meridian hospital, along with the other Confederate soldiers who had been wounded at Rich Mountain. Medical doctors in sympathy with the Confederacy were called in from several surrounding towns.

Surgery was performed on Web's leg to remove bone splinters. Because the bone was shattered, he was advised by army officials that when he was ready to travel for home, he would be released from the army. His doctors said Web would walk again, but he would limp for the rest of his life.

During Web's recovery, Mandrake stayed at his side day and night. Through Southern newspapers and *Harper's Weekly* magazine, Web kept up with the progress of the war. After the Bull Run battle, there were numerous minor battles and skirmishes between the opposing forces. Everyone knew another big battle was due, but no one could predict where it might happen.

On August 17, Web's doctors released him. He was discharged from the Confederate army at Harper's Ferry on August 20 and put on a military train for Richmond that same day. With Mandrake on the seat beside him, he could hardly hold back the tears for the elation within him. Tomorrow he would hold Abby in his arms.

It was late morning on Wednesday, August 21, 1861, when Charles opened the front door of the Ruffin mansion in response to the sound of the knocker. Only a breathless gasp came from the butler when first he set eyes on the man on crutches.

Smiling, Web said, "Hello, Charles. How are you?"

"I...I'm fine, Mister Web," the butler was finally able to get out. "I'm...just shocked to see you. I...I thought—"

"That I was dead? In the prison fire?"

"Yes, sir. That's what we all thought. But allow me to say, I am certainly happy to see you alive!" Then looking at Mandrake, the butler said with a smile, "Jedidiah told us you had gone north, Mandrake."

"Yassuh. I thought Massa Web was dead too, by what Jedidiah tol' me. Was only the han' of the Lord that put me where he was so's we could meet up again. I sho' was mighty glad to fin' him alive."

"Have you seen your parents yet, Mister Web?" asked Charles.

"Yes. I stopped at my parents' place. Needless to say, they were both shocked and pleased."

"Yes, sir," said Charles.

"Is Miss Abby at home?" queried Web, his throat tightening.

"Yes, sir," nodded the butler. "She's up in her room at the moment. She's...uh...she's not been too well, Mister Web."

Web's face blanched. "She's sick? How bad?"

Charles put his hand to his forehead. "Oh, please forgive me, Mister Web. Here I am, making you stand at the door. Please come in. You too, Mandrake."

Charles closed the door behind them, then with Web hobbling on his crutches, he led them to the receiving area, where the broad staircase wound upward. Pointing to a small couch, the butler asked, "Would you like to sit down, Mister Web?"

"Not at the moment, thank you. Right now I want to know about Miss Abby's illness."

"Well, sir, it's—"

At that instant, John Ruffin appeared, having come from the library, and gasped, "Web!"

Ruffin rushed to the wounded man and embraced him. Then with tears on his cheeks, he asked how Web had escaped the prison fire and how he had hurt his leg.

Web said, "I'll explain it all to you in a moment, Papa John, but first I want to know about Abby's illness."

"Illness?" echoed John, his brow furrowing. "What are you talking about?"

"Charles said she has not been well."

"Please allow me to explain," spoke up the butler. "What I meant was that Miss Abby has been having an awful time accepting your...death. She is not ill physically. I meant that she's not been too well emotionally." A grin spread over his face. "But she'll get well in a hurry now."

John laid a hand on Web's shoulder and said, "Abby's had such a hard time of it, Web. I knew she loved you, but I guess I never knew how much. There've been all kinds of young men here with intentions of courting her, but she won't even see them."

Web smiled. A promise unbroken, he thought to himself. Then to Ruffin he said, "I'll tell you all about my escape from the fire and all that after I see Abby. Charles said she's up in her room. May I go up and see her now?"

John looked at the old grandfather clock in the corner. "Well, you'll have to give it a few minutes, son. Right now, Abby's personal attendant is helping her with her bath."

"Personal attendant?"

John nodded and looked at Mandrake. "Excuse me, Mandrake," he said with a smile. "I haven't even spoken to you. Jedidiah told me you were here several weeks ago, and gone again. I wasn't sure if we'd ever see you around here any more. Especially since Web had set you free."

Mandrake smiled in return. "I'm still free, Massa John, but from now on, I's gonna be Massa Web's personal 'tendant. That'll be somethin', won' it? If'n Miz Abby keeps her personal 'tendant after she marries Massa Web, there'll be two personal 'tendants 'round their house."

"Oh, she'll keep her all right, Mandrake," chuckled John.

"Tell me about this attendant, Papa John," said Web.

"Nothing much to tell, son. Abby just needed another female to be close to her. Your...death left a real empty spot in her life. This young lady has been a real help to her."

Web thought of Lynne and said cautiously, "How about Lynne, Papa John? Is...is she doing all right?"

"You mean since she learned of Daniel's death?"

"Yes, sir. I saw my parents before coming here, and they told me she's spending some time at the Hart place these days."

"Lynne feels the Harts need comfort just about as much as she does. She's been there a lot since word came from the government."

"How long ago did the Harts get word?" asked Web.

"About ten days ago."

"I was with Daniel at Rich Mountain, Papa John. That's where I got this leg shot up."

"Really? Then you probably saw Reed there, too?"

Web and Mandrake exchanged quick glances.

"That's right," nodded Web.

"I got word of his death just about a week ago," said John. "Guess it takes the government quite a while to report all the deaths in battle."

"Yes, sir."

Looking serious, John said, "Web, I owe you an apology. A big apology. I was wrong about Reed, and I know it now. Did Mandrake tell you what Jedidiah told him about Hec Wheeler's confession and your being cleared?"

"Yes, sir."

"Well, Reed had me fooled, but that opened my eyes. Reed would've been convicted and hanged if he had lived to come home. I...I guess it's best that he died on the battlefield, fighting for the Confederacy. At least with him dying as a hero, it goes better for our family, wouldn't you say?"

Again Web and Mandrake exchanged glances.

"Sure. Lots better," nodded Web.

John looked at the clock and said, "Well, I know you're eager to see Abby. She should be presentable right soon, I would think. You can tell me all about how you escaped the prison fire and ended up in the army after you and she have had your reunion." Clapping his hands together, he laughed, "I sure wish I could be a fly on the wall when you walk into her room!"

There was movement at the top of the spiral staircase. Every eye flashed to the spot, thinking it might be Abby. Instead, it was Abby's attendant, clad in a brilliant white, starched dress. Her dark skin stood out in lovely contrast.

Web stood speechless at the sight of her, but it was Mandrake who was in a state of numb shock. He blinked and shook his head as if he had suddenly been swept into a heavenly dream.

At the top of the stairs, smiling and eyes brimming with tears, was the most beautiful woman Mandrake had ever seen. Orchid opened her arms and virtually glided down the stairs.

There was not a dry eye in the room as Mandrake and Orchid embraced, wept, and held each other tight. When the initial impact of the stunning surprise had eased, Orchid told Mandrake how she had escaped from Horatio Clements's place. She told about the bullet the guard had put in her side and how she had toppled into the Potomac River. Maintaining consciousness, Orchid had floated downstream a ways until she caught hold of some foliage along the bank. She was able to crawl out and make it to a small cottage near the river, where a widow woman took her in, summoned a doctor, and saw to it that she was given proper medical attention. The widow kept her until she was able to travel, then had her merchant son, who sometimes does business in Richmond, bring her home. She had arrived on July 11, the same day the battle had been fought on Rich Mountain.

Miss Abby, who was so torn up over Web's death, welcomed her, and asked Papa John if Orchid could be hired as her attendant. John was glad to do so. Since then Orchid had been living for the day her wandering husband might come home.

Holding her tight and still weeping, Mandrake looked at Web and said, "Looks like yo's and Miz Abby's household really is gonna have two personal 'tendants, Massa Web."

Smiling broadly, Web said, "I wouldn't have it any other way, my friend."

Orchid looked into Mandrake's eyes and said, "Could you let go of me long enough fo' me to give Massa Web a hug?"

"Long as it don' las' too long," grinned the happy black man.

Orchid embraced Web, then looked up at him and said, "Massa Web, that sweet lady upstairs is gonna think she's dreamin' when she sees you. But you jus' squeeze her so hard she'll know yo' real, will you?"

Balancing on his crutches, Web smiled and said, "You can count on it!"

As Orchid went back to Mandrake's arms, Web ran his gaze up the winding staircase. He could feel all eyes in the room on him as he climbed the stairs adeptly, using the crutches. When he reached the top of the landing, he looked back.

John Ruffin was wiping tears. "Sure wish I could be a fly on the wall!" he said again, lips quivering.

Web grinned, then turned and hobbled quietly down the hallway, his heart drumming his ribs. When he reached the spot, he took a deep breath, let it out slowly, and tapped on Abby's door.

EPILOGUE

When the Civil War came to an end, David Hart of Beverly, West Virginia, published a small book telling of his experience in the Battle of Rich Mountain. Still a Union enthusiast and a true patriot to the Northern cause, he wrote in part, "Our boys lit into those Rebels with their Enfield and Minié rifles, and I never heard such screaming in my life. The whole earth seemed to shake."

Edmund Ruffin, the South's secessionist leader who fired the first shot at Fort Sumter, joined the Palmetto Guard—a South Carolina militia unit—six days after Major Robert Anderson surrendered the fort to General Beauregard. At the time, Ruffin was sixty-seven years of age. He fought with that unit, facing Union guns and artillery on several occasions.

General Robert E. Lee signed the documents of surrender at Appomattox Court House on April 9, 1865. Nine days later, the seventy-one-year-old Ruffin took the rifle he had used to fight the Union and turned it on himself, committing suicide. The fall of the Confederacy was more than he could stand.